From a Single Seed

Teri Ames

Copyright © 2016 by Teri Ames. All rights reserved. Printed in the United States of America by Catamount Publishing, Middlebury, Vermont.

Cover and book design by Kit Foster Design
Cover Photographs © ver0nicka / AntonioGuillemF
Typeset in Garamond and Calibri
First edition

Publisher's Cataloging-in-Publication data
Ames, Teri
From a Single Seed/ Teri Ames
p. cm.
ISBN: 978-0-9972484-2-5
1. Crime—Fiction. 2. Law—Fiction. 3. Vermont—Fiction.
I. Title.
Library of Congress Control Number: 2016919213

To Jane Ames,

a mother who would have been there

PART I
Searching for Shannon

CHAPTER 1
Sunday, December 22, 2013

H E HOPED this phone call would be the end of it. It had taken Dustin an entire day to track down the hockey player. An entire day when he should have been getting Christmas presents for his kids. Or at least doing real police work. Instead, some prima donna college student decides to go off with her boyfriend, and he gets stuck trying to find her. All day working the phones, cutting through red tape at the college, and waiting for people to call him back. After he tracked them down in places he'd never been. Places he'd probably never see. Like Phoenix and Miami. And Pittsburgh. Christ on a stick, he needed to travel more.

The home number he'd gotten for the boyfriend had a Vermont area code. It was good to know that not everybody who went to college in his town was a flatlander.

He answered the phone. "Officer Shores."

"My mom said I should call you. You left a message on our answering machine. This is Keenan Brody."

"That's right. I'm looking for Shannon Dawson." According to the chief, when Shannon hadn't gotten off the plane in California last night, her parents had checked with the airline and learned she hadn't been on either of her flights across the country. Nor had she used her prepaid voucher on the airport shuttle that the college ran during peak travel times. The parents had contacted the Middleton Falls Police Department late last night, and the chief had called in Dustin to investigate early this morning. It was supposed to be his first full day off in over a week. "I was told you might know where Shannon is."

"Okay," the boyfriend said.

Dustin waited for more. When it didn't come, he tried again. "Keenan, can you please tell me where Shannon is?"

More silence on the line. The kid obviously didn't want to answer the question. "Keenan? Are you still with me?"

"No. I mean, yes."

"Let's try again. Where is Shannon Dawson?"

"I don't know."

It was less than convincing. Dustin glanced at the photo of Shannon he'd gotten from the college directory. She was cute. He pictured her standing next to her boyfriend, hand over her mouth, giggling. "Okay, Keenan. First of all, this is a serious matter. Shannon's parents are worried sick. Second, you may not be aware, but it's a crime to give false information to a police officer. If you have any idea where Shannon is, you need to tell me right now."

"I haven't seen her since Friday."

"Two days ago?"

"Yes."

"When did you last talk to her?"

"Friday night."

"You didn't talk to your girlfriend for two days?" There were several seconds of silence. It was a yes or no question, shouldn't take this long to answer.

"She hasn't called me back." Keenan paused before adding quietly, "I was ticked at her." Dustin could feel there was more, so he resisted the urge to fill the silence. "She wasn't really my girlfriend," Keenan finally said.

"Wasn't—or isn't?"

More silence.

"I heard you were dating her. Maybe I heard wrong. Why don't you tell me what your relationship with Shannon Dawson is?"

"We were dating. I guess."

"And are you still dating?"

"I don't know." Was this kid slow? Masterson College

students were supposed to be rich *and* smart. Maybe his head got smashed into the boards too many times playing hockey.

"Do you have any idea where Shannon is right now?"

"Not really." It wasn't an unequivocal no. He obviously knew something but didn't want to share it. Dustin could feel he was approaching the limits of his patience, so he forced himself to take a deep breath before continuing.

"If you know anything at all, you need to tell me." Despite the breathing exercise, Dustin's voice had come out louder and harsher than he intended.

"She might have gone to Maine."

"Maine? Why would she go to Maine?"

"I don't know. She said something about Maine the last time I talked to her."

"On Friday night?"

"Right."

Dustin glanced at his scant notes on the notepad in front of him. "I feel like I'm missing something here, so help me fill in some of the blanks. Were you with Shannon on Friday night?"

"Not really. I just ran into her."

"Where did you run into her?"

"At a party off campus."

"Whose party?"

"I don't know."

Yeah, right. "So you went to a party, but you don't know who was having it?"

"Yes."

"Where was it?"

"I don't remember."

"You. Don't. Remember." Dustin waited a few beats, but the kid didn't say more. With as even a tone as he could muster, he asked, "Okay, who else was there?"

"Lots of people."

"Who was Shannon with?"

"I'm not sure."

Dustin clenched his teeth and inhaled sharply through his nose. "Let me get this straight. You ran into your *girlfriend* at a party, but you don't remember where the party was or who she was with?"

"Yeah."

"Were you drunk?"

"No, I don't drink during hockey season. I mean, I'm not old enough to drink."

"Which is it?"

"Both."

"Do you understand how serious this is? An eighteen-year-old girl has been missing for two days."

"I think I recognized one of the girls from the ice rink. She's probably in the figure skating club with Shannon."

"Can you give me a name?"

"I don't know, Janie, or something."

"Last name?"

"I don't have any idea. I don't really hang out with Shannon's friends."

Dustin was done hiding his irritation, so he said, "Why not? You don't like her having friends?"

"What? It's not like that!" Keenan's voice was shrill, and Dustin smiled at having gotten the kid to break. Maybe now he could get somewhere with the interview.

"But she's in a skating club?"

"Yeah. That's how we met. At the rink."

"Can you remember the names of any of her other friends?"

"She talked a lot about Amy. I met her once, but I can't tell you her last name. I'm pretty sure they lived in the same dorm."

"Lived?"

"They lived in the same dorm last semester."

"Okay. Is there anything else you can tell me that would help me find Shannon?"

"I don't think so."

Dustin tossed his pen across the desk in resignation. "Well, if you hear from Shannon, have her give me a call. Better yet, have her call her parents." He said it just in case his original suspicion was right and Shannon was listening to the conversation.

Dustin got another pen out of the drawer and wrote down Keenan's details, then he hung up the phone and stared at it for a minute. Shit. Either Shannon Dawson really didn't want to go home—or something bad had happened to her. While Dustin was staring at the phone, it rang. Caller ID told him it was his soon-to-be-ex-wife. Just what he needed. If he didn't pick up, she'd have him paged. No sense avoiding the inevitable. He picked up the phone.

"I just wanted to let you know I'll be picking up the kids at 8:00 a.m. the day after Christmas." Joanne's Boston accent made his skin crawl. How had he ever thought it was exotic?

"The agreement says 5:00 p.m. You get them Christmas Eve and morning and I get them Christmas night and the day after. You already got the best part of the holiday."

"Our flight leaves at 11:05 a.m. We'll need to get to the airport." The temporary visitation agreement had only been in place for a few weeks and already she was stretching it to suit her needs. That was the problem with Joanne. She always had good reasons why he should bend. And he always bent. Well, not any more.

"Change it. It's my time."

Joanne laughed, a throaty hiccup. "You obviously don't understand how the airlines work. The tickets are non-refundable."

"I just don't see why you would buy tickets without asking me first."

"You can have some extra time with them after we get back." It was a bone and he knew it.

"Fine," he said. "But don't forget."

He'd better go tell the chief that the Brody kid had been a dead end. At least it was looking like there might actually be something to investigate.

CHAPTER 2
Thursday, October 10, 2013

SHE WAS the sparkliest thing he had ever seen. It was partly the lycra tights she wore with her sweatshirt, and it was partly the way the light reflected off her blond pony tail. But mostly, it was her essence. She was pure and shiny and just plain perfect.

The college had laid down ice a week ago. Today was the third time since then that Keenan had found himself in the bleachers watching the girl spin and jump effortlessly. He couldn't help it. For some reason he kept showing up early for practice, hoping she'd be there. So he could watch. Even though he probably should have been in the weight room with his teammates. Or at the library studying.

He needed to stop doing this, find out if she had a boyfriend. Hell, for all he knew, she was a lesbian. What an idiot he was, up here pining after a lesbian figure skater. Enough already. Time to shit or get off the pot as Grandpa Armand always said.

Keenan hurried to put on his gear so he could get on the ice before she finished practicing. He always wore the cumbersome pads that protected him while he played hockey, so they didn't usually bother him, but when he approached her, the pads suddenly made him feel like a Neanderthal. He should have put on the pads after he talked to her. What the hell was he thinking? He wasn't. That was the problem.

SHANNON HAD seen the hockey player watching her from the stands the week before and again that day. She pretended not to notice, but she could feel his eyes on her and wondered if he would try to talk to her.

She smirked when he lumbered out onto the ice near the end of open practice time. She skated backward by him so she could get a good look at his face. It was a handsome face, warm and aristocratic, in direct contradiction to his armor.

She continued skating backward and he joined her, matching her glides. She picked up the pace, and he did too. His agility was undeniable.

"You're pretty good," she said, "but I bet you can't do this." She touched the ice with her toe and did a double toe loop.

He did a stop, making a shower of snow. "That's not fair. I don't have toe picks."

She skated back toward him. "So do a different jump. You don't need picks for a waltz jump." She demonstrated. "Or a Salchow." She did another jump.

"What do I get if I make it?"

"The satisfaction of winning the bet."

"Not good enough. I win, you have dinner with me."

"Deal. But you have to do one full revolution and land without falling."

"Okay, but show me one more time how you do it."

She showed him the Salchow.

She watched the determination on his face as he began his approach and found herself hoping he would make it. He got some backward speed, turned, spun, and then launched. It wasn't the most graceful Salchow she'd ever seen, but he did manage to get all the way around before he hit the ice. What surprised her was that he didn't even come close to losing his balance. He skated back to her grinning broadly.

"Good enough?"

She smirked and shrugged. "I'll be at the Cameron Dining Hall at six thirty. If you find me, we can sit together."

"That's not much of a date."

"It wasn't much of a Salchow." She skated off toward the girls' locker room, glad he couldn't see the smile she couldn't repress.

CHAPTER 3
Sunday, December 22, 2013

USTIN DREW a line through another name on the skating club list. It seemed there were a lot of people who signed up but never participated. And, of course, nobody he'd talked to had heard of Shannon Dawson. It could be that the Brody kid had sent him on a wild goose chase. He switched back to the roster for Shannon's dorm. There were two girls named Amy living in McCullough Hall. He'd left messages on the home phones of both an hour ago, then decided to start with the skating club list, mostly because it was shorter. Most of the people he'd left messages for wouldn't call back. People were weird that way. He just hoped that if someone had information, they would call.

Shannon lived on the second floor, so he started with Room 201.

Finally, after five dead ends, he got a call from a girl on the third floor who said she knew Shannon.

"I got a text from Alex who got a text from Kyra who said you were trying to track down Shannon's friends. Is she okay?"

"Who am I speaking with?"

"Sorry. This is Madira Mehta. My friends call my Maddy. I hang out with Shannon sometimes. I mean, we're not 'besties' or anything, but we're friends. What's up with Shannon?"

"She's missing. Can you tell me when you last saw her?"

"I think I saw her Friday morning when she was on her way to her last final."

"So you didn't see her Friday night?"

"No, but I heard she was pretty drunk."

"Who told you that?"

"Oh, wait . . . I might be thinking of someone else."

"I'm not trying to get her in trouble. I just need to know who saw her last. Do you know who saw her Friday night?"

"Maybe Alex Jones."

"Okay. Do you know a girl named Amy?"

"Sure. She probably knows where Shannon is."

"How do I get in touch with her?"

"I'm pretty sure she's in Aspen, but she'll have her cell. Give me a sec to look at my contacts." Dustin took Maddy's information as well as Amy's and Alex's. Finally, he was getting somewhere.

Dustin reached Alex right away. Unfortunately, Alex had no idea where Shannon was.

"Did you see her on Friday night?"

"No, I didn't. I left school on Friday afternoon."

"Did you hear she was intoxicated?"

"I don't want to get her in trouble."

"Believe me, nobody's worried about that right now. We just want to find her. Do you know who she was with?"

"No, my boyfriend saw her with some friends. He mentioned how drunk they were. He wasn't with them though."

"Any idea who she was with?"

"Nope."

Before hanging up, he got Alex's boyfriend's information, but it was probably another dead end. At least now that he had a solid lead, he could stop plodding through the lists. He left a message on Amy's cell then decided to take a break.

He walked back to the break room and found his plastic container with three formerly-frozen-now-soggy burritos in the back of the fridge. Since Joanne had kicked him out, he hadn't had a good meal of leftovers. Come to think of it, he hadn't had a good meal.

He ate alone at the table in the windowless room. The flavor of the burritos was good, even if the texture wasn't. That was probably why the box said, "Keep Frozen." Not his fault the PD's fridge was freezer-less.

Amy Stevens finally called him back at 7:10 p.m. He could hear music and laughter in the background.

"Shannon's missing?" Amy said. "I had forty-eight texts about it when I checked my phone. There's no reception on the top of the mountain, so I left my phone in the lodge."

"Do I take it you don't know where she is?"

"No. I mean, I assumed she went home."

"When did you last see her?"

"Friday afternoon. We both had the cell biology final. It was the last one and probably the worst."

"How do you know Shannon?"

"We're both neuroscience majors and we live in the same dorm."

"Would you say you're close friends?"

"Sure. We only met at the beginning of the semester, but the neuroscience program is intense, so it's something we have in common. Most people don't get it."

"Did Shannon say anything to you to indicate that she might not be planning to go home?"

"No, not at all."

"Did she tell you her plans for Friday evening?"

"Yeah. She was going to a party with a couple of her friends from the skating club. She invited me, but I already had plans back in the city."

"What are the friends' names?"

"All I know is Greta and Jenna, no last names."

"Do you know Shannon's boyfriend?"

"Jake?"

"I thought his name was Keenan."

"Yeah, it is."

"Who's Jake?"

"He's her HTH."

"Huh?"

"Home Town Honey."

"They still together?"

"No, I mean, not really."

"What's that mean?"

"They agreed to see other people when they went away to college."

"And Shannon was seeing Keenan?"

"Right."

"But she was also still seeing Jake?"

"Yeah. But don't judge her. It's not like it sounds."

"I'm not interested in judging her. I just want to know where to look for her. You know how to get in touch with this Jake guy?"

"No idea, but he's from her hometown. Shouldn't be hard to find."

"Of course not." Dustin didn't appreciate the rich college girl telling him how to do his job. "I just thought you might know, save me some work. So, can you tell me who might have seen her after you last saw her?"

"You should talk to Greta and Jenna. I'm pretty sure that's who she was going out with."

"Okay, thanks for your help. If you think of anything or hear anything that would help with our investigation, please give me a call."

"I will. Officer?"

"Yeah?"

"Do you think Shannon's okay?"

"I hope so," Dustin said. But it was starting to look doubtful.

After a phone call to Shannon's parents, Dustin tracked down Jake Miller in California.

"When did you last speak with Shannon?" Dustin said.

"I don't know. It's been a while. She hasn't answered my calls or texts in a few days."

"I understand you go to Columbia. That's in New York City, right?"

"Yes, sir."

"When did you leave to go back home?"

"I flew out last Thursday."

"Can you prove that?"

"Probably, why?"

"Shannon hasn't been seen since Friday, more than forty-eight hours ago. People who knew her, like you, are going to need to account for their time, their whereabouts around the time she was last seen."

"Okay. How about a copy of my itinerary from Delta? I could forward it by email."

"Sure. That would be great."

"Officer, you think somebody did something to Shannon, don't you?"

"I hope not. That's why we investigate. To rule out the possibilities."

Using the skating club list, it was easy to locate Greta and Jenna. He called Greta first.

"Oh my God, Shannon's missing?"

"I understand you were one of the last people to see her."

"I went to the party with her, but I think she left with Keenan."

"About what time would that have been?"

"I'm really not sure. Around eleven o'clock maybe?"

"But you're sure you didn't see her after the party?"

"Absolutely. I only saw her for a few minutes after Keenan showed up."

"Was everything okay with those two?"

"What do you mean?"

"Well, for example, did Shannon and Keenan have any sort of fight or argument?"

"I'm not sure."

"Do you have any idea where she went after the party?"

"You'd have to ask Keenan."

"One more thing. Was she using drugs or anything?"

"No, Shannon's not like that."

"I heard that maybe she was drunk."

"She didn't seem like it to me."

"Okay. If you hear from Shannon or you think of anything else that might help us find her, please let me know."

Jenna called Dustin back an hour after he left her a message.

"I just heard about Shannon," she said.

"I understand you were with her last Friday, the last day of the term."

"That's right."

"Can you tell me what you remember about that night?"

"I just talked to Greta about it, and we remember it the same way. We went to the party, and then Shannon disappeared not long after Keenan showed up."

"You're sure she left with Keenan?"

"She must have because she didn't leave with us."

"Did anything seem wrong between them, like were they fighting?"

"I really can't say."

"How drunk was she that night?"

"She wasn't that bad. She drove to the party."

"Whose vehicle did she drive?"

"She drove her Golf."

"Where did she park it?"

"I don't know. Somewhere on Maple Street."

"Did you happen to notice if it was still there when you left?"

"I'm sorry. I didn't think to look."

"Okay, when you get back to town, I'll need you to give me a written statement."

POLICE CHIEF Harold Higgenbottom hated dealing with parents of college students. They usually started calling him when they were unhappy with the answers they had gotten from someone else in his department. He almost never got complaints from the local citizens, but for some reason college parents seemed to have no problem calling him whenever Junior had a run-in with the law, as if they somehow deserved special treatment because they paid as much as his salary in tuition each year.

"Chief, Olivia Dawson's on the line. Again. You want to talk to her?" the dispatcher said over the intercom.

"You'd better put her through." Two seconds later the phone rang and he picked it up.

"This is the chief." He never answered the phone, "Chief Higgenbottom," even though it might have sounded more professional. He preferred to be called plain "chief" by his subordinates, so that's what he called himself. He'd never told anyone, but it made him feel in league with Celtics great Robert Parrish, who also went by the nickname. Besides, he'd never liked his name.

"Please tell me you have some news." Olivia Dawson's voice was like sandpaper. The chief suspected she had been drinking coffee around the clock for two days.

"Sorry, Mrs. Dawson. I was hoping you had something for me."

"No, we keep hitting dead ends. You have to be doing better."

"I have one officer working full time on this, but he hasn't turned up anything yet."

"Just one? My daughter has been missing for two days and you think that's enough?"

"I'm sorry, Mrs. Dawson, but we're a small department. One man full time is a significant commitment. I have total confidence in his work. Besides, we don't know for sure that your daughter didn't just take off. College students have been known to do that."

"Not my daughter."

After he hung up, the chief rubbed his eyes and called Dustin Shores into his office.

"Please tell me you've got a lead."

"Not a realistic one."

"What have you got?"

"The girls Shannon went to the party with said she left with Keenan Brody. Nobody saw her afterward."

"What about Shannon's roommate?"

"Tessa. She said Shannon didn't sleep in the room on Friday

night, but it wasn't the first time, so she didn't really think much of it."

"Did she have any idea where Shannon might be?"

Dustin shook his head. "Tessa left town early Saturday morning. And apparently, they weren't close. Not really friends, just assigned roommates. She knew Shannon was dating a hockey player, but didn't even know his name. That's why it took so long to track him down."

"So, what are you left with?"

"The boyfriend said something about Maine."

"Maine?"

"I think he's just trying to get us to chase our tails, keep us from looking at him."

"Should we be looking at him?"

"Probably. I listened to the tape of my conversation with him again. I think he's lying. Something about him just doesn't seem right."

"What did he say?" The chief was twirling a pen around the fingers of his right hand, a habit he started when he quit smoking years ago.

"Well, at first he denied that Shannon was his girlfriend. Then he was really vague about the last time he saw her. And he kept referring to her in the past tense."

"That's weird," the chief said.

"Yeah," Dustin said. "Like maybe he knows she's dead."

"She may well be."

"I know. Missing two days. It's a long time for a kid in her circumstances."

"You really think the boyfriend has something to do with her disappearance?"

"You know the statistics. And it's not like we have any other leads."

The chief pursed his lips and nodded. "Could be random, like the Patricia Scoville case in Stowe. It took fourteen years and DNA to solve that one."

"Could be."

"When was the last time anyone saw her?" the chief said.

"Friday night at a party. She was with some girls from her skating club. Apparently, she likes to skate. That's how she met hockey boy."

"Hockey, huh?" The chief raised an eyebrow.

"That's part of why my gut's having issues with the boyfriend."

"I get that. But keep working on the timeline. We need to figure out who was the last one to see her alive, then maybe we can figure out where she disappeared."

CHAPTER 4
Thursday, October 10, 2014

KEENAN SHOWED up for dinner with a single red rose tucked inside his jacket. There was a convenience store on the edge of campus that always had a supply of roses on the counter. After practice, he had showered quickly so he would have time to detour to the store. It was cliché, but he didn't have time for anything more creative.

When he arrived at the dining hall, the sparkly girl was sitting with her friends, but didn't have a tray in front of her. She got up to meet him.

"I was afraid you wouldn't show," Keenan said.

"You won the bet, fair and square," she said.

They got their trays and went through the food line. Keenan didn't want to look like a cretin, so he took less than normal. Besides, he was too excited to eat.

"Are you really going to eat all that?" she said. She had a single baked potato on her plate.

"I burn a lot of calories at practice."

"You must, because without your pads you don't look heavy. You definitely don't look like you weigh two hundred and ten pounds."

It took Keenan a second to process. "You looked me up on the roster," he said.

"I had to. I couldn't have dinner with you without knowing your name. Could I, Keenan Brody?"

Keenan felt himself blush. "Now I'm at a severe disadvantage because I don't know yours."

"I guess you are. Why don't you go grab that empty table while I get a salad."

Keenan sat alone at the table and watched her make her way through the salad bar. Even without her sparkly tights and in the artificial light of the dining hall, she shone.

As soon as she was seated across from him, he took the rose out of his jacket and placed it on her tray. She smiled.

"It's Shannon. My name, that is."

"Shannon," Keenan tried the sound of her name and smiled. "Are you a nice Irish girl, then?" he said with a fake brogue.

"Afraid not," she said. "I'm pretty sure my mother just liked the name."

"My mother will like it too. She insisted on giving all us kids Irish names."

"Are you Irish?"

"Nope," said Keenan. "I'm one of the few Vermonters who go to Masterson. I think my mother was just rebelling against her French Canadian family when she named us. Where are you from?"

"Solana Beach, California."

"What's it near?"

"San Diego."

"You surf?"

"A little. But skating is more my thing."

"I noticed. How did you learn to skate like that?"

"I used to compete."

"I don't think of southern California as exactly a skating mecca."

"It's not. But there's a rink with a good program half an hour from our house. My mom put me on skates when I was three. I think she was hoping I would make it to the

Olympics."

"I take it you didn't make it."

"I wouldn't be here if I did."

"I guess that's two things we have in common—not being in the Olympics and skating at three. Thanks to the second one, I'm just as comfortable on skates as I am in shoes," Keenan said.

"I could tell. Now tell me the truth. Was that really your first Salchow? You have a sister that figures skates, don't you?"

"No way. Both my sisters play hockey. I'm just a quick study. And I was extremely motivated to get it right."

Shannon laughed.

"How about Saturday night you let me take you some place other than the dining hall?" Keenan said.

"Okay."

"You like Chinese?"

"Love it."

They sat and talked until the serving line closed and the workers began to pack up the remaining food. A janitor started putting the chairs upside down on the tables so he could mop. Shannon looked around. They were the only students left in the dining hall.

"They're going to kick us out," she said.

Keenan glanced at his watch. "You're right. Technically, the dining hall closed five minutes ago. We'd better get going."

Keenan insisted on walking her back to her dorm.

"You really don't have to," Shannon said. "It's not far, and it's not like Middleton Falls, Vermont is a dangerous place."

"I know. But my wannabe Irish mother would kill me if I let a girl named Shannon walk home alone."

After she had gone inside, Keenan picked up his pace. It wasn't that he wanted to get back to his dorm. He doubted that he could study if he tried right now. He just had so much energy. He found himself whistling "Something" by the Beatles. Jeezum, next he'd be singing Elton John songs in the shower.

CHAPTER 5
Monday, December 23, 2013

I CAN'T believe it took two days to get someone from the college to let us into the girl's room," Dustin said. "For all we know, we're going to find her dead body." He was standing outside Shannon and Tessa's second-floor dorm room and watching the chief read code numbers off a yellow sticky note and enter them into a keypad. He was a little surprised that the chief was actively participating in the investigation; he usually just gave advice and kept an eye on things from his office.

"No, we won't," the chief said. "You said Masterson Public Safety did a wellness check at her room on Saturday night after her parents reported her missing."

Dustin shrugged. "They said they did. So, why'd it take so long for us to get access?"

"Apparently, the college policy was unclear and the Dean of Students is out of town for the holidays. The college doesn't allow law enforcement access to dorm rooms without a search warrant or the consent of the students. Nobody wanted to be the one to go against the policy."

"Do they want us to find this girl or not?" It sure felt like the answer was not.

"The Dawsons finally got someone to see reason on this, but I had to agree we won't touch the roommate's stuff. I'm surprised they didn't send another dean with us."

"Probably all busy with the holidays. It seems overboard to be worrying about the roommate's privacy when there's a girl missing."

"Tell me about it. I think it's shorthand for 'Don't prosecute the roommate if you find drugs.'" There was a click and the chief pushed the door open. "We need to take photos as we go, in case this turns into a criminal investigation."

"Of course. I'll do it." Dustin took a camera out of its case. He snapped a photo of the blank whiteboard on the outside of the door before following the chief inside.

"And keep an inventory of everything we find that belongs to Shannon."

The room felt small for the amount of stuff that was crammed inside. There were two twin beds, two dressers, and two desks, all of which appeared to be standard issue. It was obvious which side belonged to Shannon—there were several framed and autographed photographs of figure skaters over her bed. The embroidered pillow with the name "Tessa" on the other bed was also a giveaway. Dustin moved around the room taking photos.

Tessa's side of the room was orderly. Her bed was crisply made. Her books were stacked neatly on her desk. Her closet had only summer clothing hanging.

Shannon's side wasn't messy, but it wasn't as organized as Tessa's. Her bed looked like the covers had been pulled up quickly. Her desk was still littered with papers and what appeared to be an open biology textbook. Inside her doorless closet were an insulated parka and a pair of fleece-lined boots.

"If she took off, she was going somewhere warm," the chief said.

"This doesn't look good," Dustin said.

"You look through her dresser. I'll take the desk."

"Looks like it's just clothes here," Dustin said. "And there's a rolling suitcase in the back of the closet."

"That's not good either."

"Nope."

"Here's something we're going to want to log into evidence."

"What's that?"

"Looks to me like a very expensive MacBook," the chief said and opened the laptop.

"I can't imagine she'd just leave it behind."

"Me neither," the chief said.

"Hopefully, we can figure out how to get into it. It's probably password protected."

"If the parents don't know the password, we can send it up to the tech guys in Burlington."

They spent half an hour making a list of all Shannon's belongings.

"You see anything else here?"

"Nope."

OLIVIA DAWSON had her phone in her lap during the entire flight. After she was reprimanded by the flight attendant for taking a call, she put the ringer on vibrate and started declining calls. But there was no way she was putting her phone in airplane mode. If Shannon or the police called, she was taking it. Airline regulations be damned.

Olivia called the police chief as soon as they were on the ground and the Fasten Seat Belt sign was off. "Please tell me you've found my daughter."

"I'm sorry, Mrs. Dawson. Not yet."

"Oh my God. Have you done anything to find her?"

"We're taking this seriously. I assure you."

"Then how come nobody knows where she is?"

"My investigator has figured out that she went to a party on Friday night. He's spoken with two of her friends, who said she met up with her boyfriend there."

"Jake was at Masterson?"

"The other boyfriend."

"She doesn't have another boyfriend."

"Apparently, she'd been dating a boy named Keenan."

"No, she wasn't. She would have told me."

"Her friend Amy confirmed it, as well as the boy himself."

Olivia was silent while she racked her brain, trying to remember Shannon mentioning someone named Keenan.

Nothing came to her. There had to be some mistake.

"Anyway," the chief said, "there's some evidence she may have been intoxicated."

"Nonsense. She doesn't drink." Now Olivia knew for sure that the chief was getting misleading information about her daughter.

"Okay."

"What do you know about the boy?" Olivia said. "Maybe he drugged her."

"We will consider that possibility," the chief said.

After hanging up, Olivia filled her husband in on the conversation.

"These backwoods cops don't have any idea what they're doing," she said.

"Maybe," Jack said. "But let's just hope we can get more information by talking to them in person."

"How long is the drive?"

"My memory is that it's an hour from the airport."

Olivia waited with their bags while Jack rented a midsize car at the Avis desk in the Burlington International Airport. There was only a middle-aged businessman in line ahead of Jack, but his transaction seemed to take an inordinate amount of time, probably because he was flirting with the attractive twenty-something at the counter. Olivia wanted to strangle him.

JACK CONSULTED a map before heading out of the parking area and then south in the direction of Middleton Falls. It had snowed recently, and the roadway was covered in brown slush. As the rental pulled away from the airport, a panel truck came by in the opposite direction and hit a pothole, spraying them with buckets of chocolatey snow cone. Jack had to use the wipers to regain visibility.

"What a God-awful place," Olivia said. "How does anyone live with these conditions?"

"It's really beautiful here. You'll see once we get away from the airport." Jack remembered how, four months ago when he had delivered Shannon to the Masterson campus, the Vermont mountains had been lush, seemingly much friendlier than the stark California terrain he was used to.

"I've been here before," Olivia snapped. "I just don't understand why anyone would choose this over California sun."

A few miles out of town, the traffic disappeared and sun came out. The mountains sparkled on both sides of the highway. Olivia and Jack rode in silence with their eyes on the road in front of them.

When they passed the sign that read Welcome to Middleton Falls, Jack spoke. "Should we check into our hotel first? Or go straight to the police station?"

"You really have to ask that?"

"What?"

"Your daughter's been missing for three days."

"If she'd turned up in the last hour, the police would have called. They have our cell numbers."

"That's not the point. You don't even seem like you're worried."

"Of course I'm worried," Jack said. "But I'm not sure that our presence at the police station is going to be helpful to them."

"How can you say that? She's our daughter. We know her better than anyone else."

"Then how come we didn't know she had a new boyfriend?"

"I'm sure there's an explanation," Olivia said.

"Probably. One like she wanted some independence. Privacy. A chance to live her life without having to report every detail to you."

"I don't make her report to me."

"Sure you do. How many times a day do you call her?"

"She calls me too."

"As much as you call her?"

"No, but—"

"See my point?"

"You're just jealous because I have a closer relationship with her."

"Sure. That's it. So why'd she ask me to drive her across country last fall?"

"She told me she thought you'd been working too hard. That you needed a break from work."

"That's funny. She told me that she couldn't stand the thought of five days of driving with you grilling her about her personal life."

Olivia gasped. "You're lying. Why are you taking this out on me?"

"I'm sorry. I shouldn't have said that."

"Is it true?"

"No, it isn't," he said.

"I didn't think so," Olivia said, but her tone said that she now had her doubts, and Jack wished he hadn't just lost control.

Jack thought back to the trip east at the end of August. Shannon's VW had been piled to the roof with her clothing and gear. He still remembered her expression when he'd reminded her to leave room for his carry-on suitcase. Sheepish at first, and then wry. "I figured you could keep your bag on your lap." When he shook his head, she'd laughed. "Just kidding, Dad. We can strap it on the roof." They'd eventually made room on the back seat. The trip had involved long days of driving, but they'd stopped to do a little sightseeing and managed to sample the soft-serve ice cream in various parts of the country along the way. It had been bittersweet to leave her behind when he got on the plane for home; he had known he would miss her, but felt gratified that she was clearly ready for this next phase of her life.

Jack used the rental's GPS to find the police station. He parked in one of the visitor spaces near the entrance. After getting out of the car, he waited on the sidewalk. Olivia sat with the car door open, staring at the ground, seemingly paralyzed.

"What's the matter?" Jack said.

"I forgot my winter boots."

"Me too. I was so focused on Shannon."

"My shoes are Italian leather."

"You want me to carry you to the sidewalk?"

"No. I want my boots."

"Do you want to go to the store for boots before we go see the police?"

"No."

"Then let's go."

Olivia gingerly put the tip of one toe into the slush, then the other. She slammed the car door and leapt up to the sidewalk, which was slightly less slushy.

"That was graceful," Jack said and instantly regretted it. He was usually miles better at self-censoring. It must be the stress.

Olivia glared at him as she tiptoed by and headed to the building. The dispatcher let them in almost immediately and the chief showed them to his office.

DUSTIN WAS seated in the chief's office at the work table that was piled with photos and papers. He got up and introduced himself before offering his chair to Olivia.

"Please tell me what you're doing to find my daughter," Olivia said.

"I've managed to track down a number of her friends from the dorm and the skating club. I've spoken by phone with the boy she's been dating on campus. We went to her dorm room this morning."

"And what have you learned?"

Dustin decided not to sugarcoat it. "A lot less than I'd hoped."

"Why don't you give her the timeline," the chief said.

"On Friday night, she met up with some friends from the skating club and, at around 9:00 p.m., they went to a party off campus. Shannon drove her vehicle and parked on Maple Street. They were at the party for a while and then Shannon disappeared. The boyfriend and the friends all say that they didn't see her after that."

"Is this really helpful?" Olivia said.

"Absolutely," the chief said. "Everything we nail down helps us figure out where to look next and who she crossed paths with, who to talk to." He nodded at Dustin.

Olivia was staring at Dustin and fiddling with her wedding ring. "Well. Then what?" she said.

"The only other thing is that we located Shannon's car on campus at her dormitory lot." He wished he had more.

"So she must have driven back to the dorm," Olivia said.

"Probably." The chief nodded.

"What happened at that party?" Jack said.

Dustin shook his head. "We're not sure. Everybody's been vague about the party."

"Did anyone see her after the party?" Jack said.

"Not that we've been able to find," Dustin said.

"We need to find out what happened at the party . . . who she left with," Olivia said. Dustin didn't appreciate her use of the royal we.

"We're working on it," the chief said. "We think there was underage drinking, and that's the reason for the code of silence."

"My daughter doesn't drink," Olivia said.

Dustin was impressed that the chief was able to resist rolling his eyes before he answered. "You may be right, but we need to consider the possibility," the chief said.

"I'd like to interview more students, but it's hard to conduct interviews on the phone," Dustin said.

"So, go out and do it in person," Olivia said.

"Finals ended on Friday," Dustin said. "Everyone left town on Saturday. The college is a ghost town during the holidays."

"We can't afford to send Officer Shores traipsing around the country trying to track down college students," the chief said. "Our department's yearly travel budget is in the thousands."

"I understand," Jack said.

"I don't," Olivia said.

"They'll all be back in a few weeks," the chief said.

"A few weeks is a long time," Olivia said.

"In the meantime, Officer Shores will keep working the

phones and we'll follow up on every local lead we have. Which reminds me, did you bring the key to Shannon's vehicle? We've had it towed to our garage so we can go through it more thoroughly. Like I said before, it'll be easier to move it when we're done if we have the key."

Jack pulled a ring of keys out of his pocket and unclipped a VW key. "This should do it."

"Great, thanks. Now Officer Shores has a few questions for you." The chief nodded toward Dustin.

"That's right," Dustin said. The Dawsons turned their attention to him, and he felt pressure to impress them with his investigative prowess. It was a foreign feeling. "Does Shannon have any friends from home that she's close to? People she might have told her plans to. People she might have met up with if she was going to make an unscheduled trip."

"I can give you a list of her friends," Olivia said. Jack nodded.

"Can you get us access to her Facebook page? Maybe she posted something there. Or maybe it will tell us who else we need to talk to."

"She wouldn't 'friend' me," Olivia said. "She said she wanted her Facebook page to be something she did with her friends."

"Sophie can probably help with that," Jack said. "They were best friends in high school."

"Then we need to talk to Sophie. There's one other thing. We found a MacBook in her dorm room. You wouldn't happen to know the password? We can send it up to the computer geeks in Burlington for analysis, but that will take time."

"Please don't waste any more time," Olivia said. "We got the computer just before she left for college. I remember her saying there's a login hint, in case she forgets her password. If you can show me the hint, I might be able to figure it out."

"Okay, let's try it." Dustin left the room and got the MacBook from the evidence locker. He was back a minute later.

Olivia paced while Dustin opened the laptop and waited for

it to come to life. He clicked on the login. "The hint is 'jump number sign.'" Dustin's voice fell with his hope. The clue was certainly cryptic.

Olivia barely hesitated. "Try L-U-T-Z, probably with a capital L, followed by the number seven."

Dustin tapped the keyboard. "That's it. We're in. I can't believe you figured it out on your first try."

"I know my daughter. The Lutz is her favorite jump because it makes her feel like she's flying, and she always says that her lucky number is seven," Olivia said, reaching for the laptop. "Let me have a look."

"Actually, ma'am, it would be better if you leave this to us. I'm going to ask you to sign a Consent to Search form for the computer, so I can read through her emails and see if I can access her Facebook page. When I'm done, I'll send it up to Burlington. I'll let you know what I find."

The chief presented her with a form and a pen. Olivia hesitated, looking pleadingly at her husband.

Jack Dawson reached over, took the pen, and signed the form. "Let's get out of their hair so they can do their jobs," he said.

"But—"

"I'm sure they'll check in with us after they've gone through the laptop. Right, chief?"

"We'll be in touch as soon as we have something to report. This laptop may keep us busy for a while, especially if it has all her contacts on it."

"Okay, we'll be waiting for your call," Olivia said.

Jack gently steered his wife toward the door. "Let's go buy some boots and check in at the hotel. Neither one of us slept much on the flight cross country."

As soon as they were gone, Dustin said, "Now that we've met the mother, I like the ran-away-from-home theory quite a bit better than I did before."

CHAPTER 6
Saturday October 12, 2013

SHANNON WAS surprised that Keenan insisted on walking out to the parking lot with her to get her car. "I feel bad I don't have a car, so I can't pick you up," he said.

"I don't mind," Shannon said. "I can get the car and pick you up at your dorm."

"No way. I believe in door-to-door service."

He met her at her dorm and they did the five-minute walk to the parking lot together. When they got there, he insisted on opening her door even though she was driving.

"You're nuts," she said.

"Probably. It's just awkward that I can't drive on our first date."

"Our first date was at the dining hall."

"That doesn't count."

"Why not?"

"Not romantic enough," he said.

They went to the China Palace and lingered over Moo Goo Gai Pan that was too salty and mushy. Shannon had always thought of Chinese food as full of healthy, crispy veggies. Apparently, not in Vermont. Keenan seemed to enjoy the food, and she realized she was happy to be there, the food notwithstanding.

After dinner, they parked in town and went for a walk to

the falls that gave the town its name. It was an impressive sight, a fifty-foot-wide swath of white water pouring over a ledge and plummeting thirty feet straight down. Keenan took her hand and led her down the path to the base of the falls. She felt the mist on her face when he kissed her for the first time. His warm lips and her cool skin. It made his lips seem even warmer.

"I wanted our first kiss to be memorable," he said. "After all, you only get one first kiss."

CHAPTER 7
Tuesday, December 24, 2013

HOW MUCH are we going to tell the parents?" Dustin said. He and the chief had been in the chief's office until one in the morning skimming everything on Shannon's laptop. They had agreed the night before to meet with Shannon's parents at eight o'clock, so they were both back in the office before seven, steaming mugs of coffee in front of them. Dustin had printed and highlighted a stack of emails and Facebook postings.

"Probably all of it." the chief said. "You'd want to know if it was your kid, wouldn't you?"

"Yeah, but it's going to be hard on them."

"It's not like there's no hope."

"Right, but the best case scenario at this point is that she was either abducted and is being held alive somewhere, or she hated them so much that she planned her own disappearance leaving no trace."

The chief shook his head. "The mom's overbearing, but I doubt the kid disappeared herself just to avoid spending a few weeks with her parents. She'd already managed to get three thousand miles away from her mother. You don't walk away from a free Masterson College degree."

"What about a kidnapping? Is there enough money there for that to be a possibility?"

"Anything's possible, but I think we would have heard if this was a kidnapping case."

"We should probably still explore that with the parents. In

the interest of being thorough."

The dispatcher buzzed the intercom and a few minutes later Olivia and Jack Dawson entered the room. Dustin noticed they were both sporting what looked like new winter boots and parkas.

"What can you tell us?" Olivia said.

"Coffee?" the chief said.

"No, thanks," Olivia said.

"I'll take one," Jack said. Olivia glared at him.

"I'll be right back," the chief said.

"Tell us what you found," Olivia said.

"I'd rather wait for the chief," Dustin said. Olivia glared at Jack again. Dustin felt bad for the guy. His wife had the evil-eye thing down.

Jack shrugged. "I'm tired. Not sleeping much these past few days."

The three of them sat in awkward silence for a few minutes until the chief came back with a styrofoam cup of hot coffee.

"Black okay?"

Jack glanced at his wife before answering. "Sure," he said. Jack cupped his coffee apparently absorbing the warmth, but didn't drink it. The chief settled into his chair.

JACK HATED black coffee, preferring it with a splash of cream. He wasn't really much of a coffee drinker, but he was so emotionally wrung that he knew needed some form of chemical alteration. He didn't know if the coffee would make him feel better, but he doubted he could feel worse, so it was worth a shot.

The chief leaned forward, clasped his hands, and put his forearms on his desk. "We went through a lot of what's on the laptop last night," he said, making eye contact with Jack. "We'll probably want to go back further at some point, but we read a bunch of the most recent stuff."

"Was there anything helpful?" Olivia said.

The chief turned his gaze to Olivia. "Yes. It was set up to stay logged into her Facebook account unless she logged it out.

And she didn't."

"And?"

"Shannon did a lot of messaging with her friends on Facebook, but the last time she posted anything on her page was Friday night at around 8:45 p.m. when she posted a picture of herself with two other girls. We also put in a subpoena for cell phone records with AT&T yesterday morning. The records came in from that last night."

"What do they tell you?"

"The last call Shannon took on her cell was at 8:47 p.m. on Friday. She talked to Keenan Brody for eight minutes and twelve seconds."

"Who is this guy?" Olivia was shaking her head convulsively.

"We think they were having an intimate relationship."

"What's that mean? They were having sex?" Olivia said.

"It's possible from what we've learned so far."

"I'm sure you're mistaken," Olivia said. "She's never even mentioned him to me."

"Maybe she wasn't serious about him."

"My daughter wouldn't have casual sex. That's not the way I raised her."

"I'm sorry ma'am, I didn't mean to imply anything about your daughter's morals. It's just that when kids go away to college, sometimes they like to experiment, try things their parents wouldn't approve of."

"So, what do you think happened to our daughter?" Jack said.

"From everything we've learned, she's been off the grid since Friday night at about nine o'clock. For someone like her, someone that's always connected to her friends electronically, that's a big deal."

Jack didn't want to say it, but he needed to know. "You think she's dead, don't you?"

"I'm not going to lie to you," the chief said. "It's a possibility. But usually when someone dies, there's a body."

"So do you think maybe she was abducted?" It sounded

strange to hear hopefulness attached to Olivia's question.

"That's what we're wondering," the chief said. "Is it possible this is a kidnapping? I mean, I assume you're well off, since your daughter goes to Masterson. Any reason your family would be a target?"

"I'm a general surgeon," Jack said. "I make a good living, but I don't think of us as kidnapping targets."

"Do you have any enemies? Any reason someone would use your daughter to get back at you?"

"I've lost patients, even been sued for malpractice and been cleared, but that's not unusual these days."

"Have there ever been threats against you or your family?"

"Of course not," Jack said before he realized it wasn't exactly true. He thought of the Mendez family. They had lost their son to infection after Jack had operated on a burst appendix. Jack didn't carry any guilt because he knew that Antonio's death had not been his fault. It was the fault of an extremely rare complication and also the parents' delay in bringing the boy to the emergency room. But Jorge Mendez had been in pain over the loss of his eldest son, and that pain had turned to anger. He had left a threatening message on Jack's voicemail at work after the judge had dismissed his lawsuit against Jack and his malpractice insurance company. Jack hadn't even bothered to report the threat to the police because he assumed that Jorge was just venting his anger. Jorge had needed time to work through his grief, not a criminal record. He wouldn't have taken revenge, would he? No, it was too long ago. It wasn't even worth mentioning.

"I'M SORRY to have to ask this, but . . ." the chief took a deep breath before continuing, "is there any reason that Shannon would want to run away?" Dustin was glad the chief had asked the question, so he didn't have to.

Sure enough, Olivia turned her evil eye on the chief. "That's ridiculous," she said.

"I have to ask," the chief said.

"I don't think that's likely," Jack said.

"What are you going to do to find my daughter, other than ask insulting questions, that is?" Olivia said.

"Well, at this point, this is still a missing person investigation—," the chief said.

"You've got to be kidding me," Olivia said.

"—but, we're going to treat it like an abduction slash potential homicide."

"We want to hire a private investigator," Olivia said. "We talked about it last night."

"It's not that we don't trust you," Jack said. "We just want to do everything we can to find our daughter."

"I understand. Like I told you before, we don't have the resources to traipse around the country interviewing college students, and we'll be happy to follow up on any lead that your investigator brings us."

"What are you going to do next?"

"Dustin's going out to interview the Brody kid tonight. He lives about two hours away. On Thursday, the Vermont Fusion Center will do a location trace of Shannon's cell to see if they can locate where she was when she made her last call. They're on skeleton staff for the holiday."

"We want you to keep us in the loop," Olivia said.

"Of course. How much longer will you be staying in town?" the chief said.

"Until you find my daughter," Olivia said.

"At least through the end of the week," Jack said. "I cancelled my OR schedule for a while, but at some point I need to go back to California, or I'll risk destroying my practice."

The chief nodded. "We'll keep looking for answers. I'm sorry I haven't had much for you so far."

When they were gone, the chief closed his office door. "It's Christmas Eve. I forgot about that when I promised you'd head out to Lyndonville tonight. You have plans?"

"It's okay. My ex has the kids tonight. I don't get them back until tomorrow afternoon."

"That's good. Someone needs to talk to Keenan Brody. He may be the key to this whole thing. I didn't want to say anything in front of the parents, but we both know that most homicides in Vermont involve domestic violence."

Dustin nodded. "It's supposed to snow tonight. I should probably get on the road as soon as I finish going through all the texts and emails between Keenan and Shannon. I want to be prepared for this interview."

"That's good. If the weather turns south, don't hesitate to get a motel room tonight. Just keep it cheap. You know we have big budget issues."

"Should I call the kid first?"

"No, let's not give him a chance to rehearse his answers or lawyer up before you can take a stab at him."

Dustin wandered the toy aisle at Kinney Drugs. He'd forgotten to pack a lunch that morning, so he'd had to go out for food when his stomach started panging. The cheapest and easiest thing was always McDonald's. When he pulled into the parking lot, he remembered that he still hadn't done his Christmas shopping. Shit. Only four more shopping hours until Christmas.

He'd been planning a trip up to the big mall in Burlington on Sunday, but he'd been called in to track down Shannon Dawson and ended up staying until long after the mall was closed. Then, with the investigation heating up, there hadn't been time on Monday. He'd been considering getting the kids a Wii. It was a little more than his budget would allow, but that's what credit cards were for. He'd pay it off eventually. If he ever got up to the mall. Maybe the prices would be cheaper after Christmas.

He picked up a Tonka truck. Quinn had one just like it at his old house. Joanne's house, he mentally corrected. There weren't many toys at his new place, just things the kids had left behind when they packed up to go home. A naked Barbie doll he'd found tangled up in Sienna's blankets. Some happy meal toys.

Dustin looked at his watch. He didn't have time to wander around town looking for a better toy selection. At least the drug store had an entire aisle devoted to toys. He got a cart from the front entrance and piled in cheap plastic toys, starting with the Tonka truck. He smiled when he found a section with Barbie outfits. He even remembered wrapping paper and tape before he headed to the checkout.

After the second time he felt the car drifting while going thirty-five miles per hour, Dustin wished he had taken his ten-year-old Explorer rather than the department's Chevy Impala. You just can't beat four-wheel drive in a snow storm. Route 2 from Montpelier to St. Johnsbury had not been plowed despite the six inches of snow that had accumulated. The storm had come on fast and furious, and this less traveled road was not a priority for the highway crews. Dustin reduced his speed and plodded along at twenty-five miles per hour. His shoulders were tense from gripping the wheel, so he tried to force himself to relax. When he got to St. Johnsbury, he pulled into a diner. He needed a break and a chance to regroup before the interview.

"We're just closing," the waitress said. "We close early on Christmas Eve." She was slightly pudgy with a warm smile and strangely perfect teeth. Dustin was disappointed he wouldn't get a chance to chat with her.

"That's okay," he said. "I understand."

He continued up the road and spotted a McDonald's near the interstate. Apparently, the golden arches didn't give its employees as much time off during the holidays.

For the second time that day, he ordered a coffee and a chicken sandwich. There were a few other people in the restaurant, probably people traveling for the holiday. He hoped that Keenan Brody would be home on Christmas Eve. If not, he'd try again in the morning. Failing that, it wouldn't be the first time he wasted a trip trying to get a candid interview. He quickly ate his sandwich and took the coffee to go.

Interstate 91 was in good shape. It was a welcome change from the earlier part of the trip. Dustin tucked in behind a massive snowplow and had a stress-free trip north until he reached the Lyndonville exit. When he got off the interstate, it was back to slow going. Fortunately, he didn't have much farther to travel. The GPS took him to the Brody home about ten minutes later. The trip had taken almost four hours.

Even though it was dark, Dustin could tell that the family lived pretty far off the beaten path. The house was well lit, but he couldn't see lights from any other nearby houses. The building was a white two story with a front porch that spanned the facade. As was customary in these parts, half of the front porch was stacked with firewood. A barn with weathered vertical siding appeared to be tilting away from the wind.

It struck him. This kid must be a hick. What was a California girl doing dating a hick? Something didn't add up. He parked in front of the barn, next to a Subaru station wagon that sported rust holes on the wheel wells. It only had an inch or so of snow accumulation. At least that meant someone was probably home.

As he walked up the front steps, he could see through the large-paned windows into the living room. A sparkling Christmas tree dominated the scene, but there was nobody in the room

When he knocked firmly on the door, dogs barked in response. He waited until a smiling, middle-aged woman answered the door. Three dogs were at her heels.

"Merry Christmas," she said. Her expression turned to puzzled when she didn't recognize him.

"Merry Christmas," Dustin responded. "Sorry to interrupt, ma'am. My name is Officer Shores. I'm from the Middleton Falls Police Department. Are you Keenan's mother?"

"That's right. I'm Cassie Brody."

Dustin wrote her name on his notepad before looking up. "I need to speak with Keenan."

"It's about that missing girl, isn't it? Have you found her?"

"Yes ma'am and no ma'am. Is Keenan here?"

"Of course. Come in, officer."

Dustin followed her into a large hallway that also served as a mudroom. There were hooks along both walls with winter coats in abundance. The floor was lined with boots of various sizes. A quiver of hockey sticks leaned in one corner next to a dented bookcase stacked with hockey skates. Dustin could feel the heat from a wood stove coming from the left side of the hall. In contrast, a cold draft seemed to be coming from the right. The unmistakable aroma of roast turkey mostly masked the odor of well-used athletic gear. Mostly. The dogs sniffed Dustin thoroughly before losing interest and heading back toward the turkey. He noticed that one of the dogs had three legs and another was missing half an ear.

"Can I take your coat?" Cassie Brody was still smiling.

"No thanks, I need the stuff in my pockets."

"I'll be right back," she said, her smile drooping.

She returned a minute later with a well-built young man in a T-shirt and jeans. A slender middle-aged man with wire-rimmed glasses followed them.

"Good evening, officer." The man extended his hand. "I'm Greg Brody, Keenan's father. I assume you're not here with good news."

"No news, sir, but I need to speak with your son. From everything we've determined, he was the last one to see Shannon Dawson last Friday."

"Of course, Keenan will do everything he can to help. Right, Keenan?"

"Yes, sir."

"Would it be possible for me to speak with Keenan alone? He's over eighteen, right?"

"He's nineteen. But we'd like to hear what you have to say."

"Some of my questions may be . . . a little personal in nature. It would be better if we speak alone."

"Our son doesn't have secrets from us, officer. We'd like to be a part of this."

"Why don't we leave that up to Keenan?" Dustin said, looking in Keenan's direction.

"They can stay." Keenan shrugged.

Dustin could hear voices in the back of the house. He wondered how many people were there eating dinner.

"Is there somewhere private we can talk?" Dustin said.

"Sure, let's go into my office." Greg led them to a room on the cold side of the house. Once they were inside, he shut the door and the air was instantly colder. Dustin was glad that he'd kept his coat. Greg pulled two chairs over in front of a small sofa. Dustin took a hard chair as he'd been trained to do in case he needed to get up quickly. He pulled a digital recorder out of his pocket and tapped the Record button before placing it in his lap. Greg took the other chair. Keenan sat on the sofa with his mother.

"We've gotten copies of Shannon's phone records. She hasn't used her phone since last Friday night. It appears that Keenan here was the last person to speak with her by phone. I'd like to know what was said." Dustin looked at Keenan. The kid looked pale.

"She's dead," Keenan said. His expression went completely slack.

"How do you know that, son?" Dustin said.

"I just do." Keenan was slowly shaking his head, staring as if he were somewhere else, remembering something that happened.

"Did you kill her?" Dustin said softly.

"What?" Greg Brody was out of his seat. "Don't answer that, Keenan."

"What?" Keenan blinked before alarm registered on his face. He turned toward Dustin. "No, I didn't kill her. I . . . I really liked her."

"Then, how do you know she's dead?"

There was a long pause before Keenan answered. "You just said she hasn't used her phone since Friday. She's always on her phone."

"That was our impression from her phone records."

"She wouldn't go anywhere without her phone."

"Is there something else you want to tell me about Friday?"

"Like what?"

"Were you with Shannon that night?"

"No. She went out with her friends."

"But you said you ran into her at a party."

"That's right."

"Okay. Let's start with the phone conversation at 8:47 pm. What was that about?"

"I called her."

"I know that much. What did you talk about?"

"She was at a party at a dorm."

"How do you know that?"

"She must have told me."

"Why did you call?"

"I was hoping to see her that night, but she had other plans."

"What else was said?"

"She said she had something to tell me, and that it couldn't wait until after break."

"What was it?"

"I don't know. She said she had to tell me in person."

"Anything else?"

"That was pretty much it."

"You were on the phone for more than eight minutes, you had to have talked about something else."

"Not really. I was hanging out in my dorm watching TV with my roommate. I kept watching TV, and she kept doing whatever she was doing with her friends."

"And what were they doing?"

"It sounded like they were having a party."

Dustin noticed that, despite the chilly temperature of the room, Keenan was showing sweat rings in the armpits of his T-shirt.

"Okay. So, how did you run into Shannon?"

"I decided to stop by the party."

"Did you go looking for her?"

"Not really. I figured if I ran into her, I'd talk to her."

"Who did you go to the party with, your roommate?"

"Nah, he wanted to watch the rest of the game. I went by myself."

"Are you friends with the people who threw the party?"

"Not really, but I knew a lot of people were going."

"How did you get to the party?"

"I walked."

"How far was it?"

"I don't know. It took about fifteen minutes."

"Okay, what happened when you got to the party?"

"I ran into Shannon."

"Who was she with?"

"When I saw her, she was with two girls."

"Who were they?"

"I'm really not sure."

"Did you talk to Shannon?"

"Only for a minute."

"Did you find out what she wanted to tell you?"

"Nope, she seemed like she wasn't in the mood for anything serious."

"Was she drinking?"

"Yes, sir."

"Was she drunk?"

"I thought so."

"Were you drinking?"

"No, sir."

"Did you leave the party together?"

"Huh?"

Dustin recognized the stalling tactic. "I asked, 'Did you leave the party together?'"

"No, sir."

"Did you see her again after that?"

"No, sir."

"Do you have any idea what happened to Shannon after you talked to her at the party?"

"No, I do not." The redundant answer was a red flag for deception.

"How long have you known Shannon?"

"We met in October, when they first started making ice."

"How did you meet?"

"She used to practice until three thirty. We had ice time starting at four."

"'We' means?"

"The hockey team. She was an awesome skater. I used to watch her practice until I had to get dressed."

"And you started dating?"

"Something like that."

"Were you intimate with her?"

Keenan first looked toward his mother, then back at the officer. "I don't see how it's any of your business."

"We have a missing eighteen-year-old girl. There's a chance this is going to become a murder investigation. Everything about her is my business."

Greg stood up. "Officer, I think Keenan here has tried to be helpful. We all have, despite your timing." Dustin winced involuntarily, but Greg didn't seem to notice. "We want you to find this missing girl, but I resent the implication that my son might somehow be involved in her disappearance. Do we need a lawyer?"

"I'm just conducting an investigation here." Dustin remained seated. "The only reason Keenan would need a lawyer is if he has something to hide. Of course, you're always welcome to hire an attorney."

"I have nothing to hide," Keenan said. "I don't know what happened to Shannon."

"Anything else you want to tell me about Shannon?"

"I think we're done here, officer," Greg said.

"I really don't know what happened to her," Keenan said.

"For your sake, I hope not," Dustin said. He didn't turn off the digital recorder until he was outside.

CHAPTER 8
Saturday, October 19, 2013

KEENAN FELT the warmth of Shannon's body snuggled against him in his twin bed. He breathed the smell of her citrus shampoo and rubbed his cheek against her silky blond hair. He liked that she was wearing his T-shirt.

It was almost too good to be true. He'd worked hard to make their first few dates memorable, even sat through a film with subtitles last night, but he still couldn't believe his luck. The sparkly girl had spent the night. Thank God his roommate had gone away for the weekend.

SHANNON OPENED her eyes to find Keenan staring into them. It took a second before she remembered where she was. It was the first time she had ever woken up next to a boy. It wasn't the first time she had ever had sex. She'd been intimate with Jake during senior year of high school. But that was different because she had always had a curfew. There was something even more intimate about the act of sleeping side by side. It was liberating and frightening at the same time.

"Good morning, Sparkly," he said.

"Sparkly?"

"That's what I used to call you before I knew your name."

"Huh?"

"Because of your sparkly skating tights."

"Well, now that you know me, maybe you can call me Shannon."

"Oh, is that your name?"

"Very funny."

He kissed her deeply and she felt her body respond. She should get up and go before this turned into something she wasn't ready for. He pulled away first.

"I'm really glad you're here. I mean, it was really nice to spend the night with you, and I want to spend the day with you." He sounded so sincere it was scary.

"I have homework."

"Perfect. We can study together. After we have breakfast together."

"Don't you have practice today?"

"Not until late afternoon."

"I was planning to go skate for a while this morning," she said.

"I'll go watch you."

"Are you always this intense?"

"Nope. I've just never met anybody like you before."

CHAPTER 9
Tuesday, December 25, 2013

USTIN HAD spent Christmas Eve at the Colonnade Inn in Lyndonville. He'd chosen it because it was the first motel he came to after he left the Brody house. The snow had still been coming down hard and he was not up for another epic drive across the state. Once was enough in those conditions.

He'd pulled into the motel at around eight o'clock, a little surprised to see several large SUVs with out-of-state plates and roof racks full of skis and snowboards. The Colonnade didn't seem the sort of place anyone would go for a Christmas getaway, even if it was only a few miles up the road from Burke Mountain ski area. But then, he'd never understood the fascination with skiing. As far as he was concerned, it was a sport for rich people and flatlanders. Real Vermonters preferred ice fishing.

At least the trip had been worth the effort. That Brody kid knew a lot more than he was letting on. He probably even knew where Shannon Dawson was. Or rather, where her body was. Dustin was having a hard time putting his finger on it, but there was something "off" about the kid. He admitted that he knew she was dead, but there was more to it. It was probably time to take a harder look at him. Besides, it wasn't like they had any other suspects.

Dustin drove back to Middleton Falls on Christmas morning. He was planning to spend the afternoon and evening with his kids and first thing the next morning start going back through Shannon's laptop with a fine-toothed comb. Maybe if he did a search for Keenan's name in the emails, he would find out what was really up with those two.

Dustin was finishing wrapping the last of the drugstore toys when Quinn and Sienna bounced into his apartment. Joanne stood just inside the door holding two backpacks. She looked around with obvious distaste.

"You can just set those on the floor," Dustin said.

Sienna did a cartwheel across the nearly empty living room. "Daddy! Daddy! Santa got us a Wii. And the Toy Story game. And the Cars game. And the Lego Harry Potter game."

"I'm a really good driver," Quinn said, "and I beat Lightning."

"Wow. That's great," Dustin said, trying to show more enthusiasm than he felt. He looked at his pile of gifts. He should have gotten a tree. Hell, even a second color of wrapping paper and some bows would have made it seem more festive.

"When are you going to get some furniture? It's been a few months." Joanne was still standing in the doorway.

"When I have time." And money.

"I like it this way," Sienna said "There's more room for cartwheels."

"That's exactly what I was thinking," Dustin said.

"Sure you were," Joanne said. She called the kids over for hugs before she left.

"You want to open presents?" Dustin said as soon as she was gone.

"Yeah!"

It took two minutes for the kids to tear the paper off the presents. When they each had a small pile in front of them, they both sat on their knees and looked at him.

"Don't you want to play with your toys?" he said.

"Can we watch TV?" Sienna said. Quinn nodded.

"Sure," Dustin said. "But first let's go pick out something for dinner."

The kids followed him into the kitchen, and he opened the

fridge. There was milk, a brick of cheddar, and some condiments. He should have planned something for Christmas dinner. He would have if he hadn't been so wrapped up in the Shannon Dawson case. He tried the freezer.

"How about frozen pizza?" Dustin said.

"I like it better cooked," Quinn said. Both kids were looking at him with big eyes and serious expressions.

"You know what? Let's do something special. After all, it's Christmas." The kids nodded, eyes widening with anticipation. "How hungry are you?"

"Not very," Sienna said. "We ate ham at home already."

"Then, let's have a snack night. I can make popcorn and nachos and we'll eat in front of the TV. How's that sound?" Quinn was bouncing with excitement.

"I call the chair," Sienna said, referring to the stuffed chair he'd found on the side of the road the week after he'd gotten his apartment.

"I was thinking we could have a camp-out tonight. Why don't you grab the covers from your beds and set them up in front of the TV."

"Yeah!"

"And we can have gummy bears for dessert," Dustin said, remembering the package he'd picked up at the gas station on his way home that morning.

Dustin was studying the printouts from the laptop at eight o'clock that evening when the chief knocked on the conference room door.

"I hope you didn't cancel Christmas with your kids so you could work on this case," the chief said.

"No, we had dinner and opened presents, but they really wanted to go back to their mother's house for the night. Apparently, they got a ton of new toys from 'Santa' this year that they wanted to go play with. I hate that Joanne's dating a rich guy. I can't compete with that."

"Don't try. Eventually, they'll see through it."

"Yeah. In another decade or so. I just hope she doesn't

marry him."

"There's nothing you can do about it either way, so you might as well let it go."

"I know, but it's easier said than done." Dustin shook his head and exhaled loudly.

"Where are you at with the laptop," the chief said.

"It's more where I'm at with Keenan Brody."

"What's up?"

"Well, I told you last night I thought he was less than honest with me."

"Yep. Did you find anything more?"

"Sure did. I looked for Keenan's name in all of Shannon's Facebook chat messages."

"And?"

"Apparently, Shannon realized she still had feelings for her high school sweetheart. Sounds like maybe she and Jake got it on when they saw each other at Thanksgiving."

"I can see it happening."

"Here's where it gets interesting. Shannon polled her friends by a private group message a few days before she disappeared. The overwhelming majority said she should tell Keenan about Jake."

"Whatever happened to don't kiss and tell."

"Or in this case, don't screw and tell."

"Are we sure this guy Jake isn't a suspect?"

"Yup. He was already back in California when Shannon disappeared. I confirmed it with his plane ticket and his parents."

"Okay, so what did the Brody kid say about it?"

"That's just it. Nothing. He claims Shannon said she had something important to talk to him about, but she never told him what it was."

"Wasn't there a long call between them right before she disappeared?"

"Exactly. He claims they never talked about whatever it was."

"But you don't believe him."

"Nope. They were on the phone for eight minutes. And the kid was sweating bullets when I questioned him."

"What else do we have on him?"

"At this point, it's more instinct than evidence. Except the part of the interview when he admitted that she was dead."

"Yeah, you mentioned that in your email last night."

"It was definitely odd. He said it with such certainty. I think we should search his dorm room."

"You think he'd give us permission?"

"Maybe, maybe not. I was hoping we could get a warrant."

"With what? We need to be able to articulate what crime was committed and what evidence we think we'll find."

"It's either an abduction or a murder."

"Okay, but how do we link it to the kid's dorm?"

"I don't know. Yet."

"Keep looking."

"Will do. There's one other thing that's odd. According to Shannon's friends, Greta and Jenna, Shannon drove them to the party. When she met up with Keenan, they found another ride home. But he says he didn't see her after the party."

"Public Safety found her car back in a lot near her dorm, so she must have gone back there," the chief said.

"But her roommate didn't see her that night, assumed she spent the night with Keenan."

"So, there's two possibilities. One, she got abducted by a total stranger somewhere between the parking lot and the dorm. Two, the boyfriend's lying."

"My money's on the boyfriend," Dustin said.

"Has Steve finished going through the car?"

"He's still working on it."

"Find anything yet?"

"Nothing obvious. He took a bunch of prints. We'll find out if there's been anyone with a record in that car. Hey, chief?"

"Yeah?"

"Why are you here on Christmas?"

"I was going over the case notes again. We've got to find that girl."

CHAPTER 10
Thursday, December 26, 2013

OLIVIA DAWSON didn't bother with formalities, so the chief didn't bother to offer coffee.

"What did you learn from that boy?" Olivia was standing in the middle of the chief's office, a puddle growing around her from the snow melting off her boots. The chief motioned her into a chair, but she remained standing. Her husband took a seat, leaving behind his own puddle on the chief's floor. Apparently, Californians didn't know how to wipe their feet on the way in. Dustin seemed happy to remain leaning against the wall in the corner of the room.

"He says he doesn't know anything," the chief said.

"And you believe him?" Olivia said.

"We're still taking a hard look at him."

"What does that mean?"

"It means a few things came up during the interview and after that don't make sense. We're continuing our investigation."

Olivia finally sank into a chair. "My daughter has been missing for more than five days."

"I know, I'm sorry."

"What are you doing to find her?"

"Public Safety at the college has been combing the campus."

"I asked what *you've* been doing."

The chief tried to ignore Olivia's tone. "We've been working the phones and picking apart this laptop."

"What about the cell phone trace?"

"It looks like the last time her phone was used, she was still on campus. It's another dead end."

"Her car. What about her car?"

"There was nothing obviously amiss. We took a bunch of prints. We ran them through NCIC, but got no hits."

"What does that mean?"

"It means nobody with prints on file left a print in that car. At least not one we could lift."

There was silence as everyone seemed to ponder the import of the dead end.

Finally, Olivia spoke. "Where is she?" The dark circles around her eyes were starting to resemble the zombies in *The Walking Dead*.

Jack Dawson looked no better. "Is our daughter alive?" he asked.

"I don't want to give you false hope," the chief said.

"Is there any hope?" Olivia said. "Have you found any clue to where she might be?"

The chief shook his head. "I'd like to issue a press release. On the off chance that someone in the community saw something or knows anything."

"Do it," Jack Dawson said.

The chief nodded. "I'll do it right away. It might not be too late for tomorrow's paper. Have you hired a private investigator?"

"We're meeting with one this afternoon."

"Good. Maybe they can turn up something we missed. If she's alive, that's your best bet."

"You don't think she's alive."

"I hope she is, but in all honesty, every day it gets less likely."

As soon as the Dawsons were gone, the chief started drafting a press release. It should have been a simple thing, but it wasn't, because like everything else about his job, it involved politics. It seemed like he was always walking a tightrope between the town and the college. There was a chance this case involved a drunk college student engaging in risky behavior, but if he painted it that way, he'd get in trouble with the college. Masterson College had a big endowment because the administration was always mindful of public relations. Not to mention he'd piss off the Dawsons. On the other hand, the police budget for the town was woefully inadequate. If the townspeople thought he was wasting valuable resources on a matter that really fell under the college's jurisdiction, he'd draw public criticism. He needed to garner sympathy for the family of the missing girl without lying about the situation. Getting caught in public lies was the fastest way to end a public service career.

After deleting the beginnings of three drafts, he decided that the safest thing was a minimalist approach.

<u>PRESS RELEASE</u>

The Middleton Falls Police Department is asking the public for assistance in locating a missing Masterson College student. Shannon Dawson was last seen on the evening of Friday, December 20, 2013 on Maple Street in Middleton Falls. Dawson is a freshman from Solana Beach, California. She is 5 feet 5 inches tall with blond hair and blue eyes. If anyone has any information relating to her disappearance, please contact Officer Dustin Shores at the Middleton Falls Police Department.

He printed it and faxed it over to the *Adams Gazette* along with the photo of Shannon from the college directory. On his way back to his desk, he got another coffee. By the time he got there, the dispatcher was announcing Manny Rodriguez from the *Gazette* on his intercom. He didn't want to pick up, but he had to.

"What's this about a missing college student?" Manny sounded eager.

"You got my press release."

"Pretty bare bones. Can you at least tell me whether you have any leads?"

"All I'm going to say is that the investigation is ongoing."

"But you suspect foul play?"

"We haven't ruled it out."

"Any suspects?"

"We're just investigating at this point."

"But you have Dustin working full time on this?"

"Yes."

"What about the girl's family?"

"Her parents are here, helping look for her."

"Where do I find them?"

"I'd rather not say."

"You can tell me or I can call the local hotels. It's faster if you tell me."

It was probably better to keep Manny as an ally. "They may be at the Marriott. But you didn't hear it from me."

"Thanks, chief."

After he hung up, the chief called Dustin back to his office.

"Okay, what's your theory at this point?" the chief said.

"I think that Keenan and Shannon left the party together. Nobody I've talked to so far reported seeing them leave together, but a few people said they saw them together at the party. Nobody remembered seeing Shannon after that."

"Okay, makes sense."

"I think she told him about Jake. Either during that eight minute phone call or when he found her at the party."

"Probably."

"He got mad."

"I can see that."

"She ends up dead. Maybe it was even an accident, manslaughter instead of murder."

"It's possible. But how drunk do you think she was?"

"I don't know. She was drinking."

"What if she just had an accident? I don't know, slipped on the ice and whacked her head, something like that."

"There'd be a body. We've got no body."

"Good point."

"I think Keenan killed her and hid the body."

"That would explain the lack of a body. But do you really see the kid as a killer?"

"He's a hockey player. Those guys all have short fuses. He probably just got angry. Hit her, strangled her, I don't know."

"Look, I'm not saying your theory isn't a possibility, but we don't actually have any evidence. All we have is a lack of evidence."

"That's why I want to search Keenan's dorm room."

"We don't have any more PC today than we had yesterday. No Vermont judge is going to give us a warrant."

"Maybe we won't need one. The hockey team is due back in town on Saturday. They resume practice that afternoon."

"What are you thinking?"

"I'm going to ask the kid for consent to search. Before he has a chance to get rid of any evidence."

"I guess it can't hurt to ask, but in the meantime don't shut down the other avenues of investigation."

"What avenues?"

"Another good point. Just try to keep an open mind. Everything we have right now is speculation."

OLIVIA THOUGHT she could hear the blood pounding in her ears in the still air of the hotel room. She and Jack were waiting for the private investigator. They'd had no idea how to find one. The yellow pages were woefully inadequate for such an important job. Jack had finally contacted a friend who was an attorney in California. That friend made a few calls and got him in touch with Evan Halliday. The man was driving to Vermont from Connecticut. The expense seemed irrelevant.

There was a knock on the door and Halliday entered. The men shook hands. Olivia didn't have the energy to get up from where she was seated on the corner of a bed. When Jack introduced her, she raised her hand a few inches from her lap and fluttered her fingers. It was a rude greeting, but she was beyond caring.

"I know I said it before on the phone," Halliday said, "but I'm sorry you folks are going through this."

"Thank you for coming up here," Jack said.

"The police here just don't know what they're doing," Olivia said.

"Well, that's why I'm here. I can make sure they're doing everything they can, and I can also do things they can't."

"Like what?"

"Let's just say I don't have to play by the same rules the cops do."

"I don't care how you do it," Olivia said. "I need you to find my daughter."

"I will do my very best."

"What should we be doing?"

"Take care of yourselves. By that I mean try to eat and sleep, if you can."

Both Dawsons nodded.

"And keep in contact with friends and family. If anyone hears anything or has any idea at all where Shannon may be, I want to hear it."

"Of course," Jack said.

"Where will you start?" Olivia said.

"I'm going to start by going through the police file."

"They promised to cooperate," Jack said.

"That's good. After that, I'll start conducting my own interviews. I can look for video surveillance cameras at local businesses that may have recorded some clues. There are avenues the police have yet to explore. I'm sure of it."

"It helps to know that someone competent is stepping in," Olivia said.

After Halliday left, Jack went out for a walk. Olivia tried turning on the TV, but she couldn't focus on it, and the noise just made her head pound even worse. After a few minutes she turned it off. She checked her cell phone again in case someone had left a message and she had somehow missed it. She was pacing in her hotel room, cell phone in hand, when the phone on the nightstand rang.

"Mrs. Dawson?"

"Yes."

"This is Manny Rodriguez from the *Adams Gazette*. I'm sorry about your daughter. I was hoping you could give me a little more background information for an article."

"Do you think it will help locate her?"

"I do. The more people who hear about this, the more likely someone will remember something."

"Okay, then. What do you want to know?"

"How about I come to your hotel room and we can talk about your daughter?"

At least it would be more useful than pacing.

CHAPTER 11
Friday, November 1, 2013

T WAS the first hockey game of the season. Officially, it was only a scrimmage with a nearby rival, but the stands were packed with college students, faculty, and families from Middleton Falls. Hockey was more than a sport at Masterson College; it was a tradition.

Shannon sat in the bleachers with her friends and watched the team circle the ice in preparation for the game.

"What number is Keenan?" Greta said.

"Number five," Shannon said. "There he is, the fourth one in line." The starting players took their positions. Keenan stayed back by the goalie. "Keenan said he plays right back."

"I have no idea what that means," Greta said. "This is my first hockey game. Ever."

"Me, too," Shannon said. "Hockey's not big in southern California."

"I went to a few Rangers games with my dad," Amy said. "It's fun, in a barbaric sort of way."

"You mean like gladiators fighting to the death?" Greta said.

"Nothing that dramatic," Amy said. "It's no worse than football."

"I hate football," Greta said. "I've never understood the point of overgrown monsters plowing into each other at full speed."

Amy rolled her eyes. "Hockey's got more finesse and it's a faster game, so it's much more fun to watch."

"I'm just psyched to see Keenan play," Shannon said.

"Sounds like we have a starstruck fan in our midst," Greta said.

"More like lovestruck," Amy said.

"Give me a break, guys. I've only known him for a few weeks," Shannon said.

"It only takes a minute to fall in love." Greta raised her eyebrows. "Or so I've heard."

"I can't fall in love," Shannon said. "I'm still technically dating my high school boyfriend."

"In California?" Jenna said.

"No, he's here on the east coast, down at Columbia."

"Then how come he hasn't been up to visit?" Jenna said. All three of her friends turned to face Shannon.

"I don't know. It's complicated. Let's watch the game." They all smirked but dropped the subject. Thankfully. Shannon didn't feel the need to reopen that wound, especially now that she had someone else to take her mind off it.

There were a couple of players on the other team who seemed like they just liked to hit people gratuitously. Shannon gasped when one of them took Keenan out from behind when he was nowhere near the puck.

"Are they allowed to do that?" Shannon asked.

"I don't think so," Amy said. "The refs must not have seen it."

"I don't like their number twelve," Shannon said.

The Masterson team was down four to nothing at the beginning of the third period. The other team was in front of the Masterson net and Keenan was defending the goal when Number 12 checked Keenan into the boards. It was hard to see exactly what happened, but by the time the referees separated them, there was blood on the ice. The coaches called a timeout and both Keenan and Number 12 ended up in the penalty boxes.

"Oh my God. Is that normal?" Shannon said.

"It's hockey," Amy said. "Shit happens."

"Wow," Greta said. "I'd be careful of Keenan if I were you, Shannon. It looks like he has a vindictive streak."

AFTER THE game, Keenan sat in the locker room and listened to the coach lecture the team about how unnecessary penalties only served to penalize one's teammates. It was a lecture he'd heard before by every hockey coach he'd ever had, but it had rarely been directed at him. Of course, the coach had a point. There had been too many Masterson penalties in the game. And it probably contributed to their losing by so much. The problem was that the other team had been playing dirty, and the refs had only seemed to give Masterson penalties. Keenan knew he shouldn't have taken the bait when Number 12 came after him, but the guy had been the dirtiest player on a dirty team and Keenan hadn't been able to stop himself from retaliating. And, truth be told, it had felt good to sock him.

When the coach was done and gone, the players started getting out of their gear.

"Hey, Keenan, nice swing at twelve." Rob McPherson was smiling. "He deserved it."

"He sure as hell did," Taylor Browning called from the end of the locker room. "There was something seriously wrong with that guy."

"The coach was right," Keenan said. "I should have let it go."

"No way." Rob was shaking his head. "If you hadn't set him straight, the guy would have kept walking all over us."

Brian Lattrelle was the goalie. He came over and clapped

Keenan on the back. "All I can say is, thanks, man. I'm glad you had my back. In the first two periods, that goon shoved me four times after the ref had blown the whistle. And got away with it every time. He needed a lesson."

CHAPTER 12
Saturday, December 28, 2013

D USTIN READ his *Gazette* over breakfast on Saturday morning. The biweekly paper had arrived a day later than usual in most people's mailboxes. The front page featured an article about Shannon's disappearance. Since the police had released so few details about the investigation, most of the article was about the interview with Shannon's parents, who described their daughter's accomplishments in loving detail. Manny Rodriguez also quoted the Masterson Dean of Students, who assured people that the Masterson campus was safe and there was no reason to suspect a predator was on the loose. Shit. Despite the dean's assurances, every parent in town was probably now thinking Predator. You plant an idea and it has a way of growing. It wouldn't be long before high school basketball games would be poorly attended as parents kept their kids home. They needed to give people answers. And soon.

Dustin checked in at MFPD before heading to campus. The Dawsons' private investigator was already entrenched in the conference room with the Dawson file when he arrived. Evan Halliday had introduced himself in the chief's office the previous morning, making sure to let them know that he was on a first-name basis with the New York City chief of police. As if Dustin cared. Every time Dustin had walked by the conference room yesterday, he'd heard Halliday making loud blowing and clucking noises, like he couldn't believe Dustin had screwed up the investigation so badly.

Dustin was waiting outside Keenan's dorm room late that

morning when Keenan arrived hauling two large duffle bags. A guy Dustin had gone to high school with now worked for Masterson Public Safety and had let him into the building so he could catch the kid by surprise. Keenan looked exhausted when he approached. Probably the stress of knowing they were onto him. The good news was that Keenan was alone and did not appear to have been inside the room yet.

"Did you find her?" Keenan asked.

Dustin shook his head. "We're still looking."

Keenan's shoulders sank. Dustin had to give it to him. He was putting on a good act.

"You want to help us find Shannon?"

"Of course I do."

"Let me search your room."

Keenan opened the door to his room using the keypad and placed the two duffles inside. "I didn't have anything to do with her disappearing."

"Then you have nothing to hide."

"If I didn't have anything to do with her disappearing, how does letting you search my room help find her?"

"Because it helps us rule you out as a suspect. We can focus in another direction."

"Why am I a suspect?"

"Most homicides are committed by someone the victim knows, usually a spouse or boyfriend."

"But this isn't a homicide, is it? What have you not told me?"

"I think the question is, what have you not told us?"

"I've answered all your questions. I'm not sure what else you want from me."

"I want the truth. All of it. And I want to search your room."

Keenan started to shut the door. "I want to talk to my dad."

Dustin put his hand out to keep the door open. "Look, I don't have any reason to believe you had anything to do with Shannon's disappearance. But if I didn't investigate every possibility, I wouldn't be doing my job."

"I didn't do anything to her."

"Then there's no reason not to consent to a search."

Keenan was clearly thinking about it. He pulled out a phone. "I just want to see what my dad says." Dustin had to wait while Keenan tried to reach his father. After about thirty seconds, Keenan put his phone back in his pocket. "He's probably driving, so he can't pick up."

"Are you worried I'll find drugs or alcohol? Because that doesn't concern me right now."

"No, nothing like that. I'm subject to drug and alcohol testing as a student athlete. I don't want to get kicked off the team, so it's not an issue. I can't promise my roommate doesn't have something stashed away, but it doesn't have anything to do with me."

"Sounds like we're on the same page."

"I don't know."

"Let me have a look. I don't find anything, there's no reason to keep looking at you."

"There was no reason to start looking at me."

"So, let me in."

Keenan stepped to the side and gestured with one arm. "If it will get you to leave me alone, then go ahead."

Dustin pulled a folded form out of his coat pocket. "Great. I just need you to sign this Consent to Search form."

Keenan studied the form for a minute, signed it against the open door to his room, and handed it back.

"Why don't you stay out here in the hall while I search?"

"I'd rather not."

"It's protocol," Dustin said. He pulled a pair of blue nitrile gloves out of his pocket and put them on. Keenan leaned against the hallway wall. He looked smug, which probably meant this was a waste of time.

Dustin took in the room. The furnishings were standard. He didn't see anything suspect or unusual on the walls or on the surfaces of the furniture. He decided to start with the desk and pulled the center drawer open. Amid the jumble of pens and pencils something jumped out at him. A set of keys with a VW key fob. He gently placed the keys in a clear Ziploc evidence bag.

"You have a car here on campus?"

"Nope."

"What are these?"

"They're Shannon's."

"How'd they end up in your desk drawer?"

"I put them there."

"When was this?"

"Right before I went home for break."

"You didn't think it was worth mentioning?"

"I forgot."

"You forgot something this important?"

"It was a week and a half ago."

"How'd you end up with the keys, son? Did you take them from her after you killed her?"

"What? No. I keep telling you. I didn't kill her."

"Maybe it was a mistake. You argued, you hit her, harder than you meant to. Then, you panicked and hid her body, used her car get back to campus."

"No. That's not what happened."

"Or you strangled her. It's easy to choke someone to death by mistake."

"No."

"How did it happen? How did she die, Keenan?"

"I have no idea. I just wanted her to be safe—for all the good it did."

"What did you do with her body, Keenan?"

"Nothing. I didn't want anything to happen to her."

"Of course not. But it happened anyway. She died anyway, didn't she?"

"I don't know what you're talking about, but I think I need a lawyer."

"You're not under arrest. Why would you need a lawyer?"

"Because you're turning this into something it wasn't."

"So what was it? What happened to Shannon?"

"I'm not talking to you any more. You're not listening to me."

"Okay. When you're ready to talk, here's my card. In the meantime, this search is going to take longer than I expected. I need to call for help. You might want to go somewhere else to wait."

"Can I at least get my parka out of my duffle?"

"Sorry, it's in the room, so it's part of the search."

"It's twelve degrees out. I need my parka."

"You can have it after we clear the room."

"You have got to be shitting me." The kid walked away but kept looking over his shoulder. Dustin waited until he was out of sight to call for assistance.

They didn't turn up anything else in the search. As soon as Dustin finished, he headed to the chief's office. "Do we have probable cause to arrest him?" Dustin said.

"On what charges?" the chief said.

"I don't know. Murder?"

"To charge a murder we either need a body or a confession. Or at least evidence of foul play. We have none of the above."

"You're right. But my gut says he killed to her."

"So, try again for a confession. That might also help us find the body."

"I doubt he'll talk to me again. He knows we're onto him."

"What about getting him to submit to fingerprints? If we find his prints on the driver's side of Shannon's car, that proves he drove it back to her dorm. That's solid proof he was the last one to see her."

"He won't willingly give me prints. I had to play all my cards to get him to consent to the search. He already mentioned talking to a lawyer. He'll lawyer up for sure if I ask for prints."

"Go talk to the state's attorney first thing on Monday. See the man himself, not one of his deputies. This case is too big. Fred already told me he wants to be in from the get-go. Ask him if he can get you a court order. Maybe the Brody kid will say something when we bring him in for prints."

"Okay, I'm on it."

"And talk to Public Safety today. See what it'll take to get access to the kid's gym locker."

CHAPTER 13
Monday, December 30, 2013

USTIN WAS always nervous when he had to talk to the state's attorney. Fred Dutton was a career prosecutor who had been getting elected to the chief prosecutor's job for as long as Dustin had been on the force. Nobody had tried to run against him in decades. The man clearly knew his business. When Dustin arrived, Fred was on the phone, but Dustin only had to wait a few minutes before the receptionist sent him back to Fred's office.

"Tell me about the investigation. What's going on?"

Dustin filled him in on the Facebook messages on Shannon's MacBook, the trip to the Northeast Kingdom, and the searches of Shannon's Volkswagen and Keenan's room. "My theory is that Shannon told Keenan she slept with Jake, he got angry, and he killed her. He told me he doesn't keep a car on campus, so he must've used her car to take her body somewhere and dump it. Then, he drove the car back and left it in her usual parking area. It was careless. If he'd disposed of the keys or brought the car back to the party, we might not have picked up on it."

"It's not a bad theory based on what you have, but I'll need a lot more evidence before I charge anyone. And it's still possible that Shannon drove that car back herself."

"So, why did Brody have her keys?"

"I don't know. What did he say?"

"He didn't give much of an explanation."

"That's troubling." Fred furrowed his brow. "Where are you

going with the investigation?"

"I'm going to talk to the students as soon as everyone gets back in town. It's hard conducting an investigation when all your witnesses are out of state."

"Okay. What else?"

"That's what I wanted to talk about. I'd like an order for fingerprints from the Brody kid. His prints aren't in the system because he has no record. If we find his prints in the vehicle, it's one more piece of circumstantial evidence."

"Let's look at the rule." Fred picked up a green legal volume from the corner of this desk. He flipped through the pages for about ten seconds. "Here it is. It says we can ask for a non-testimonial order if we have probable cause to believe a crime was committed. Do we?"

"Definitely. A kid like Shannon doesn't disappear at Christmastime unless something happened to her."

"That's probably true. But what crime?"

"I don't know."

"Maybe it doesn't matter. The judge might cut us some slack, but we also need a reasonable suspicion that Brody is the perpetrator. I'll draft a request for an order. I need you to write an affidavit in support. Write it like you would a search warrant request, but be vague about the charges. Make sure to be convincing that this is more than just a missing person case, and explain why fingerprint analysis might help us identify the perpetrator. I'll file it under seal so we don't tip our hand just yet."

"Yes, sir. I'll get something to you as soon as I can. Thank you, sir."

Dustin made two trips to the hockey locker room the next day. The first time, he searched Brody's locker without a warrant after he secured the cooperation of the college athletics director. Unfortunately, it had contained nothing more than overripe hockey gear.

The second time, Dustin waited outside the door for practice to end. At least the Brody kid was easy to locate; the college posted the ice arena schedule on its website.

"Keenan Brody, I have a court order requiring you to submit to fingerprinting. You are hereby ordered to appear by five o'clock today at the MFPD offices." Dustin pulled a folded copy of the court order out of his pocket and handed it to Keenan.

"I want a lawyer," Keenan said. Spoken like a guilty person, Dustin thought.

"You're not under arrest, so we're under no obligation to provide an attorney. You just come to the station for prints, then you'll be free to go."

"What if I refuse?"

"You'll be in contempt of court and we'll arrest you for that." Dustin turned and strode quickly out of the building. He was looking forward to the fingerprinting. In his experience, sometimes suspects let things slip during routine processing, especially if you were able to goad them a little. This situation was perfect for that type of thing. The kid would not be in custody, so there would be no legal requirement to issue a *Miranda* warning. He hoped the kid didn't get spooked and bring a lawyer, though he doubted that would be the case. The kid was just cocky enough to think he could outsmart Dustin. Not happening.

Keenan arrived alone later that afternoon. Dustin made him wait in the lobby for ten minutes just to establish the upper hand. Then, he led him to a small room set up with finger-printing equipment and cameras.

Dustin was surprised at how much pressure he was feeling. He knew this might be his last chance to talk to the Brody kid. If the prints came back matching the prints from Shannon's car, they would have solid evidence that Keenan had driven the car. That would make it likely that he had disposed of the body. They were still waiting on a forensic report, but there were some blond hairs found in the trunk of the car. If the forensic analysis proved they matched the hairs taken from Shannon's brush in her dorm room, that would be strong circumstantial evidence that her body had been in the trunk of the car.

He needed to be careful here. Brody had already mentioned a lawyer a couple of times.

"Thank you for coming in. This should only take a few minutes."

"It's not like you gave me a choice."

Dustin shrugged. "We just want to find the girl. Give her parents a little peace."

"Sorry, I can't help you."

"Can't or won't?"

Keenan just glared at Dustin.

"Where's Shannon?" Dustin asked.

"Oh my God. How many times do I have to tell you? I have no idea."

"But you had her keys."

"Because I didn't want her to drive. I told you. She was drunk." Keenan shook his head and crossed his arms. It was definitely body language that indicated lying.

"Are we going to find your prints on the steering wheel?" Dustin knew they hadn't been able to recover any usable prints from the steering wheel, but the kid didn't need to know that.

"Of course you are. I drove the car back to the dorm."

Bingo. His strategy had worked. He needed to keep the pressure on to get the full confession, so he quickly asked, "Where was Shannon? In the trunk?"

"No, she left the party before I did."

"Did you put her in the back seat?"

"No."

"You put her in the front seat then."

"I keep telling you, she'd already left."

"So why'd you drive her car back to the dorm?"

"I was trying to be nice."

"Really? Chivalry? That's your explanation?"

"Is that so hard to believe?"

"Actually, yes." The kid must have come up with the explanation after Dustin found the keys. He sure as hell didn't mention anything about taking her keys to keep her from driving or driving the car back to the dorm the last time they "chatted" when Dustin had searched Keenan's room. The circumstantial evidence against the kid was mounting.

CHAPTER 14
Friday, November 14, 2013

"YOU REALIZE you've been talking about Keenan nonstop for ten minutes," Amy said. "I think you're in love with him." Shannon was walking with her friend from their dorm to their chemistry class. The air was crisp, and they were both wearing winter coats and fleece-lined boots.

"I can't be. I told you I'm still technically involved with Jake."

"Love doesn't care about technicalities. Besides, whose idea was it to see other people, yours or Jake's?"

"It was mutual, I guess. Jake didn't want to go off to college tied down, so we agreed." Not that she'd had a choice. "Plus, we said if we came back to each other, it was meant to be."

"Were there any rules?"

"Rules?"

"You know, like it's okay to date, but don't sleep with anyone."

"No, but I don't want Jake sleeping with anyone else."

"Why not? You are."

"I know. And I feel guilty about it."

"So, stop."

"I don't want to."

"Because you're in love with Keenan."

"Maybe."

Amy laughed. "Sweetie, you can't have it both ways."

"I know."

"You probably ought to tell Jake about Keenan."

Shannon knew her friend was right. Deep down she'd been thinking the same thing for a couple of weeks. "I can't do it on the phone. Not after two years."

"Are you guys going home for Thanksgiving?"

"No, the break is too short to fly across the country. I'd been planning to go down and stay with Jake at his dorm for a few days, but that was before Keenan. Now I need to come up with a new plan. I might just stay here."

"I have an idea. Come home with me. We'll go out in the city. You can have Turkey Day with my family and you can get together with Jake without having to stay with him. You can tell him about Keenan in person."

It was the perfect solution. "Do you think your parents would mind?"

"Of course not. We have plenty of room. They'll love you."

"Thanks, Amy. Now I just have to figure out what I'm going to say to Jake."

"You still have two weeks. You'll come up with something." She hoped Amy was right on that count as well. The problem was, she didn't want to think about it.

KEENAN SLIPPED into his seat just before the professor started her lecture. His friend Aarav Chadha looked at him out of the corner of his eye but didn't smile. Aarav was slight and dark with wire-rimmed glasses and a perpetually creased brow. They had met during freshman orientation and become friends when Keenan had commented on Aarav's well-worn copy of *The Stand*.

"You like Steven King?" Keenan had asked.

Aarav had tensed and looked around, as if he expected that Keenan was talking to someone else. "Yes," he said slowly.

"Me, too. I've read all his books. He might even be the reason I'm an English major. I want to write books someday."

Aarav nodded and his shoulders relaxed. "I'm an English major too, although my father doesn't approve."

"Why not?"

"He's an engineering professor. He thinks the only things worth studying are math and science."

"So you're the family rebel?"

"No, that's my Uncle Raj. He's in jail in India."

"Really? Are you from India?"

"No, I'm from Baltimore. My parents moved to the U.S. when my dad was in graduate school."

They had continued talking and discovered that they shared many of the same favorite books. And it turned out they had a few of the same classes the first year. They had frequently had lunch together after their writing seminar.

When the lecture was over, Keenan watched Aarav pack up. "Are you okay?" Keenan asked.

Aarav shrugged.

"What's going on, Aarav? We haven't talked much lately."

"You've been busy."

"Yeah, it's hockey season. I've been out straight between school and hockey. I lift in the morning, then we're on the ice from four to six every day. It feels like I'm always rushing to get to the dining hall before it closes."

"You're always with the team when I see you."

"That's just 'cuz we usually all walk over together after practice. Is there something you want to talk about?"

"Not really. I thought maybe you were mad at me."

"Not at all. It's just my busy time of year, and"—Keenan grinned—"I met a girl."

"Okay, that explains it," Aarav said. He sounded disappointed, but he smiled. "You want to have lunch today?"

"I can't. I promised Shannon I'd meet her for lunch."

"That's her name? Shannon?"

"Yeah, she's great. You want to have lunch on Monday?"

Aarav nodded.

"Better yet, let's try for lunch every Monday. I miss talking with you."

Aarav's smile gleamed. "Maybe you can help me figure out how to ask out this girl in my poly sci class."

CHAPTER 15
Thursday, January 2, 2014

I WANT the truth. Who did this to us?" Olivia Dawson sat in the chief's office and wiped a tear from her cheek with the back of her hand. The woman looked gaunt. The chief figured she hadn't slept in almost two weeks. Her husband was motionless in his chair. Their private investigator, Evan Halliday, leaned against the back wall of the office with Dustin. Halliday's eyes had been on his phone since entering the room.

The chief shook his head. "At this point, we can't be sure."

"That's not good enough."

"I assure you, we will not stop investigating until we have answers, but that doesn't mean we'll find them."

"I just want my baby back." Olivia was sobbing. Her husband seemed too wrapped up in his own grief to console her.

The investigator lowered his phone and stepped forward. "We need to know everything that's going on with this investigation."

"I assure you," the chief said. "I'm not holding out on you. There just isn't much there."

"What about the new boyfriend?" Halliday said.

Dustin looked at the chief and raised an eyebrow in obvious question. The chief nodded at him. "At this point, he's our prime suspect," Dustin said. "Our only suspect."

"So, get him to tell you what he did to our daughter." Olivia sounded understandably bitter.

"I've spoken to him multiple times. He denies any involvement."

"And you believe him?"

"Not really."

"So, do something to get him to talk."

"Believe me, I've tried."

"So, arrest him. That's what they do on TV," Olivia said.

The chief knew he needed to regain control of the conversation. "There just isn't enough evidence," he said.

"What exactly do you think you have?" Halliday said, without looking up from his phone. He appeared to be texting.

"We have a motive. Apparently, Shannon was planning to tell Brody she had been with Jake over Thanksgiving and that she still had feelings for Jake. We have evidence of a phone conversation between Brody and Shannon the night she disappeared."

Evan nodded but continued to text. "You also have opportunity. According to the file, you can put them at the party together. Are there any new developments?"

"We found Shannon's keys in Brody's dorm room and his prints near the headlight switch of her car as well as several places on the passenger side."

Olivia's eyes opened wide. "Oh my God! And you think that's not enough evidence?"

"He says she was drunk, so he took her keys and drove her car back to the dorm for her."

"And you believe him?" Olivia said.

"Not really." The chief frowned.

"Then why haven't you arrested him?"

"Forgive me, but we don't even have a body."

"That's because he did something to her."

The chief nodded. "Possibly."

"So, arrest him," Olivia said with more force this time.

"The state's attorney said it wasn't enough."

"What more do you need?"

"A body or a confession."

"So he gets away with this. He takes my child from me and he gets away with it."

"Not necessarily. The students will start coming back to campus in a few days. It'll be easier to track down everyone from the party. I assure you, we'll interview everyone and get more details about what happened at that party."

"Do you mind if I have a crack at the boyfriend? I might be able to get him to talk," Evan said.

The chief glanced at Dustin, who nodded. "Go for it," the chief said. He no longer cared how the case got solved. The private investigator was a bit of a prick, but if he could get some answers and give the Dawsons some peace, the more power to him.

CHAPTER 16
Friday, January 3, 2014

DUSTIN HAD a list of students he wanted to interview in person. At the top of the list were Greta and Jenna, the two girls Shannon had been with the night she disappeared. Fortunately, Greta was registered for a January term class and was due back on campus.

He made an appointment to interview her at the station the day she returned. When she arrived, he showed her to an interview room and turned on the recording devices.

"Thanks for coming," he said.

"My dad told me not to."

"Why?"

"He's a lawyer. He said you should never talk to the police."

"Don't you want to help us find your friend?"

"That's why I'm here."

"So, tell me about the last time you saw Shannon."

"She came over to my room after dinner on Friday night, the last day of the term."

"Who else was there?"

"Jenna and Ruby."

"What were you doing?"

"Just hanging out and listening to music."

"About what time was it?"

"I think Shannon got there around six thirty or seven."

"Were you drinking?"

"It's against the rules to have alcohol in the dorms."

"What about smoking weed?"

"That too."

"Look, I'm not trying to get you in trouble with the college. I just want to know exactly what we're dealing with. Did Shannon ingest any substances while you were with her?"

"I'm really not sure."

"Is it possible?"

Greta looked around the room uncomfortably. "Sure," she said.

"Did you talk to Shannon about her relationships with Keenan Brody and Jake Miller?"

"Sure."

"What did she have to say?"

"Mostly that she was confused."

"About what?"

"She was definitely wheeling and dealing with Keenan, but Jake was still a question mark."

"What exactly do you mean by wheeling and dealing?"

"Sorry. They were in a relationship."

"So, why was Jake a question mark?"

"Well, when she left for college, Jake told her he wanted to see other people. So, when she met Keenan, she decided to go for it."

"Sounds straight forward."

Greta shook her head. "Except that she actually liked Keenan. She was pretty happy with him until she went to the city for Thanksgiving. Then, she and Jake hooked up."

"Hooked up as in . . . ?"

"Had sex." Her expression added, "Duh."

"Okay."

"She felt guilty."

"Hence, the poll?"

"You know about that?"

Dustin nodded.

"So, she decided to tell Keenan about Jake. But she didn't really want to because she was afraid of how Keenan would react. That might be why she had a couple of drinks."

"A little liquid courage?"

Greta shrugged. "Maybe."

"Do you know if she did in fact tell Keenan?"

"I didn't hear her, if that's what you mean."

"But, it's possible she told him?"

"Sure."

"Likely even?"

"She said she was going to."

"Did anything else happen at the dorm?"

"Not really. We went over to Lila and Grace's room for a while."

"Was there drinking in that room?"

"I can't be sure."

"Did you see anyone drinking?"

"Not that I can recall."

"Okay. What time did you leave?"

"We left to go to the party at about nine o'clock."

"Where was the party?"

"Off campus."

"Do you know the address?"

"I'm not sure. Somewhere on Maple Street."

"Was there alcohol at the party?"

"There might have been."

"Look, Greta, I know you're trying not to get anybody in trouble because of what your dad said, but I can't find Shannon unless I get honest answers from you. What was going on at the party?"

Greta chewed her lip. "A few people were drinking."

"Were you drinking?"

"I'm going to take the fifth."

"Okay. How much did Shannon have to drink?"

"I really can't say."

"Was she drunk?"

"I don't know."

"Greta, this is important. How drunk was she?"

"I'm not her, so I can't say how drunk she was."

"Spoken like a lawyer. Are you planning to follow in your father's footsteps?"

Greta shrugged. "We were just having a good time. She didn't seem drunk to me."

"Did you see Keenan Brody that night?"

"Yes, I did."

"Where?"

"At the party."

"Was he there when you got there?"

"No, he arrived after. He wanted to talk to Shannon."

"Did Keenan seem agitated when you met up with him?"

"Now that you mention it, yeah."

"So, it's likely Shannon had already told him about Jake by that point?"

"Yeah."

"What happened when Keenan got there?"

"He made Shannon go out on the back deck to talk."

"Did it look like she wanted to go?"

"Not really."

"So, he forced her to go with him?"

"You could say that."

"What happened while they were out there?"

"I wasn't out there, but I saw them through the glass door. It looked like they were arguing."

"Did Shannon seem intimidated?"

"Probably. Keenan's a big guy."

"And he plays hockey."

"Yeah."

"So, she would have been afraid?"

"I guess so."

"How were they standing?"

"Just facing each other a few feet apart."

"Did they stay that way? Or did he get physical with her?"

"You know, I think I remember him grabbing her."

"Okay, good. What do you mean by grabbing?"

"You know, grabbing. Like, he put his hands on her arms."

"Could you hear anything they said?"

"Not really, it was noisy inside the house."

"But he was yelling at her?"

"Yeah, probably. I mean, wouldn't you yell if your girlfriend just told you she slept with another guy?"

"Did they leave the party together?"

"They must have."

"Did you see them?"

"I'm not sure."

"Did you see Shannon again that night?"

"I haven't seen Shannon since I saw her on the deck. They must have left through the backyard."

"Why do you say that?"

"Because I would have seen them if they left through the house."

"Do you think she would have gone with Keenan willingly based on what you saw?"

"I don't know. Maybe not."

"How much longer did you stay at the party?"

"Not long. When we realized Shannon had ditched us to go with Keenan, Jenna and I caught a ride back to campus."

"Who with?"

"Joe something."

"Do you have contact info for him?"

"I don't know him that well. He was getting ready to leave, so we asked him for a ride."

"Okay, is there anything else that happened that night?"

"No."

"What about planning a trip to Maine?"

"Maine? No, that was a joke."

"Did you try to call Shannon after you left the party?"

"I wish I had, but I didn't. I was a little salty because she left us without a ride. Now I wish I'd called her. Or that I hadn't let her go out on the deck with Keenan."

"Anything else that you think would help us figure out what happened to Shannon?"

"Not really."

"If you think of anything, I want you to call me. Now, I need contact information for all the girls you mentioned, and I need a few minutes to type up a statement of everything we just talked about. Then, I want to take a drive down Maple Street so you can show me where the party was."

After he had dropped Greta on campus, Dustin went to see the chief. He put Greta's statement on the desk.

"I knew I was on the right track. Now, we have evidence of an argument with the Brody kid right before she disappeared and a witness who saw him grab her. Please tell me we have enough to charge him now."

The chief took a minute to read the statement.

"This helps, but I still don't think it's enough."

"What else do you want me to do?"

"I want you to track down as many kids from the party as you can. Get statements from them. Somebody at that party saw something. They had to have."

"Okay. What else?"

"Let's get a search warrant for the house. If the kids aren't back yet, it may look like it did the night of the party. It's clear there was alcohol being served to minors, and it was the last place she was seen. If you write it up right, the judge will give you a warrant. For all we know, her body is under the back deck."

"I guess I can do that. What specifically are we looking for?"

"Evidence of a party. Evidence that Shannon was there. Her phone. Anything belonging to her . . . Her body."

"But I think the Brody kid used her car to move her body."

"You may be right. But, we don't have any witnesses that saw him put her body in the car. While you're at the house take lots of photos. I wouldn't be surprised to learn that house or yard is the crime scene. Actually, I think I'd like to go with you on this one."

EVAN HALLIDAY could tell that the local police were less than thrilled about his involvement in the case. No big surprise, and nothing he wasn't used to from his years in the FBI. Local cops were almost always smalltime and incompetent. And it was becoming clear they'd royally screwed up the investigation by dragging their heels in the beginning. It would be fun to solve the case under their noses and show them up.

Evan watched hockey practice from the bleachers at the ice arena. He'd played hockey for a few years as a kid, so he was impressed with the level of play, the agility and power the team demonstrated on the ice. He had done some research before coming down to the rink and learned the Brody kid's jersey number, but there was a mishmash of jerseys on the ice during practice, so it was hard to tell who was who. Fortunately, the team photo was on the college website, so he knew what Keenan Brody looked like. He'd track the kid down after practice.

Keenan was one of the last to leave the locker room. He came out looking freshly showered.

"Keenan?"

The kid looked at him, clearly confused that he didn't recognize the middle-aged man in a suit.

"I'm Evan Halliday." He held out his hand. "Shannon's parents hired me to find her. I was hoping I could ask you a few questions."

Keenan shook hands with apparent reluctance. "I didn't do anything to her. The police have it all wrong."

"I don't have anything to do with the police investigation. I'm just trying to help the Dawsons find their daughter. You may have information that will help us. Can we go somewhere, get a cup of coffee? Maybe some food?"

"I suppose."

"It's my treat. Where would you like to go?"

"The Commons Cafe is the only thing open on campus right now." Keenan gestured toward the center of campus.

"Is it a good place to talk?"

"Yeah, and we can walk." Keenan glanced down. "Without destroying your loafers. The college does a good job keeping the paths around campus clear."

"Let's go, then," Evan said.

Keenan hesitated, as if he might change his mind. Evan smiled brightly and started walking. "This way?" he said looking over his shoulder.

Keenan nodded and followed.

It was best to keep the conversation light for a while, try to get him comfortable. "So, how long you been playing hockey?" Evan said.

"Since I was four."

"Wow. That's young."

"It's a family tradition."

"You're lucky. I tried skating once in Central Park. Couldn't sit down for a week."

They both laughed, though Keenan sounded more polite than genuine. "I am lucky," Keenan said. "I know I wouldn't have gotten into Masterson if I wasn't a good hockey player."

"You getting a full ride?"

"No, it's against the rules for Division III, but they want me here, so I got a lot of need-based aid."

"Your parents helping you?"

"Yeah, but I have an older brother at Tufts and two younger sisters in high school, so they're stretched a little thin."

"Your brother play hockey too?"

"Everybody in my family plays hockey. But my brother doesn't play college hockey, if that's what you mean. He's too focused on his grades, trying to get into vet school."

"Good for him. What's your dad do?"

"He's a large animal vet."

"Ah, your brother's following in dad's footsteps. What about you?"

"Nope. I'm not good with gross stuff. I'm an English major."

Evan laughed. "What's your mom do?"

"She was always a stay-at-home mom, but now that us kids are older, she has a business selling medicinal herbs on the internet. She grows the stuff in the fields and even has a little greenhouse."

"You mean like medical marijuana?"

"What? No. I mean like St. John's Wort."

Evan chuckled. They arrived at the cafe, and Evan was glad

to get out of the icy wind. It was much colder in Vermont than Connecticut.

The cafe was more a cafeteria than a restaurant. They went through the line and Evan got coffee. Keenan got a burger and a large coke. When they got to the cashier, Evan insisted on paying.

"I invited you, remember?" Evan knew that a college student with loans would be unlikely to turn down a free lunch.

"Okay, if you insist."

They got a table in a remote corner, though it was probably unnecessary. The cafe was quiet, awaiting the return on the students the next day.

"So, tell me about Shannon."

"What do you want to know?"

"What's she like?"

"She's smart and pretty, with a good sense of humor, but a competitive side too."

"She have a lot of friends?"

"I guess so. I don't know. We were only dating for a couple of months."

"You really like her?"

"A lot. But I don't think it was going to last."

"Why not?"

"I think I liked her more than she liked me."

"What makes you think that?"

"Just how cool she was."

"What do you mean?"

"I don't know."

"Did you have a girlfriend in high school?"

"Yeah, but it wasn't serious, mostly because I didn't want it to be."

"But you wanted to get serious with Shannon?"

Keenan shrugged. "I don't think it was heading that way."

"Tell me about the last time you saw Shannon."

"She called me and said she wanted to talk before we left for break. I could tell she was drinking. I'd never seen her drink before."

"Were you concerned?"

"A little. Plus, I knew she was leaving to go home the next day, and I didn't want to leave things up in the air, so I decided to go find her."

"So you went looking for her?"

"Yeah."

"How'd you know where to find her?"

"She said they were going to the keg party on Maple Street."

"So you went to the party?"

"Yeah. And she was there with her friends."

"What happened next?"

"I tried to talk to her, but she was too drunk."

"How do you know?"

"It was obvious she was wasted. She was acting clumsy. She's never clumsy. And she and her friends had this stupid idea of driving to Maine. It was crazy."

"Did you guys talk about anything else?"

"Not really. It was clear she didn't want to talk to me right then."

"So what happened next?"

"I took her keys."

"Why did you take the keys?"

Keenan looked puzzled. "So she couldn't drive, obviously. If she'd tried to drive to Maine in the condition she was in, she would have killed herself and her friends."

"How did she react to you taking the keys?"

"She wasn't happy, but she didn't go crazy or anything. She just left."

"Did you see her again?"

"No. I assumed she had found her friends, and they'd gone off somewhere. I couldn't find any of them at the party, so I drove the car back to her dorm."

"What were you thinking?"

"I was thinking she needed to catch a plane the next day and it would be easier for her if she didn't have to worry about going back for her car."

"Was it a shorter walk for you from her dorm?"

"Actually, it would have been shorter if I'd walked home from the party."

"So you were just being a nice guy?"

"Yeah."

"Even though you thought she was going to break up with you?"

"Is that so hard to believe?"

Evan looked away for a few seconds while he pondered the possibility. "Why didn't you tell the police any of this when they came to your house?"

"They didn't ask."

"Maybe not specifically, but they asked you to tell everything."

"That Shores guy isn't exactly easy to talk to."

Evan laughed. "Yeah, he's a bit uptight. So, who do you think I should talk to to figure out what happened to Shannon?"

"I would talk to the two girls she was with that night. They were probably the last ones to see her."

"Did you try to get in touch with her after she left the party?"

"Yeah. I called her cell a bunch of times."

"Did she answer?"

"Not once. So I walked over to her dorm room to return her keys."

"But she wasn't there?"

"Nope. That's why I threw her keys in my desk drawer. I didn't know what else to do with them, and my brother was coming to pick me up."

"Okay, thanks for talking to me."

"Thanks for lunch. Can I ask you something?"

"Sure, go ahead."

"Do you believe me?"

"Why wouldn't I?"

"Because the police seem to think I did something to Shannon. It's crazy."

"The police are conducting a criminal investigation. I'm

trying to find a missing person. We have a different focus."

"You didn't actually answer the question."

"Do I believe you? I don't know yet."

"At least you've been honest with me." Keenan sighed.

"Can I contact you if I have more questions?"

"Sure, but next time call my cell, okay? I'm getting sick of people coming to practice to find me."

After Keenan left, Evan turned off the digital recorder he had in his pocket.

DUSTIN WAS supposed to pick up Sienna and Quinn after school. He hadn't seen them since Christmas because they'd been away with Joanne for the rest of school vacation.

He waited in his Explorer in the pickup line at the elementary school with his engine running. There were No Idling signs everywhere in front of the school, but lots of the drivers were ignoring them. It was too cold to care about air quality. With the heat blasting into the car, he closed his eyes and, without meaning to, dozed off.

He woke up when the car door slammed. Quinn was strapping himself into the back seat.

"Anson got a bloody nose so we couldn't have art today," Quinn said.

"I'm sure you'll get to do art another day."

"Art's my favorite class."

"I'm sorry," Dustin said. He hadn't seen his son in ten days, the longest they'd been apart since Quinn was born. It felt like their reunion should have been more momentous, at least warranted a hug.

Sienna was getting in her side. "Mrs. Bevins gave us homework," she said. Dustin saw that tears were forming in the corners of her eyes.

"I'm sure you'll get it done. I can help if you want."

"We need to use a computer, Dad. You don't have a computer at your apartment."

"I'm sorry," he said. "You know what? You can do your homework at Grandma's. I need you guys to go there tomorrow anyway."

"I thought we were spending the weekend with you."

"You are. I just need to work for a couple of hours tomorrow."

"Oh."

"How was Florida?" Dustin said, hoping to change the subject. "Did you have a good visit with Nanna and Papa?" Joanne's parents had moved to Florida the previous fall.

"We ended up going to Puerto Rico. It was too cold and cloudy in Florida, so Gregor decided we needed to go somewhere warmer. He wanted to go to the Dominican Republic, but we didn't have passports."

"Gregor went with you guys?" Dustin said.

"Yeah," Sienna said.

"Wow." Dustin wanted to say more, but didn't know where to start. His kids had spent Christmas break with Joanne and her boyfriend in Puerto Rico. Which he had just learned did not require passports. He pictured Gregor and Joanne lounging on a beach while his kids splashed in the waves. It was so totally fucked up, he didn't know where to fucking start.

It was quiet in the car while he drove to the apartment. He had meant to do something to make the apartment more like a home, maybe get a couch. But there hadn't been time while the kids were away. He'd been working around the clock on the missing girl case. Hell, he'd even forgotten about getting a Wii. He needed to find Shannon Dawson so he could get on with his life.

"Can we watch TV?" Quinn said.

"Sure," Dustin said.

"I call the chair," Sienna said. At least he had food in the house this time.

CHAPTER 17
Sunday, November 24, 2013

KEENAN AND Shannon had spent Saturday night in her dorm room since her roommate was out of town for a change. They got up too late for breakfast at the dining hall, so they decided to jog into town for bagels before going for a workout. Keenan needed to lift weights. Shannon had her own workout routine.

They sat in the back of The Bagel Shoppe drinking hot coffee and eating warm bagels with cream cheese. Shannon's phone made chiming noise, so she picked it up.

"What's up?" Keenan asked.

"Just a text from my friend Sophie in California. She wants me to look at a video she just shared on Facebook." Shannon put her phone between them on the table and played the video. The video was entitled *Restoring Your Faith in Humanity*. It combined clips of ordinary people saving wild animals in trouble around the world.

"That's totally cool," Keenan said. "My parents would love that."

"Yeah. I'm going to share it and post a comment to Sophie. That way you can share it too."

While Shannon typed, Keenan caressed her cheek. He couldn't help it, he just wanted to touch her all the time. When she finished, she smiled at him and took his hand, but let go a minute later so she could finish her bagel.

"We can't sit here all day, you know," Shannon said.

"I know. We both need to work out. Then, there's practice and studying."

"I've got a chemistry lab report due on Tuesday, so I probably won't see you for a couple of days."

"That's okay. But I want to see you before you leave for Thanksgiving."

"I'll make sure to save Tuesday night for you."

"You could always come home with me for Thanksgiving, you know."

"I'm not sure I'm ready for that. It's a little soon."

He wanted her to change her mind, but he had a sense that, if he pushed too hard, she would pull back from him. He feigned nonchalance. "My parents are cool. And my mom's a great cook. They'd put you in the guest room, of course, but I could sneak in and visit you."

"It's tempting, but I already told Amy I'd go home with her. Besides, I want to do some things in the city."

Keenan realized he had been holding his breath, hoping for a different answer. He exhaled and tried to give her a smile that looked genuine. "You'd rather spend the weekend in New York City than Lyndonville, Vermont. Are you crazy?"

"Yup. Crazy for you."

Keenan smiled for real.

CHAPTER 18
Saturday, January 4, 2014

THE JUDGE was quick to sign off on the warrant to search the Maple Street house. The chief was a little surprised, but with a young woman missing, the judge probably thought it prudent to do what he could to help. The chief recruited Sergeant Dave Patterson to help him and Dustin execute the warrant. They went to the house first thing the next morning.

"Is anyone staying here now?" Patterson asked as they mounted the front steps.

"I don't think so," Dustin said. "The property is owned by Ken Perkins. He owns a dozen or so rental properties near the campus. He said this one is rented to three male seniors. I drove by last night after I submitted the paperwork to the judge. There were no lights, so I figured we could wait until this morning to search."

"The students probably won't be back for another week or two," the chief said.

"That's what I figured," Dustin said.

Except for a lone red Solo cup tipped sideways and wedged under the porch railing, there was no evidence of the party from a few weeks before. The chief knocked. There was no sound or movement within the house.

"You want me to break the door down?" Patterson asked.

"Let's see if we can find a less destructive means of entry first," the chief said.

"On TV, they would just break the door down," Patterson

said.

"Good thing we don't just play cops on TV," the chief said. "Look around for a hidden key."

"A key, really?" Patterson said with a snort.

"Humor me," the chief said.

"Got it," Dustin said a minute later, holding up a key. "It was stuck to a magnet under the mailbox."

"Hmph," said Patterson. "How'd you know?"

The chief shrugged. "They're a group of college students. Probably always forgetting their keys."

The three cops let themselves in and shut the front door against the cold. It was clear that the house was uninhabited. The thermostat was set just high enough to keep the pipes from bursting.

"If the girl's here, she's dead from hypothermia," Patterson said.

The chief nodded. "Don't touch anything without taking photos first."

"What are we looking for?" Patterson asked.

"Signs of a party. Signs of a struggle. Particularly on the back deck. That was where the witness said Shannon and Keenan argued. Look for blood."

"Who cares if there was a party?" Patterson asked.

"We have a working theory on what happened to the girl, but we don't know for sure. We may never pin a murder on anyone, but if people find out that the renters of this house were serving alcohol to minors, and we didn't do anything, that looks bad. We may need to charge them with the alcohol violation as a public relations move."

"How thoroughly do we search?" Dustin said.

"Just look through everything, but don't tear the place apart. For all we know one of these kids has a parent who's a high-powered lawyer. The warrant gives us authority to search for evidence that alcohol was served to minors and evidence of a struggle on or near the back deck, anything belonging to Shannon Dawson, and a body. I think that gives us a right to look around the whole place, but don't go overboard.

Capisce?"

"Gotcha," Dustin said.

The house was surprisingly clean. The garbage can in the kitchen was empty. As was the larger can in the garage. There were two six packs of empty Budweiser bottles in the garage and a nearly full bottle of Stolichnaya vodka in the freezer. The officers poked around in the three upstairs bedrooms, but found nothing. Either the party was a low-key affair or someone had taken the time to clean up afterwards.

By unspoken agreement, they were saving the deck for last. It was the place they most expected to find something useful. It turned out the deck was not sheltered from the elements, and everything was covered by twelve inches of crusty snow.

"This is a wild goose chase," Patterson said.

"Sure looks that way," Dustin said.

"Take photos," the chief said. "I'm going to get some shovels from the vehicles."

The chief was back a few minutes later with two shovels. "Let's look under the deck first. Just in case."

Dustin got down on his hands and knees. "There's nothing here."

"Let's start slowly and carefully removing the snow," the chief said.

"What are we looking for?"

"Evidence of foul play."

"Can you give me some idea what that looks like?"

"Not really. Just wing it."

An hour later, the deck was clear.

"That was a waste of time," Patterson said.

"No, it wasn't," the chief said. "Sometimes when you investigate, it's just a matter of ruling things out. We now know the girl's not here and there's no evidence that anything happened to her here. Whatever happened probably happened after she left. We need to keep talking to witnesses. Somebody saw her leave the party."

"Where does the backyard go?" Dustin said.

"That's a good question. Go check," the chief said.

Dustin carefully made his way across the backyard, stomping the icy crust to reach solid footing. A few minutes later, he made his way back using the same footprints.

"It backs up to Mear Woods."

"Maybe we need to search the woods?" Patterson said.

"I think we'd be remiss if we didn't," the chief said.

"It's a couple hundred acres," Patterson said.

"We'll need volunteers," Dustin said.

"We won't have trouble getting them," the chief said. "The disappearance has gotten a lot of press. People will step up."

Dustin scowled. "Hey chief, do we really want some local yokel finding this girl's body? It could really screw up our crime scene. Besides, if she was killed two weeks ago, she's buried under a foot of snow. She's nothing more than a mound."

The chief nodded. "If we round up all the law enforcement officers in the county, how many you think we can get on the search?"

"Thirty?" Patterson said, shrugging.

"Is that enough to canvas the woods?" Dustin said.

"Depends on what we're looking for," Patterson said.

"At this point, I just want to find her body," Dustin said.

"It'll probably do," the chief said.

CHAPTER 19
Sunday, January 5, 2014

THE DAY of the search dawned clear and painfully cold at minus twelve degrees Fahrenheit. It was still twilight when everyone gathered at 7:00 a.m. in the backyard of the Maple Street party house. Dustin counted twenty-seven law enforcement officers. Most of them were off the clock, but everyone was wearing their department-issued parkas. Two departments brought their K-9 units. The air was cloudy from respiration and steaming coffee. Every few seconds someone stomped to stay warm.

Glenn Peterson had a German Shepherd named B.J. "It may be too late for the dogs," he said. "How long has the girl been missing?"

"Fifteen days." Dustin said.

"I've heard of dogs picking up a scent ten to twelve days old, but the conditions have to be right," Glenn said.

"The snow probably killed the trail," Dustin said.

"Actually, the snow could have the effect of preserving it. Dogs can smell through snow. But fifteen days is still a long time."

"Will the dogs be able to help find the body, assuming there is one?"

"B.J. and Duke aren't trained as a cadaver dogs, but if her body is out there, they may pick up on her scent somewhere near the body."

"So it's worth a try?"

"Definitely."

At 7:10, the chief started speaking. "Okay, everyone. First, thanks for coming out today, You're all a credit to our profession. Second, we've got two hundred acres of woods to comb. This house was the last place anyone saw Shannon Dawson. I want you all to fan out from here, form a line, then head north. The woods border Route 57 on one side, Route 12 on the other and residential properties on the other two. It's not really a rectangle, but it's close. If everyone gets to the north end and we haven't found anything, we'll try it again going east to west.

"Also, there's a fair amount of snow and there's been some drifting. As soon as possible, find yourself a long stick. If you see anything that looks like it could have a body buried in it, poke it with the stick. It's a lot faster than digging up every snowdrift in the woods. If anyone finds anything, call my cell. If you don't have my cell, hang back and I'll give it to you. Good luck, and thanks again."

The dogs were shown a piece of Shannon's clothing, but neither one seemed immediately to pick up any trail. The crowd started moving.

By eight thirty, the first of the officers reached the other side of the woods. At nine o'clock, the group started again in a perpendicular direction. As they trickled out of the woods, they got into their cars and left. They were probably all feeling as deflated as Dustin, and just as eager to get back to a heated building.

At noon, Dustin and the chief met with the Dawsons and their investigator at the station. Evan Halliday had been invited to help with the search, but had apparently thought it beneath him. The guy had probably spent the morning in the sauna at the Marriott while everyone else had been out freezing their nuts off.

The chief described how they had conducted the search. "We knew it was a long shot," he concluded.

"The time to search was right after Shannon disappeared," Halliday said. "I'm not saying it was a complete waste of time, but—" His phone vibrating in his pocket was audible in the quiet room. He pulled it out and swiped the screen, not bothering to finish his sentence.

"Maybe you needed more people to be more thorough," Olivia said.

"We got every available law enforcement officer in the county to come out."

"What about using volunteers? I'd be willing to search." Jack said.

"That's not a good idea."

"Why not?"

"You're not trained to deal with what you might find."

"Oh." Jack Dawson slumped in his chair. "Is there any place else worth searching?"

"There's ninety thousand acres of national forest in Adams County. We can't search it all on foot."

"Would the dogs have been able to find her trail if you had searched that house sooner?" Olivia asked.

Dustin started to say, "Probably," but changed his mind. The Dawsons already thought MFPD was incompetent. No need to give them more reasons. Fortunately, Halliday seemed to be more interested in his phone than running them down at the moment. "If she got into a vehicle, the dogs would have lost the scent regardless," Dustin said.

"There's no point second-guessing," the chief said. "The holiday slowed our investigation. We can't change that. Besides, every time we eliminate a possibility it brings us closer to figuring this out."

"We appreciate that you're still working on this," Jack said. "We know you don't expect to find our daughter alive."

The chief looked at both Dawsons before continuing. "We're sending up a plane to search a broader area. They'll take aerial photos. But if she's buried under the snow, we may just have to wait until it melts. We want to bring you folks some closure . . ."

Jack nodded. Olivia's eyes welled with tears.

"We won't get closure until we know who did this," Olivia

said, "even if you do find her."

"What's your theory on what happened at this point?" Jack said.

"I'd rather not share it yet," the chief said.

"Don't you think we deserve to know?" Olivia said. "It's our daughter we're talking about."

"Everything we have is very circumstantial. It's dangerous to jump to conclusions this early." The chief pursed his lips before continuing. "The students are trickling back onto campus right now. Dustin's got interviews scheduled. We'll let you know as soon as we have something concrete. How much longer are you folks going to stay in Middleton Falls?"

"I'm moving to an efficiency apartment on campus next week," Olivia said. "The college has some apartments they use for visiting professors. I'll be here until you find my daughter."

"I'm going back to California at the end of the week. I have to make sure I don't lose my practice."

"That's understandable," the chief said.

"I guess we all have different priorities," Olivia said.

JACK KNEW that Olivia was still clinging to hope that Shannon would turn up alive and well, but he also knew it was no longer realistic. That realization led to his decision to make plans to go back to California and start the process of grieving. He'd keep trying to convince Olivia to come with him, but he knew her well enough to know that, as long as Shannon was missing, it would be a hard sell.

"YOU NEED to find out what they're not telling us," Olivia said. She and Jack were meeting with their private investigator in their hotel room. The small round table was designed for two people to drink coffee. It felt too intimate for this meeting even though it had accommodated the addition of the desk chair.

"They're probably trying to protect you," Evan said and set his phone in the middle of the table.

"We don't need protection, we need information," Olivia

said.

"What are they protecting us from?" Jack said.

"The inner workings of a college freshman," Evan said.

"What does that mean?" Olivia said.

"That Shannon had things going on in her life that you'd rather not know about."

"That's ridiculous. I know my daughter," Olivia said. "You're not going to convince me she was a drug addict or anything." Olivia realized that she had used the past tense. She waited for one of the men to correct her, to tell her there was still hope.

After a few seconds, Jack said, "Look, Evan, have you reviewed the entire police file?"

"Yes."

"You did some interviews of your own?"

"I did. I spoke with everyone on the list of friends from California that you gave me."

"What else have you done?"

"I've been scouring the internet once a day. I also went around town looking for surveillance videos for that Friday between 10:00 p.m. and midnight. Frankly, I can't believe the police didn't do it themselves. Then again, there are a lot of things I would have done differently in this investigation."

"Did you find anything?"

"Yes and no. This place is amazingly backward. There's not a single traffic cam in town. The gas stations had the only cameras with views of the street. I got copies of four tapes, but there was no sign of Shannon or her car on them."

"What does that tell us?"

"That her car didn't go up Main Street on its way back to the dorm."

"Is that helpful?"

"It means that if Keenan used her car to dump her body, he probably didn't head north toward the national forest." Evan's words cut through Olivia's soul, bringing images of her beautiful daughter dumped like trash in the lonely woods. Where she would be eaten by starving animals trying to survive the harsh winter. Olivia rubbed her eyes trying to erase her own imagination.

"But it doesn't rule him out as a suspect?" Jack said.

"Not at all. It just rules out some exit possibilities."

"Do you think he did it?" Jack said.

"I don't know. He comes across as a nice kid. Good family. No criminal record whatsoever. But it could be an act. Ted Bundy was the epitome of clean cut."

"We need to know what the police have on him," Olivia said. "I'm tired of people withholding information from us. We're capable of making our own judgments."

CHAPTER 20
Wednesday, November 27, 2013

SHANNON WAS glad she and Keenan had his room to themselves on the night before they left for Thanksgiving break. There were no classes on Wednesday, so they slept late again. After breakfast, they went for a run. Then, Keenan went back to her dorm with her and sat on her bed, watching while she packed. When she was done, he carried her suitcase out to her car.

"What time are you leaving?" Shannon said as they were walking back to her room.

"My mom's picking me up after lunch, around one o'clock," he said. "Stop for a second." He took her hand and led her to a nearby bench. He sat and pulled her into his lap and kissed her. After a minute, she pulled away, but stayed in his lap.

"I should go," she said. "I'm supposed to meet Amy in a few minutes."

"I love you," Keenan said.

Shannon looked up at him. She wanted to say it, but something was holding her back. She could see his mood falling with each second that she didn't respond.

After about fifteen seconds, he said, "I've never said that to anyone before. Anyone outside of my family, that is. I'm underwhelmed by your response."

Shannon still hesitated. Maybe it was time for the plunge.

The past month with Keenan had been magical. This was the happiest she'd ever been. She didn't want to blow it, but she still had this unresolved thing with Jake.

"I love you, too. There. I said it. Now do you feel better?"

"I'll feel better when you get back from Thanksgiving and I can be with you again."

"It's only four nights." Shannon stood.

"I know. Have a great time with Amy."

Keenan wrapped her in a hug that made her feel safe and loved. Then, he kissed her one last time so tenderly she almost changed her mind about leaving.

Shannon pulled away.

"I have to go or I'll be late."

"I know. Drive safely."

She started to walk away, then looked over her shoulder and waved. He was still standing there watching her walk away. He waved back, but didn't move. It was the most romantic thing she'd ever experienced.

WHEN KEENAN'S mother arrived, she had his younger sister in tow.

"I call shotgun," Kaitlyn said before he even said hello. He hugged his mom.

Riding alone in the back, it was hard to participate in the conversation, so Keenan balled up his jacket, wedged it between his head and the window, and closed his eyes. He thought about Shannon, imagined her driving to the city with Amy. He was smiling when he dozed off.

When they got home, his father and brother came out to greet them.

"When did you get in?" Keenan said, embracing his brother.

"An hour ago," Liam said. "We managed to get ahead of the Boston traffic."

Keenan hugged his dad. "How's the ice?"

His father laughed. "One-track mind. Some things never change."

Liam smiled. "I haven't been down to check yet, but Meg said it was solid yesterday. And it's been hovering below freezing all day," he said.

"What are we waiting for?" Keenan said. "We've only got an hour till it gets dark."

"Are you girls in?" Liam said.

"I promised Mom I'd help with the baking for tomorrow," Kaitlyn said, "but I'll definitely be on the ice with you guys tomorrow afternoon."

"Meg's still over at a friend's house," his dad said.

"Their loss," Keenan said and grabbed his bag from the trunk of the car.

Ten minutes later Keenan and Liam were down at the pond playing one-on-one. As ponds went, it wasn't much. His grandfather had made it using a backhoe when Liam was a toddler. There were better, less muddy swimming holes nearby in the summer, but in the winter it was a great place to skate as long as they put the effort into keeping it clear. Someone had carried down a goal and cleared the ice. A shovel leaned against a nearby tree.

"We need to get the other goal out of the barn before tomorrow's game," Keenan said as he drove by his brother, keeping the puck out of reach and slapping it into the goal.

Liam recovered the puck. "Let's try to remember to bring the big brown bucket too. We'll need to resurface and I don't see any Zambonis parked around here."

The brothers skated until the darkness made it hard to see the puck. As they collected their discarded jackets, three deer came out of the woods and stared briefly before scampering across the field. Liam and Keenan both stopped to watch them.

"That reminds me . . . that Facebook video about rescuing animals was awesome," Liam said.

"I was hoping you saw that."

"Yeah. I shared it too. It looks like it's going viral." They sat down on a log and started unlacing their skates.

"How's it feel to be a senior?" Keenan said.

"I don't know. I was so busy this fall, getting my applications done for vet school on top of my regular coursework."

"When will you find out where you got in?"

"You mean *if* I got in. It's more competitive than med school."

"Wow. I had no idea Dad went through that to be a vet."

"Neither did I, until recently. They send out acceptance letters in the spring, but first there are interviews."

"You probably don't have time for girls," Keenan said. He put his skates over his shoulder and picked up his stick.

"I don't have time to date, if that's what you mean," Liam said. "But, I certainly have time to notice them."

Keenan laughed. "I guess being pre-vet is like being a priest."

"Not exactly. I have a 'friends-with-benefits' thing with a girl in my major. Her name's Bree and she's cool."

"I had a deal like that with a girl at St. J Academy," Keenan said as they started across the field toward home.

"Really? Who?"

"Her name was Bethany. She liked to have sex in the locker room after hockey games."

"Bethany King?"

"Yeah."

"She was in *my* class." Liam said. "I had no idea you dated her."

"I didn't. We just had sex my sophomore year. Then she graduated." Keenan thought about Bethany for the first time in ages. The summer after she graduated, she had sexted him a few times. He had considered responding, but ultimately decided he would feel too exposed. He assumed she was off at college somewhere giving him no more thought than he was giving her.

"You're unbelievable," Liam was shaking his head. "My brother, the stud. And here I thought Anna was your first girlfriend."

"She was."

"If you say so."

"And for the record, I dated Anna all of senior year and never had sex with her."

"Correction. My brother, the enigma."

"Look who's talking. That 'friends-with-benefits' thing working for you and Bree?"

"It has to. I know she's not The One, but I don't have time for dating. And celibacy isn't my thing either."

"How do you know she's not The One? She ugly or something?"

"No, she's cute and smart and funny. I like spending time with her, but something's missing. I'm hoping I'll know it when I find the right girl."

"Yeah, you'll know it all right," Keenan said. He wondered where Shannon was. Probably just getting into the city.

CHAPTER 21
Thursday, January 9, 2014

THE AERIAL search had been conducted by a medical rescue team out of Maine. They went up in a bush plane and took hundreds of high-resolution aerial photos and then sent them to a lab in Ohio for analysis. Dustin had clicked through his copy of the DVD full of photos. There was too much snow for him to see anything. He hoped the experts would see something he couldn't.

While waiting for the expert analysis, he had gone back through all the evidence. What they had was really a lack of evidence. They had ruled out just about every possibility. Wasn't it Sherlock Holmes who said that when you have eliminated the impossible, whatever remains, however improbable, must be the truth? Shannon probably didn't get lost in the woods behind the party house. They would have found her. She didn't drive her car back to the dorm. Keenan admitted that he did that, although only after they had him dead to rights with the keys in his possession. If she had left on her own, they would have found her or her body. Public Safety had been searching the campus for weeks. As far as Dustin was concerned, there were only two possibilities: (1) Keenan killed her and disposed of her body; or (2) an unknown perpetrator (serial killer?) abducted her. In light of the argument on the back deck, there was an obvious choice. Now, he just needed to prove it.

Jenna Davidson was waiting for him in the interview room when Dustin walked in. She was wearing earbuds and texting furiously. She pulled out the earbuds and stowed her phone in an oversized shoulder bag.

Dustin introduced himself. "I need you to think back to that last night on campus. I know it was three weeks ago, but the details of that night are extremely important. We need to figure out what happened. So, try to put yourself back there, remember what you were feeling, and let's see if we can fill in the details. Okay?"

"Sure."

"What were you and Shannon up to?"

"We were just letting off steam. It had been a hard week."

"Okay. Were you drinking?"

"I was not." She said it like she was expecting the question and had rehearsed the answer. Dustin didn't believe her, but it didn't make sense to alienate a key witness at the beginning of an interview.

"Was Shannon drinking?"

"She might have had a few."

"Did you go to the party on Maple Street?"

"We did."

"How did you get there?"

"Shannon drove."

"What time did you go to the party?"

"I don't know, ten or ten thirty."

"What happened when you got to the party?"

"We ran into some friends. We danced."

"Was there alcohol at the party?"

"I'm really not sure." Again, the answer didn't sound credible. Again, he let it go.

"Okay. Who did you talk to at the party?"

"I talked to some people from my dorm."

"Who did Shannon talk to?"

"We were all together."

"Did you see Keenan Brody at the party?"

"Yeah, he showed up looking for Shannon."

"About what time?"

"I don't know. We'd been there for a while."

"But you said he was looking for her?"

"Definitely."

"Because she told him she had slept with her old boyfriend?"

"Yeah, that's right." At least she was being honest about the stuff that mattered.

"Did he seem agitated to you?"

"Yeah. He really wanted to talk to her."

"Did she want to talk to him?"

"I don't think so."

"Why not?"

"I don't know."

"Was she afraid of him?"

"Well, I know she was afraid to tell him about Jake."

"Because he was going to be angry?"

"Yeah, I guess. He's a jock. Definitely not my type."

Dustin knew the next few questions were critical. He set his pen down and leaned back in his chair, studying Jenna. "So, what happened when Keenan got there?" he asked slowly.

"He tried to get her to leave."

"What exactly did he say?"

Jenna shook her head. "I don't remember, but he got her to go outside with him."

"You mean on the back deck?"

"Right."

"Did you see them struggle?"

"Yeah, that sounds right." Dustin watched Jenna carefully, looking for signs she was holding back. He didn't see any. She was staring into the middle distance as if searching her memory.

"Where were you when this was happening?"

"I was in the kitchen."

"Did you see him hit her?"

She shook her head. "I don't know, but I know he grabbed her pretty hard."

"Did he shake her?"

"Yeah, a little."

"Okay, good. Was he yelling?"

"Yeah, he was mad."

"Why didn't you do something?"

Jenna scowled and looked Dustin in the eye for the first time since the interview started. "I figured it was between them. How was I supposed to know he was going to hurt her?"

"No, you're right, what happened isn't your fault. I wasn't trying to blame you. What makes you think that Keenan did something to Shannon?"

"Well, you guys are investigating him. And it's all over Facebook."

"What exactly are people saying on Facebook?"

"Just that Keenan is a suspect in Shannon's disappearance."

"Anything else?"

"That he was the last one to see her alive."

"How do you know that?"

"People have been posting when they saw her. Somebody from the party posted that Shannon and Keenan left together."

"Who was that?"

"I don't remember."

"Can you help me find it later?"

"Sure."

"Did you talk to Shannon after you saw her fighting with Keenan?"

"No, I didn't."

"Why not?"

"She left."

"Did you see Shannon and Keenan leave together?"

"I'm pretty sure."

"How did they leave?"

"Must have been out the back. I'm pretty sure they didn't come back in through the kitchen."

"Did it look like Shannon went willingly?"

"Yeah. I mean, if he'd been dragging her, I would have stopped him."

"Yeah, okay. Did you call Shannon to check up on her?"

"No."

"How did you get back to campus?"

"Greta and I caught a ride from a guy in her sociology class."

"Do you know him?"

"No."

"Anything else that you remember about that night?"

"Not really. I mean, I just never thought it would be the last time I saw Shannon."

"Well, you can help us get justice for her. Can you find those Facebook postings on your phone?"

"Sure."

After a minute of thumb movement, Jenna showed Dustin a series of Facebook postings about Shannon's disappearance. He made a note to track down a kid named Jeremy Rollins. When they were done, Dustin had Jenna wait a few minutes while he typed up a written statement for her to sign. He put it in front of her.

"I'm going to read you what I wrote," Dustin said. "If you agree, I need you to sign this statement at the bottom and we'll notarize it. Okay?"

"Sure."

"It says: 'I, Jenna Davidson, was with Shannon Dawson on the evening of Friday, December 20, 2013. We went to a party at 853 Maple Street. While we were there, Keenan Brody came to the party looking for Shannon. He wanted her to leave with him, but she did not want to go because she had just told him that she had slept with her old boyfriend and he was angry. I saw Keenan grab Shannon hard and shake her. He was also yelling at her. Eventually, the two of them left together. I did not see or talk to Shannon again after she left with Keenan.'"

Jenna signed the statement. "Can I go now?"

With the help of Public Safety, Dustin tracked down Jeremy Rollins. When Jeremy finally arrived, Dustin put him in the interview room.

"Thanks for coming in."

"Man, it's not like you gave me much choice, calling my parents."

"Look, Shannon Dawson is missing, presumed dead. Don't you want to help us figure out what happened to her?"

"I don't know anything."

Dustin had a gut feeling that Rollins did not think highly of cops, but he decided to try to win him over. "That's not necessarily true. You were one of the last people to see her. You're an important witness."

"What makes you think that?"

"The stuff you posted on Facebook."

"Oh, that."

"Was it true?"

"Was what true?"

"That you saw Shannon the night she disappeared?"

"Yeah."

"And that you saw Keenan?"

"Yeah."

"And that he was looking for Shannon?"

"Sure."

"That they had a fight?"

"I don't know."

Dustin decided to back off. "An argument?"

"Keenan lives in my dorm. I don't want to say anything against him."

"But you made some posts on Facebook about a fight?"

"Yeah, but that was just Facebook."

"So? Are you saying you lied about what happened that night on Facebook? That's not good." More likely he was lying to Dustin to protect his friend.

"No, it's not like that."

"What is it then?"

"Look, I can't really remember what happened that night. It was weeks ago." Okay, it was clear they were going to have to do this the hard way.

"But you saw Keenan and Shannon together that night?"

"Sure."

"Did you see them leave together?"

"I don't know."

"What do you mean, you don't know? You posted on Facebook that they had a fight and then they left together."

"That's because I heard it."

"From who?"

"I don't know. There's been a lot of rumors in the past few weeks."

Dustin was beyond frustrated with this kid. "I'm not the bad guy here. I'm trying to help this girl's parents find some peace, some closure."

"I get that. But I'm not the guy to help you."

Dustin stared at the kid for half a minute. "Okay, who can help me? Give me some names."

"You want me to rat out my friends?"

"No, I just want to know who was at the party. Who saw something?"

"Like I said."

"Look, I've been reasonable with you, but we need answers. If you're not telling me something, I can go to the state's attorneys. They can haul you into court and make you answer. You don't answer, you go to jail. You want to go that route?"

"What the fuck? I already told you everything I know."

"Did you? How about who saw Shannon and Keenan leave together?"

"I don't know, man."

"How about who was at the party? Who might have seen them leave together?"

"I can tell you who was at the party, but I don't know what they saw."

"Okay, do it."

"There's some girl named Heather from my English class. I don't know her last name."

"Okay, who else?"

"Kyle Perkins from our dorm. That's who I went with."

"Anyone else?"

Jeremy shook his head. "I don't know. I recognized a bunch of people, but I don't know them."

"Okay. This is a start. What else are you not telling me?"

"Nothing."

"Are you friends with Keenan?"

"I wouldn't say friends, but I know him."

"Are you protecting him?"

"What? No, I just don't know anything."

Dustin typed up a short statement for Jeremy to sign. It helped put Shannon and Keenan together that night, but little else. Rollins was definitely protecting Keenan. His Facebook posts made it sound like he saw the whole thing, including the argument and the physical stuff. According to Jeremy's Facebook posts, Keenan had practically dragged Shannon off. But Facebook wasn't usually admissible evidence, at least that's what the state's attorneys always told him. He needed to find someone from the party who saw something and could swear to it.

A few more phone calls located Kyle Perkins and Heather, whose last name it turned out was Turner, from Rollins' English class. They both agreed to come for interviews that day.

Kyle Perkins described Keenan as an acquaintance from his dorm, but had no idea who Shannon was.

"That missing girl was at the party on Maple Street?" Kyle said. "I had no idea. I mean, I saw a bunch stuff on Facebook, but I didn't realize it was the same party I was at."

"Did you see Keenan that night?"

"Yeah, that's right. He was there."

"Did you see him with a girl?"

"Maybe."

"Blond girl?"

"Could be."

"Were you drinking that night?"

"Me? No way. I'm under age." Dustin scratched the corner of his eye in an effort to disguise his eye roll.

"Did you see Keenan do anything with a girl?"

"Sorry, I wasn't paying attention. I don't know the guy well enough to care."

"Do you know anyone who might help us?"

"Nope, sorry." Dustin had a feeling that Perkins had already spoken to Rollins and that he was playing dumb, but there was nothing he could do about it.

Fortunately, Heather Turner had a much better attitude.

"Yeah, I know Shannon," she said.

"Did you see her on the night she disappeared?"

"I did."

"Did you see her with Keenan Brody?"

"I saw her with a guy, but I didn't know who he was."

"Did you see them talking on the back deck?"

"I did."

"Were they arguing?" Dustin stressed the last word.

"Yes, they were."

"Did you see him do anything physical, like hit her or grab her?"

"Yeah. He hit her." The answer was surprising, but not necessarily disappointing.

"Are you sure he hit her?" Dustin asked.

"You're right, maybe he grabbed her too." Heather's expression was serious.

"Was it rough?" Dustin said.

"Definitely."

"Did it look like he was mad?"

"Very much so."

"Where were you when you observed this?"

"I must have been in the living room."

It had been a while. It wasn't a surprise she was having a hard time with the less important details. "Could you see the back deck from the living room?" he asked.

"You're right. I must have been in the kitchen. Can you see the deck from there?"

"Yes." Dustin nodded.

"Then, I was in the kitchen."

"Who were you with?"

"I really don't remember."

"That's okay. You've been helpful."

"Is there anything else you remember?"

"Like what?"

"I don't know, just anything you noticed about Shannon or Keenan, the guy she was with. Did you see them leave?"

"Yeah. She left first like she wanted to get away from him, and he followed her."

"Okay. That's good. Let me type up a statement for you to sign."

CHAPTER 22
Monday, January 13, 2014

I WANT something done!" Olivia said. The chief leaned back, looked over at Fred Dutton, and decided to let the state's attorney be in charge of the meeting.

"What do you want us to do?" Fred said, taking the cue. He had made the trek to the police station to attend the meeting with Olivia Dawson and her investigator. Dustin also seemed happy to let Fred handle things.

"I want him charged with murder."

"I'm sorry, Mrs. Dawson, but the evidence isn't there," Fred said.

"Officer Shores just finished reciting all the evidence against Keenan Brody. Does anyone here doubt that he killed my daughter?"

Nobody answered. The chief would have felt more certain if the case was less circumstantial, but it wasn't the time to say that. After an appropriate pause, Fred broke the silence. "Unfortunately, there's a difference between having a good idea of what happened and proving it in a court of law. I have a sworn duty to only bring cases that are supported by the evidence." It was definitely good to have Fred be the one facing off with Olivia for a change.

"I know some AUSAs who'd have no problem getting a conviction on these facts," Halliday said, raising an eyebrow. "But they're used to high-profile trials."

"And what about your duty to my daughter?"

"Hold on. Both of you. I wasn't finished. From what

Officer Shores has said, there may be enough evidence for a domestic assault charge. We know Brody grabbed her and shook her and hit her. That may qualify as an assault. They were dating, so it would be a domestic."

"Why would she be with someone like that?" Olivia said.

"I don't know. But, if I can get Officer Shores to go back and get more statements, we can probably get enough for a domestic assault charge."

"How long would he be in jail?"

"There's an eighteen-month maximum, but judges in this state rarely impose the maximum."

"You've got to be kidding me. He murders my daughter and he might go to jail for eighteen months. *Might?*"

"I can't charge a murder without a body. At least not on these facts. And it's my call to make, not some AUSA in New York City."

Halliday shrugged and smirked. He really was a prick.

"Just do something. Anything," Olivia said. "I can't take any more waiting around for something to happen."

"I understand. I am truly sorry for what has happened to your family."

"She was all I had, my only child." Olivia closed her eyes and bowed her head.

"I know, ma'am. We'll do our best to get you some form of justice."

"Are you a religious man, Mr. Dutton?" Olivia met his eyes.

"I am."

"I'm sure that young man will burn in hell for what he did to my daughter. In the meantime, please do what you can to avenge her death."

"I'll do my best."

WHEN OLIVIA and Halliday were gone, Dustin and the chief continued their meeting with the state's attorney.

"What do you need from me?" Dustin said. He was kicking himself that he hadn't thought of the assault angle. It had been right there in front of his face.

Fred Dutton shook his head. "As domestic assault cases go, this one is weak. I probably wouldn't charge a case like this if it weren't for the fact that the girl is presumably dead. You did a good job getting all those kids to describe the altercation on the deck. But you were focused on the murder aspect of this case." Dustin was grateful that the state's attorney wasn't dressing him down in front of his boss.

"The girl's got to be dead. It seemed like the right course," Dustin said.

"I'm not blaming you. But, if you were investigating an assault on the deck, what would you have asked?"

Dustin sat and thought for a moment. "The only thing I would have done different is ask the victim if she was hurt."

"That's right. Vermont law requires us to prove that the victim experienced some pain."

"But I couldn't have asked her. She's missing."

"Of course. But you can go back to the witnesses and ask them if she was hit or shaken hard enough that she would have been caused pain. That's how we get around the missing victim. We do it sometimes in domestics when the victim won't cooperate."

"That should be easy enough."

"Okay. When can you get supplementary affidavits from the witnesses and get the whole thing to me?"

"It's going to take time to round up the students again and write up the affidavit of probable cause. Day after tomorrow?"

"That's fine. Take your time. For the sake of the girl's parents, I want this thing airtight."

It felt like they were finally getting somewhere. Finally.

CHAPTER 23
Wednesday, November 27, 2013

AFTER A long drive in holiday traffic, Shannon and Amy arrived at Amy's Lexington Avenue apartment. Shannon was used to suburban California, so the uniformed doorman and the elevator ride to the fourteenth floor felt weird. Exciting, but weird. "I can't believe how old everything feels. And gray. It's so different from L.A."

"You've never been to New York before?"

"I'm a California girl, remember?"

"I just assumed . . . Well, in that case, I can't wait to show you my town."

"I can't wait to see it. But don't forget, I'm meeting Jake on Saturday."

They had a late dinner with Amy's parents that night. Then, Amy offered to take Shannon clubbing. But only after she had spent an hour doing Shannon's makeup. Shannon giggled when she saw herself.

"You expect me to go out looking like this?"

"You'll fit right in, trust me."

"I suppose it doesn't matter. It's not like I know anybody here."

Amy laughed. "Exactly. And I have the perfect dress for you to wear."

They waited in line for an hour to get into a club that Amy said was the edgiest place around. "And they never card the hot-looking girls," she added. Shannon was just glad to get in out of the cold when it was finally their turn at close to midnight.

Inside, the music was loud and discordant with a strong beat. The girls danced together until Amy's friends from high school showed up. Then, there were introductions that Shannon couldn't hear over the music.

A tall, thin boy with a spiky haircut took an interest in Shannon. "I can get you drinks if you want—I have a fake ID." He leaned in close so they could hear each other. She could smell smoke on his breath.

"Thanks, but I'm happy just dancing."

"I have some really good weed, if you like that better."

Shannon smiled. "Thanks, but I'm good."

The group danced until three o'clock in the morning. The club was still raging when Amy and Shannon took a cab back to Amy's apartment. Shannon probably would have called it quits sooner, but Amy was having a good time with her high school friends, and Shannon hadn't wanted to ruin it for her.

"I can't believe you didn't drink anything," Amy said in the back of the cab. "We're not at school, so they can't kick you out for drinking."

"I know. I didn't need it. It was just fun being there. Seeing it."

CHAPTER 24
Thursday, January 16, 2014

K EENAN BRODY, you are under arrest for domestic assault. Please turn around so I can cuff you." Dustin had been waiting for Keenan to walk out of the locker room after practice for five minutes. It had been five minutes of pleasant anticipation.

"What? Who did I assault?" Keenan turned around so the Shores could handcuff him.

"Shannon Dawson. You have the right to remain silent . . ."

Dave Patterson grabbed his arm and led him from the building while Dustin continued the *Miranda* warning. There was a police car idling in the No Parking zone in front of the athletics complex, white exhaust billowing from the tailpipe into the frigid late-afternoon air. Dustin opened the back door and pushed Keenan into the back seat.

"There has to be a mistake," Keenan said once the car was moving.

"There's no mistake," Dustin said.

"Is Shannon back? Did she accuse me of this?"

"Nice try, kid. You know she's not coming back."

"Then, how could I have assaulted her?"

"We have witnesses to the fight you two had before she disappeared."

"What fight?"

"At the party."

"We didn't fight."

"Save it for your lawyer, kid," Patterson said. He was driving and didn't see the exasperated look that Dustin gave him. Patterson was a sergeant, for Christ sake. He should know better than to discourage a subject from talking post-*Miranda*.

A few minutes later, they arrived at the MFPD building. They took Keenan to the booking room, the same room where he had provided fingerprints, and removed his cuffs. Dustin was relieved that Patterson left, locking the door on the way out.

"When can I talk to my father?" Keenan said.

Dustin was shuffling papers and took his time answering. "You can call someone as soon as we're done with the paperwork. What do you weigh?"

"Two-ten. What's going to happen to me?"

"When we're done here, you'll have a chance to tell your side of the story."

"When do I get a lawyer?"

"Do you want one? Because if you do, you can call one as soon as we're done with the booking. Or, if you can't afford one, we'll call the public defender for you. Benny doesn't like to make cell calls, but he'll talk to you on the phone. But, if you go that route, you may not have a chance to tell us your side of the story."

"What story? I have no idea what I'm accused of."

"Do you want to talk to me? If you do, I can give you the details, but first you need to sign a written *Miranda* waiver." Dustin pulled a half-sheet of paper out of the desk drawer. "It just says that you understand your rights, but you're willing to waive them. It's pretty straight forward." Dustin put a pen on the table next to the form.

"I want to talk to a lawyer."

Shit, Dustin thought. The law was clear. If a suspect in custody clearly requested a lawyer, the police were prohibited from asking any more questions. "Doesn't surprise me at all," he said.

"I need to call my father. He's got the name of a good lawyer."

"Of course he does."

Dustin painstakingly filled in the printed form. He wanted to drag this out as long as possible. He may not be allowed to ask questions, but there were other ways to get people to talk. Sometimes impatience caused people to make admissions. Finally, Dustin got up and stretched.

"I'll get you the phone now."

"Can it be a private conversation?"

"Got something to hide?"

"I just want to know."

"Yeah, we don't record attorney phone calls."

"I'm calling my dad so he can call an attorney."

"I'll shut off the sound, but the video will be rolling. It's a security issue."

"Okay. Thanks."

Dustin watched the kid on the closed circuit. As promised, he had turned the sound off. He didn't want the case thrown out on a technicality. The kid looked scared while he was talking on the phone. That was good. He was more likely to let his guard down and give them something they could use. Dustin waited and watched him for five minutes after Keenan had hung up. Then, he went back into the interrogation room and sat across from Keenan.

"What will it be?" Dustin said.

"My dad's calling a lawyer."

"That's okay, I'm in no hurry. I'll sit here with you until someone shows up."

"I'd rather be alone right now, if that's okay."

Damn. This kid was tough. Of course, he'd have to be to kill his girlfriend in cold blood and then go about his business like nothing happened. It was clear he wasn't going to get anything more from the kid tonight. He'd better get on the phone with a judge and see if he could get the kid held without bail until morning. The judges didn't usually do that for misdemeanor domestics, but maybe they would make an exception.

While Dustin was faxing his affidavit of probable cause to Judge Whippet, Barry Densmore came to the window and asked for Keenan. That was not good. Barry was arguably the best defense attorney in the county. He exuded confidence in a tailored suit. His shoulder-length silver ponytail was evidence of his contempt for convention. The kid had to be guilty if he was hiring Barry.

As expected, the judge set temporary bail. The lawyer made some calls and a half hour later the kid strolled out of the station like his arrest was nothing more than a minor setback. Of course, the kid probably wasn't worried because he was only looking at a misdemeanor. Dustin knew that he needed to find the body. It was probably only a matter of time. Unless he buried her. Or hid the body somewhere so he could bury it later. God, it would piss him off if the kid actually got away with this.

Dustin planned on being in court in the morning. He didn't usually go to arraignments. But, then again, he didn't usually handle homicide cases either. He wanted to be there every step of the way.

CHAPTER 25
Friday, January 25, 2014

OLIVIA HAD sat behind the prosecutor at the arraignment and studied the boy who had in all likelihood killed her daughter. She should have felt relieved that they were finally doing something, but Olivia knew in her heart it was not enough. When his lawyer had said, "not guilty," she'd wanted to scream. There had to be something more she could do.

A few days later, the Adams Gazette had run the story front and center.

MC Hockey Player Arrested in Disappearance of Coed
By MANNY RODRIGUEZ

Masterson College Sophomore Keenan Brody was arraigned in Adams County District Court last Friday on charges related to the disappearance of freshman Shannon Dawson. Dawson has been missing since December 21 of last year and is presumed dead. According to an affidavit filed by MFPD Officer Dustin Shores, the investigation into Dawson's disappearance revealed that she had been dating Brody for several months, and that on the night of her disappearance the two had quarreled at an off-campus party.

According to witnesses, during the quarrel, Brody struck and shook Dawson with significant force. Dawson left the party and Brody followed her. Dawson was never heard from again.

Brody is a left wing for the MC varsity hockey team. His teammate, Rob McPherson, described him as a solid defender who knows how to play rough. When asked whether he thought his teammate was capable of killing his girlfriend, McPherson replied, "Everybody's capable of murder." Brody could not be reached for comment. His mother said, "Our hearts go out to Shannon's parents, but I know my son. He would never have done anything to harm her. I'm sure of it."

Brody was charged with misdemeanor domestic assault. If convicted, he could be imprisoned for up to 18 months. He is represented by Attorney Barry Densmore. Densmore did not return a call to his office.

When asked why he had not charged Brody with the murder, State's Attorney Fred Dutton said, "It's hard to prove murder without a body. There was clear evidence of an assault, so we decided to charge that. If more evidence comes to light, we will reevaluate the charges."

A day later the story went statewide. A week later it went national and viral. Shannon's picture was too pretty to resist.

The *Times* and the *Post* both carried stories insinuating that Keenan was getting away with murder. There were numerous quotes from Manny's first story on Shannon's disappearance, when her parents had talked about her bright future and her dream of following in her father's footsteps and becoming a doctor.

The local CBS affiliate offered to sponsor a candlelight vigil for Shannon.

"I'm not sure," Olivia said when they called her.

"It will help keep your daughter's story in the news. Make it more likely she's found."

"What will you do?"

"We'll put up posters, get some candles and some flowers."

"What do I have to do?"

"You just get up and talk about your daughter. And, of course, give us the exclusive interview afterward."

The vigil was scheduled for Friday. That night, a blown-up picture of Shannon was placed on an easel at the top of the chapel steps, which were adorned with lusterless dried flower arrangements.

Olivia stood on the steps and watched as students came forward to speak about Shannon. It was surreal. She didn't know these people, had never even heard of them. Yet, they were crying for her lost daughter. Did they really know Shannon? Their grief somehow felt as fake as the flowers.

After half an hour, Olivia was invited to speak. She had prepared something earlier in the day. Her hands shook as she took off her gloves and unfolded the piece of paper. She had to breathe deeply for a few breaths before she was ready to begin.

"Thank you all for coming here tonight. It means a lot to my husband and me that Shannon is so respected and missed by her college community. I would give anything to have my daughter back. But today marks the five-week anniversary of her disappearance. I know that means that she is probably not coming back, no matter how hard I wish it." Olivia bowed her head and tried to compose herself. When she looked up, tears were streaming down her face.

"My daughter was a special person. Bright, loving, giving. I will love her forever. Her father and I both will." Olivia swallowed, her hand moving to her throat. "She never did anything to harm anyone. She doesn't deserve whatever happened to her. And I will see that the person responsible for taking my daughter from us pays for what they have done. I will not rest until my daughter gets justice."

After a brief statement from the dean, assuring everyone that the Masterson campus was still as safe as ever, the attendees raised their candles to a verse of "Kumbaya."

All the local television stations ran footage of the vigil. The thousand lights on the lawn of the chapel were a powerful image as was Olivia Dawson's tearstained face when she delivered her vow to avenge her daughter's presumed death.

The next day, the Burlington paper ran a story about the vigil with the headline "Mother of Missing Masterson Coed Vows To Seek Justice Against Hockey Player." There were three pictures: Olivia, Shannon, and Keenan. Keenan's picture was cropped from the hockey team photo taken at the beginning of the season.

Olivia was exhausted. She didn't relish the media attention she was getting, but she knew that if there was any hope at all of finding Shannon, the media was her best bet. The police sure as hell hadn't been effective. Even the private investigator had not come up with anything useful and had returned to New York after submitting a hefty bill.

She knew she looked like crap on the television, but for the first time in her life she was beyond caring. After an entire month in this winter wasteland, she would give anything to get back to California, but there was no way she was leaving until they found Shannon. She was still pissed at Jack for leaving her here alone to cope, but she knew that if she joined him, her daughter's case would go on the back burner. She was determined to do whatever she had to do to keep her daughter's memory alive and people looking for her.

CHAPTER 26
Friday, November 29, 2013

SHANNON AND Amy spent the day after Thanksgiving shopping and going to museums. They returned to Amy's apartment just before dinner laden with handled, logo-labeled shopping bags.

"Do you want to go out tonight?" Amy said.

"Would you be disappointed if we stayed in and watched a movie?" Shannon said.

"Not at all. I live here, so I can do New York any time. I just wanted to give you a chance to see it."

"I feel like I saw all of it today. I'm exhausted."

"Are you ready for your talk with Jake tomorrow?"

"I'm dreading it, if that's what you mean, but I have to tell him."

"I've been thinking about that. If you guys agreed to see other people, then you don't have to tell Jake anything."

"I'm in love with Keenan. And he's in love with me. I think this is it. You know what I mean?"

"That's pretty intense."

"That's why I owe it to Keenan to end things with Jake."

"Have you heard from Keenan this weekend?"

Shannon smiled. "He's sent me about a hundred text messages."

"Do you want me to go with you to Jake's?"

"No, he's going to come here to get me tomorrow

morning. I'd never find his dorm on my own."

"Great. I can't wait to meet him."

KEENAN READ Shannon's text message. It sounded like she and Amy were having an action-packed weekend in New York City. He missed her so much he ached, but he was glad she was having a good time. He only had one more day to hang out with his family before he had to go back to campus for hockey practice. At least he'd be busy and the time would go quickly.

"CWTSY Sunday!" he texted before he went to sleep. He really couldn't wait to see her.

SHANNON LAY in bed and rehearsed what she would say to Jake. She loved him. She would probably love him forever. But she was *in love* with someone else. She hoped they could stay friends. She tried it out a zillion different ways, but none of them felt right. Because no matter how she said it, Jake was going to hurt. And she knew from experience how that felt.

CHAPTER 27
Tuesday, April 8, 2014

USUALLY, MARCH came in like a lion and went out like a lamb. That year, the entire month of March was colder and snowier than normal. Then, almost as if a switch were flipped, the temperatures soared at the beginning of April. After three days in a row in the seventies, on April 7, the sun warmed things up to a record-breaking eighty-two degrees. Everything started melting, and melting fast. The rivers rose to flood stage, causing flood watches for the entire northeast including Northeastern New York, Vermont, Northern New Hampshire and Northern Maine.

Then, as if to add insult to injury, the heavy rain came.

The chief was eating lunch when the dispatcher buzzed his intercom.

"I think we found her."

The chief did not have to ask who, and the next question was obvious. "Dead?"

"Unless she's got gills."

"Where is she?"

"Bunch of whitewater kayakers found her a quarter-mile below the falls. They're waiting for you on the west bank."

It only took the chief a minute to find Dustin and three more minutes to get down to the river. Four brightly colored kayaks marked the spot along the creek.

"Thank you for calling us. Can you show us where the body is?"

"It looks like it's hung up under a strainer about twenty feet off shore." A kayaker pointed.

The chief squinted at them. "What's a strainer?"

"An underwater log."

The chief surveyed the landscape and saw no realistic way to retrieve the body. He excused himself and called Colchester Technical Rescue. They were an hour away, but they were also the only ones in the area equipped for an underwater retrieval.

The chief and Dustin took statements from each of the four kayakers. When they were done he said, "I don't think you guys should hang around here for the next part. It's not going to be pretty."

"We could go out there and get a rope around her for you," the kayaker said.

The chief was only half listening. "I appreciate the offer, I really do. But this is a law enforcement matter. I'd better let the rescue experts handle it."

"You mind if we put back in here? We have a car parked a mile downstream."

The chief figured it wouldn't make much difference. "Yeah, just go downstream a bit."

A few minutes later, the first of the curious bystanders appeared. The kayakers had probably called their friends while they were waiting for the police. The chief had Dustin string up yellow tape to keep the area clear for the rescue people to work.

While they were waiting for CTR, the chief called the state's attorney. Five minutes later Fred Dutton showed up at the waterfront.

"What do you want me to do about a medical examiner?" the chief asked. "Normally, I would call one of the assistant MEs, but . . ." The Office of the Chief Medical Examiner was in Burlington. Two physicians covered the entire state, but each county had its own assistant medical examiners who handled the routine cases. They were usually nurses or paramedics who had received special training in forensics.

"Let's send this one straight to Burlington."

"That's what I was thinking. I'll call them."

Even though time was not of the essence, Colchester

Technical Rescue arrived exactly sixty-five minutes after the chief called. They took the temperature of the water, studied the currents and the terrain, then mapped out a plan.

An hour later, they were pulling Shannon Dawson's body out of Moose Creek. It was an impressive rescue that would have been more impressive if the rescuee had survived. The camera crew behind the yellow tape got footage of the limp body being pulled from the river. Dustin realized the horror of what was being recorded and grabbed a blanket from the cruiser to cover the body until they could get it into a body bag. It wasn't the smartest of crime-scene procedures, but the chief knew that they weren't going to get much evidence from a body that had been underwater for several months anyway. He hoped for the sake of the girl's parents that the media would not show that footage. Dustin should have put the yellow tape farther away, but it wasn't like any of them had experience with high-profile homicide investigations.

After they shipped the body off to Burlington, the chief and Dustin returned to the MFPD barracks. The chief spent several minutes in his office trying out different versions of the wording before he called Olivia Dawson. He considered driving to her apartment, but he didn't want to take the time. It would be awful if she heard the news from someone else. He picked up the phone.

"Mrs. Dawson, I'm sorry to tell you that we found your daughter's body this afternoon."

Olivia inhaled sharply. "Are you sure it's her?"

"Yes, the body matches your daughter's description."

"Where did you find her?"

"Some kayakers spotted her in Moose Creek."

"Can I see her?"

"I wouldn't recommend that, Mrs. Dawson."

"Why not?"

"The body has probably been submerged for a while. We've ordered an autopsy."

"Then, how do you know it's her?"

"Mrs. Dawson. Nobody else has been reported missing

around here, and there was an iPhone in a pink case zipped into the pocket of her jacket. Just like the one you described for us. We'll check dental records, but I wouldn't be calling you if I had doubts."

There was silence for about fifteen seconds. The chief wasn't sure what to say next.

"Mrs. Dawson, do you have someone who can be with you until your husband gets here?"

"I don't know anyone here in town." Olivia Dawson started sobbing.

"Are you at your apartment?"

"Yes."

"Do you want me to come there and help you figure out the next steps?"

"Yes. Please."

Olivia was alternately catatonic and hysterical that evening. The chief called a local doctor, who was also a friend, and had him call in a prescription for valium. Then, the chief stayed with Olivia until an advocate from the local women's shelter showed up. Olivia wasn't technically a victim of domestic violence, but he didn't know who else to call, and they were willing to help. He picked up the prescription just before the pharmacy closed and dropped it off for her. Her husband was taking the redeye and would arrive midmorning. Hopefully, he'd be in better shape and could help with the grim task of bringing their daughter home for a funeral after the autopsy.

CHAPTER 28
Friday, April 11, 2014

THREE DAYS after the body was recovered, Dustin found himself summoned to the state's attorney's office with the chief. Fred Dutton had received the autopsy results by email. He handed out copies of the report and gave them a few minutes to study it.

"What do you think?" the chief asked.

"It sounds inconclusive," Dutton said.

"I agree," the chief said. "Except for the dental match."

"Yeah, it feels like the ME is hedging," Dutton said. "She might have drowned and received the two head injuries post-mortem. Or she might have died from the head injuries and just gotten water in her lungs during the months she spent underwater."

"It doesn't leave us much to work with," the chief said.

"I agree," Dutton said.

"Can I say something here?" Dustin said. It was really getting to him. All along, Dutton had been saying they couldn't charge a homicide without a body. Well, they had a body. What the hell was the reluctance about? Of course, he couldn't say that. He needed to tread lightly.

The state's attorney nodded. "Go ahead."

"Nothing in this report is inconsistent with our theory of what happened."

"Which is what exactly?" Dutton said.

"Keenan and Shannon argued. He assaulted her. She left. He followed her. They argued some more. He killed her. Now, we know he probably hit her on the head. Then he used her car to take her to the river below the falls and dumped her in the water. He drove the car back to the dorm and went home for Christmas."

Dutton and the chief were both sitting still, obviously thinking.

The chief was the first to speak. "If he had killed her first and then put her in the car, there would have been traces of blood in the car."

"Not necessarily," Dustin said. "He could have wrapped her in something."

"That would have taken some premeditation," Dutton said, "which I'd be hard put to sell to a jury."

"Or he could have gotten lucky." The chief was twirling his pen. "There might not have been much blood. It's not inconsistent with the autopsy results. It says here the injuries to her head were possibly antemortem."

"What if they went down to the water and he killed her there?" Dustin got up and started pacing. "Maybe he held her under until she drowned."

"Then he would have been wet," Dutton said. "The car seat would have gotten wet when he drove it back to the dorm. The only wet place in the car was the driver's foot well, and it wasn't all that wet. No more than you'd expect anyway. Besides, the water would have been cold, even in December."

"Okay." Dustin wasn't ready to give up. "Or he hit her with a rock down by the water and threw the body in. Does it really matter exactly how he did it?"

"Juries like theories that make sense," Dutton said. "And they like it when the evidence matches the theory. Isn't it possible that she just slipped and fell into the water?"

"You'd have to be an idiot to be wandering around on an icy river bank in the dark," Dustin said.

"Or drunk?," the chief said. "We have witness accounts that she was drinking, but the toxicology report was inconclusive."

Dustin stopped pacing and shook his head. "The only one who says she was wasted is the Brody kid. And he knew she would turn up in the river eventually. It's his get-out-of-jail-free card."

Dutton looked up at him. "What did her friends say about the drinking that night?"

"Just that she'd had a little," Dustin said.

The chief nodded. "Nobody said she was so intoxicated she might fall in the river and drown. If they had, we might have considered that possibility long before now. I think we have enough to charge the murder, now that we have a body." Dustin was relieved the chief had finally taken his side.

Dutton started drumming his fingers. "As far as I'm concerned, the real question is whether we have enough to convict. Three months under water destroyed most of the evidence. The way I read this autopsy report, she might have drowned and gotten the injuries postmortem or she might have been killed by a head injury and dumped. If it's the first one, it's hard to pin it on the boyfriend."

"He could have pushed her," Dustin said, "and watched her drown."

"I understand what you're saying. The circumstantial evidence leads to his involvement, but I can't go in front of a jury and say, 'We have three theories on how he killed her—pick one.'"

"Why not?" Dustin said.

The prosecutor picked up the pace of his drumming. "It's too messy. And Barry's too good a lawyer to let me get away with it."

"So, the kid gets away with murder?" Dustin was shaking his head.

"What about the iPhone?" Dutton said. "Any chance we'll get more evidence from that?"

"I sent it up to the tech guys in Burlington for a data retrieval," Dustin said, "but they said they probably won't get anything we haven't already gotten from the MacBook and the phone records."

Dutton nodded. There was a minute of silence while the three men pondered the situation.

"What's your leaning, Fred?" the chief said.

"I don't know yet."

That night, Dustin made macaroni and cheese for Sienna and Quinn. His mom had brought over an old table and chairs. The table was formica with corroded metal legs, and the matching chairs had cracked vinyl upholstery. The set had probably come out of Uncle Vic's trailer. It was undeniably ugly, and Dustin hadn't seen that particular shade of orange in a kitchen for several decades. But, for the first time since he had moved out of his former house, he was able to eat dinner with his kids not seated on the floor in front of the television. He even made peas, which would technically meet Joanne's green vegetable rule and which he wouldn't have bothered with if he was eating alone. He used his phone to play music while they ate.

It was good. The kids seemed happy. They chattered about school and friends. It was the most normal meal he'd had in a long time. He should have gotten a table months ago. Unfortunately, all his plans for furnishing his apartment had gone on hold when it became clear that he and Joanne were not going to work out the divorce thing without lawyers. He'd scraped up every penny he could to hire a lawyer. Joanne basically wanted to keep everything they had owned together and the kids. She'd offered him visitation every other weekend and two weeks during the summer. Then she'd acted surprised when he'd balked.

"You gave up so many of your scheduled weekends, I just assumed you didn't want the kids more than that," she'd said.

"I gave up one weekend."

"And you had your mom watch the kids a lot when you had them."

"I was working a homicide investigation."

"You think the kids care about that?"

"No, but—"

"But nothing. You don't see me asking you to take the kids on my weekends. Even though it would mean Gregor and I could go away."

"You work part time."

"Which means I can make the kids first priority."

"They're my first priority too."

"Doesn't look like it."

"The investigation is over."

"It doesn't matter. You don't even have a suitable place for them to stay with you."

"I would. If you'd let me have some of our furniture."

"I don't think so."

It usually wasn't worth fighting with her. Which was why she always won. But there was no way he was going to give up his kids, let some other guy raise them. His kids.

After he tucked the kids into their mattresses on the floor, he got out his copy of Shannon's autopsy report and spread the photos on the table. There had to be something they were missing. There had to be a logical explanation for how the injuries matched up with his theory of the case. He closed his eyes and imagined Keenan and Shannon. Standing beside her VW. Arguing. Him hitting her.

"Daddy?" Dustin opened his eyes and saw Sienna staring at the photos on the table. "What's wrong with that girl?" she said.

Shit. He did not want Sienna seeing the photos. "She's dead," he said and scooped them up.

"Why's she naked?"

"Because that's what they do with dead bodies."

"How'd she die?"

"Someone killed her."

"Are you going to catch them?"

"Yes, I am, honey."

"Because you're a police officer and you catch bad guys."

"That's right. Now let's get you back to bed."

PART II
Justice for Shannon

CHAPTER 29
Monday, April 14, 2014

BARRY DENSMORE sat in his office with the door closed. He had asked Marcy to tell everyone he was unavailable for the rest of the day. It wasn't fair to leave his secretary on the front line while he took cover, but he didn't want to deal with the media. And there was certainly a lot of interest in the Brody case that week after Shannon's body was found. Besides, he had a lot of work to do if there was any chance of getting Keenan Brody acquitted of the assault charges.

Barry knew lawyers who were able to use the media to their advantage, but he'd never been one of them. He never talked to the media until a case was over, and he always instructed his clients to do the same. Albeit for different reasons. He didn't blame the reporters for getting things wrong any more than he blamed the cops, who seemed to get things wrong more often than they got them right. It was all a matter of psychology. People hear what they want to hear, and they tell things in ways that make themselves look good. The bottom line was, if you don't say anything at all, you can't be misquoted. At least in theory.

Unfortunately, Barry feared his policy of silence was harming the Brody kid emotionally. It's one thing to zip your lip when a few thousand people are speculating whether you're guilty of a petty crime. It's another to keep quiet when the nation is judging you guilty of murder.

He wouldn't care so much if he weren't also starting to

wonder if the Brody kid might be one of those rare but occasionally sighted animals: the innocent client. Most of his clients were guilty, if not of the actual crime they were charged with, then something else, usually something worse. Any lawyer doing criminal defense for a few years knows that. But the Brody kid had been adamant from day one that he was innocent.

Barry remembered his first meeting with the kid at the police station back in January, three months ago. Like most first-time offenders, Brody had looked shell-shocked when Barry walked into the interview room.

"I had a brief conversation with Officer Shores before I came in here," Barry had said. "You're being charged with domestic assault of the missing college girl. I take it you knew her?"

"We were dating."

"Okay, that explains why it's a domestic."

"But, I didn't assault her."

"I make it a practice not to ask my clients if they're guilty. It's usually irrelevant and my job is the same either way."

"I don't understand."

"My job is to help you navigate the criminal justice system, make sure that things are done as fairly as possible, and get you the best result I can."

"But I didn't assault anybody."

"Most people don't realize that the legal definition of assault is broad. You don't have to punch someone to assault them."

"I didn't lay a hand on her."

"It can also include pushing or slapping, lots of things."

"You're not listening. I didn't do anything to her. This is a mistake. I should have just told the cops my side of the story. Then they'd realize they got it wrong."

"That would absolutely be a mistake."

"Why?"

"Because there's never anything to be gained by talking to the police. Besides, they already arrested you. They wouldn't have done that if they didn't have enough evidence to justify the charge. They're not interested in your side of the story. They're just interested in tripping you up so they can bolster their case."

"You're not interested either."

"Yes, I am. I'm just trying to set the ground rules. I need you to know that I will represent you to the best of my ability no matter what you've done."

"And I need you to know I haven't done anything."

"Okay, then. I have a couple more grounds rules. First, from here on, you don't talk about what happened, or didn't happen, to anyone but me."

"Nobody? Not even my parents?"

"You're going to need their support, so it's okay to involve them, but you need to be aware that anyone you talk to could become a witness against you. There may be some conversations that you and I need to have privately. Whatever you tell me alone is confidential."

"Wow. What else?"

"Everything you tell me has to be the truth. You don't have to tell me anything, but I can't do my job if you lie to me. Tomorrow you can come to my office and tell me as much as you want to." Barry had glanced at the camera in the corner of the room. "The police station is not the best place for open conversation."

The kid had looked relieved. And he had sounded earnest when he came to Barry's office the next day with his father. Keenan had sworn that he never assaulted Shannon Dawson and seemed genuinely perplexed that there were witnesses who saw him do it.

Most people assume that, when there are witnesses to a crime, it must have happened the way they said. But Barry knew better. Though he would wait to form an opinion until after he'd studied the evidence.

The problem with the case was that it was emotional and political at the same time. That was obvious from the get-go. The night Barry met Keenan, the judge had set temporary bail at $10,000. That was high end for a misdemeanor assault and a first-time offender. Then, Fred Dutton himself had handled the arraignment. As far as Barry knew, Fred hadn't done an arraignment in at least a decade. He usually left such routine matters to his underlings. Of course, Fred was never one to miss a public relations opportunity.

Fred must have been disappointed that the camera crews hadn't been at the arraignment. It was probably only because they hadn't yet gotten wind of the case. They had been at every court appearance since.

To make matters worse, soon after Keenan's arrest, the college judicial board had summoned him to an emergency hearing. Keenan had called Barry, who met him on campus. Barry understood that there was pressure from the media and Shannon's parents, but it wasn't fair to make the kid fight a two-front war. He had needed the college to back off. Barry spent nearly two hours explaining to the board how participation in the college judicial process would make it impossible for Keenan to get a fair trial in state court.

A few days later, Barry had gotten an email from the chairman of the judicial board indicating that they had decided to postpone the proceedings until after Keenan's criminal trial. Barry considered it a victory. If Keenan got convicted on the assault charges, the college investigation was moot. If not, they would cross that bridge later.

For many lawyers, the realization that most clients are guilty becomes an excuse. The system is designed to reward defendants who plead guilty, and it's much easier to negotiate a plea deal than investigate and try a case. But Barry also knew that, if you dug deep enough, you could frequently find reasonable doubt. The result was that he had secured acquittals for a few clients he honestly believed were guilty. It didn't bother him much. He figured on the karmic scale he was even because he also knew that a few of his innocent clients had opted for plea deals rather than risk the crap shoot of a jury trial.

And a trial was always something of a crap shoot. He'd once heard Bob Kessler talk a client into a plea deal with the line,

"Are you going to trust your future to twelve people too stupid to get out of jury duty?" Barry wasn't that much of a cynic. Then again, he knew he was a better lawyer than Bob.

As soon as his secretary had transcribed the interviews done by the police, Barry went through them carefully. He winced when he read Keenan's second interview with the police. He always advised his clients to not speak with the police under any circumstances, but people who have done nothing wrong assume that the best course of action is to be helpful to the police. As children we're taught that, when we're in trouble, we can always go to a police officer if we need help. That might still be good advice for anyone under the age of eight. But only because children are rarely prosecuted for misdeeds. As far as Barry was concerned, everyone else should avoid talking to the police, especially if there was any chance at all they might be the target of an investigation.

By the time Barry had done his first thorough pass through the evidence, he knew it was possible that Keenan was telling the truth. It was clear that nobody the police had talked to in the first few days after Shannon's disappearance had mentioned an assault or even an argument between Shannon and Keenan at the Maple Street party. There had been early reports about how drunk Shannon had been. It wasn't until after the police had decided to target Keenan that there was any actual evidence of his guilt. It occurred to Barry that Keenan might be a victim of the *misinformation effect*. It was a possible defense at least. Whether it would be enough to create reasonable doubt, he had no idea.

Then, Shannon's body had been discovered, and the phones had started ringing off the hook. Barry hoped things weren't about to get worse for his client.

At five o'clock, Marcy poked her head into his office.

"I'm heading out. You should do the same."

"I will. Soon."

"The phones have been slowing down, but they probably won't stop for a while. If you go home, they won't bother you. Your home number's unlisted."

"That's a good point."

"I also happen to know that you have nothing pressing to attend to tonight. Remember, I keep your calendar."

"Are you mothering me again?"

"Somebody needs to take care of you. Besides, I get away with it because I have job security."

"How's that?"

"You couldn't run this place without me. And we both know it."

"Yes, we do."

"Good night, Barry."

"Good night, Marcy."

The phones stopped ringing at about six o'clock. Barry thought about ordering takeout and eating at his desk. Instead, he found leftovers from his last takeout order in his office fridge and heated them in the microwave.

At nine o'clock, he was still at the office. He couldn't help it. There was too much to do and too many people depending on him. If there was ever a good day for a glass of scotch, this was it. Just one, like always. He'd rather have it at home, but that wasn't really an option. He went to his credenza, knelt down, and pulled out a bottle of Johnnie Walker Red Label and a glass from the back of the cabinet. He poured two fingers and took a sip. Then, he put on a jacket, went outside, and sat in the old porch rocker on his back porch. He could see his breath in the light from his office window. The scotch would keep him warm for a few minutes.

When he finished his scotch, Barry rinsed the glass in the bathroom, dried it, and put it away with the bottle. Time to get home to Sam.

FRED DUTTON sat on the edge of his bed and watched Olivia Dawson on his television. Olivia was in California for her daughter's funeral, but was being interviewed by Sarah Chase, the chubby brunette news anchor at Channel 4, through a live feed at a California TV studio. Sarah was in the local studio with Stephanie Beasley, a local law professor and frequent commentator on all things legal.

"How do you feel about the assault charges that have been filed in your daughter's case?" Sarah said.

The screen zoomed to Olivia's image. "I'm furious. That boy killed my daughter, and he's going to walk away from this with a slap on the wrist. They told me he'll probably serve a year in jail. My daughter is missing the rest of her life and he only misses a year. It's unbelievable."

"I'm sure it's frustrating. Adams County State's Attorney Fred Dutton has refused to comment so far, but we are joined in the studio today by Professor Stephanie Beasley from Vermont Law School. Professor, what do you think of the lack of murder charges?"

"Well, I understand why Mr. Dutton declined to file the homicide charges when there was no body. There's not much precedent in Vermont for homicide charges without clear proof of death."

"But now things are different?"

"Absolutely," Beasley said. "We now have all the elements of a winnable homicide case."

"Can you explain what they are?"

"First, we have motive."

"How do you know that?"

"The affidavit of probable cause in the assault case describes a love triangle. That's a pretty strong motive."

"Sure. What else do you know about the case?"

"There's also a means."

"I thought the autopsy report was inconclusive."

"Only because of the underwater burial. I understand there were clear signs of blunt force trauma. On the heels of the assault that people witnessed, it's not unexpected that there was more violence."

"But there were no witnesses to the murder."

"First of all, on these facts, we're probably talking about manslaughter instead of murder. And you need to keep in mind that most criminal cases are based on circumstantial evidence."

"So, professor, why is Fred Dutton dragging his heels on

this case?"

"You'd have to ask him, but I think he's being overly cautious. Like I said, I understand why he only charged the assault when he didn't have a body. A homicide conviction on those facts would have been a long shot. But the facts have changed."

Fred clicked the TV off. He had never liked Stephanie Beasley. As far as he was concerned, she was a shameless self-promoter-slash-know-it-all who taught the law because she was too slow on her feet to actually practice it.

Olivia, on the other hand, he felt bad for. She wasn't making his job any easier, but under the circumstances, it was hard to hold it against her. He'd probably be doing the same thing if he were in her shoes. The problem was that he had aways prided himself on his integrity as a prosecutor, and he didn't like outsiders telling him how to do his job. It made him want to dig in his heels. Olivia had sworn to stay in Vermont until her daughter was found and the case was solved. And she'd been a rock in his shoe since he'd filed the assault charges. He hoped to convince her to stay in California for a while, although he had a feeling that would only happen if he filed a homicide charge.

"You really shouldn't watch the news about your cases. You know it makes you crazy. Always has." Kathy Dutton was already in bed, a book in her lap.

"I know. But I need to figure out how people feel about this case."

"You're not going to figure that out by watching the news."

"You're right."

"I know. Now come to bed."

"I'm still too keyed up."

"So, read for a while and then sleep on it. I have no doubt you'll do the right thing, whatever that turns out to be."

"What did I do to deserve you?"

"I can't remember. It was too long ago. Now I need to get to sleep. I'm watching Tanya's kids tomorrow morning so she can go up to the mall. Those two take all my energy."

Fred kissed his wife. "I promise to turn out the light soon. Good night, Grandma."

KEENAN WATCHED the news clips on his laptop alone in his room. He'd had a double room to himself since the beginning of the term when he had come home from an away hockey game to find his roommate's stuff gone. He and Brendan had been roommates since the start of freshman year. They weren't best friends, but they'd been compatible roommates. Or so Keenan had thought. He guessed that Brendan was pressured by his parents to change roommates. It still would have been nice to hear it from Brendan. The college had a housing shortage, so Keenan had expected they would assign him a new roommate from the long list of people who had been crammed into temporary housing. But it never happened. It was probably for the best. He'd been in tears many times during the past months and he'd rather nobody saw him that way.

Keenan searched his own name on Twitter and realized that he now had his own hashtag, #KeenanBrody. People around the country had retweeted photos of him with captions like "Another college athlete gets away with a crime of violence" and "Hold Brody accountable, make college campuses a safe place to date." He scanned through the recent tweets, but couldn't find any suggesting he might be innocent. It wasn't a surprise, given how much his peers had vilified him on Facebook in the aftermath of Shannon's disappearance. He'd stopped checking Facebook a while ago. What was he thinking, checking Twitter?

Most people had retweeted his mugshot, but there were other photos that looked familiar, probably taken during one of the court hearings that Barry said were routine. It seemed the media was always there, even when the hearing only took a few minutes

He remembered waiting in the courtroom with Barry and his dad before the first hearing. The judge had taken a fifteen minute break so the camera guys could set up.

"If nothing is going to happen today, why are they here?" Keenan had said.

"This case is big," Barry had said. "None of them wants to be the one who missed something. Besides, if something does happen with the case later, they can use the footage from today and talk over it."

"So, they're just here to get footage of me in court?"

"Basically."

"You're saying *I'm* the news."

Barry nodded, and Keenan felt like he might get sick. He breathed deeply and focused his gaze on the front of the room to control the nausea.

"Why does the judge allow it?" his dad had said. "It seems awfully disruptive given how many people are here waiting for hearings."

"It's partly the First Amendment and it's partly political. Judges in Vermont are appointed, but they get reviewed every six years. No judge wants a media campaign against him, especially if he's nearing the end of a term."

When Keenan's case had finally been called, he and Barry were already waiting at the counsel table. The hearing itself had taken less than a minute. Then, the judge had left again so the crews could disassemble their equipment.

Thinking about his decimated reputation made Keenan's stomach churn and the bile rise in his throat, so he popped two extra-strength Tums from a flip-top container he had started keeping on his desk. Then, he called his dad.

"They're saying I killed her," Keenan said.

"I know," his dad said.

"Why is this happening?"

"I don't know. Only God knows. How are they treating you at the college?"

"No different than before they found her. The only person who still talks to me is my friend Aarav."

"What about your teammates?"

"Now that the season's over, I only see them in the weight room. But, yeah, they avoid me too." For the first time in his life, Keenan was glad that the hockey season was over. Normally, he thrived on the locker-room camaraderie, enjoyed the good-natured teasing that seemed to get piled on everyone in turn. But, even before Shannon's body was found, it was clear his teammates had their doubts about him. The locker room had become eerily silent every time he'd walked in. The bus rides to away games had seemed longer, sitting alone, not talking to anyone. He'd been thankful for the earbuds that he wore even when he wasn't playing music. At least his teammates hadn't let their distrust affect their play. On the ice, they had still passed to him, let him do his job as a defender. After all the years of training and playing, the game must be too ingrained to ignore.

"Do they really think you killed Shannon?" his dad asked.

"It sure feels that way," Keenan said, remembering that Rob McPherson had pretty much said so to a reporter.

"I'm sorry, son. All I can say is that it will all blow over, eventually."

"I sure hope so."

"And if it gets too bad, you can always come home."

"There's nothing I'd rather do right now, but I need to try to stick this out. If I leave, everyone will assume it's because I'm guilty. Besides, a degree from Masterson College is a big deal."

"I'm proud of you, Keenan."

"Yeah, right. Your son, the accused murderer."

"You're still the same kid to me. I know none of it's true."

"Thanks, Dad."

Somehow the media had gotten Keenan's cell phone number again. He had gotten a new one after his arrest when he'd been barraged by calls. These past few days, the calls had been constant again, so he powered down his phone as soon as he was done talking to his dad. He would walk to the Sprint office in town and get a new number the first time he could make time. Or more accurately, muster the energy.

Keenan made himself a peanut butter and jelly sandwich for dinner. His weight was down at least fifteen pounds since

Christmas. He should probably go to the dining hall more often, but the only person who had sought out his mealtime company was Aarav. They had eaten together a couple of times, but Keenan had been hyperaware of the accusing stares in his direction and decided early on to minimize the amount of time he spent in the dining hall. He'd gotten in the habit of having cereal in his room in the morning. The mini-fridge fit two gallons of milk, which he could stretch out to a week. One of the advantages of living alone was that he didn't have to leave room for his roommate's food. He should probably stock up on snack food again soon.

CHAPTER 30
Saturday, November 30, 2013

JAKE ARRIVED at Amy's apartment on time and the doorman buzzed him up. When Shannon opened the door, he swooped her into a big hug, picking her off the ground and swinging her around.

"I can't believe we haven't seen each other in three months," Jake said. "It's so great to see you."

Shannon introduced Jake and Amy.

"How was your Turkey Day?" Amy asked.

"I went to my cousin's house in New Jersey," Jake said. "Now I see why Shannon decided to stay with you. Nice place you have here."

"Thanks."

"Are your parents here?"

"No, they're both at some emergency association meeting. Someone in the building must have broken a rule." Amy rolled her eyes.

"I'll call you later, Amy, okay?" Shannon said.

"Sure. Enjoy the city, guys."

"Thanks. It was nice to meet you." He shut the door and, before Shannon could say anything, pulled her into a kiss. Shannon closed her eyes and kissed him back for a second before she remembered that she shouldn't. She pulled away.

Jake grinned at her. "I have a few ideas for today," he said. "I was thinking we could be tourists."

"Sounds like fun," she said.

"Super. I already got tickets."

"Tickets for what?"

"You'll see."

Shannon wasn't sure when she should tell Jake about Keenan. He seemed so excited that she didn't want to ruin the day by starting off with the bad news.

It turned out the tickets were for the ferry to Liberty Island and the crown of the Statue of Liberty. They stayed on deck for the ride to the island and watched the wake from the back of the boat.

"It's pretty cool, isn't it?" Jake said. "Us being here in New York City together. It's a long way from Solana Beach, California."

"It sure is."

"I've missed you. I've been so busy with school that I didn't realize how much until I saw you."

"I've missed you too, Jake." It was true, but she knew she needed to tell him the rest.

Without warning, he kissed her. His lips felt cold against hers, but familiar. This time she just let it happen. As the kiss deepened, she tasted his breath. Jake. It was like coming home. But better, because when she opened her eyes she could see the New York City skyline.

Jake pressed his forehead against hers. "I've wanted to do this," he said, "see the statue, that is, since I got to New York. But I've been saving it for your first visit. You should have come down here sooner."

"It's not like you came up to Vermont to visit me." This was the perfect segue. "If you ha—"

"I know. It's just been so overwhelming. The architecture program here is brutal. Pre-med at Masterson is probably just as bad. Aren't you overwhelmed?"

"Yeah, but I find time to do other things. Like skating." She had another chance to say it, but she just couldn't do it. It would ruin the day and she didn't want to do that.

They climbed the statue, then took goofy pictures of each other and a few joint selfies with the statue in the background.

On the ferry ride back, the wind picked up.

"Let's go inside," Shannon said.

"No, it's more fun outside and it smells better. I'll keep you warm."

They sat on the bench, arms wrapped around each other, and talked about their friends from high school. Shannon put her head on Jake's shoulder. It reminded her of their prom night, sitting side by side on the beach.

He gave her a tour of the Columbia campus.

"Wow. This is so urban. You need to come up to Masterson. There are cows wandering around on the quad."

"You're kidding."

"Yeah. But it's nothing like this. This is incredible."

Jake took her to his favorite burger place for dinner. It was a hole-in-the-wall near campus, but Shannon agreed that the burger was one of the best she'd had. And the fries were salty and browned to crispy perfection.

"Now you get to see my room."

"Is your roommate here?"

"Nope. Gone to Boston for the holiday."

The rooms were smaller than the ones at Masterson, but something about being in the city made them feel more chic. She sat on the bed. It was time to tell him.

"Jake—"

He silenced her with a kiss. After a minute she pulled away.

"Jake—"

"Let's talk later. Right now, I just want to be with you. It's been three months."

"But—"

"You used to like it when I did this." He kissed her neck. "And this." His hand worked its way under her shirt.

How could this be wrong? It was Jake. The boy she'd lost her virginity to two years ago. The boy who had nearly severed her heart from her body when he suggested they see other people at the end of last summer. Maybe she only thought she was in love with Keenan because she was getting back at Jake. This didn't feel wrong. It felt way too good to be wrong. What the hell.

Afterward, she lay beside him in his twin bed. "I need to call Amy."

"Don't go back there tonight. Stay here with me."

"What about her parents?"

"She can cover for you. I want to wake up next to the woman I love tomorrow."

"I thought you wanted to see other people."

"I said that, didn't I?"

"You did. Didn't you mean it?"

"I thought I did when I said it, but that's just because I didn't know what to expect at college. I was scared, weren't you?"

"Yeah, but I would have tried to do the long distance thing if you had wanted."

"I made a mistake. I realize it now. I want you here as much as you can come."

"I can't come down here all the time. I have to study too. Besides, we have final exams coming up in a couple of weeks."

"I know. We do, too. Then, as soon as finals are over, we'll both be home for Christmas break."

"That's true."

"And the watchful eye of our parents."

"Ugh. Don't remind me," Shannon said.

"That's why it's extra important that you spend the night tonight. It may be our only chance before next semester."

Shannon thought about it. It was so great to be with Jake. She had thought she had it all figured out, but now she wasn't sure. She owed it to herself to figure out which guy she was actually in love with.

"Okay. I'll ask Amy to make up an excuse," she said.

That night Shannon and Jake went out to listen to blues music. They held hands and laughed. Then, they made love in Jake's single bed. Shannon realized that it was actually the first time they had really made love. All the times they'd had sex before had been the desperate gropings and grindings of horny teenagers. Here, away from their friends and parents, it felt different. More mature. Much better.

Shannon woke up with Jake spooning her and his arm holding her tight. It felt right. She was glad she hadn't told him about Keenan. It would have hurt him too much.

CHAPTER 31
Tuesday, April 15, 2014

WHEN KEENAN walked out of his dormitory to go to his political science class, there were four reporters waiting to ambush him. A television news van was parked at the curb, doors open.

"Keenan, did you kill Shannon?" a male voice shouted from the bottom of the steps. He wanted to turn around and go back to his room, but he couldn't afford to miss any more classes. There had been so many days at the beginning of the semester when his grief had made it too hard to get out of bed for his first class of the day. With hindsight, he wasn't even sure what he had been grieving most: Shannon's lost life or just the loss of control over his own life. It was probably a toss-up. He had stopped skipping classes when he realized he needed to regain even a smidgen of control. He couldn't go back there.

"Keenan, how did you kill her?" It was a female voice.

Keenan threaded his way through the reporters and started walking.

"Did you dump her body in the river?" someone called after him.

Keenan kept walking, but they followed him. He picked up his pace as he made his way across campus and managed to lose all but one. The blonde in her mid-twenties looked like she ran marathons in her spare time. She wasn't even breathing hard when she said, "How about an exclusive, Keenan? Tell me how Shannon died."

"You're sick," he said, and he ducked into the English

building. Once he was alone, he wished he could take it back. There was nothing to be gained by antagonizing the reporters. Of course, you'd have to be sick to do what they were doing to him.

When the class was over, Keenan and Aarav sat in silence while the professor cleared the podium and packed her bag. As soon as she had left the room, Keenan said, "Aren't you going to ask me if I killed her?"

"No."

"Why not?"

"I know you. I know how you felt about her."

"That doesn't seem to matter to the police. Or anybody else for that matter."

"From what my family says, the police in India imprison people for things they didn't do all the time. I guess it happens here too."

Keenan nodded.

"Besides, you're my best friend. What does it say about me if my best friend is a murderer?"

Keenan looked into Aarav's near-black eyes and was grateful for the compassion he saw.

BARRY GOT the autopsy results a few days after Fred did and apparently even after the results were leaked to the press. He met with Keenan in his office that afternoon.

"Does it say how she died?" Keenan said.

"Not really."

"Poor Shannon. I figured she was dead months ago, but now it's so real." The kid sounded sincere. Of course, he might be a good actor.

"I'm sorry for your loss," Barry said.

"Thanks."

"Now that he has a body, Fred Dutton may decide to pursue a homicide charge, but I don't think this autopsy report does much to help him."

"Is there anything in there that points to murder?"

"The report says that she either drowned or was killed by

head trauma."

"If she drowned it was probably an accident, and they have to know I didn't have anything to do with it."

"Except that the toxicology report on her blood alcohol content was inconclusive."

"But I'm telling you she was drunk."

"We need more than just your word. Her friends said she wasn't that intoxicated, and people that are barely intoxicated don't fall into the river and drown on their own."

"She was a lot more than a little intoxicated when I saw her. That's why I took her keys."

"That's the problem we've been having with this investigation. Everybody my investigator talked to downplayed Shannon's intoxication."

"That's because they don't want to get in trouble. They were drinking with her and they're afraid of getting kicked out of school."

"We've got to find someone, or better yet a few people who will say she was intoxicated. It would also help if we had someone who would testify about the party and the fact that they were serving alcohol to minors. I'm going to have my investigator make that her top priority. Toni's good at getting people to talk to her." Toni had her own investigations firm, but she spent half her time working on Barry's cases. Barry found her to be quick witted, thorough, and worth every penny that his clients paid for her services.

"Nobody's going to rat them out. There's a code. That's why I didn't tell the police everything right up front."

"We need to get someone else to break it," Barry said. "Otherwise, you may become the scapegoat."

FRED DUTTON hadn't been reelected as Adam's County State's Attorney every four years for more than two decades by being politically imprudent. He understood his role well. His constituents wanted to know that he was keeping order in Adams County, that the drug addicts were prosecuted when they broke into houses while the hard working were at work.

But the voters also wanted to know that Junior wouldn't get the book thrown at him when he screwed up. Even the kids of the upstanding were known to make mistakes. Fred had always been good at finding the right balance.

The problem was that, even after discussing the case with everyone he could think of, he still wasn't sure how the Brody case would play with the voters. Of course, if he were really sure that Brody had committed murder, the decision would be easy. The problem was, he wasn't. The assault looked solid on paper, but he knew that an attorney as skilled as Barry might pull off an acquittal. And there was no sugarcoating it—the autopsy results were undeniably inconclusive. Was it worse to lose a high-profile homicide case or to walk away from one?

All Fred really wanted was to get reelected one, maybe two, more times, preferably without an opponent. After that, he'd retire with a full pension from the state and spend all his free time on the golf course. He was pondering his dilemma when it came to him. He could pawn it off on the grand jury.

Grand juries were rarely used in Vermont. Prosecutors ordinarily charged crimes by filing informations, which were reviewed by judges. Occasionally, prosecutors invoked a grand jury, especially when dealing with crimes committed by law enforcement officers during the course of their duties—it helped to be able to say to the cops, "Don't look at me, the grand jury made the call." Fred had used a grand jury for that purpose once in his second term.

Fred called Jerry Niven, the clerk of the court. "How soon can you empanel a grand jury?" Fred said.

"I don't know. Never done one." Jerry had only been the clerk for five years.

"Well, have a look at Rule 6 and get back to me."

A few hours later, Fred and Jerry met with the judge. The next day, Jerry sent summonses to thirty people. The super secret grand jury would convene the following week.

CHAPTER 32
Thursday, April 17, 2014

EVEN THOUGH it was a routine status conference, the camera crews were at the courthouse again. Now that this might become a murder case, they were hoping for a tidbit. Barry met Keenan and his parents before the hearing. He had told Greg and Cassie that their support at every stage was critical, that their faith in their son sent a strong message—although he suspected he wouldn't have been able to keep them away if he'd tried.

As soon as the cameras were ready, the judge came back to the bench.

"Mr. Densmore, I see that you did not file any motions. Have there been any plea negotiations?"

"Mr. Dutton and I have discussed the case on multiple occasions. I'm afraid there's no middle ground. This case is on a trial track, Your Honor."

The judge peered over his reading glasses. "Very well. When do you expect to be ready for trial?"

"My client will be finished with his courses for the semester the third week in May. After that, he'll be better able to assist in his defense. We'd like a trial in June, if we can get dates."

"That's awfully quick." The judge took off his glasses and looked at the cameras.

Fred Dutton was on his feet. "May we approach, Your Honor?"

The judge nodded and waived both attorneys to the front of the room. The air was filled with a mild static noise that teetered between peaceful and irritating.

As soon as the sound blocking was on, Fred began. "As Your Honor is aware, there is the possibility of additional charges. Perhaps we should hold off on scheduling."

"If Mr. Dutton is going to charge my client, I think, in all fairness, he should not delay," Barry said.

"The delay is not Mr. Dutton's fault," the judge said.

Barry looked back and forth between the two men. What the hell did they know that he didn't?

"You'll find out in a few days anyway, so I might as well tell you," Fred said. "We're convening a grand jury on the homicide charges."

Barry stood up straighter. "When is this happening?"

"Next week."

"When were you going to tell me?"

"You know you're not entitled to notice."

"Right, so the state can stage another ambush on my nineteen-year-old client."

"Come on, Barry. You know me better than that. I'm telling you now because I trust you'll respect the secrecy of the proceedings. I'm giving you time to decide if you want to let your client testify before the grand jury. You know he's the target, so there's no point pretending otherwise."

"And if I don't let him testify?"

"Then they can consider the evidence and decide whether to indict without hearing from him."

"Of course they'll indict without his side of the story. Damned if I do, damned if I don't."

The judge frowned, raised a finger, and took a deep breath.

"Sorry, Your Honor," Barry said.

The judge exhaled, but gave Barry a stern look. "Okay gentlemen, where does this leave us on the assault charge?" he said.

Fred was the first to speak. "We see the assault and the homicide as two distinct events, separated in time, which makes them two separate counts. Whether or not the defendant is indicted, I plan to keep the assault charge. I can't say whether the defense will want to try them together or separately. I'd be inclined to join them."

Barry shook his head. "If my client ends up facing a homicide charge, I'm not sure what we'll want to do."

"Under the circumstances, we should wait and see what happens next week. If there's no indictment, we can come back the following week to discuss scheduling," the judge said.

With grim expressions, the attorneys walked back to the counsel tables.

"The clerk will issue scheduling notices," the judge said. "Court is in recess." The judge rose and strode quickly from the room.

There was a moment of stunned silence in the courtroom. As far as the reporters could see, nothing had happened. All that time setting up cameras and not one thing had happened. Served them right, the vultures.

Barry whispered to Keenan, "It'll take the press a few minutes to regroup. Get out of here as fast as you can and don't let them corner you. Meet me at my office. Bring your parents."

"What just happened?" Keenan said.

"I'll tell you when you get to my office. Now, move."

As soon as Keenan was moving, Barry decided to take a minute to talk to Fred. He caught up with him in the elevator.

"Hey, I want to thank you for giving me the heads up on the grand jury. I know you didn't have to do that. I'm sorry if I reacted badly."

"That's okay," Fred said. "I get it. You're stuck between a rock and a hard place."

"I guess you are, too."

"What do you mean?"

"Try a case with weak circumstantial evidence or leave the only possible homicide in Adams County this decade unsolved."

"Those are your words, not mine."

"You really want to ruin my client's life over weak circumstantial evidence?"

"A girl is dead."

"And it was probably her own fault."

"He had a motive."

"Lots of people have motives. Almost none of them commit homicide." Barry waited for Fred to respond, but he didn't. Instead, the elevator was filled with a whirring sound as it climbed. "I have a feeling this is one of the those cases where we agree to disagree."

"It won't be the first time," Fred said.

"No, it won't."

"But given the media attention, we probably shouldn't go golfing together until after this thing is over."

"Yup."

They both got off the elevator. Barry took the back stairs down to the parking lot. He had hoped for a different reaction from Fred, but wasn't surprised by the one he got. He knew enough about psychology to know when to back off—the more you try to convince someone with a lot to lose that they're wrong, the more firmly convicted they become. There was still a sliver of hope that Fred would be able to assess the evidence objectively, and Barry did not want to be the one to get Fred's back up.

Keenan and his parents had arrived at Barry's office ahead of him. They were standing in his reception area when Barry bustled in. He led the way into a conference room, slapped his briefcase on the table, and shut the door.

"Have a seat." Barry gestured toward the chairs, but remained standing himself. He could feel the worry radiating from the parents and knew that nothing he was about to say was going to assuage it.

"What's going on?" Greg said.

"Fred Dutton is summoning a grand jury."

"What does that mean?" Keenan said.

"It means that next week a grand jury will hear the evidence about Shannon's death and decide whether to indict you for homicide."

Cassie Brody grabbed her husband's arm.

"But, he hasn't been charged yet?" Greg said.

"No, but he likely will."

"Is there anything you can do to stop the indictment?" Greg said.

"I don't even know what 'indict' means," Keenan said.

"Okay. Let's all take a breath. First of all, an indictment is just a different way of filing charges. It's rarely used in Vermont."

"So, why is it being used for Keenan?" Greg said.

"Without knowing if there's new evidence, I can't say for sure, but my educated guess is that Fred Dutton has a weak case. He's feeling pressure to charge a homicide, but he's not sure what the right move is. Politically, that is."

"I don't understand," Cassie said.

"The grand jury gives Fred a scapegoat. If they don't indict, he can tell the press that they made the decision, not him. If they indict, and he loses at trial, he can say he thought it was a weak case all along, but that he took it because of the grand jury."

"So, it's not all bad news," Keenan said. "You're saying they have a weak case."

"No, it's bad news," Barry said. "Good news would be Fred admitting that he doesn't have enough to charge you. I just talked to him and he's not going to do that."

"So, what do we do about the grand jury?" Cassie said.

"There's not a lot we can do. Ultimately, it's Keenan's decision whether to testify. Keenan's the target, so if he wants to take the Fifth, Fred won't be offering immunity. Without immunity, I always advise clients never to talk to the grand jury."

"Why?"

"Let me explain how the grand jury works. To get a grand jury, the court pulls eighteen to twenty-three people off the juror rolls. They're just random people. They're supposed to not be biased against you, but for all we know, they all read the paper and think you're a murderer. We don't get to screen them. In fact, I'm not even allowed to participate in the proceedings. It's the state's attorney's dog and pony show. He gets to parade a bunch of witnesses in front of the grand jury and ask them anything he wants any way he wants, and the grand jurors can ask questions as well. Witnesses can be represented by attorneys, but the attorneys have to stay out in the hall. Then, when the state's attorney is done, the jurors get to vote. As long as twelve of them vote to indict, the charges get filed. The more grand jurors he has, the lower the percentage required for an indictment."

"Maybe they won't indict Keenan," Cassie said.

"Miracles do happen," Barry said.

"So, why would Keenan risk talking to them?" Greg said.

"Because there's no guarantee they'll hear Keenan's version of events if he doesn't tell them. Without his story, it's almost certain he'll get indicted. Of course, if he testifies, he probably still will get indicted."

"So, it might help," Keenan said.

"It might, but in my professional opinion, the risks outweigh the benefits."

"Explain the risks," Greg said.

"Well, like I said, they can ask you anything they want, any way they want. I can't be with you to object."

"I didn't murder Shannon and I didn't even assault her. All I have to do is tell the truth."

"It's not that simple. If it were, you might not already be facing assault charges."

"It should be simple," Keenan said.

"You're right. It should be—but it isn't. The criminal justice system isn't all that good at truth finding. And the grand jury proceedings don't even pretend to be aimed at finding the truth. It's too lopsided. Only one side gets to present its version of events, and as long as there's 'good and sufficient evidence,' there's an indictment. It's not a high standard and the rule against hearsay doesn't even apply."

"So, what's the worst-case scenario if Keenan testifies?" Cassie said.

"Good question. The worst case is they indict him, and then at trial everything he says gets used to impeach him."

"Impeach?" Keenan said.

"Make you look like a liar."

"But if I'm telling the truth, how can I look like a liar?"

"Trust me, it's not that hard. What juries don't understand is that the human memory is imperfect. In fact, it's downright unreliable. If you go in there and say anything inconsistent with what you said before, or say after, Fred will claim it's because you're not telling the truth."

"So, why might Keenan want to testify for the grand jury?" Greg said.

"Because it's the only chance he has to head this off before trial."

"Why are you so convinced he'll be indicted?" Cassie said.

"There's this saying, 'A grand jury would indict a ham sandwich.' And in my experience, they always indict. The state courts here in Vermont rarely use them, but the feds use them in all their cases, so I have some experience with it. And we already know what the evidence against Keenan is because of the assault charge, unless Fred's been holding out on me. Which I doubt. Fred may be a political animal, but he's a straight-shooter."

"I need to testify for the grand jury," Keenan said.

"I think you should talk it over with your parents before you make a final decision."

Keenan looked first at his mother, then his father. "I need to do this. I'm innocent and they have to believe me. If I just tell the truth, they'll see it."

Barry couldn't resist. "I bet you thought the same thing when you let Officer Shores interview you."

"But that's different, he was trying to make a case."

"What makes you think the grand jury will be any better?"

"They have to be."

"My advice is to stay away from the grand jury. I can't do anything to protect you if you walk in that door."

KEENAN UNDERSTOOD why Barry wanted him to stay away from the grand jury, but he was tired of people saying things about him that weren't true. If there was any chance of avoiding a murder charge, he needed to do it.

His parents stayed in Middleton Falls that afternoon. They said they wanted to discuss the options, but it felt like they were just trying to talk him out of testifying. The three went for a walk around campus until a fifty-degree drizzle made the walking uncomfortable.

They had an early dinner at a local diner with high-backed booths. Keenan was glad for the quasi privacy. They ordered greasy burgers with fries, but most of the food got cold, uneaten. His mom asked for a doggie bag. Keenan knew she would actually feed the leftovers to the dogs when she got home.

Keenan insisted on walking back to campus, so they said good-bye in the parking lot.

"I think you should take Barry's advice, Keenan." his dad said. "It's obvious the man knows what he's talking about."

"But if I don't do this, I'm going to be tried for murder, Dad. Murder."

"I'm sorry, son. If I could take your place right now, I would."

"I know, Dad."

"This just isn't fair," his mom said. She hugged Keenan long and hard before getting in the car to head back to Lyndonville.

CHAPTER 33
Sunday, December 1, 2013

JAKE ACCOMPANIED Shannon back to Amy's apartment when it was time to leave. They said good-bye at the corner so Amy's parents wouldn't realize that the "friend from high school" she ran into was actually a boy.

"I'll see you in a few weeks."

"They're going to be long weeks." She was thinking of the studying.

"Just remember I love you and we'll be together soon. You'll get through it."

They shared one last kiss before Jake had to go. Shannon felt a hollow feeling in her chest when Jake's dark hair disappeared from view as he descended into the subway entrance.

Shannon told Amy everything that had happened during the drive back to Vermont that afternoon.

"What are you going to do?" Amy asked.

Shannon took her eyes off the road and glanced at her friend. Amy's expression was somber, which only made Shannon feel worse. "I don't know. I can't be in love with both of them. I need to figure it out, but I can't right now. Finals are coming up."

"Tell me about it. We've only got two weeks until the first one."

"I need to keep my head in my studies. If I don't, then medical school won't happen."

"I hear you. But, you know it's not right to be sleeping with two guys at the same time."

"I know. Believe me, I know. And Keenan wants to see me tonight. He's been texting me since yesterday morning. I told him my battery died and that's why I was incommunicado."

"Nice lie. Are you going to see him?"

"I have no idea."

CHAPTER 34
Friday, April 18, 2014

BARRY KEPT Keenan in his office all the next afternoon going over his testimony.

"The most important thing here is consistency," Barry said. "Keep it short, sweet, and consistent." He gave Keenan copies of his statements to study and coached him on how not to appear too defensive.

"Whatever you do, don't lie. It will come back to bite you."

"I would never lie."

"And don't get angry. Even if you feel like they're accusing you. If you get angry, they'll think you're capable of murder."

"I won't. I promise."

"And call me this weekend if you have any questions." Barry wrote his cell number on the back of a business card.

"Thanks."

"You don't have to do this, you know."

"I do. Have to do this. If I don't, I'll wonder if I could have stopped it."

As soon as Marcy left at five o'clock, Barry poured himself a Red Label and brought it back to his desk. He imagined Keenan in a jail cell for a decade, doing push-ups instead of playing hockey, reading instead of studying. It would be a waste of a promising life. He took a sip and realized his glass was empty. He got up and poured another scotch. That one seemed to disappear too quickly as well. He should go home. But Sam had been spending less and less time there. Probably because

Barry had too.

CHAPTER 35
Tuesday, April 22, 2014

BARRY MET Keenan at the courthouse on the morning of his grand jury testimony.

"Are you sure I can't convince you to not do this?" Barry said.

"I have to."

"I'll be right here in the hall if you need me. If you say you want to consult with your lawyer, they'll take a break so we can talk."

Keenan walked through the courtroom door and Barry sank onto the bench outside the door. He probably should have tried harder to talk the kid out of testifying. But, if he were feeling framed for murder, he'd want to tell his side of the story as well. Ah, the psychology of being a lawyer. They should teach a course on it in law school.

FRED DUTTON knew he could put the Brody kid through the wringer, but truth be told, he wasn't hellbent on indicting the kid. In fact, his life would be a hell of a lot easier if he didn't have to try a high-profile homicide case with very circumstantial evidence at this point in his career.

He had tried to present the evidence to the grand jury in an orderly and neutral fashion. He didn't leave anything out, but he didn't try to spin it either. His only witness before the grand jury had been Dustin Shores, who had spent a day and a half giving a good summary of the evidence. Fred's final submission was a copy of the autopsy report. He didn't even bother to bring the medical examiner down to testify.

As icing, he let the kid tell his own story his own way. Without interruption. When it looked like the kid was done, he said, "Anything else the grand jury should know?"

"I can't think of anything right now, sir," Keenan said. He'd sounded polite throughout his testimony.

"Any questions from the grand jurors?"

It wasn't surprising there were few. The poor schmucks had only been grand jurors for two days; they didn't have the job down yet. Nor would they likely before their careers as grand jurors ended in a matter of hours.

Fred told the kid he was excused.

The beauty of the grand jury was that it was so super secret that nobody would ever know how hard he hadn't tried. Except for Barry, who would figure it out when he read the transcripts. But Barry knew better than to tell on him.

KEENAN WALKED out of the grand jury room and collapsed on the bench next to Barry.

"Are you done?" Barry said.

"He said I could go."

"You didn't come out to consult with me."

"They didn't ask anything you hadn't prepared me for. It wasn't that bad."

"Really?"

"No. I just told them the truth. I didn't do it."

"Don't get your hopes up," Barry said.

But Keenan couldn't help it. He'd put so much time into preparing for his testimony. Just like it had been a final exam. And just like with a final exam, he knew he'd aced it. There hadn't been any questions that he didn't know the answers to. He knew he'd sounded sincere while he was testifying. He had to have. Because it was the truth. Nothing but the truth. And the grand jurors would be able to see that.

He talked to both his parents by phone as soon as he got back to the privacy of his room. By the time he was done recounting everything, he felt like a weight had been lifted. He still had to deal with the assault charges, but at least people would stop calling him a murderer.

That night, he slept for seven hours. It was the longest he'd slept since Shannon had disappeared.

CHAPTER 36
Wednesday, December 4, 2013

I CAN'T believe we've been back for three days and I haven't seen you," Keenan said. Shannon had begged out of seeing him on Sunday night, claiming that she was exhausted from the late nights and travel. She'd rejected his calls on Monday and Tuesday and sent him texts saying she was at the library and couldn't talk. She'd even avoided open ice time at the arena so they wouldn't run into each other. Finally, on Wednesday, she knew she had to deal with it. She accepted a call.

"I'm sorry. I've just been busy."

"Are you okay? You don't sound okay. Did something happen in New York?"

"I've just got a lot on my mind. It's the pre-med thing. Where are you guys playing this weekend?"

"We have a home game on Friday night and an away game on Saturday in Rochester. I won't be back until 2:00 a.m. on Sunday. I know you're busy studying, but I really want to see you before I go. How about tomorrow night?"

"Okay. I'll meet you after practice."

"Great. I can't wait."

Thursday came and she just couldn't do it. While Keenan was at practice, she sent him a text: *Im sick. Dont want u to get it too. TTUT.* Talk to you tomorrow. Maybe she'd have it figured out by tomorrow. Unlikely. The only thing she knew was that she couldn't sleep with Keenan right now. Not after she'd just slept with Jake.

She got a text back that said: *Get better soon. ILU.* I love you too, she thought. But she didn't answer. Instead, she checked her Facebook account and noticed that Jake had posted one of their selfies from the Statue of Liberty. The memory of their excursion made her smile. Automatically, she started to click on the Like icon, but fortunately she stopped herself in time. If she "liked" the photo, it would be accessible on her Facebook page. And anyone could see it. Including Keenan. She exhaled sharply as the close call registered.

KEENAN WAS beginning to wonder if Shannon was avoiding him. It didn't make sense. A week ago she had said she loved him. Of course, girls had never made much sense to him. He needed to find out what was going on. He walked out to the convenience store where he'd bought the rose and bought a can of chicken soup, a bottle of ginger ale, and cough drops. On impulse, he threw a *Cosmopolitan* magazine on the counter. That should cover whatever kind of illness Shannon had.

When she opened the door to her room, Shannon smiled.

"I brought home remedies." He held up a plastic bag.

"I'm feeling much better."

"Are you even sick?"

"I haven't been feeling right."

"Can I come in?"

"I guess."

He couldn't resist scooping her into a hug. "You feel so good," he whispered in her ear. He set her down. "How's the studying going?"

"I'm having a hard time."

"Did something happen? Oh my God, you're pregnant!"

"No, I'm not pregnant. At least I don't think so."

"So, what's the problem?"

When she didn't answer, he tried again. "Is it me?"

"Sort of."

"Did I push you too fast? I know you said you weren't sure if you were ready."

"Maybe."

"You could have just told me, you know."

"I know."

"I would have given you space if you needed it."

"I know."

"Is that what you want?"

"I don't know."

"Look, Shannon. I'm in love with you. I want to be with you. But if you need me to back off a little, I will."

"Keenan, you know I care about you. I'm just not sure I'm ready to be in a relationship. You know how important grades are if I'm going to get into med school."

"I don't think this is about grades. Is it the sex?"

"I don't know."

"Are you having regrets about the sex? Because I'm not. But if you want to take sex out of the equation, I can do that. For a while, anyway. I just want to be with you."

"Could you? Forget about sex? It feels like it complicates things too much."

"I'm not going to forget about it. It was too good to forget. But we can step back a little if it's what you need."

Shannon grinned. "Okay."

"But don't expect me to give up kissing." He bent over and kissed her deeply.

"Wow. I forgot how good you are at that."

"Try to keep it in mind while you're studying this weekend. I'll call you after we get back from Rochester."

Keenan felt better as he was walking home. It seemed like Shannon was just getting cold feet. He would back off a little, but he wasn't ready to give up by any means.

AFTER KEENAN left, Shannon sat on her bed and opened her calculus textbook. She was glad she had finally seen Keenan, and that he had offered her a solution to her problem. Well, a temporary solution anyway. The problem wasn't dating two guys at the same time, but having sex with both of them. Without sex involved, she could take a little time to figure things out.

She started her homework problems and felt relaxed for the first time since she'd left Jake.

CHAPTER 37
Wednesday, April 23, 2014

THE MORNING after he testified, the grand jury indicted Keenan on a single charge of voluntary manslaughter. Barry wasn't surprised when Fred called to give him the news.

"The indictment was sealed," Fred said. "And the court staff isn't supposed to say anything to anyone about the grand jury."

"Which means that Manny Rodriguez is already writing his story for the *Gazette*."

"That's what I was going to say next."

"How much can you afford to play this down?"

"Why are you asking?"

"My client obviously knew there was a chance he would be indicted, but he showed up to testify."

"What do you want?"

"You've already got bail on him from the assault charge. How about you flash cite him for tomorrow on the manslaughter charge?"

"A flash cite instead of an arrest? On a homicide charge?"

"I know it's unconventional, but the kid's not going to flee. He's known all along this was a possibility. That way, we might be able to avoid some of the media circus." Barry waited while Fred considered his unusual request.

Fred sighed. "I'm getting pretty damned tired of the media myself."

"Imagine how the Brody family feels about now."

"But if he doesn't show, I'll look like an idiot."

"He'll show."

"Okay, but consider it a favor."

"Thanks, Fred." Barry was truly grateful for the favor. He knew it was a big one. And he wondered why he had used it up on Keenan Brody. Was he sure the kid was innocent? Or was he, too, falling prey to psychological phenomena?

"You were indicted on a charge of voluntary manslaughter," Barry explained to Keenan on the phone a few minutes later.

"How?"

"I told you it would be stacked."

"I'm screwed, aren't I?"

"I don't envy the position you're in, but it could've been worse. At least it wasn't a second-degree murder charge. You never know. If you hadn't gone in to talk to the grand jury, it might have been." Barry wasn't sure that was true, but he wanted the kid to feel better.

"So, what happens if I get convicted?"

"Manslaughter has a one-year minimum and a fifteen-year maximum."

"Fifteen years is a long time. I'd be an old man when I got out."

Barry was glad Keenan couldn't see him smirk. He was thinking that thirty-four isn't even considered middle-aged anymore. At least he hoped not, since he'd passed that mile marker a long time ago. "I could probably negotiate a plea deal that would get you out sooner."

"I can't go to jail for something I didn't do. This is so fucked up."

"I'm sure it feels that way."

"Tell me something. Can you win?"

"I'm not going to make you any promises, other than that I will do my best. But, yes, there's a chance I can win."

"I really didn't kill her, you know."

"I already told you it doesn't matter if you did."

"But it does. To me. You ever lost a trial you should have won?"

"I've lost a few over the years."

"Were those clients innocent?"

"I don't think so."

"That's why I need you to believe me."

"Point taken. I really will do my best. That's all I can promise. Now, you promise me you'll be at the courthouse tomorrow at 8:45 a.m. Your arraignment's set for nine o'clock. I had to use up a favor to keep you from spending the night in jail tonight."

"Thanks."

"Just be there. And bring your parents. Actually, you should probably have your dad call me. We need to talk about money."

CASSIE BRODY clutched her husband's hand while he talked to Barry on the phone. She was shivering despite the warm spring day. Usually spring was her favorite time of year. She loved when everything came to life again after the dormant winter. This year everything was ahead of schedule because of the sudden shift into spring. The azalea outside her kitchen window had its first flower. The willows were budding out, an electric yellowish green, getting ready to burst, and the marsh marigold around the pond was in full bloom. But, though she noticed, it didn't bring her joy; all she could think about was the cruelty of a world that would persecute her child.

"How could they do this to him?" she said as Greg hung up the phone. "He's such a good kid, an honest one."

"I don't know. I really don't understand this," Greg said. "None of it makes sense."

"Remember when he was eleven? And he put a hole in the drywall playing knee hockey in the living room?"

"After we told him no knee hockey except in the basement. I remember."

"He came to me, found me out working in the garden. To tell me what he'd done. And to apologize. None of our other kids would have done that."

"You're probably right."

"I know it. Liam would have rearranged the furniture so we

wouldn't find out."

"Or blamed Keenan."

Cassie sobbed. "I know they don't know him like we do, but they should have believed him."

"Barry warned us that they probably wouldn't."

"I know. But I was hoping he was wrong."

"Me, too."

"What else did Barry say just now?"

"He said that we should plan on at least another hundred thousand dollars for the trial. He needs eighty thousand by next week."

Cassie gasped. "Where are we going to get that kind of money?"

"We're going to take a second mortgage. But first, we're going to go to Middleton Falls tomorrow morning and stand by our son while he gets arraigned."

"Oh my God. How is he going to survive this?"

CHAPTER 38
Thursday, April 24, 2014

KEENAN WAS in the bleachers at the ice rink. He had put his phone on mute. The enormous arena was empty, the rink nothing more than a slab of concrete.

How had his life gone so bad so fast?

He knew that he needed to get to the courthouse, but he just wanted to check out. He could hitchhike back to the Northeast Kingdom and spend the summer living in the woods. Thanks to his grandpa, he knew how to hunt and fish. He could survive and they'd never find him, even if they figured out where to look. It might even be peaceful. Except he'd always be looking over his shoulder. And by October, the nights get mighty cold. He'd need shelter and a fire. Once you lay down roots, you're easier to find.

Who was he kidding? He couldn't do that to his family. If he ran, everyone back home would think he was guilty. His family would pay the price and he wouldn't get to be with them. There was no choice here, but he still couldn't get up.

He heard footsteps and saw his coach approaching.

"I was sorting through some equipment, saw you up here. I sometimes come here to think too."

Keenan wished he would leave, but he nodded.

"It was a good season. The team played well."

"Except the game against Trinity. We lost six to nothing."

The coach shrugged. "That wasn't good, but the important thing is that you guys didn't let it psych you out. It was hard to lose so heavily first game of the season. It could have set the tone. I've seen it in other years, but you guys made it your Alamo. That's what a winner does. Keenan, you're a hard worker."

"Thanks, coach."

"You know, I was under a lot of pressure to suspend you from the team."

"Pressure from who?"

"The other players' parents, the administration." The coach rubbed the top of his balding head before he continued, "But in this country, a person is innocent until proven guilty. That's part of what makes this country great. I don't know if you had anything to do with that girl's death—"

"I didn't."

"—but, whether you did or didn't is in the past. What you do from here on speaks to the kind of man you are. Anyway, I hope you're back on the team next year."

"Thanks, coach."

FRED WASN'T sure whether he was more pissed at Barry or his client. He sat at the prosecution table doodling geometric patterns on his yellow legal pad. Barry appeared calm at the adjacent table, but Fred could tell by the way he was jiggling his right leg that he was using his game face. The massive clock on the courtroom wall moved to nine o'clock and there was no sign of Keenan Brody. The kid's parents were in the gallery behind Barry looking rumpled and weary. They had probably gotten up in the middle of the night to come and watch their son get labeled a fugitive.

Olivia Dawson was at the back of the courtroom, both her hands clutching the arm of a woman he recognized as an advocate from Safe Haven, the local women's shelter. He had told Olivia about the grand jury in hopes that she would stay in California, but she had insisted on returning "to see things through," whatever that meant. It wasn't a huge surprise that she wanted to be involved—the families of victims frequently needed to feel a part of the court process to get closure. But that usually meant driving an hour to get to court proceedings, not moving across the country.

The only other spectator was Manny Rodriguez from the local paper. Thanks to his contacts in the courthouse, he would scoop the other journalists. And it might be a bigger story than expected. Something like, "Brody Indicted for Homicide, On The Run After Prosecutor Cites Him." He should have just had Dustin arrest the damn kid.

Barry got up and walked back to the Brodys. He maintained a studied calm, but it was obvious he was asking them where their son was.

Finally, at 9:10 Keenan burst into the courtroom and made his way to his seat next to Barry, who somehow managed an aura of nonchalance. The parents were visibly relieved.

Barry pushed the mute button on his microphone and waived his client into a huddle. Even without hearing it, Fred had a pretty good idea what Barry was saying to his client. It could only be a form of the riot act. However, the conversation ended abruptly when the clerk bellowed, "All rise, the Honorable Edmund Whippet presiding." The judge strode quickly across the front of the room, his black robe floating behind him. As soon as the clerk had announced the case, the judge began.

"We're here for an arraignment on a charge of voluntary manslaughter. Mr. Densmore?"

"Waive the reading, waive the twenty-four-hour rule, enter a plea of not guilty, Your Honor."

"I see that the defendant appeared today on a citation. We already have ten thousand dollars' bail and conditions in place. Are you seeking anything more, Mr. Dutton?"

Fred wanted to ask for $100,000. It was a homicide charge after all, and the kid had been late. But then Barry would be pissed at him. And the kid had showed up. On the other hand, if he didn't ask for an increase, Olivia would surely communicate her displeasure. "In light of the more serious charge, we believe an increase in bail is appropriate. We'll leave the amount to Your Honor's discretion." Fred glared briefly at Keenan, who probably didn't understand just how much his tardiness could have cost him.

"Okay, I'm ordering another ten thousand dollars in bail. How much time do we need for initial discovery?" the judge said.

"I've already turned over most of the evidence in connection with the related assault case," Fred said. "I should be able to do the rest within two weeks."

"Let's come back in four weeks on both cases. I want preliminary witness lists exchanged within three and the first round of depositions scheduled before the next status conference. I want to fast-track this case if we can. Any objection?"

"No, Your Honor," both attorneys said simultaneously.

"May eighteenth at 9:00 a.m.," the clerk said.

Fred nodded at Barry as he walked past the defense table. Fred had been fair throughout the whole process. He was pretty certain of that. Mostly because he had wanted to believe that Brody was innocent. There were probably a lot of complex reasons for that, some of them relating to his friendship with Barry. He probably let Barry take advantage more than he should. After all, Dustin and the chief had been convinced of the kid's guilt long before there was even a body. He probably should have listened to them. Of course, the grand jury hadn't been influenced by politics or friendship. They had heard an unbiased version of the evidence and decided to indict. That meant the kid was probably guilty. He should have realized it sooner.

CASSIE STILL couldn't believe that her son had been charged with manslaughter—it was surreal. She hadn't slept because she'd been worrying about Keenan and what might happen in court. Even though Barry had told them it was unlikely that Keenan would go to jail that day, she had still been afraid that Barry might be wrong. Thankfully, he hadn't been.

After posting the additional bail, they met with Barry at his office. "We have some decisions to make," Barry began. "First, the judge is giving us an opportunity to fast-track. I suspect it's because he doesn't want to deal with a prolonged media circus any more than we do."

"I want to get this over with," Keenan said.

"I can do that," Barry said. "I don't have any other cases that will require this level of attention in the short term. But you need to understand that, if we rush this, we're more likely to make mistakes."

"I need my life back," Keenan said.

"Okay. When do you start school in the fall?" Barry said.

"Classes start the first week in September."

"I'll try to get trial dates at the end of August," Barry said. "That might work to our advantage anyway. I like Judge Whippet, and Adams County is supposed to be getting a new judge in September."

As the thought of a trial brought back images of her son in the courtroom, Cassie felt the now all too familiar turmoil in her stomach. She had to force herself to pay attention to Barry's words—there might be something Keenan needed her to remember later.

"Right now, because of the timing, Keenan is facing charges under two separate docket numbers. The judge will want to join them, try the assault and manslaughter charges together. The prosecution too. We have to decide whether to oppose it."

"You mean ask for two trials. Why would we want to do that?" Greg said.

"The biggest reason is that even if they're not convinced of the assault, the jury may convict him of it as a compromise."

"I don't get it," Cassie said. "Compromise?"

"Being a juror is a tough job. There's pressure to be fair, but also not to let people get away with crimes. If we convince them that there's not enough evidence for the manslaughter charge, they may convict on the assault charge to hedge their bets on whether they got it right. I'm not saying they do it consciously. It's just psychology. The conventional wisdom is that we're better off splitting the charges if we can. That way we can also try to keep the evidence of Shannon's death out of the assault charge."

"But everybody around here already knows she's dead," Keenan said.

Barry shrugged. "I'm hoping to find fourteen jurors who don't read the papers."

"And two trials will cost twice as much, right?" Greg said.

"For the most part."

"I don't want to go through two trials," Keenan said. "I just want to get this over with." So did Cassie. But maybe she should try to talk him into two trials. If that would help keep him out of jail. It felt so counterintuitive. How was she supposed to know what was the right thing?

"I don't blame you," Barry said. "Ultimately, just like everything else we do, it's your decision. I'll tell you what I think is the best way to go, but I can't force you to do things my way unless there's a matter of ethics involved. Now for the second question. We need to decide if we're going to file a motion to change venue."

"What does that mean?" Keenan said.

"If we do nothing, the trial in this case will take place here in Adams County. If we don't think we can get a fair trial here, we can ask to have it moved to another county here in Vermont. It's generally within the judge's discretion whether to allow it, but given the amount of media attention, there's a good chance he'd grant it."

"What are the pros and cons?" Cassie said. It was so much to process. She needed it distilled.

"If we keep it here, we'll probably get to keep Judge Whippet. If we move it, we don't know who we'll get."

"Judge Whippet's good?" Cassie said.

"He's fair. And that's more than I can say for a lot of judges I've encountered. There's also the expense. If we move it to another county, I'll have travel expenses."

"That could add up," Greg said.

Barry nodded. "But by far the primary consideration is whether we'll be able to find enough unbiased jurors in this county to get a fair trial. The media coverage may make that difficult. It's been front page on the *Adams Gazette* for months.

If we move it to a different county, it may be easier to find jurors that don't read the bigger papers and their local papers may not have covered the story, or at least not have given it as much attention."

"Other than expense and the judge, are there any other reasons we should consider keeping the trial here?" Cassie said.

"Yes. The demographics of Adams County."

"What's good about Adams County?"

"It's the most liberal county in the state. On average, seventy-five percent of Adams County voters are Democrat or Progressive. Statewide, it's closer to sixty percent. In general, Democrats are more likely to acquit. And, in this county, even a good number of people who vote Republican are suspicious of the government."

"What do you think we should do?" Greg said.

"I've had good luck with Adams County juries. I would probably keep the trial here. But, like I said, it's up to you. If you don't think you can get a fair trial here, I'll try to get it moved."

"We'll do what you think is best," Greg said. Given the apparent complexity of the decision, Cassie was glad to hear him say it.

"Keenan, are you okay with that?" Barry said.

Keenan nodded once slowly.

"Of course, it's possible we won't be able to get enough jurors here," Barry said. "If that happens, the court will have no choice but to move the trial."

CHAPTER 39
Friday, December 13, 2013

THE WEEK before final exams Keenan was a perfect gentleman. He walked Shannon to the library every night, and he walked her home. He kissed her gently and held her hand, but nothing more.

Shannon found that it was easier to study when she was with Keenan because she didn't think about Jake.

The last weekend before exams Keenan was busy with hockey.

"We're away again this weekend," he told her. "You'll have to study without me."

"Next week, I really need to hunker down. Monday's history. I've got calculus and chemistry on Tuesday, English on Thursday. Then cell biology. I won't have time to see you."

"Okay, but I want to see you before you go home for the holiday."

On Saturday, while Keenan was away, Jake called her on FaceTime. They had texted during the previous two weeks, but it wasn't the same. Seeing his face on her laptop reminded her of her dilemma.

"How are finals going?" Jake said.

"We haven't started yet. My first one is on Monday. How about you?"

"Two down, two to go. I'm flying out on Thursday."

"My flight is on Saturday."

"How are you getting to the airport?"

"There's a shuttle leaving from campus."

"I can't wait to see you."

"Yeah. It'll be good to be home for a few weeks."

"We'll have to find a way to get away from our parents."

"I don't know."

"Where there's a will, there's a way," Jake said.

Why did it have to be so difficult? "See you in a week."

"I love you."

"You too."

She clicked End, closed the laptop, and pushed it away. The problem was she did love him. She loved them both. What the hell was she supposed to do? She needed an advice column like they had in her local paper. That gave her an idea. She could ask her friends for advice. She reopened her laptop, clicked on the Facebook icon, and found the private Facebook group she had with her Masterson friends. She thought for a minute before initiating a group chat.

Is it possible to be in love with two guys at the same time?

Do I have a moral responsibility to tell Keenan that I slept with Jake?

Do I have a moral responsibility to tell Jake that I slept with Keenan?

Do I really have to choose?

Is it okay to keep both of them if I'm not sleeping with either?

The query went out to her six closest friends at Masterson. Responses came back quickly. Everybody must have been looking for an excuse for a study break.

Jenna wrote: *Wish I had your problems. I don't know Jake, but Keenan is a hottie. I think the answer is simple. How would you feel if one of them was sleeping with someone else? You either need to choose or you have to tell them and let them choose. Just be prepared that if you let them choose, you may lose them both.*

Carly wrote: *I think either you need to tell them or you need to stop sleeping with them. It's high school health class 101. Condoms aren't fool proof. You could get pregnant. You could get an STD.*

Greta wrote: *Whatever happened to "Don't kiss and tell." I say keep it to yourself until you're ready to decide. That's what a guy would do.*

Gwen wrote: *I'm in favor of honesty. You can't have a relationship with either of them if it's based on lies.*

The last response struck a chord with Shannon. She realized that the lies were what was making her a wreck. She would tell Keenan before she left for break. She would tell Jake as soon as she got home.

There. It was decided. Why didn't she feel better? Probably because it might mean losing them both. That would really suck.

CHAPTER 40
Friday, May 9, 2013

WITH ONE mile to go, Keenan picked up his pace. He'd already pounded out six miles and his legs were heavy with exhaustion. His lungs ached in suffocation, but he didn't back off. Instead, he focused on the horizon, concentrated on pushing as hard as he could, and with each step, he willed the pain away.

When he reached the college field house, he doubled over, relishing the feeling of air filling his lungs. Was that how Shannon had died? Gasping for air, finding only water to breathe? He shuddered.

Keenan had never been much of a runner. Running just felt so inefficient compared to skating. But the rink had shut down at the beginning of April and he'd forgotten his inline skates back in Lyndonville. His frustration had been building to the point he thought he'd explode, so one night in April, he'd put on his gym shoes and gone for a run. He had savored the anonymity of running in the dark. Nobody noticed him as he passed the dimly lit downtown storefronts and ran out into the semi-rural neighborhoods on the edge of town. He felt almost normal. Before long, he was going out every night. At first, for a few miles. Then more, and more.

When the days got longer, he started running in the early mornings. He was always awake early, might was well take advantage of the insomnia. Middleton Falls was like a ghost town just after sunrise. Unfortunately, the morning runs reminded him of the times he'd gone for weekend jogs with

Shannon, which made him sad. But he'd found that the harder he pushed himself, punished himself, the better he felt afterward.

It was only six o'clock in the morning, which meant that the weight room would be mostly empty except for a few faculty members. He could lift weights in peace for an hour and still make it to his eight o'clock class.

He just needed to get through one more week of classes, a week of finals, and one more court date, and then he could head home for the summer. He'd still need to make regular trips to Middleton Falls to meet with Barry and prepare his defense, but at least he could spend one last summer fishing and hanging out with his family. A regular job would be too hard to manage, but he'd arranged to work for Grandpa Armand at the farm all summer.

Barry had told him a few months ago that if he was convicted of the domestic assault charge, he would be prohibited from touching a gun for the rest of his life. It seemed like the least of his worries right now, but it would be a shame if he could never go hunting with his uncle and grandpa again. Maybe they could get in a day of turkey hunting before the season closed at the end of May.

IT HAD taken a couple of meetings, but Fred finally convinced Olivia Dawson to return to California until the beginning of the trial. He had explained that he would be tied up with depositions and trial preparation for months and promised to keep her updated.

As part of his preparation, Fred made the trip to Burlington to meet with the medical examiner at her office. Dr. Grace Collins wasn't scheduled for a deposition until later in the month, but Fred wanted to make sure they were on the same page before Barry locked her into testimony that could damage his case. Once it became clear that he was going to have to try the case, Fred had gone through the evidence more thoroughly. And he realized why the grand jury had indicted. It might all be circumstantial, but the evidence was overwhelming. He wondered why he had been so reluctant to see it in the beginning.

"It's been a while," Fred said as he shook hands with Grace Collins.

"Yeah. I think the last time I had to testify in Adams County was that shaken baby case a few years back," Grace said.

"Your testimony was crucial in that case. We're always grateful."

"It's my job to give the dead a voice. That's all I did."

"I need you to do it again in the Shannon Dawson case."

"I saw you charged the boyfriend. You sure he did it? If I recall, my autopsy was inconclusive."

"We're sure. They fought, and he assaulted her just before she disappeared. We have witnesses."

"That changes things."

"It sure does. We also have evidence that he used her car to transport her body."

"How solid?"

"It's solid. DNA. Fingerprints."

"What do you need from me?"

"I need you to support our theory of the case. If you think your autopsy results are consistent, that is."

"What's your theory?"

"We think he hit her again after they left the witnesses. Probably killed her first, then dumped her body in the river. I need to know if you can support that fact pattern."

"Give me a minute to look through the file." She opened a legal-size manilla folder and started thumbing through the pages. While she was reading, Fred studied her as unobtrusively as he could. She was a handsome, middle-aged woman. Not pretty, really. But that could be more due to her authoritative nature than her physical characteristics. It was hard to separate the two. While she was reading, her eyebrows arched a few times. Five minutes later she looked up. "It could have happened the way you think. There's nothing here that's inconsistent."

"That's what we thought, but I wanted to hear it from you.

Can you say unequivocally that the blunt force trauma to the head was sufficient to kill her? If you can, it makes my job a lot easier."

"I can. The only reason I didn't conclude that the head trauma was the cause of death is that it's impossible to prove scientifically whether she drowned first."

"I understand. But can you also say that the head injuries were consistent with an assault?"

"I can definitely come up with a scenario that fits the injury pattern."

"Good. That's good."

"As long as you're sure this wasn't just an accidental death."

"It would be too much of a coincidence. All the facts point to manslaughter."

"I'm not a big believer in coincidence."

"Me neither."

CHAPTER 41
Thursday, December 19, 2013

SHANNON HADN'T expected the history test on Monday to be as hard as it was. She hadn't put much time into it because she was more concerned about her required courses. Obviously that was a mistake, but one she hadn't had time to regret because she'd had to get ready for chemistry and calculus. At least English hadn't been that bad. From what everyone said, five exams in one week was as bad as it got. She felt like a hamster running on a wheel, not sure why she was running, but not daring to stop. Maybe she should have taken a lighter course load her first semester. What was she trying to prove anyway? Stop. This wasn't the time for self-recrimination. She just needed to get through this week. She'd gotten less than four hours of sleep each of the past few nights, but she knew she could go one more night without sleep if that's what was needed.

KEENAN KNEW he was lucky. Two of his English professors had assigned papers in lieu of final exams, so he'd only had three exams and they were well spaced. He'd tried to give Shannon space by sending her texts of encouragement, but resisted calling and interrupting her studying. The last thing he wanted was to be responsible for Shannon doing poorly on one of her tests. Finally, when he couldn't resist any longer, he called her on Thursday night.

"You have one exam left, right?"

"Yup. Cell biology."

"How do you think you did so far?"

"I don't know. The exams were harder than I expected."

"Don't worry. I always think I did worse than I did. You'll do fine."

"I hope so. I pretty much need to get straight As if I'm going to get into med school. What do you have left?"

"Just political science. It shouldn't be too hard."

"You're lucky. Cell biology is my hardest class. I'll be sooo glad when it's over tomorrow."

"You're leaving on Saturday, right?"

"Yeah, my flight leaves at two o'clock."

"Can I see you tomorrow night?"

"I already made plans with my friends from the skating club. We're going to a party."

How could she have made plans for the last night they would have together for a few weeks? Was he being played? She wouldn't respect him if he acted like a whiner, that was for sure. "That's cool," he said. "Maybe I can see you after the party."

"I don't know. Maybe."

"Just to say good-bye."

"Maybe."

"If it doesn't work out, we could say good-bye on Saturday morning."

"That might be better. I'll call you tomorrow night."

"Good luck tomorrow."

"You, too."

Keenan wanted to throw his phone. Instead, he set it down on his desk and clenched his fists. He could understand why guys sometimes punched walls. He'd give anything for a punching bag right now. How could she have made plans with her friends? This thing with Shannon was getting more and more fucked up by the minute. Shannon seemed happy when they were together. What the hell was going on?

He should probably stay at his desk and study for a few more hours, but all he wanted to do was go to the gym and work out. Hard. Maybe he could even find a punching bag.

BARRY WOULD have liked to spend all his time preparing for the Brody trial, but he had other clients. He had won a DUI trial in early June. The client's blood test results had come back just below the legal limit, but the state had insisted on prosecuting based on the argument that the guy's blood alcohol was higher at the time he was driving. Years of experience had taught Barry that the police weren't good at following their own procedures, so he was able to convince the jury that the field sobriety tests were unfairly administered and that there was insufficient evidence of intoxication at the time of driving. It would have been his client's second DUI conviction, which would have meant a mandatory jail term. Fortunately, the jury would never know about the prior DUI. He hoped the guy would take the close call as a wake-up call.

Whenever he wasn't working on other cases, Barry worked on Keenan's case. He had no choice. The Brody case was moving along faster than any other case on the docket.

The May status conference had been perfunctory, and the court had seemed happy to excuse Keenan's attendance at future conferences. The court just wanted to make sure that the attorneys were keeping to the schedule with as little fanfare as possible.

And they were keeping to a schedule. Barry had taken depositions of the student witnesses in May before they left for the summer. Barry only had a few questions for each of them, so the depositions were brief. The next week Barry had deposed Officer Shores and the medical examiner. The week after, Fred deposed Barry's expert. At the June status conference, Fred and Barry let the court know they would be ready for trial in August.

Barry met with Keenan and his parents a week later.

"The court couldn't make time for the trial in August," Barry said. "The best they could do was the first week in September."

"That means Keenan will miss the beginning of school," Cassie said.

"I may miss a lot more than that," Keenan said.

"He'll make it up. Right, son?" Greg said.

"Seems like the least of my worries right now," Keenan said.

"The judge keeps asking about the possibility of a plea deal. Have you thought any more about the state's offer of eight to fifteen years?"

"Eight years?"

"Like I said, you'd be eligible for parole in about six. Whereas, if you're convicted at trial, the judge can sentence you to up to fifteen years."

"I can't spend six years in jail for a crime I didn't commit."

Barry nodded.

"What happens next?" Greg said.

"We have a hearing set for August for some pretrial matters. The judge has excused Keenan's appearance again. The clerk told me they're hoping the media will stay away if Keenan's not there. It seemed to help last time."

"Works for me," Keenan said.

"In the meantime, I'm going to keep getting ready for trial." Barry said.

"How do things look? From your perspective, that is." Cassie said.

"I have a plan for the defense. I hope it will be enough."

"Well, you get paid win or lose," Keenan said.

Cassie and Greg both frowned. "Keenan?" Cassie said. She shook her head before turning to Barry. "I'm sorry."

"No need," Barry said, raising his hand. It was easy to forgive the sarcasm. He could only imagine the frustration the kid was feeling.

AS HIS father pulled the car into their driveway, Keenan's mother reminded him that his grandparents would be arriving soon for his birthday dinner.

"The big two-oh," she said and laughed.

Keenan didn't respond. He knew she was just trying to keep things normal, but they weren't, and probably never would be again. As soon as the car stopped moving, he jumped out, not even bothering to shut the car door, and ran straight for the pond. He stripped his shirt, tossed it on the ground, kicked off his shoes, and dove in. He hovered near the bottom, eyes open but not seeing much in the murky water, and relished the painfully numbing cold. Fifteen years. Fifteen fucking years. Why did Shannon have to die? He didn't want to breathe ever again.

BARRY WAS at his desk at seven o'clock that evening when Marcy walked in.

"You scared me," Barry said. "I thought you left hours ago."

"I did. But I was driving by and saw the lights on. What are you still doing here on a Friday night?"

"I'm working on the Brody trial."

Marcy crossed her arms. "When was the last time you had dinner with Sam?"

"He doesn't care whether I come home for dinner."

"I bet he cares that you never come home for dinner."

"He's old enough to take care of himself."

"He is."

"So why are you pestering me?"

"His mother left you because you didn't pay enough attention to her. You're smart enough to learn from your mistakes."

If anyone else talked to him that way, he'd be pissed. But Marcy was not just his secretary, she was a trusted friend and sometimes confidante. And she was rarely wrong. So he shrugged. "He's twenty-four. He doesn't want his father breathing down his neck. He wants a roof over his head and a little independence."

"You're right, but he may be getting more independence than he should right now."

"Do you know something I don't?"

"Pete said he saw Sam at Mr. K's Place last night."

"Was he drinking?"

"I don't know. Maybe you should ask him. And make sure he's taking his meds."

"Okay, I will."

Marcy's face softened and she sat down in his visitor chair. "This Brody case has you worked up, doesn't it?"

"Yes. There's something about Keenan that reminds me of Sam a few years ago. Before his diagnosis."

"They're both smart, good-looking. Is there something else?"

"I can't put a finger on it. It's this potential, an energy that radiates, but hasn't found a direction yet. It's how I used to see Sam before. Now it's like all Sam's energy turned inward and is burning itself out. I'd hate to see that happen to Keenan. And it will if he's convicted."

"You can only do your best."

"I'm trying, but my secretary wants me to go home."

Marcy stood. "Don't give up on your own son yet."

"I won't."

"And don't think I haven't noticed how much you've been slashing your billings on the Brody case."

"It's like a puzzle. I can't bill for the time I spend just shuffling the pieces around."

"Go home, Barry."

"You got it, boss."

A S HOPED, the courtroom was bare of spectators, leaving Barry and Fred alone in the courtroom with Judge Whippet and his clerk. The judge was flipping through papers on the bench.

"My notes say we're here to tackle motions *in limine* and other housekeeping matters," the judge said.

Barry got to his feet.

"You have something to say already, Mr. Densmore?" the judge said.

"Actually, Your Honor, I'm wondering if Your Honor will be the judge presiding over this trial."

"Ah. I see your concern. It's true that I'm getting reassigned to Chittenden County in September. However, I've decided to stay and preside over this trial. I've been with it since the beginning, so I'd like to see it through."

At least they didn't have to worry about the judge. The rumor was that Judge Jenkins would be returning in September. Jenkins clearly had a pro-prosecution bent. He had only been on the bench for a few years, and the last time he had been in Adams County, Barry had not been impressed.

"Before we get started, any chance of a plea deal in this case?"

Fred answered first. "We've given the defense our best offer. We can't go lower for a crime of this magnitude."

"My client is innocent. It's hard to stomach jail time for a crime you didn't commit."

"Sounds like an impasse," the judge said. Both attorneys nodded.

The judge decided to start with Barry's three pretrial motions. The first was routine and Barry expected no objection from Fred.

"I'd like an order prohibiting the state and its witnesses from referring to Shannon Dawson as a 'victim,'" Barry said when called upon.

"Mr. Dutton?" the judge said.

"I object," Fred said. "Shannon Dawson is dead. She had to be a victim of something to end up that way. It puts an undue burden on the state to have to censor all the witnesses."

Really? He was opposing a routine motion? Barry looked over at Fred, who had sat back down without looking at Barry as he stood. "My problem with it is that if we label her a victim, the jurors may be predisposed to think she was the victim of an assault and a homicide. It's our position that she was neither and the use of the term 'victim' may bias the jurors against my client. I submit that the burden on the state is minimal compared to the potential prejudice to my client."

The judge nodded. "I'll grant that motion. What's next?"

Barry continued. "We also have a motion to prevent the state from submitting evidence of text messages and Facebook group chats among Shannon Dawson and her friends regarding her love life, especially ones in the week prior to her disappearance."

"What's the basis for the motion?"

"First, they're irrelevant. Second, they're hearsay."

"Okay. What do you say, Mr. Dutton?"

"Those messages are hardly irrelevant. They establish a clear motive for homicide. They show that Shannon was not sure if she wanted to continue her relationship with the defendant. And for that reason, they fall squarely within the state-of-mind exception to the hearsay rule."

"Not all those messages meet the exception. And there's another problem with them. They may show how Shannon was feeling, but they don't show that she ever communicated those feelings to my client. Without that link, her feelings are irrelevant and obviously highly prejudicial to my client."

"We do have evidence that she told the defendant. I believe there were two witnesses who testified in depositions that Shannon intended to tell Keenan about her relationship with Jake prior to the winter break."

"That's even more circumstantial."

The judge was rubbing his jaw. "It cuts both ways. The fact that she was going to tell him is proof that she had not yet told him. I see that you've both cited case law in your memoranda. I want to review those cases. I also want to look through those messages. What else do we have, Mr. Densmore?"

"I want to make sure the prosecution makes no mention of most of my client's statements to Officer Shores. They're almost all hearsay."

"Some of them are admissions," Fred said. "We all know there's a hearsay exception for those."

"It's our position that my client never admitted to anything of consequence," Barry said.

"He admitted that he went to the party to find Shannon," Fred said.

"He did," Barry agreed.

"He admitted to driving her car back to campus," Fred said.

"That's true."

"He admitted to knowing she was dead."

"No, he didn't. He expressed his concern. There's a big difference."

The judge looked over the top of his reading glasses at the attorneys. "Obviously, I need to review the referenced transcripts as well. I'll issue a written decision."

FRED AVOIDED looking at Barry as he hastily gathered his papers and exited the courtroom. Barry was probably pissed at him. The problem was that Barry was used to Fred giving in to him. But it was one thing to cut him some slack on a misdemeanor plea deal. This was a homicide case and Barry was clearly on the wrong side of it. After all the preparation he had done for trial, Fred had no doubt. He probably hadn't wanted to see it at first because he didn't want to have to deal with a high profile trial. Against one of his oldest friends.

But Fred hadn't forgotten how to play hardball, so Barry had better get used to it.

KEENAN FINISHED stacking the fourth cord of firewood at his grandparents' house just as his brother, Liam, showed up.

"Your timing is impeccable as always," Keenan said.

"I was doing you a favor."

"How's that?"

"You need to stay strong for hockey next year."

"Yeah, right."

"I'm serious. You've got to stay positive."

Keenan wiped the sweat from his eyes and slumped against the side of the woodshed. "I've been thinking maybe I should take the plea deal. I'd be out in six years. My lawyer says I can change my mind up until the trial starts."

"But you didn't kill her."

"Of course not. But six years is a shitload less than fifteen."

"That's true. But you have to have faith that the system works."

"I don't have faith in much of anything right now," Keenan said.

CHAPTER 44
Friday December 20, 2013

S HANNON WALKED out of the cell biology final and tried to breathe. It was easier if she just focused on breathing, because when she let herself think, she felt like a pinball in one of those old-fashioned machines, pinging up and down, side to side, out of control. One minute she was just glad it was over and that a much-needed break was on the horizon. The next minute she was sure she had failed all the exams. Her parents would be so disappointed. But then she would be free of their expectations. Maybe she'd be happier if she failed her classes and had to change majors. Unfortunately, no emotion seemed to last more than a few seconds. She felt like she was going crazy. What she needed was to let off steam.

Fortunately, there was open ice time from two o'clock to five o'clock that afternoon. Shannon skated hard for nearly two hours. She thought only about the ice, her skates, and the technique that had been drilled into her during the years of competition. It was an effective meditation that calmed her mind. She was drenched in sweat when she got off the ice, but she had temporarily slain the demons of self-doubt

Until she remembered that her love life was a mess. She'd been putting it off for weeks and now she needed to deal with it. Later. But soon.

She had a couple of texts and a voicemail from her mom,

but Shannon didn't feel like telling her mom about the exam. Her mom would just say, "You always worry too much about your grades, and you always do fine." Well, maybe not this time. She sent her mom a text explaining that she was meeting friends for the evening and that she would be on the plane the next day.

After she showered, Shannon considered stopping at the dining hall to eat, but she couldn't find anyone at her dorm who hadn't already eaten, and she wasn't in the mood to eat alone. She grabbed a PowerBar and got a bottle of orange juice out of her room fridge. Maybe Jenna and Greta would be up for ordering pizza later.

When she got to Jenna's room, there was already a party in progress. Jenna handed her a wine cooler from the room fridge.

"Where'd you get this?"

"My friend Holly on the second floor has a fake ID. Don't you want it?"

"Sure, why not? Just one. I earned it this week."

"We all did," Greta said, then added, "Cheers!" Shannon clinked bottles with her friends, then unscrewed the cap on the wine cooler and took a sip. It was sweet and didn't even taste alcoholic. It probably wasn't all that strong.

Shannon drank her wine cooler quickly, mostly because she was still dehydrated from her marathon skating session. About halfway through it, she started to feel more relaxed. Wow, what a week.

When Jenna handed her a second wine cooler, Shannon didn't even think. She opened it and started sipping. Greta was telling her friends about her family's beach house in Maine. "It's the coolest place ever. I want to take you guys there."

Shannon smiled. "We should definitely go sometime. I love you guys. I can't even believe I didn't know you guys a few months ago. I feel like I know you so much better than my high school friends."

"To all my new best friends," Greta shouted, raising her wine cooler.

There was a chorus of hollers and much clinking of glass bottles. Shannon beckoned Greta and Jenna so she could take a group selfie with her phone. "Hide your bottles," she said before pushing the virtual button.

"That's a great picture," Jenna said when Shannon held up the phone.

"I'll post it on Facebook, so you can have a copy," Shannon said. She clicked the Facebook icon and posted it with the caption, "Chillin' after a long week of finals."

Greta got out her phone. "I'm adding a comment."

A few seconds later, Shannon smiled as she read it aloud from her phone. "Good friends always mean good times."

Shannon's phone rang in her hand. It was Keenan. Time to face the music.

CHAPTER 45
Monday, September 1, 2014

CLASSES HAD not yet started at the college, but with a week and a half to go until trial, Keenan and his parents were settling into the Maple Tree Manor Motel so they could have daily meetings with Barry. They were able to get two rooms at the monthly rate of $600 each on the condition that maid service would be weekly. The rooms were dark and a little musty, but clean. Keenan was staying in one, and his parents were in the other. His sisters and grandparents would be joining them once the trial started. His brother had gone off to vet school a week earlier. Keenan hoped the trial wouldn't distract Liam from his studies. His own studies seemed trivial, almost irrelevant. He would have opted to take the semester off if he could have done it without giving up the entire hockey season.

It made sense to be in Middleton Falls, available for meetings, but in some ways there was too much down time. Too much time to think about what was coming, how many ways his family would be even more damaged.

Keenan and his parents went to Barry's office the first afternoon.

"There's good news and bad news," Barry said.

"I always like to hear the good first," said Keenan.

"Okay, we just got a ruling. The judge ruled that most of what you said in your interviews with Officer Shores can be kept out of evidence. It was legally the right call, and it helps to have it decided up front."

His parents were nodding. Keenan wasn't sure how the

ruling helped, but Barry seemed pleased, so he forced himself to relax a little.

"What's the bad news?" his dad said.

"The judge is allowing Officer Shores to testify that Keenan said, 'She's dead,' during his interview at your house. The judge also decided that Shannon's Facebook chat messages will be admissible. I'll still object to their admissibility at trial in case there's an appeal."

Barry seemed almost academic about it, which rubbed Keenan the wrong way. "You mean in case I'm convicted," he said. He needed to remind Barry of the stakes.

"We have to plan for that possibility," Barry said.

"How much does that ruling hurt us?" his dad said.

"It's hard to say. The messages are tangible evidence of a motive. Evidence that the jury will be able to take into the deliberation room. I hate giving them something so concrete. But, as the judge pointed out, the messages are also proof that less than a week before the night in question, Shannon was still struggling with whether to tell Keenan the whole truth. Since the messages are coming into evidence, I'll try to hammer that home."

"So, it all comes down to spin," Keenan said.

Barry shrugged. "There's actually another issue we need to discuss today. We need to decide if you're going to testify. I strongly advise against it, but I recognize that it's your call to make."

"Can't we wait and see how the trial goes?" his dad said.

"That's a possibility." Barry looked at Keenan. "But, if you're certain that you won't testify, I can spend some time at jury draw making sure the jurors don't hold it against you."

"What do you mean?" his mom said.

"Well, if I know for sure that a client isn't going to testify, I like to talk to the jurors about that right from the beginning. During voir dire, I can ask if any of them would have a hard time acquitting someone who did not testify in their own defense. I can talk about Constitutional rights and then ask the judge to strike for cause anyone who thinks you should have to testify."

"Can't you do that even if he decides to testify?" his mom said.

"I could." Barry was looking at Keenan. "But if I spend a lot of time talking to the jurors about your right to not testify and then you to decide to testify, they may hold it against us. It might even be subconscious. They could resent the fact that we wasted their time with it. They could also think that you're desperate, that you weren't planning to testify, but that you decided you needed to because the state's case was stronger than you expected."

"I want to testify." Keenan knew he could be convincing, convince them.

"I know you've told me that several times, but I was hoping that now that the trial is upon us, you'd reconsider."

"Explain to us the disadvantages of testifying," his mom said.

"First off, the research shows that defendants are less likely to be convicted if they don't testify. The theory is that, even though the judge explains that the burden is on the state to prove the charges, whenever a defendant testifies, the jurors subconsciously shift the burden back to the defense."

"But, if he's convincing, that could help, right?" his dad said.

"Maybe. But it's not likely that he'll be convincing." Barry said.

"Why not? I can do this," Keenan said. He had to. If he didn't and got convicted, he would spend the rest of his life wishing he had. He had thought about it enough to know that he was not going to change his mind.

"Because you'll be nervous. And any mistakes you make, however minor, will be held against you. The jury will be scrutinizing your every reaction and expression. And when the state's attorney cross-examines you, he'll bring up every inconsistent statement you ever made. The judge ruled that most of your statements to Shores are inadmissible, but if you testify, it's a game changer. All that stuff that we just managed to keep out will come in."

"What kind of stuff are we talking about?" his dad said.

"Anything that Keenan said before that's not completely consistent with what he says on the witness stand. Fred Dutton's been doing this for decades. He knows how to cross-examine a defendant. He'll paint Keenan as a liar and we'll have a whole lot of explaining to do." Barry looked back at Keenan again. "And even if we do manage to explain away all the inconsistencies, the jury's not likely to believe you. They know you'll say anything to get out of these charges."

"But I'm not going to lie. They've got to know it's the truth." Why were they still talking about this? Barry kept saying it was his decision.

"In a perfect world or in a perfect system, that might be true. But what we have is an adversarial system, and like I said, Fred Dutton is going to do everything in his power to make you look like a liar."

"This isn't fair," his mom said.

"You're right. It's not, but it's what we have to work with. My advice is to make the decision not to testify and let me start working the jury during jury selection."

"I'm innocent," Keenan said. "I need to tell them that."

"Take a few days to think about it. Talk it over with your parents. You hired me because you wanted my advice. This is one time you should take it. And keep in mind that ideally you give me your decision before we draw a jury. And I need to say this one last time . . ." Barry made eye contact with each of the Brodys individually before he continued. "It's still not too late to take a plea deal."

CHAPTER 46
Saturday, September 6, 2014

BARRY SAT at his desk with a fresh legal pad in front of him. He needed to come up with a theme for his case. Something that would tie the defense case together. Something the jury could come back to when they were trying to decide whose version of events was more believable.

"This case is about . . . ," Barry said aloud to the empty room.

"Police ineptitude." He snorted. It was troubling how flawed the investigation had been, but blaming the police would likely not sit well with the jury.

He tried again. "Finding someone to blame." That could work. He would need to build on it, but it was a good starting point. He started scribbling notes.

Two hours later, he had an outline for his opening statement. He would need to tweak it and practice it, but it helped to go into jury draw with a clear idea of how he planned to present his case.

With five days to go until jury draw, Keenan was still insisting on testifying. Barry wished there was some way to get through to the kid, but he understood it. On some level it was probably Barry's fault for insisting that the kid keep his mouth shut during all the months that the media had been painting him as a monster. If he had let the kid publicly proclaim his innocence, even briefly, it might have helped to suppress the need that was clearly growing inside him, threatening his judgment.

Barry took it as a personal learning experience. He'd had high-profile cases before, but never anything with this level of media attention. Combine that with a young client and a reputation worth protecting, and it was a recipe for disaster. He should have seen it coming. Next time he would. If there ever was a next time.

FRED WAS getting tired of working weekends, especially while there was still good golfing weather. The golfing season in Vermont was short to begin with. When he was a young prosecutor, Fred had worked more than his share of weekends. And he knew that his deputies put in a lot of weekend time. But it seemed like he'd worked most of the weekends in August getting ready for the Brody trial, and there was still a lot to do.

The trick to beating Barry was to anticipate his defense and head him off. Much easier said than done. It had always felt like the discovery rules were unfair to the prosecution. Fred had to let Barry know everything about the state's case, but Barry didn't have to tell him anything but the names of potential witnesses. It was like playing Battleship where the other side could see your ships, but you couldn't see any of theirs.

Fred had used a summer intern to summarize and catalog all the witness statements and depositions. It had taken the law student most of the summer, but could prove invaluable. You never knew when Barry would pull out a witness that had seemed inconsequential and make his or her testimony pivotal. Fred had gone through all the summaries looking for such witnesses but had no luck. The problem was he couldn't think the way Barry did. And he didn't have access to the same information, even if he could.

That morning, after Fred's wife had commented that he'd gained weight that summer, she'd packed him a lunch. By ten thirty he was starving, so he got his lunch out of the fridge. Tuna fish on wheat with almost no mayo. And a bag of carrot sticks. He loved his wife, and he knew that Kathy was watching out for his health, but she didn't understand that, in times of stress, a man needed comfort food. He called the deli down the street and ordered a pastrami grinder with cole slaw and a bag of chips. Delivered. While he was waiting for his comfort food, he ate the tuna fish.

Dustin Shores arrived as Fred was finishing his second sandwich.

"I went over the files this morning, like you requested," Dustin said.

"Is there anybody else we should interview before the trial?"

"Not that I can see."

"Okay, then let's focus on your testimony. We're going to go over direct and cross until you know exactly how I want you to answer every question. We're going to be ready no matter what Barry throws at you, so don't make any plans for next weekend either."

CHAPTER 47
Friday, December 20, 2013

YOU SAID you'd call," Keenan said before he realized it was the wrong thing to say. He hoped he didn't sound desperate.

"I'm sorry. I've been meaning to."

"That's okay. Sounds like you guys are having a good time." Keenan could hear loud music and voices in the background.

"Yeah. Give me a minute. I need to find a quieter place to talk." After a few minutes of muffled conversation Shannon came back on the line. "I can't believe finals are finally over. It was the week from hell."

"I bet. Having three was bad enough. I can't imagine having five. Where are you guys?"

"We're in Jenna's room."

"Sounds like you guys are drinking."

"Just a little. You know I'm not much of a drinker."

"What's the plan for the rest of the night?"

"I don't know. I think we're going to that party."

"The one on Maple Street?"

"Yeah."

"Do you want to come back here afterward? My roommate's going to be here, but we can still hang out."

"I don't think so. I said I'd drive, so I need to stay with my friends."

"Okay." Keenan was disappointed, but it was the answer he'd expected.

"Keenan?"

"Yeah."

"There's something I need to tell you."

"Okay. Go ahead."

"In person."

"Okay, I can meet you at the party."

"No. Not tonight."

"Tomorrow then."

"Okay. Tomorrow. I'll tell you tomorrow."

SHANNON PUT the phone back in her pocket. She'd managed to buy herself one more day.

"Was that Keenan?" Jenna asked.

"Yup."

"Did you tell him about Jake, yet?"

"Nope."

"When are you going to?"

"The next time I see him. I can't go home for break without coming clean. I just hope he doesn't hate me."

"He's not going to be happy."

"I know, but it's the right thing to do."

KEENAN POCKETED his phone. He didn't like the sound of the pending conversation. Shannon probably wanted to break up with him. So why make him wait? Now, he got to spend the whole night wondering if it was over. It sucked. Mostly because he really loved her, and he had thought maybe, just maybe, she was falling in love with him. Was love always this painful?

Wait a minute. If she wanted to end their relationship, he deserved to know. He was going to find her and make her tell him. It was a free country and there was nothing stopping him from going to the party on Maple Street.

CHAPTER 48
Tuesday, September 9, 2004

BARRY WAS studying the jury questionnaires when Fred called.

"I don't suppose you're calling to tell me you've decided to dismiss the charges against Keenan Brody," Barry said. "I won't hold it against you that I spent the last week preparing for trial."

"Wishful thinking, Barry. Actually, I'm calling because I just got the inside scoop on Judge Whippet from Jerry Niven."

"What's that?"

"You probably know we had an acting judge for arraignments today?"

"Yeah. I saw that Bill Jensen was covering for Whippet."

"Apparently Ted Whippet had a heart attack last night."

Barry dropped his pen as the potential impact registered. "Oh my God. Is he alive?"

"Yeah. But he's in the ICU up in Burlington."

"Are they going to continue the Brody trial?"

"No. Apparently, Jerry had a discussion with the court administrator in Montpelier. They don't know how long Whippet is going to be out, or if he's even coming back. They decided that, since the trial is going to be here in Adams County, Judge Jenkins should just step in. It will be least disruptive for the system."

Oh shit. If he had known they were going to get Jenkins, he would have filed a motion to change venue. Jenkins would be a disaster. And now that they had two hundred people coming on Thursday morning, a request for a change of venue would not be well received. His best hope was to pull out all the stops to get a fair panel. Failing that, he would have to show it would be impossible to get an impartial jury in Adams County.

CHAPTER 49
Thursday, September 11, 2014

FRED SAT at the counsel table facing the twenty-four people who were the first juror candidates for the Brody trial. There were another hundred and fifty or so sitting on the gallery benches and in the folding chairs brought in to accommodate the large numbers summoned in hopes of empanelling a jury. The few reporters who bothered to attend this first phase of the trial were forced to stand in the back by the door.

Barry and the defendant sat to his right. The Honorable Patrick Jenkins reigned at the bench. Fred had chosen at least a couple hundred juries in his career. He knew it was more art than science, despite what the so-called jury consultants would say. He had reviewed the questionnaires that the jurors had completed. Unfortunately, the rule requiring jurors to complete the questionnaire was never enforced, so not everybody had turned one in. That wasn't a big problem. The fact that someone chose not to submit the requested information was information in itself. He preferred to stay away from those nonconformists—they were too likely to acquit. Fred had also had the state police run records checks on all the jurors, information he had no intention of sharing with Barry because it was technically not required.

From the records and completed questionnaires, Fred had made a list of the people he wanted to keep off the jury. They included anybody with any sort of criminal record and anyone who said they would have difficulty judging others. He also included on that list anybody with a background in engineering or science—their personalities tended to demand more certainty than most, and a case as circumstantial as his would not sit well with them.

Fred also had a list of people he wanted as jurors. Tops on the list were those who had been on juries before and convicted. He also liked people who were older with long-term employment. Anyone with a college-aged daughter would have sympathy for the Dawsons and want to give them justice, so he had to consider that factor as well.

Each side would get six peremptory challenges plus two more for alternates. Given the number of possible jurors, it wasn't many. Fred was planning to save his peremptories as long as possible. It only took one problem person to hang a jury, and he didn't want to go into the trial with anyone who might screw up the process.

Fred prepared mentally while the judge explained the process to the jurors. Fortunately, Vermont was one of the states that allowed the attorneys a lot of leeway in voir dire. Unfortunately, voir dire was more a popularity contest than anything else, and his friend Barry had undeniable charisma. Fred's best bet was to make the jurors feel comfortable with him and use the questions as an opportunity to plant some bias in his favor.

Fred stood, took a deep breath, and began.

He asked standard questions, trying to weed out anybody who knew anybody involved in the case or anyone unlikely to convict due to personal bias. Then, he got to the meat of his voir dire.

"How many of you have watched *CSI*?" Approximately half the jury pool raised their hands.

"Come on. Let's be completely honest." Fred raised his own hand slowly. "I watch it sometimes. Anybody else seen it? Maybe *CSI Miami* or *CSI New York*?" A few more hands went up.

"Okay. *CSI* is a great show. I really enjoy it. I've even learned a few things from those guys. But it's not real, is it?

Anybody think *CSI* is real?" There were a few dubious looks from the jurors, but nobody raised their hands.

"In real life, we're rarely able to prove our cases with scientific certainty. In real life, we have to prove our cases with circumstantial evidence. Can anybody explain what circumstantial evidence is?"

A young guy in the first row raised his hand. Fred pointed to him. "Circumstantial evidence is evidence that relies on inference to prove a fact," he said.

"I'm impressed. Are you a lawyer?"

"No, I'm a criminal justice student." Excellent. Fred looked down at his seating chart.

"Mr. Bledsoe, right?"

"Yes."

"Mr. Bledsoe is correct. If a witness sees someone commit a crime, that's direct evidence. But if we find evidence that a person was the perpetrator, such as a fingerprint, that's circumstantial evidence. Mr. Bledsoe, would you be able to convict someone if all the evidence against him was circumstantial?"

"I don't see why not. I mean, fingerprints don't lie."

Fred nodded. He loved this kid. Too bad Barry would likely strike him.

Fred explained reasonable doubt to a sea of blank faces, emphasizing that the state did not need to prove its case beyond *all* doubt.

He had been questioning the jurors for well over an hour, and they were probably getting bored, but he needed to address the issue of the media. He wanted to touch on it, but not belabor it. Barry would have to do that. Better to let Barry bore them. Fred decided to ask only one question.

"There's been a lot of media coverage in this case, so it's been hard to avoid all exposure to the case. Does anyone think that the media coverage will affect their ability to be fair in this case?"

There were no hands. Good. He decided to end strong.

"I have only a few more questions and then I'll pass you

over to Mr. Densmore. How many of you have children?"

Three-quarters of the jurors raised their hands.

"How would you feel if you lost your child, Ms. Bauer?"

"Just awful. I can't imagine." The jurors were all nodding. It was a good place to leave things.

"Thank you, ladies and gentlemen, for your patience. I will now turn you over to Attorney Densmore for his questions."

CHAPTER 50
Thursday, September 11, 2014

BARRY WAS a little surprised Fred didn't have a deputy sitting with him as second chair. It was always helpful to have a second set of eyes and ears during the trial. Fred had probably decided it would sit better with the jury if the prosecutors didn't outnumber the defense lawyers. During trial, every decision involved strategy. Barry always sat alone at the counsel table, but for complicated trials, he frequently had his investigator in the gallery to take notes and run down any last-minute gaps in the testimony. In this case, Barry had also had Toni do basic background checks on the potential jurors. He didn't normally do that, but with the stakes so high, he figured it was worth the expense to weed out anyone likely to convict. She had flushed out one security guard and one former Navy SEAL who had not filled out questionnaires.

Barry nodded reassuringly at Keenan as Fred made his way back to the counsel table. The kid looked petrified. Barry had met with him for a few minutes that morning for last-minute instructions.

"You need to keep your head up and make eye contact with as many jurors as possible," Barry had said. "Watch their faces. I'm going to give you a notepad and pen. Take notes if anything concerns you."

"What kinds of things should I be looking for?"

"Just reactions to the questions. If somebody has a strong reaction, sometimes they involuntarily nod or shake their heads. They don't always raise their hands, even though they're supposed to. Sometimes it's because they don't want to call attention to themselves, but the reality is, most people don't even recognize their own biases. That's why if you see anybody who should not be on this jury, you need to make a note of it."

"I'll do my best, but what if I miss something?"

"I'll be watching and Toni will too. She's good at reading people."

"That helps. I'm so nervous, I'm afraid I'll screw up."

"I'm sure you'll do fine." Barry didn't actually think Keenan would contribute much, but it helped the client to give them something to do during voir dire. The assignment would keep Keenan from burying his face in his hands and looking dejected and encourage him to make eye contact with the jurors. The only risk was that he would take the assignment too seriously. Better nip that in the bud. "But there are two things you should not do during voir dire. Don't talk to me, even while the other side is doing the questioning. It looks rude and you don't want the jurors labeling you before the trial even begins. Same thing goes for passing notes. We'll have a minute or two to talk before we have to make decisions on the jurors. Save it for then."

"Okay."

"And Keenan?"

"Yeah?"

"Try not to look panicked. I know you're scared. That's natural. But we want the jury to think that you trust them."

"I'll try."

"And, whatever you do, don't look cocky. If they think you think you're getting away with something, they'll hold you accountable."

"Okay, so don't look too scared, but don't look cocky. What the hell does that look like?"

"I don't know. Just be aware that they're watching your every move so it's important to be likable."

"Should I smile?"

"No. That would look fake."

"Okay. Serious, but likable. You're not making this easy."

"That's because it isn't." Barry wished he could give him more concrete advice. "One last thing—it would really help if you would decide right now that you're not going to testify."

Keenan had shaken his head.

Barry knew that a trial was more about spin than truth. He also knew that there had been a fair amount of spinning going on in the media, most of it not good for his client. The media had presented the circumstantial evidence as if there were little room for interpretation, which had garnered a lot of sympathy for Shannon and her family and almost none for Keenan.

Barry was hoping to get a group of jurors who had not been unduly influenced by the media, but realistically he knew that was impossible. His best bet was to use voir dire to negate some of the damage already done and try to identify people who could keep an open mind. Unfortunately, the jury selection process was as flawed as the rest of the system. It relied on prospective jurors being honest and forthright about personal beliefs and biases in a very public setting. And normally that didn't even involve a risk of being on TV. Very few people would be forthright with the reporters in the courtroom. One more way the media was influencing justice.

Barry rose from his seat. "Good morning."

He spent a few minutes talking about Keenan and his love of hockey. He let them know that Keenan had volunteered at clinics for their local hockey program. He wanted them to think about Keenan as a real person and hockey players as athletes, no more prone to violence than the average person. He also asked questions designed to get the jurors thinking about reasonable doubt as an incredibly high standard.

Finally, he got to the media issue. "How many of you have read news stories about Keenan Brody?"

All the jurors raised their hands.

"Mr. Kearns. If you had to decide my client's guilt based on what you read in the paper, how would you decide? Honestly."

"Sounds like he's guilty."

"Thank you for your honesty. Anybody have a different opinion?"

Nobody raised a hand. Barry had expected the response, but actually seeing it drove home the enormity of the task before him. He stood staring at the jurors, trying to decide what to ask next.

"I think now would be a good time for a recess," the judge said. "Let's resume at one o'clock. And I want to remind everyone that they are not to talk about this case with each other or anybody else. Attorneys, I want to see you in my chambers."

"I want most of them struck for cause," Barry said. "They all just admitted they think my client is guilty."

"Wait a minute," Fred said. "I asked them if they could be fair despite the media coverage and they all said yes."

"You can't seriously expect them to overcome a bias as serious as a presupposition of guilt."

The judge rubbed his chin for a few seconds before answering. "I'm inclined to agree with Mr. Dutton. They said they could be fair."

"But that doesn't mean they can or will. It just means they don't want to admit they can't, whether it's to us or to themselves. Or to the press."

"They haven't heard the evidence yet. I've allowed you to educate them that there's more to the story than what's in the paper."

"Then I'll need more time with this panel."

"I want a jury before we leave here today. Don't drag this out."

"Are you saying I can't take the time to explore the biases of each juror?"

"I'm saying I want to finish this by five o'clock today."

"You just sent them off for a one-and-a-half-hours' lunch. My client can't get a fair trial in Adams County if I can't do a proper voir dire."

"You'll have all afternoon."

"I need to talk to my client. If Your Honor won't permit me to thoroughly examine the potential jurors, we'll be filing a motion to change venue."

"And I'm telling you based on what has happened so far, I'll deny it. The law is clear that I have broad discretion on the issue. If you had filed the motion before we dragged a couple hundred people in here, I might have given you a different answer. But now that they're here and they're telling us they think they can be fair, I see no reason to waste the resources." Before Barry could open his mouth, Jenkins snapped, "Especially if you're really just judge shopping."

"I want to put the motion on the record."

"We can do that after lunch. I'll allow a verbal motion."

"I'd also like to file a motion to increase the number of peremptories. If Your Honor is going to insist that we draw a jury today, I can't get a fair jury with only six. Obviously, both sides would get more. Does Your Honor want that in writing?"

"I'll take a verbal motion on that after lunch as well. My law clerk can research it during the break. I'll see you both back here at twelve thirty."

Fred and Barry left together but did not speak. Fred headed toward the stairwell, presumably to go to his office. Barry went in search of his client and found him in the conference room where Keenan's parents had been waiting all morning.

"What happened with the judge?" Keenan said. "Anything we should know?" Barry didn't believe in keeping things from his clients, but there was not much to be gained by getting the Brodys more worked up than they were.

"Just housekeeping matters."

"What do you think of the jury so far?" Cassie asked.

"There are six people on that panel I could live with as jurors."

"Can you get rid of the rest of them?"

"I can, but I'd have to use all my peremptories. Unfortunately, this is one part of the trial where the judge can make a big difference. Jenkins is not giving me a lot of leeway. We only get six peremptory challenges for the panel of twelve, then two more for the alternates. Do you have any thoughts about any of the jurors?"

"I tried to do what you said and watch them," Keenan said. "I'm afraid they all think I'm guilty."

"You may be right. So, we need to get people who we think can keep an open mind. I like Mrs. Hiller. She'll be able to identify with you because she has a son a few years younger than you who plays hockey. Mr. Martin is probably okay. Billings and Kramer too. Beyond that, I don't have much confidence."

"So, what will you do?"

"I'm going to file a motion to increase the number of peremptories. It's worth a shot. I'll also do my best to get the people on the panel to admit their bias so we can get them struck for cause. There's no limit to the number we can get rid of for cause, only the peremptories."

"What can we do to help?" Greg said.

"Get something to eat. After today, you should bring lunch to court. It will give us the opportunity to use the lunch break to discuss the case."

"We have a little kitchenette in our motel room. I'll make sandwiches for everyone including you, Mr. Densmore," Cassie said.

"Thanks, Cassie. I'll take one as long, as you call me Barry. When you go out today, get something quick. Remember, you need to avoid the jurors."

Barry called Marcy and had her bring him a sandwich to the courthouse. While he was waiting, he met with Toni, who had been watching from the back of the courtroom. She filled him in on her observations. Unfortunately, he couldn't strike everybody she recommended. He'd give anything to have Judge Whippet back.

At twelve thirty, Barry and Fred met with the judge in the courtroom. The jurors were still at lunch, so the courtroom was empty. Barry put his two motions on the record. The judge promptly denied them both.

CASSIE AND Greg both embraced their son before he headed back into the courtroom. They could have waited back at the motel, but they wanted to be there with their son, supporting him. Cassie was frustrated with being isolated in the conference room, but Barry had been clear that they could not risk contact with the potential jurors. It could mean a mistrial and having to start over. Which might not be a bad thing, except that it would anger the judge. Barry had explained that, although the judge would not decide if Keenan was convicted, he definitely had the power to influence the outcome. At least the conference room had more windows than their motel room, and a better view.

FRED LIKED Judge Jenkins. He was relatively new, having been on the bench for three years. This was his second stint in Adams County. Fred's underlings in the State's Attorney's Office were glad Jenkins was back.

Fred knew that both he and Barry would have benefitted from an increase in the number of peremptories, but Fred had figured that Barry would benefit more. It was clear that, in general, the panel was on Fred's side.

Fred watched as Barry spent the afternoon trying to get the jurors to admit their bias against his client so he could get them struck for cause. He was only moderately successful. There were three rounds of culling, each of which involved an odd dance of musical chairs and another group of potential jurors being called from the gallery.

Finally, at five thirty, all the peremptories had been exercised. "We have a jury," the judge said. "Now let's get two alternates and call it a day."

When he was back in his office, Fred looked over his final seating chart. He felt pretty good about the jury. They were all law-abiding citizens. More than half were women. Almost all had kids. There was one guy who was retired from the army. There were no engineers or scientific types. It was definitely a jury that could convict.

He filed the chart away. That phase was over. It was time to gear up for trial. He had met with all the witnesses during the previous week. He would meet with them all again over the next few days. He had some notes ready for his opening statement. He would need to polish that before Monday, but for the most part, he was ready.

Despite the hard work, it felt good to be trying a case again. He had forgotten how much he enjoyed the challenge. Besides, Barry might be his friend, but it would still feel good to beat him.

KEENAN WAS going crazy. During the whole jury selection process, he felt like a freak. People wanted to see him, study him, but they didn't want to get caught doing it. And he was supposed to sit next to Barry, looking friendly and pretending it wasn't bothering him. Like a contestant in a beauty pageant. On top of it, there was this false air of joviality to the whole thing. During the break, Barry had explained that conventional wisdom was that getting the jurors to like you was the most important part of jury selection. But every time someone laughed, he wanted to pull his hair out. Didn't they understand that his life was at stake? That it was his life they were treating casually, as if he weren't sitting right there watching the whole thing.

After the voir dire, Barry met with Keenan and his parents again.

"What do you think of the jury?" Greg said.

"I think they're a reasonable group. That's the best we can hope for under the circumstances."

"What do we do now?"

"We get ready for Monday."

"Is there anything we can do?" Cassie said.

"Try to keep Keenan from going crazy and make sure he shows up on Monday morning. I'll meet with you guys on Saturday afternoon. I'll update you then. In the meantime, I'm going to prepare our other witnesses and get ready for opening statements."

Now even his own lawyer was talking about him like he wasn't there. He mentally searched for a word to describe how he was feeling. Dehumanized. That was it. He imagined it was how a slave up for auction would have felt—completely without control of his own future.

KEENAN FOUND the party easily. Out on the porch, coeds in sweatshirts and unzipped coats let off the tension of the end of a semester, laughing and howling. On-campus drinking was against the rules, so it had to be low key, but off-campus parties could be rowdier, as long as they didn't call so much attention that the police showed up.

The temperature was in the low fifties, unseasonably warm for a December evening, which provided another cause for celebration. Below-freezing weather and snow showers had reigned during the weeks leading to final exams. It had rained most of the day, washing away much of the snow that had fallen earlier in the month. The patches that remained were compressed to translucent by foot traffic making them extra slick. Although the rain had stopped, the air still felt thick with moisture.

Keenan searched the faces on the porch as he made his way up the front stairs. He recognized Jeremy from his dorm leaning against the wall, smoking a joint.

"Have you seen Shannon?" Keenan said.

"I did," said Jeremy. "She was hanging with her friends tonight. You should be too. Here, have a hit."

"No, thanks."

"Why so uptight? You need to mellow out, dude," Jeremy

said, holding out the joint.

Keenan shook his head. "I'd get kicked off the team if I got caught."

Jeremy shrugged and inhaled from the joint. Keenan waited until he opened his eyes.

"Is she still inside?"

"You are so whipped, it's pathetic."

"It's not like that. I just need to talk to her for a minute. Do you think she's still here?"

"She was in the kitchen a while ago."

"If you see her, let her know I'm looking for her."

Jeremy waved and went in search of another beer. Keenan tried to follow, but got stopped by the guy at the door collecting money. Reluctantly, he pulled five singles out of his wallet and let the guy put a smiley face on his hand with a Sharpie.

Bass-heavy music blared from the living room speakers. A trio of girls danced enthusiastically, spilling drinks onto the already stained floor. Two boys watched them from the tattered couch, not trying to talk over the music. Red plastic cups, some half full of warm beer, adorned every surface.

Keenan had to weave his way through a crowd in the dining room. He poked his head into the kitchen. Two girls in skinny jeans and sweatshirts were perched on the counter engaged in conversation. A bucket of red "punch" sat in the middle of the kitchen table, available for anyone brave enough to try it. A plastic soup ladle rested nearby amid blood-like splatters. A group of boys hovered around a keg. A few people loitered on the nearby back deck.

Keenan found Shannon coming out of the upstairs bathroom. Two other girls came out behind her. The first two in line for the bathroom scurried to take their place and shut the door.

"We're gonna drive to Maine. Jenna's family 'ss a cottage

there," Shannon said. Her eye makeup was smudged and her blond ponytail was uncharacteristically off center.

"You're going tonight?" Keenan said.

"Sure. S'not that far. Jenna said so. We can be back by lunch."

"That's crazy. It's too far. And you're drunk. Please don't go. Besides, you said you had something to tell me."

"I don't want to talk to you now." Shannon started down the stairs and Keenan followed.

Keenan took Shannon's hand and pulled her onto the back deck, which was now deserted. He tried to pull her into a hug, but she pushed him away.

"Shannon."

"I can't talk to you."

"Okay. But promise me you won't drive."

"I'm not that drunk."

"Shannon, you're not driving anywhere." Keenan held out his hand. "Give me the keys."

"Ss my car."

"You can have the keys back tomorrow when you're sober. Hand them over."

Shannon tottered backward shaking her head.

"I'm not kidding. You're in no shape to drive."

Shannon reached into her pocket and pulled out her keys and phone. "I s'pose you want this too."

"Not really. Just the keys. And only because I'm worried about you."

"Well you can have them because I'm leaving." She thrust the phone and keys at him. He picked up the keys, glad that she wouldn't be driving to Maine that night. She shrugged and stuffed the phone into her jacket pocket. She fumbled with the zipper on the pocket for a few seconds, then turned away.

"Where are you going?"

"Away from you."

"You said you had something to tell me. I'm going crazy. I just want to know what it is."

"I can't deal with this right now." She stumbled as she walked down the back stairs and onto the lawn. He wanted to follow her, but if she wanted space, he should give it to her. He wished he knew what had changed since Thanksgiving. Things had been going so well before that.

Keenan found an Adirondack chair with peeling yellow paint up against the back of the house and sank into it. He didn't feel like going inside. It's hard being the only sober person in a group of partyers. He didn't feel like sitting on this deck all night either. He'd wait a few minutes and see if Shannon came back. Maybe he could give her a ride home. Her behavior tonight was completely out of character. It was the first time he had seen her drunk in the two months he had known her. As far as he knew, she didn't drink.

As long as he had her keys, she couldn't drive. At least he would be able to sleep better tonight knowing that. He waited until he started feeling chilled. Then, he walked through the house looking for Shannon's friends. When he couldn't find anyone he recognized, he went out front and spotted Shannon's car a block and a half away. He drove it back to the parking area near her dorm where she usually parked. He considered dropping off her keys at her dorm, but he wanted to see her before she left. She didn't need a key to get into her dorm room which had an electronic keypad. The car keys would give him an excuse to see her in the morning.

CHAPTER 52
Monday, September 15, 2014

IT HAD been the longest weekend of Keenan's life. The Brodys had spent it in their motel rooms. The TV had perpetually chattered in his parents' room, filling the void of conversation, but attracting nobody's attention. His mother had seemed intent on playing solitaire on her iPad, but studied the moves much longer than warranted. Keenan frequently caught her rubbing the corners of her eyes in an ill-disguised attempt to hide her tears. His father had pretended to read some veterinary journals, but turned the pages too infrequently to be convincing.

Fifteen years would be a very long time. And everyone knew it.

Nobody felt like going out to eat. They picked up some Subway sandwiches for lunch on Saturday and ended up finishing them for dinner.

Keenan tried to study the transcripts that Barry had given him, but the words swam on the page. Was this how it felt to be dyslexic?

The meeting with Barry on Saturday afternoon was the main event of the day, but when they arrived, Barry had little to do with them. He was too busy getting ready for trial. He told them what he had done, what he still planned to do. They found themselves back in their dreary motel rooms a short while later.

On Sunday morning Keenan and his dad walked to the convenience store for coffee and the papers. Keenan's upcoming trial was the front-page story in the Burlington paper. Keenan wondered how something that hadn't yet happened could be big news. It turned out that the article was a recap of everything that had already been published.

Grandma Helene and Grandpa Armand arrived with Keenan's sisters on Sunday afternoon. It helped to have them there, made the time pass a little more quickly. But it also reminded Keenan that it might be years before the family would be together again.

Liam called on Sunday night. Keenan walked circles in the parking lot while he filled his brother in.

"I wish I could be there for you," Liam said.

"It's enough that you called. You worked hard to get into vet school. I don't want this mess to screw up your career. Mom and Dad are so proud of you."

After he hung up, Keenan had to do a few more laps while he regained his composure. He'd hoped his family couldn't tell he'd been crying when he reentered the motel room.

Keenan was in his place next to Barry on Monday morning when the judge strode into the courtroom, his black robe billowing.

"This is the case of State versus Keenan Brody," the clerk announced.

"Are the parties ready to proceed?" the judge asked.

"Yes, Your Honor." Both attorneys answered simultaneously.

"Then, please remain standing while we bring in the jury." The judge nodded toward the clerk who opened the door to the deliberation room.

As the jurors filed in, Keenan studied the twelve people that would decide his fate. Did he trust them? He didn't have any choice. How had his entire future been put in their hands? That was the kicker. He just didn't understand how he had come to be sitting in this courtroom wondering if next week he would be back in class or sitting in a jail cell.

The jurors were seated. Keenan tried to listen as the judge

explained the trial to them.

Manslaughter. The word jumped out from the drone. It was such a violent-sounding word. The air in the courtroom felt hot and thick, too heavy to breathe. He wished he could loosen the tie his attorney had advised him to wear. The one he usually wore only for hockey awards ceremonies.

The judge was telling the jurors not to look things up on the internet, that they could only consider what they heard in court. The instructions were seemingly exhaustive. Exhausting. Keenan wanted it to be over and he didn't at the same time. He hated sitting there, but at least, while he did, there was still hope. When it was over, there wouldn't be.

Keenan forced himself to make eye contact with the jurors. He tried to telepath "Innocent" to each and every one. He liked the gray-haired woman at the end of the second row. She had looked kindly at him while Barry questioned the jury. Perhaps he reminded her of her grandson. Perhaps that would be enough to preserve his freedom.

The judge finished speaking and the prosecutor rose. He walked to the podium that was facing the jurors, but didn't stand behind it. Instead, he stood beside it and started speaking to each juror as if they were in his living room. Fred Dutton looked as if he had been speaking to jurors for decades.

FRED BREATHED deeply, composing himself. He was aware that he was being filmed by the television cameras. He forced himself to speak slowly, deliberately.

"Good morning, ladies and gentlemen. By all accounts, Shannon Dawson was a vibrant young woman with a bright future. In high school, she was an A student, which earned her a place in the Masterson College Class of 2017. She was an accomplished figure skater, who was ranked highly at the Southwest Pacific Figure Skating Championships in 2010 and 2011. She wanted to be a doctor, specializing in sports medicine. She came to our community to get an education.

"On April fifth of this year, the police pulled the body of eighteen-year-old Shannon Dawson out of Moose Creek. It ended nearly four months of torture for her parents who had no idea what had happened to their daughter. And it began a lifetime of agony. An unspeakable agony—the loss of an only child." Here Fred paused, giving the jury a chance to feel the pain of the parents' loss, and looked toward Shannon's parents, who were seated in the front row, somber and pallid. He knew that his last statement had technically violated the prohibition against mentioning family and half expected Barry to object. When Barry didn't, he assumed Barry was planning to take some liberties with his own opening. Fred moved casually to the other side of the podium.

"During that four months, the police were busy looking for Shannon and piecing together the details of her last hours. What they learned was that Shannon had finished her last final exam on Friday and had gotten together with her friends, to celebrate a little, say good-bye for the winter break. But her night with her friends was interrupted by the defendant, who was in a jealous rage. He tracked her down because he wanted to confront her. You see, on the night of Shannon's death, the defendant, Keenan Brody, had learned something about Shannon that drove him crazy. He had learned that the young woman he adored had been intimate with another man.

"Jealousy is a powerful emotion. This is not the first time in history a man has been driven to homicide by sexual jealousy, nor will it likely be the last. And the defendant's jealous rage was fueled by the fact that the other man was Shannon's high-school boyfriend that she had seen during the Thanksgiving break. Not only had she cheated on the defendant, but she was going home to California for a month where she could see the other guy every day.

"It was just too much. The defendant lost control.

"As you will see, there was no witness to Shannon's death. And there is no forensic evidence directly proving that the defendant was the perpetrator. The defendant was too careful for that. But you can still hold him accountable for his crime. Because there were witnesses to his jealous rage that night. They saw the defendant assault Shannon. He grabbed her. He hit her.

"And there's plenty of circumstantial evidence to help you piece together what happened afterward. What happened is this. On December twentieth of last year, the defendant tracked down Shannon Dawson where she was at a party with her friends, and he confronted her. They argued. He grabbed her and struck her. She left the party and he followed her. They argued some more, and he killed her.

"Nobody is suggesting that he planned it. But he just couldn't control his jealous rage. He punched her, and she fell, hitting her head on something hard, probably a rock. The medical examiner will explain how we know that." Fred paused and nodded sagely.

"Now, the defendant is a smart kid. When he realized what he had done, he knew that he needed to cover it up. And what better way to wash away any evidence than with water? He took Shannon's limp body and carried it to her car. He took her keys from her pocket and drove her to Moose Creek. Then, when nobody was around, he dumped her in the river.

"Then, he drove her car back to her dorm and went home for Christmas. He spent Christmas with his family while the Dawsons searched for their daughter." Fred paused again for effect and glanced toward the Dawsons, who unwittingly played their role perfectly by visibly tensing. After three beats, he resumed his casual pacing in front of the jury, attempting eye contact with every juror.

"Meanwhile, Shannon's body got washed downstream until it lodged under a felled tree. It stayed there. The body of Olivia and Jack's daughter stayed in the icy water until the ice went out in April and she was discovered by a group of kayakers.

"The defendant might have gotten away with what he did if the police hadn't found Shannon's keys in his dorm room. And his prints on the dashboard of her car. But they did, and when they did, the defendant had an explanation for them. And it was a pretty good one.

"Unfortunately, it wasn't until after the police had found the keys and he knew they would find his prints that he came up with his explanation. And that is why it doesn't ring true.

"During this trial, you will likely see the face of a composed young man with a bright future. Well, ladies and gentlemen, it's not his only face and it's not the face he was wearing when he killed Shannon Dawson in a fit of jealous rage.

"Thank you."

Fred sat down.

BARRY KNEW that the research showed that eighty to ninety percent of all jurors come to a decision during or immediately after opening statements. He also knew that Fred Dutton had just delivered a powerful opening. Barry could see that the jurors were mesmerized by Fred's recitation of the facts. He had considered objecting to the beginning of Fred's opening, but didn't want to appear antagonistic so early in the trial. Now, he had his work cut out for him.

Even after thirty years, he was always nervous on the first day of trial. The worst part was waiting through the other side's opening. Once he started talking, he knew he would be okay. His nervousness would abate and he would appear like the shark everybody judged him to be.

Showtime. He rose and casually walked to stand in front of the jury.

"Good morning, ladies and gentlemen. We're here today because there's been a tragedy. A beautiful, precious young woman is dead from a tragic accident. Our hearts go out to her family." Barry paused respectfully and looked at Shannon's parents.

"Whenever something tragic happens, people tend to look for someone to blame. It's only natural. And that's exactly what the police did when Shannon Dawson went missing at the end of last year. They looked for someone to blame.

"Unfortunately for my client, they didn't have to look far because there was an obvious choice—the young man on campus that Shannon had been dating. Keenan Brody. But, as you will learn from the testimony you will hear, the problem with thinking you know the answers is that you frequently ask the wrong questions. Or at least ask them the wrong way.

"And sometimes there is nobody to blame.

"If Keenan Brody had been there when Shannon died, he might have been able to save her. But sadly, he wasn't.

"In fact, he had tried earlier in the evening to protect her, to keep her from driving while intoxicated. Because, on the night she died, Shannon Dawson was intoxicated, and not just a little bit.

"When Keenan saw Shannon that night, he could tell she was drunk. She was talking about taking a road trip. He was worried about her. So, he did what any responsible person would do in his circumstances. He took her keys.

"And Shannon did what almost any drunk person does when someone tries to take their keys. She got angry with him. They argued about the keys and Keenan finally got them from her. He didn't hit her. He didn't grab her. He didn't assault her in any way. He just took the keys.

"Mr. Dutton told you there were witnesses to an assault. As you will learn, the witnesses got it wrong. They didn't get it wrong at first. In fact, in the first few days, even weeks, after Shannon's disappearance, nobody reported an assault. The witnesses got it wrong later, after someone suggested to them that Keenan might be responsible for Shannon's disappearance and then the police painted a picture for them with the way they asked questions. When you hear from those witnesses, you may be convinced that they are telling the truth. Because at this point, they most likely believe it's the truth. But what they really saw was an act of caring, perhaps even chivalry. If they even witnessed anything at all. Keenan didn't assault Shannon. He just took the keys.

"Mr. Dutton talked to you about circumstantial evidence because sometimes that's all there is. But the problem with circumstantial evidence is that it frequently cuts more than one way. We'll show you that the circumstantial evidence actually supports the facts we've outlined for you today. After Keenan took Shannon's keys, he committed another act of chivalry. He drove her car back to the dorm for her.

"Because that's the kind of guy Keenan is. He's a Vermonter, born and raised in the Northeast Kingdom. His father is a veterinarian. His mother runs a small business. He has two younger sisters and an older brother. Like Shannon, he was an honors student in high school and an athlete. He is twenty years old and just finished his sophomore year at Masterson College where he plays for the varsity hockey team. Most importantly, Keenan is a gentleman. Because that's how he was raised." Barry paused and looked at Keenan's parents before finishing. He wanted the jury to know there was another family's future on the line.

"People do act out of character when they are jealous. And if Keenan had known that Shannon had cheated on him, he might have been jealous. He might have even been angry. But, he didn't know. All he knew that night was that a girl he'd been dating, someone he cared about, was drunk and planning to drive. And he needed to stop her.

"It's tragic that Shannon Dawson is gone and her family has suffered the unthinkable." Barry again looked toward Shannon's parents. "But it would also be tragic to end the bright future of a young man who is guilty of nothing more than chivalry. Let's not turn a tragic accident into a tragic mistake."

CHAPTER 53
Monday, September 15, 2014

KEENAN WATCHED as Barry made his way back to their table. For some reason, he felt better when his lawyer was beside him. Less exposed. He wondered what would happen next.

"You may call your first witness, Mr. Dutton," the judge said.

"The State calls Jake Miller." The prosecutor remained standing in the silent room.

A minute later, the rear door of the courtroom opened and a young man walked quickly to the witness box.

Keenan studied Jake while he took the oath. So, this was the guy. The other guy Shannon had been sleeping with. His lawyer had told him that Jake was on the witness list, would undoubtedly be testifying. He knew that whatever emotion he felt at finally seeing the guy, he needed to keep it in check. Because while he was studying Jake, the jury was studying him. Keenan noted that, like himself, Jake was wearing a shirt and tie, but not a jacket. They were both over six feet tall and athletic looking. Jake was dark and handsome and well poised.

The prosecutor began the questioning. "Where do you go to school?"

"Columbia University."

"What year are you in?"

"Sophomore."

"What are you studying?"

"Architecture."

"Did you know Shannon Dawson?"

"Yes, I did."

"How long did you know her?"

"I met her during our first year of high school."

"You went to high school together?"

"Yes."

"Tell us about Shannon."

"She was beautiful and smart and she had this great sense of humor."

"How did you feel about her?"

"I loved her."

Keenan felt a pang of jealousy at the words. But, surprisingly, the overwhelming emotion was emptiness. They had both loved Shannon and she was gone.

"What was your relationship with her?"

"She was my girlfriend."

"Girlfriend or ex-girlfriend?"

"I still considered her my girlfriend."

"Can you explain that?"

"We dated during our junior and senior years of high school. Then, she decided to go to Masterson, and I decided to go to Columbia. We knew we would only be five hours away from each other, but we weren't sure we wanted to have a long-distance relationship. We knew we would both be busy with studying, so we agreed to see other people during the fall term."

"I'm going to show you what's been marked as State's Exhibit 1. Can you tell the jury what it is?" Dutton placed a photo on a machine and it appeared on the AV screen that was set up on the wall opposite the jury.

"It's our prom photo. Shannon and me. Before we went to the senior prom."

Barry had told him that the prosecutor would probably introduce a photo of Shannon early on to give them a face to go with the name, but the prom photo caught him off guard. It was almost as if the prosecutor was trying to legitimize Shannon's relationship with Jake and paint Keenan as the interloper.

"Did you stay in contact with Shannon during the fall term?"

"I did. We texted a fair amount and FaceTimed a few times."

"Did you see her?"

"Only once."

"When was that?"

"Thanksgiving break."

"Where did you see her?"

"In the city."

"New York City?"

"That's correct."

"What happened when you saw her?"

"We had a great time. Did some sightseeing. Got caught up. We made love."

The words stabbed. Barry had been clear that Keenan needed to be careful about the emotion he showed. The jury was watching him. What was the appropriate emotion for hearing that your girlfriend was making love with someone else? He took a deep breath and tried to keep his face blank, his eyes on Jake.

"At that time, did you know whether Shannon was seeing someone else?"

"I didn't ask. She didn't mention it. I assumed she wasn't."

"Did you see Shannon again after Thanksgiving?"

"No, I did not. She didn't come home for Christmas."

"Thank you, Jake. No further questions."

Barry rose.

"When you saw Shannon in November, did the two of you drink alcohol?"

"No, we didn't."

"Did Shannon drink much in high school?"

"No."

"Did she drink at all?"

"I remember she had a glass of champagne on prom night. She might have also had some at graduation."

"But she wasn't an experienced drinker, was she?"

"No, not at all."

"And you said that Shannon never communicated to you that she was involved with another guy?"

"That's right. She did not."

"Did you talk to her during the week before she disappeared?"

"I believe we FaceTimed once."

"Did you have any other communication with her?"

"Yes, there were some texts."

"But, despite the fact that you had been communicating with her, she never gave you any indication she was in another relationship, did she?"

"No, she didn't."

"No further questions for this witness, Your Honor."

"Any redirect, Mr. Dutton?"

"No questions, Your Honor."

Jake was excused and they moved onto the next witness.

"The State calls Amy Stevens," the prosecutor said.

Keenan watched Shannon's friend walk toward the front of the courtroom. He had met Amy only once, but he had heard a lot about her. It felt strange that she was testifying against him.

Amy raised her right hand and swore to tell the truth.

"Did you know Shannon Dawson?"

"Yes. We were friends."

"Would you say you were close?"

"Yes."

"How long had you known her?"

"We met at the beginning of last year, but we had a lot in common. We lived in the same dorm and we were both neuroscience majors."

"Did you spend Thanksgiving with Shannon?"

"Yes. She came home with me for the holiday break."

"Where is your home?"

"New York City?"

"How did you get there?"

"Shannon drove."

"Anybody else travel with you?"

"No, it was just the two of us."

"So you had a lot of time to talk?"

"We sure did. With the traffic, it took us about six hours to get there. The way back was closer to five."

"Other than that trip, did you talk to Shannon?"

"A fair amount. She was probably my closest friend first semester of freshman year."

"Did you talk to her about her relationship with Keenan?"

"I did."

"How did she feel about him?"

"She loved him."

"Did you talk to her about her relationship with Jake?"

"Yes."

"How did she feel about Jake?"

"She loved him too."

"She loved both of them?"

"Yes. When she was with Keenan, she loved Keenan more. When she was with Jake, she loved Jake more."

"That's a bit of a quandary. What did she do about it?"

"It was eating her up, so she asked a bunch of her friends for advice. She basically polled everyone."

Barry stood. "I know the court has already ruled on this issue, but I would like my objection noted for the record. The witness is testifying about hearsay."

The judge nodded. "The objection is noted. The prosecution may proceed."

Fred lifted his chin and looked toward Amy. "I'm going to show you what's been marked as Exhibit 2. Can you identify it?"

"It's a Facebook group message I got from Shannon."

"When was it sent?"

"December fifteenth."

"When was that in relation to her disappearance?"

"The weekend before."

"And what does it say?"

"It asks for advice about Jake and Keenan."

"To your knowledge, did she come to a decision?"

"She told me she was going to tell both of them in person. She said she was going to tell Keenan before she went home for Christmas. She was going to tell Jake once she got home."

Barry rose for cross-examination.

"Did Shannon have a habit of getting intoxicated?"

"No. She was too focused on her studies."

"In the months that she was your closest friend at Masterson, did you ever see her intoxicated?"

"No, I did not."

"Did you ever see her drink alcohol?"

"No."

Barry paused and looked down at his legal pad for a few seconds, leaving the answer hanging in the air.

"Where were you on the Friday night after final exams that semester?"

"I was back in the city."

"So, you don't know for sure that Shannon told Keenan about Jake, do you?"

"I didn't hear her, if that's what you mean. I just know she was planning to tell him."

"But, it's possible that she chickened out, isn't it?"

"I suppose."

"Because she loved Keenan and didn't want to hurt his feelings?"

"Maybe."

When the judge announced the lunch break, Keenan couldn't wait to get out of the courtroom. What he wanted more than anything was to go outside and run. And run. And run. And never come back. Instead, he ate lunch in a conference room with his family and his attorney, trying to listen as everyone congratulated Barry on his opening and commented on how the first two witnesses had not really done much damage. Keenan knew they were just trying to give him hope. That's why he loved his family so much. They were stick-by-you kind of people. The one-hour lunch break flew by, and it seemed like minutes later they were back in the stuffy courtroom.

CHAPTER 54
Monday, September 15, 2014

CASSIE AND Greg Brody sat behind their son, clutching each other's hands. In her wildest dreams, Cassie had never imagined she would be watching her son on trial for manslaughter. Keenan had always been the more easygoing of her two boys. Not that she could imagine Liam killing anyone either. The whole thing was surreal. She studied the back of Keenan's head. His dark blond hair still curled up a little at the ends. He'd had a mop of curly blond hair as a baby. Such a beautiful child, who became a handsome young man. At the moment, it felt like a curse. What if the jury somehow held his looks against him?

In high school, girls had always seemed to swoon around Keenan. Not that he seemed to notice. He was always more interested in playing hockey than chasing girls. Cassie had listened to her friends' horror stories about their sons having sex in high school. Evelyn's son had even gotten a girl pregnant. Cassie had felt so lucky at the time, maybe even a little superior. Her sons were both heading to top-notch colleges instead of dead-end jobs and teenage parenthood. Maybe God was punishing her for her sin of pride.

All she knew was that at that particular moment, she would gladly make a deal with the devil if she could get her son out of this mess. She knew Barry Densmore had a good reputation, but with her son's life at stake, the devil might offer better odds.

Jenna Davidson had just been sworn as a witness.

"Were you with Shannon Dawson on that Friday night, the last day of final exams last fall?"

"Yes, I was."

"What did you and Shannon do?"

"We hung out in the dorm for a while, then we went to a party off campus."

"Were you drinking?"

"A little."

"Were you drunk?"

"No."

"Was Shannon drinking?"

"Some."

"Was she drunk?"

"She said she wasn't."

"When was that?"

"When she offered to drive to the party."

"Do you know what she was drinking?"

"I think she had a wine cooler."

"Just one?"

"I really don't know."

"Where was the party?"

"It was on Maple Street."

"And did Shannon drive to the Maple Street party?"

"Yes, she did."

"When Shannon drove to Maple Street, who was in the car?"

"It was just Shannon, Greta and me."

"Where did Shannon park at the party?"

"She found a parking spot a couple of houses down from the party."

"What happened at the party?"

"We danced, talked to some people. Then Keenan showed up."

"How long were you at the party before Keenan showed up?"

"About an hour."

"Did Keenan and Shannon talk?"

"Yes."

"Where?"

"Well, he pulled her out on the back deck."

"What happened when they were out on the deck?"

"They argued, and he grabbed her and shook her."

Cassie felt herself tense at the description of violence. She hadn't raised boys who were physically violent with women, had she? Of course, it's hard to find out that your girlfriend is involved with another guy. Anyone would get upset at that. And grabbing is hardly the same as punching. She could remember grabbing the kids in anger when they were fighting and she just couldn't take the bickering any more. Maybe that's all it was.

"How hard did he grab her?"

"Pretty hard. It looked hard enough to hurt." Cassie willed herself to keep her face blank.

"Could you hear what they were arguing about?"

"No, I could not."

"Why?"

"Because I was inside and the door was shut."

"If the door was shut, how did you know what was happening outside?"

"It was a glass door, a slider."

"Did you see them leave?"

"Yeah."

"What happened?"

"Shannon left and Keenan followed her."

"How did she leave?"

"She walked off the back deck."

"How was she moving?"

"Quickly, like she wanted to get away from him."

"Did you see Shannon again after that?"

"No, I did not."

"Did you talk to her?"

"No, but I wish I had."

"Why didn't you?"

"At first, I was upset that she'd left us without a ride. Later,

I was just too busy, what with going home and seeing old friends."

"For the record, can you identify the person you saw arguing with, grabbing, and shaking Shannon Dawson on that evening?"

Jenna pointed at Keenan. "It was him."

"Let the record show that the witness has identified the defendant, Keenan Brody," the prosecutor said.

"So noted," the judge said.

Cassie wished the girl would put down her hand. She kept her finger pointed in obvious blame until Barry began his cross-examination.

"What's your understanding of the Masterson College policy on underage drinking?" Barry said.

"It's not allowed."

"During the hour that you were at the party before Keenan arrived, you said you danced and talked to people. Is that right?"

"Yes."

"You also drank, didn't you?"

"A little."

"But when Officer Shores interviewed you on January ninth, you denied drinking, didn't you?"

"Yes."

"Because you didn't want to get in trouble, right?"

"Yes."

"The party on Maple Street was a keg party, wasn't it?"

"There may have been a keg."

"There was other alcohol, too, wasn't there?"

"I'm not sure."

"What were you drinking?"

"I think I had a beer."

"Was Shannon drinking?"

"Yes."

"In fact, she was drunk, wasn't she?"

"I don't think so."

"But you weren't paying attention, were you?"

"I don't know, maybe."

"Just like you weren't paying attention when she was out on the deck with Keenan, right?"

"No, I was paying attention for that."

"You guys were planning a road trip, weren't you?"

"No."

"But you talked about driving to Maine, didn't you?"

"It was a joke."

"What's funny about driving to Maine?"

"You had to be there."

"It was funny because you were drinking and lots of things seemed funny, right?"

"It was just conversation."

"Drunken conversation, right?"

"No, just conversation."

"When was the first time you talked to the police about Shannon's disappearance?"

"I talked to an officer on the phone a few days after the party."

"At that point, you knew that Shannon had been missing for several days, right?"

"Yes."

"That her family was worried about her?"

"Yes."

"That the police were looking for any and all leads as to what might have happened to Shannon, right?"

"Yes."

"You knew that the police were interested in whoever might be responsible for Shannon's disappearance, true?"

"Yes."

"And yet, you didn't mention that you had seen any sort of altercation between Shannon and Keenan, did you?"

"No."

"You didn't mention that you saw Keenan grab Shannon, did you?"

"No."

"You didn't mention that Keenan may have hurt Shannon,

did you?"

"No."

"You didn't mention that Keenan followed Shannon, right?"

"No."

"Those are all important facts, aren't they?"

"I suppose."

"So, why didn't you mention them the first time you talked with the police?"

"I guess I didn't remember until later."

"You have a Facebook account?"

"Yeah, doesn't everyone?"

"There was a lot of speculation on Facebook about what happened to Shannon in the first days and weeks after her disappearance, wasn't there?"

"Objection, hearsay." Fred Dutton shot out of his chair.

"It's not being offered for the truth, but the effect on the witness."

"I'll allow it. The witness can answer."

"Yeah, it was a big deal."

"And you read what people were saying, right?"

"Yes."

"Nothing further for this witness."

Cassie felt like the girl had stood her ground. Cassie looked toward the jury as the girl exited the courtroom. Several of them were studying Keenan. She wished she could see his face and know what they might be seeing.

The next two witnesses were more of the same. Heather Turner and Greta Paraiso both claimed to have seen Keenan grab Shannon forcefully. Heather saw him slap her. They both pointed at her son. Barry cross-examined both girls the same way he had with Jenna, but the damage was done. Three witnesses had seen Keenan assault Shannon the night she disappeared.

Barry managed to score a minor point with Greta on cross-examination.

"You got a Facebook chat message from Shannon the Saturday before she disappeared, right?"

"Yes."

"Asking for relationship advice, correct?"

"Yes."

"What did you advise Shannon?"

"I'm not sure exactly."

"Let me show you what's been marked as Defense Exhibit A. Do you recognize that?"

"It's a copy of my response to Shannon."

"You wrote those words to her?"

"Yes."

"What do they say?"

Greta blushed. "It says: Whatever happened to 'Don't kiss and tell.' I say keep it to yourself until you're ready to decide. That's what a guy would do."

"So, if Shannon had followed *your* advice, she wouldn't have necessarily told Keenan about Jake, right?"

"I guess so."

"Well, wasn't your advice to hold off until she was sure?"

"Yes."

"And did she ever express to you whether she had made a decision about which young man she wanted to be with?"

"As far as I know, she wasn't ready to decide."

"Thank you. That's all I have."

The prosecutor was able to fix most of the damage during redirect.

"Are you aware of the advice given by Shannon's other friends?"

"Yes."

"What did they say?"

"Objection, hearsay." Barry was on his feet.

"It's not offered for the truth," the prosecutor said.

"You opened the door, counselor. I'll allow it. The witness can answer."

"Most people thought Shannon should tell them both. That it was the fair thing to do."

"Were you under the impression that Shannon was planning to follow the more popular advice?"

"Objection, speculation." Barry jumped up again.

"Overruled. The witness can answer," the judge said.

"I thought she was going to tell them both," Greta said.

As Cassie watched the girl leave the stand, she felt something foreign brewing in her soul. It was the same feeling she had felt in the fifth grade when she found out her best friend Clara's uncle had been touching Clara sexually. Clara's family had moved away and young Cassie had been left with a bitterness that took years to fade. It had to be hate. She actually hated those college girls for publicly painting her son as a monster.

When Greta left the stand, it was four o'clock. The judge conferred briefly with the attorneys before announcing the evening recess. Court would reconvene the next day at 9:00 a.m.

KEENAN ALTERNATED between watching the jury and watching the witnesses. Even the hockey mom in the second row had stopped making eye contact with him, but he could feel the jurors stealing looks at him while he watched the testimony.

Officer Shores was the first witness on the second day of trial. It was the first time he had ever seen the officer dressed in uniform. The prosecutor spent what seemed like half an hour going through his training and experience before asking him about his investigation. Keenan was sure the jury would believe his every word.

"Were you involved in the investigation into the disappearance of Shannon Dawson?" the prosecutor said.

"Yes, I was."

"How did that come about?"

"The parents contacted MFPD when Shannon didn't arrive on her plane flight home to California."

"When did you get involved?"

"The chief assigned the matter to me the morning after the parents contacted us."

"What did you do?"

"I made contact with the college, had public safety do a wellness check on her dorm room."

"What else?"

"When they had no luck, I started trying to track down her friends."

"How did that go?"

"It was a challenge. Everyone had left town for Christmas."

"Did you get any useful leads?"

"I learned that Shannon had a boyfriend on the hockey team."

"Did you learn the identity of the boyfriend?"

"It took a while to identify him, but I eventually figured out it was the defendant, Keenan Brody."

"Did you speak with the defendant?"

"I did. I first spoke with him on the telephone."

"When was this?"

"On December twenty-second of last year."

"What did the defendant tell you?"

"Objection, hearsay." Barry said it with a bored tone.

"The witness can answer in accordance with the court's previous order, but the objection is noted." The judge's tone was equally bored.

Officer Shores didn't miss a beat. "At first he denied that Shannon Dawson was his girlfriend, then he admitted that he was dating her. He also said something about being upset with her."

"What else did he tell you?"

"He admitted that he saw her the night that she disappeared."

"Did he say anything else?"

"He referred to Shannon in the past tense a couple of times."

"Objection, hearsay." Barry sounded less bored this time.

"It's an admission." It was the prosecutor who sounded bored.

"I'll allow it," the judge said.

"Why was that notable?" the prosecutor continued.

"Well, at that point, she'd only been missing for a couple of days. In my mind, we were still dealing with a missing person case. I wouldn't have been surprised to find out that Shannon was alive and well and hanging out with the defendant."

"Was that phone interview recorded?"

"Yes, it was."

The prosecutor produced a CD and had it marked for evidence.

Keenan was floored. They had made it sound like it was different than it was. He remembered the day he spoke to Officer Shores. How could he forget? It was the day his life changed. It was probably the last day he would ever be happy.

He had been down at the pond playing hockey. The score had been tied when his mother showed up. Cassie Brody's face had been flushed. She looked like she had pulled on her mud boots and grabbed her barn coat before hurrying down to the pond. Keenan took off his helmet and skated over to his mom when he heard her call his name.

"What's up, Mom? You come down to root for the better team?" Keenan started to laugh and then stopped when his mother's demeanor registered.

"There was a police officer on the phone. He left a message about a missing girl. Asked you to call him."

"Who's missing?"

"I don't know. But it sounds important. I think you should come up to the house and call him."

"Okay. I'll be right up."

Keenan only took a few minutes to change out of his skates and sprint up the hill to the house. He had paced the kitchen while waiting for Officer Shores to come to the phone. He had been afraid of what the officer would say, but half expected it. Then, after he confirmed that it was Shannon who was missing, he'd felt mad at her and himself. Whatever the reason for her disappearance, he knew the relationship was over. He now realized that his emotional turmoil had come across the wrong way.

Unfortunately, Officer Shores had more.

"What happened with the investigation after that?" the prosecutor asked.

"Well, we got phone records from AT&T."

"I'm showing you what's been marked as Exhibit 4. Can you identify that?"

"It's the phone records we got from Shannon's cell."

"Is there anything notable on there?"

"The last call Shannon got on her phone was from the defendant."

"When was that?"

"It was 8:47 p.m. on Friday, December 20, 2013."

"How long was that call?"

"Eight minutes."

Keenan remembered that call. Shannon had said she had something to tell him, but that it had to be in person. Why were they on the phone so long? Nothing else important was said. How could this be evidence?

"What else did you do?"

"We searched Shannon's dorm room. We found her suitcase and her winter clothing. We also found her laptop, a MacBook, and started going through it."

"Did you find anything on it?"

"There were a lot of messages. All done through Facebook."

"Who did she communicate with?"

"A bunch of girls. Also, the defendant and Jake Miller."

"What else did you do?"

"We located Shannon's vehicle in the parking area adjacent to dormitory."

"Did you search it?"

"We did. We did not find her keys in her dorm room, but her father had an extra key."

"Did you find anything during the search?"

"No, but we did take fingerprints from various places around the car."

"What did you do with the prints?"

"We ran them through all the databases, but we didn't get any hits."

"Why would that be?"

"Not everyone has prints on record. Usually only people with criminal records or certain types of jobs are in the databases."

"Did you have occasion to talk to the defendant after that?"

"Yes, I did."

"When?"

"On December 24, 2013."

"Where?"

"I went to his house. I spoke with the defendant in the presence of his parents."

"What did he tell you?"

"Objection, hearsay," Barry said loudly.

"The objection is overruled," the judge said. "The witness can answer within the bounds of the court's written order."

The officer continued. "When I told him that he was the last one to speak with Shannon by phone, he spontaneously said, 'She's dead.'"

The prosecutor paused for effect. "When the defendant said, 'She's dead,' what did that mean to you?"

Barry jumped out of his seat. "Objection. Speculation."

"Overruled. The witness can answer." The judge sounded bored again. Like none of this really mattered to him.

Officer Shores sat up straighter. "I took it as an admission that he knew what had happened to her."

"How long did you spend at the defendant's house?"

"I was there for about half an hour."

"How did the defendant seem?"

"He seemed nervous. I could see that he was sweating, even though the temperature in the room was cold enough that I was glad that I was wearing my coat."

Keenan was kicking himself. Of course, they were making it all sound so incriminating. As soon as the officer had told him that Shannon had not used her phone since Friday night, he knew she was dead. It had hit him so hard that he had said exactly what he was thinking without censoring it. He should have been more careful. And he should have realized that he was a suspect in Shannon's disappearance.

That night, after Officer Shores had left, Keenan and his parents had gone to sit in front of the fire.

"I didn't like the way that went," his dad had said. Keenan mentally agreed. He didn't like the eagerness he had heard in the officer's voice.

"He was just doing his job," his mom said.

"He showed up here on Christmas Eve. Unannounced," his dad said. "That felt more like an ambush than an interview."

"It wasn't that bad," his mom said. "He just wants to find that girl."

"Shannon's dead," Keenan said.

"You don't know that, Keenan," his mom said. "She might have just lost her phone."

Keenan shook his head. "If she lost her phone, she'd get a new one and have all her stuff transferred. That's what people do these days."

"He's right, Cassie." his dad said. "Although, she might have had an accident and gotten amnesia. Maybe she's in a hospital somewhere wondering who she is."

"You sound like a bad movie," his mom said.

"Better that than the alternative," his dad said.

"Are you okay, Keenan," his dad said. "I know this is probably a shock for you."

"I'm okay, sort of. I had the feeling she was going to break up with me, so I was prepared for the end. Just not like this."

"I'm sorry, Keenan," his mom said.

"Me, too. You know, I'd rather that she ran off with some other guy than have her be dead."

"Maybe that's what happened."

"Let's hope so," he had said. Now Keenan couldn't help thinking how much better his life would be if that had been the case.

The prosecutor was continuing to examine Officer Shores.

"So what else did you do?" Dutton said.

"We searched the defendant's room."

"And did you find anything?"

"Yes, we did. Shannon's missing car keys. They were in the defendant's desk drawer."

"What did the defendant say when you showed him the keys?"

"He said that he forgot they were there."

"Did you speak with the defendant at any other time during the investigation?"

"Yes. We got a court order to get fingerprints from him. He came into the station to comply."

"What did he say to you?"

"At that time, he said he'd taken Shannon's keys because she was too drunk to drive. He also said that he'd driven her car back to the dorm for her."

"Was that the first time the defendant had mentioned taking the keys to keep Shannon from driving?"

"Yes, it was."

"And was it the first time he had mentioned driving her car that evening?"

"Yes, it was."

"And how many times had you previously spoken with the defendant?"

"Three. Once on the phone and twice in person."

"So, it was the fourth time you spoke with him that the defendant came up with his explanation?"

Barry stood suddenly. "Objection. Asked and answered."

"Sustained," the judge said.

Fred shrugged before continuing. "Where did your investigation lead you after that?"

"Well, the students started returning from winter break, so I interviewed a lot of the people I had spoken to on the phone earlier. I took statements from all of them."

"What else did you do?"

"We got a search warrant for the house where the party was on the night Shannon disappeared."

"Did you find anything?"

"No, sir."

"Did you look anywhere else?"

"We did a search of the nearby woods."

"Did you find anything?"

"No, sir."

"What were you hoping to find?"

"At that point, we had given up hope of finding Shannon alive. The truth is, we were looking for a body."

"When did you find Shannon's body?"

"Not until April fifth of this year."

"Tell us about that."

"A bunch of kayakers spotted the body in the river. Moose Creek, that is. And called it in."

"What did you do?"

"We called Colchester Technical Rescue. They pulled the body out of the water. Then, we turned it over to the medical examiner."

Barry rose for cross-examination.

"You said that Keenan admitted to being upset with Shannon, right?"

"Yes."

"But, isn't it true that his exact words were that he was 'ticked' at her?"

"Maybe."

"Let me show you what's been marked as Exhibit B. What were Keenan's exact words?"

"He said, 'I was ticked at her.'"

"Do people who are 'ticked' usually kill people?"

"Objection," the prosecutor said. "Calls for speculation."

"Sustained," the judge said.

Barry seemed to take it all in stride. "Okay, let's talk about context. What were Keenan's words immediately preceding the comment about being 'ticked?'"

"He said that Shannon hadn't called him back."

"In your experience, is it unusual for people to get ticked when other people don't call them back?"

"I guess not."

"But, it's not usually a motive for homicide, is it?"

"Objection."

"Sustained."

Barry paused briefly to look at his notes.

"Did you have a search warrant to search my client's dorm

room?"

"No, we did not."

"But you didn't need one, did you?"

"No."

"That's because my client gave you permission to search his room, right?"

"Yes."

"He signed a Consent to Search form, right?"

"Yes."

"Because he was trying to cooperate with the police, right?"

"I suppose."

"Just like he had been cooperative when you called him on the phone just after Shannon disappeared, true?"

"I didn't feel like he was being forthright with me."

"Move to strike, Your Honor."

"You opened the door, Counselor."

Barry paused. "Can counsel approach, Your Honor?"

The judge nodded. The attorneys had a heated discussion with the judge while white noise filled the room. Keenan could tell that Barry was not happy. After a minute the attorneys returned.

"When you called my client the first time, he called you back promptly, right?"

"Yes."

"And he answered your questions?"

"Yes."

"And he was cooperative with you when you showed up at his house on Christmas Eve, wasn't he?"

"Again, I didn't feel like he was completely truthful."

"Objection, move to strike."

"Sustained," the judge said. "The jury will disregard the answer." No they won't, Keenan thought. They'll remember that the officer thought I was a liar.

"But, he and his family let you in, right?"

"Yes."

"And my client answered your questions, true?"

"Yes."

"Despite the fact that you had interrupted their Christmas Eve, right?"

"Yes."

"You said when you found Shannon's keys, they were in a drawer, right?"

"Yes."

"Out of sight, correct?"

"Yes, they were hidden."

"Or perhaps 'out of sight, out of mind.' That's possible, isn't it?"

"I don't think so."

"Did you ask my client why he had Shannon's keys?"

"I don't recall."

"Let me show you what's been marked as Defense Exhibit C." Barry handed him a stack of papers. "Why don't you refresh your recollection." Keenan had seen that the document was a transcript of the conversation during the search warrant. The officer took a few minutes to review it. When he was done, he looked up. "Okay, I've reviewed it."

"Good. Let me ask you again. Did you ask my client why he had the keys?"

"No, I did not."

"Because you were busy accusing him of murder, right?"

"I was interrogating a potential murder suspect."

"Which involved making accusations, didn't it?"

"There are techniques we use to get people to talk, admit to things they've done."

"And those techniques involve making accusations, right?"

"Sometimes."

"But Keenan didn't admit to doing anything, did he?"

"No."

"Your accusations made him uncomfortable, didn't they?"

"I wouldn't know."

"Don't most people get uncomfortable when they're accused of murder?"

"Objection. He's not a psychologist."

"Sustained."

"Did my client appear uncomfortable to you?"

"Yes, he did. Because he knew he'd been caught."

"Or because he was being accused of something he didn't do. That's possible too, isn't it?"

"That wasn't my take on it."

"My client never admitted outright to killing Shannon Dawson, did he?"

"He admitted that he knew she was dead when, as far as everyone else was concerned, she was just missing."

"Let's talk about that. When you interviewed Keenan on Christmas Eve, did you think Shannon was dead?"

"I knew it was a possibility."

"Why?"

"Because she'd been missing for four days."

"That's a long time for a girl her age, isn't it?"

"Yes."

"Why else?"

"Because she hadn't used her cell phone for four days."

"That's unusual for someone her age too, isn't it?"

"Yes."

"Because kids her age are constantly on their phones. Don't put them down unless they have to, right?"

"Yes."

"Was Keenan aware that Shannon had not used her cell when he used the words, 'She's dead'?"

"I don't know."

"Let me refresh your recollection." Barry handed the officer the transcript again and waited while he read it. "Isn't it true that just before Keenan used those words, you told him he was the last person to have phone contact with Shannon?"

"Yes."

"Four days before?"

"Yes."

"So, isn't it true that when Keenan said, 'She's dead,' he was actually just stating the obvious?"

"That's not the way I took it."

"Of course not. Because you wanted him to be guilty,

right?"

"No, I wanted to find out what happened."

"Did you? Or did you want to confirm what you believed?"

"I didn't believe anything." Keenan didn't believe him. Hopefully, the jury didn't either.

"Let's talk about your interviews with the students. How many Masterson students did you interview in the days after Shannon's disappearance?"

"I don't know. Lots."

"What does 'lots' mean? Ten? Twenty? A hundred?"

"I'd have to go through my records. Definitely more than ten, probably at least twenty."

"During your first round of interviews, how many of them reported witnessing an assault on the night Shannon disappeared?"

"None."

"How many of them reported seeing any sort of altercation?"

"None."

Barry paused and crossed out some items on his notepad before he continued. "Do the AT&T records show missed calls?"

"I don't believe so. We didn't request them soon enough to have the data preserved."

"So, if Keenan had tried to call Shannon on the day after he last saw her, those calls wouldn't show up, right?"

"That sounds right."

"Same for texts, true?"

"Yes."

"That's all I have." Barry turned and walked toward the counsel table.

Fred rose for redirect.

"Of those twenty or so students that you interviewed in the days after Shannon's disappearance, how many were at the party on Maple Street?"

"I believe only two. Greta Paraiso and Jenna Davidson."

"So the students that you interviewed wouldn't have been able to witness the assault because they weren't there, right?"

"That's right. I didn't start interviewing the people from the party until later in the investigation." The officer looked toward Barry, his expression smug.

"Why was that?"

"The students had all gone away for the winter break. I did what I could over the phone, but I wasn't able to do all the interviews I wanted until the students started coming back to campus."

"And once you did, did you find any other witnesses to the assault?"

"Yes, I found one. Heather Turner."

During lunch, Keenan and his family met with Barry in a small conference room.

"That officer was a good witness for them," his dad said.

"And those girls yesterday sounded so convincing," his mom said. Keenan didn't like the way she said it. He wondered if his own mother was doubting his innocence.

"That's okay," Barry said. "We warned the jury that they would. And police officers always come across well. They have a lot of experience testifying. At this point in a trial, it always feels like the other side is going to win. It will feel better when we have a chance to present our evidence."

Barry's phone chirped, and he glanced at what appeared to be a text message.

"I need to go check in with my secretary. I'll be back as soon as I can. Save me a sandwich." Barry smiled, but it looked fake to Keenan. He wondered if his lawyer was giving up hope despite the pep talk. That would be a bad sign.

Barry was back right before it was time to go back to court. He wolfed down half a sandwich before ushering the family into the courtroom.

"Is everything okay?" Keenan said.

"Don't worry. Everything's fine." Keenan wasn't convinced.

CHAPTER 56
Tuesday, September 16, 2014

FRED WASN'T sure how many more witnesses he should try to squeeze into the second day. He wanted the jury to go home feeling like the evidence was strongly in favor of conviction. On the other hand, he didn't want them to be so exhausted that they stopped paying attention. Ultimately, it would be up to the judge when to take a break for the day, but Fred could control the pace of the remaining witnesses. He figured three more witnesses would make for a good second day.

Fred called Evan Halliday. As he made his way to the stand, Fred noticed that Halliday's tailored suit was clearly more expensive than Fred's.

Halliday was sworn and gave a description of his experience, which included twenty years in the FBI, first in Los Angeles, then in New York. He explained that the Dawsons had hired him. Fred wished all the law enforcement witnesses would come across as comfortable and confident on the witness stand. Fred had Halliday highlight his extensive training in domestic violence.

"Did you meet with the defendant during the course of your investigation?"

"I did. On January 3, 2014."

"Did he make any admissions to you during that conversation?"

"Objection."

"The witness may answer in accordance with the court's

previous ruling."

"He did. First off, he admitted he had gone to the party on Maple Street specifically to look for Shannon."

"What was the significance of that?"

"My understanding is that he had previously told Officer Shores—"

"Objection. Hearsay." Barry rose after the words were out.

"Sustained," the judge said.

"What else did he admit to you?"

"He told me he knew that he liked Shannon more than she liked him. He basically admitted he was insecure about his relationship with her."

"What was the significance of that for you?"

"Objection. Speculation," Barry said.

"Overruled. I'll allow it," the judge said.

"Insecurity and jealousy. As an investigator, those are red flags for domestic violence."

"Did you record your conversation with Keenan Brody that day?"

"I did," Evan said.

"Thank you. That's all," Fred said.

As expected, Barry's cross-examination was brief.

"My client cooperated with you, didn't he?" Barry said.

"Yes."

"He willingly answered all your questions?"

"Yes."

"He never said anything about physically harming Shannon, did he?"

"No."

Next, Fred called Officer Steve Maroney. He went through Maroney's qualifications. Maroney had been with MFPD for fifteen years and had gone to numerous trainings on forensics.

"What was your involvement in the investigation into the disappearance of Shannon Dawson?"

"I processed her car."

"What did processing involve?"

"I lifted fingerprints and collected hair and fiber samples from the interior and the trunk."

"How did you lift the prints?"

"I used a fine brush and aluminum power, then transferred the prints to fingerprint tape."

"How many sets of prints did you lift from the driver's side of Shannon's car?" Fred said.

"I was able to lift prints from five different individuals, but most of the prints were from the deceased."

"And how did you process the prints?"

"I scanned them into the computer and ran them against the FBI database."

"Did you find a match?"

"Not at first. We didn't get a match until we ran them against the prints we got from the defendant."

"Where were the defendant's prints inside the vehicle?"

"There were some on the passenger door and others on the driver's side dashboard, including the headlight switch."

"Did you recover anything else from the car?"

"Yes. We recovered several strands of blond hair from the trunk of the vehicle."

"I'm going to show you State's Exhibit 5. What is that?"

"It's a photograph of the trunk."

"Who took it?"

"I did."

"What does it show?"

"The hairs I recovered."

"What did you do with those hairs?"

"I submitted them to the Vermont Forensic Laboratory."

"Thank you, officer. That's all I have."

Barry rose. "Good afternoon, officer."

"Good afternoon."

"Did you find any blood anywhere in Shannon Dawson's car?"

"No, we did not."

"I'm going to show you what's marked as Defense Exhibit E. What is it?"

"It's a photograph."

"Did you take it?"

"I did."

"At about the same time as the photograph Mr. Dutton just showed you?"

"That's correct."

"What does it show?"

"It shows the passenger compartment of the Volkswagen when we first opened it."

"What was in there?"

"A beach towel and a water bottle."

"Did you examine the beach towel?"

"I did."

"Did you find any blood on the beach towel?"

"No, I did not."

"Did you find any hairs on the towel?"

Steve sat up straighter in his chair. "Yes, there were a few," he said.

"Isn't it possible that the hairs in the trunk of the car came from the beach towel?"

"Anything's possible." Maroney's voice dripped with derision.

"Are you familiar with Locard's Exchange Principle?"

"Yes."

"Can you explain it to the jury?"

"Basically, every contact between objects leaves a trace."

"Okay, so according to that principle, it's possible that, if Shannon had used the towel to dry off after swimming or working out, her hair could have been left on the towel, correct?"

"Well, yes."

"And, if the towel was placed in the trunk, the towel would have left a trace, right?"

"Yes."

"And that trace could have been the hair you found in the trunk?"

"But—"

"Yes or no, officer."

"Yes."

"That's all I have. Thank you."

Fred decided to take the time to counter with the obvious argument. "Where were the hairs located in relation to the towel?"

"The towel was on the floor of the passenger compartment."

"Not in the trunk?"

"No."

"How much distance was there between the hairs and the towel?"

"At least three feet and the back seat."

"Under those circumstances, was an exchange likely?"

"No, sir."

It was almost three thirty. His timing was good. He wanted to get in one more witness.

Karina Messinger from the Vermont Forensics Laboratory was eminently qualified, and it took fifteen minutes to give the short version of her education, employment, and training history. Barry didn't object to her qualification as an expert.

"Did you do any analysis of the hair found in the trunk of Shannon Dawson's car?"

"I did."

"What did you do?"

"I did a mitochondrial DNA comparison with a blood sample obtained from the medical examiner."

"What did that comparison tell you?"

"That the hair in the trunk came from either Shannon Dawson or one of her maternal blood relatives."

"Did you do any other analysis?"

"I also did a microscope comparison of the hair from the trunk and hair samples obtained from Shannon Dawson's body."

"And how did they compare?"

"They were consistent in length, diameter and

pigmentation."

"Thank you."

Barry's cross-examination was brief. "How many hairs per day does the average person lose?"

"I'm not sure."

"Would it surprise you to learn that it's between fifty and one hundred?"

"Objection," Fred bellowed. "Defense counsel is testifying. The witness said she didn't know."

"Sustained. The jury will disregard the question."

Barry thanked the witness, and as hoped and expected, court adjourned for the day. Fred felt pretty good about the day's testimony. Hopefully, the jury was left with the mental image of Shannon Dawson's body in the trunk of her car.

CHAPTER 57
Wednesday, September 17, 2014

BARRY SAT at the counsel table on Wednesday morning and tried to focus on Keenan's trial, but his head throbbed from sleep deprivation. Unfortunately, thanks to Sam, he hadn't been able to do all the prep work he had planned for the night before. And he'd been distracted during the previous afternoon's testimony. He hoped he hadn't made any critical mistakes. Why did Sam have such bad timing?

Marcy's text at lunchtime the day before had caught him off guard.

"Sam's out of control," Marcy had said when he had called her back.

"Where is he?"

"In the emergency room."

"Is he hurt?"

"No, the police brought him there when he wouldn't leave Mr. K's Place."

"Is he under arrest?"

"No, he's on a temporary psych hold. They wouldn't tell me much, but it sounds like he's refusing medication."

"Shit. I can't deal with this right now."

"I know. I'm sorry. I wouldn't have contacted you if I knew what to do."

"I know. I know. Can you try to get him a bed at Brattleboro Retreat? Or another program?"

"I can try. Are you sure you don't want to go talk to him first? Maybe you can get him to calm down, take his meds."

"I can't babysit him this week. Besides, there's no way the judge would grant a continuance in this trial."

"You know better than I do. It's just that he's your son and he needs you."

"Do you have any idea what triggered him?"

"You live with him. Have you seen signs he's been drinking or smoking marijuana? Has he been taking his meds?"

"I don't know. I haven't seen him since last week. I've been busy. I thought maybe he met a girl or something. He hasn't been around."

Fortunately, by the time Barry finished court that day, Marcy had finagled a bed at Brattleboro Retreat, a private mental health facility. When Barry arrived at the emergency room, the sheriffs had already left to transport Sam to Brattleboro. Barry knew that Sam was probably pissed at him. On some level he didn't blame him. He probably should have tried to get a continuance. He went home to pack a bag for Sam. He opened the drawers to the dresser, but none of the clothes looked familiar. He took the ones on top figuring they were the ones Sam had worn most recently. He found Sam's meds in the medicine cabinet. He considered counting the pills and calculating based on the refill date, but realized it was moot. He threw the pills in the bag along with some shampoo and toothpaste.

When he was done, he looked around Sam's room. Barry hadn't spent much time there in a long time. He sat on the bed and noticed a book with a bookmark on the night table. It was one of Barry's favorites, *The Hitchhiker's Guide to the Galaxy*. Sam must have borrowed it from his bookshelf. He unzipped the duffle bag and shoved it on top.

Barry didn't even want to think about how much a week at Brattleboro was going to cost him. At least he knew Sam was safe and he could focus on the trial.

There was little traffic on a Tuesday night, so Barry pushed the speed limit a little and was able to make the drive to Brattleboro in just over two hours. He passed an Adams County Sheriff's cruiser heading north an hour south of

Middleton Falls. Probably returning from exiling his son. Barry pictured Sam in the back of the cruiser, angry and belligerent.

At the facility, Barry waited at the admissions desk for half an hour, hoping he would be allowed to talk to his son. Finally, a nurse had come out to talk to him. She smiled while she explained that it would be better if Sam had a chance to settle in before seeing visitors. Barry left the duffle with her and drove home more slowly.

When he got home at midnight, he just wanted to crash. Instead, he forced himself to review the depositions of the witnesses he expected for the third day. He also made some notes about the second day in preparation for his closing arguments. The three hours of sleep he'd managed hadn't been particularly good quality.

The clerk announced the judge and Barry rose to his feet automatically, coming out of his thoughts and back to the trial. Barry wondered how many more witnesses Fred was planning. He only hoped that he himself wouldn't be expected to put on witnesses that day. He wanted to use his expert as his lead witness because he wanted to switch the direction of the tide as soon as possible in the presentation of evidence. However, Dr. Lapitas wasn't due to arrive until Thursday morning.

Barry gave Keenan what he hoped was a confident look. The kid looked haggard. Hard to avoid under the circumstances. Barry hoped his own feelings of doubt and exhaustion weren't getting conveyed to the jury. Confidence was such a big part of the show.

The third day of trial started on schedule. It seemed that Judge Jenkins liked to run a tight courtroom. For his first witness, Fred called Shannon's father. It was an obvious play on the jury's sympathy and a strong opening to the third day.

"Tell us about your daughter," Fred said. Barry could object on the grounds of relevance, but it would be a dangerous move. It would be better to use the same tactic for the defense later.

Jack Dawson's voice shook as he spoke. "Shannon was our only child. We had hoped for others, but it never happened." He paused, his breathing heavy with emotion. The judge offered him a box of tissues, but he shook his head. "Shannon was always such a good girl."

"Tell us about her skating," Fred said.

"Right. Ever since she was a little girl, Shannon loved to skate. We, well mostly my wife, took her to the rink almost every day for practice. They were both so dedicated to it."

"She competed?"

"Yes. She made it all the way to the semi-finals of the Southwest Pacific Figure Skating Championships in 2010 and again in 2011."

"How many skaters did she compete against to get that far?"

"I don't know. It's extremely competitive. Hundreds of girls try out, but only a few make it that far."

"Was Shannon competitive in other realms?"

"She was an exceptionally good student. She tried hard at everything she did."

"How did she end up at Masterson?"

"She wanted a small but prestigious college. She knew that medical schools were competitive, so she wanted a good name on her applications."

"What do you do for a living, Dr. Dawson?"

"I'm a general surgeon."

"So your daughter wanted to follow in your footsteps?"

"I think she had her own dreams. She wanted to specialize in sports medicine. She was an athlete and an academic at the same time."

"Did you visit Middleton Falls prior to Shannon attending Masterson College?"

"No, my wife came out here with her during her senior year of high school. To visit the campus. But I drove out with her when she first started."

"Did you have any concerns about her safety?"

"No. In fact, we were relieved that she was at a place so rural. It seemed so much safer than if she had gone to a bigger school or one in a city. We never dreamed something so horrible could happen to her."

"Thank you. That's all I have."

Barry considered waiving cross-examination. There was nothing to be gained by antagonizing someone who was so sympathetic to the jury, but he needed to make one point.

"How long did Shannon have the Volkswagen?"

"We got it for her used when she was a junior in high school. So, I'd say two years."

"And she used it to transport her belongings to and from the beach on occasion?"

"Yes."

"And she used it to transport her belongings from California to Middleton Falls last fall?"

"Yes."

"Thank you."

Next, Fred called Dr. Grace Collins. Barry had seen her testify before so he knew that Grace deserved her reputation as a solid witness.

"How are you employed?" Fred began.

"I am the chief medical examiner for the State of Vermont."

"How long have you held that position?"

"Twenty-one years."

"What sort of training did you do to become a medical examiner?"

"I graduated from the University of Minnesota Medical School, followed by a four-year residency in forensic pathology at Johns Hopkins University and a one-year fellowship at the University of North Carolina."

"Was all of that after you attended a four-year college?"

"Yes, of course. I have an undergraduate degree in biochemistry from the University of Wisconsin."

Barry stood, and the judge nodded in his direction. "The defense does not object to Dr. Collins being qualified as an expert," Barry said.

"The witness is qualified," the judge said.

"Did you perform an autopsy on Shannon Dawson in early April of this year?" Fred said.

"Yes, I did," Dr Collins said.

"Tell us about that."

"The body was brought in by Colchester Technical Rescue. I understand it was retrieved from the Moose Creek, which was consistent with what I observed."

"What did you observe?"

"First of all, the body was well preserved, probably due to the cold water and the presence of adipocere."

"What's adipocere?"

"It's when the fatty layer beneath the skin transforms into a waxy, almost soap-like material."

"What causes that?"

"In general, it's caused by extended submersion in water postmortem."

"Were you able to determine how long the body had been in the creek?"

"I can't say definitively, but it would have had to be at least several weeks."

"From what you observed, is it possible that the body was in the water for nearly four months?"

"Absolutely. The normal decomposition of the body could well have been delayed by the cold water temperatures in Moose Creek."

"How did you determine the identity of the person whose body was recovered from Moose Creek?"

"We used dental records to confirm that it was the missing college student, Shannon Dawson."

"And you performed a full autopsy?"

"Yes, I did."

"Were you able to determine the cause of death during the autopsy?"

"Not with medical certainty."

"Why not?"

"Underwater recoveries are extremely difficult."

"Why is that?"

"Because there is no universally accepted diagnostic laboratory test for drowning. We can never be one hundred percent sure whether somebody was dead when they hit the water or whether they drowned. And when you're dealing with a long-term submersion, it's even more difficult."

"Understanding that you can't say with medical certainty, was there any evidence in this case that indicated the cause of death?"

"Yes, there was evidence of blunt force trauma to the head."

"Would that trauma have been sufficient to kill Shannon Dawson?"

"Yes, absolutely. It was significant."

"Tell us about that."

"There was a closed depressed skull fracture to the right parietal bone."

"Where is the right parietal bone in layman's terms?"

"The upper right back of the head."

"And what is a closed fracture?"

"A fracture where the overlying skin not been lacerated."

"So, would there be any bleeding?"

"No, not with a closed fracture."

"And what is a depressed skull fracture?"

"It's when a piece of bone in the skull gets pushed inward, putting pressure on the brain."

"Have you seen that type of injury before?"

"Yes. It's consistent with a backwards fall. You see them a lot in older people who slip and fall on the ice."

"Did you observe any other injuries on Shannon's body?"

"Yes. There was also a contusion to the upper left cheek near the temple."

"Have you seen many of those?"

"Yes. It's what happens when someone gets punched in the face, usually by someone right-handed."

"Under what circumstances do you tend to see those two injuries in combination?"

"It's a common pattern for assault victims. The victim gets punched and either knocked out or knocked off balance. Their head gets turned away from the punch, they fall, and they hit the back of their head."

"Did you see any other signs of trauma to the body?"

"No, I did not."

Fred presented pictures of Shannon's face in death and the injury to the back of her head and had Dr. Collins confirm that she felt blunt force trauma likely contributed to Shannon's death. Barry knew that her testimony was damaging. As he rose for cross-examination, he reminded himself that he only had to create reasonable doubt.

"Isn't it true that your autopsy report indicated that the cause of death was undetermined?" Barry asked.

"Like I said, the conditions made it impossible to determine the cause of death with certainty. My report simply recognized that fact."

"But today, you're telling us that Shannon Dawson died from blunt force trauma to the head?"

"No, I'm telling you that Shannon Dawson suffered a blunt force trauma to the head sufficient to kill her, and that it likely contributed to her death. I can't tell you with scientific certainty what actually killed her."

"You sometimes put the likely cause of death on a death certificate, don't you?"

"On occasion."

"But you didn't in this case, did you?"

"No."

"Because at the time you didn't think the head trauma was the *likely* cause of death, right?"

"That's correct."

"Has your opinion changed?"

"No."

"Because you can't say with any certainty whether Shannon drowned completely by accident all on her own, or was killed by someone else, can you?"

"Not with medical certainty."

"Let's talk some more about the head trauma. Can you say with medical certainty that the head trauma occurred prior to the body entering the water?"

"No. But only because the body was submerged for so long. The normal signs that I would look for had been washed away or diluted by the water."

"So, it's possible that Shannon Dawson fell into the water and drowned, and that the trauma to her head occurred after she was already dead, isn't it?"

"It's possible."

"And it's possible that Shannon Dawson fell into the water and hit her head after she was in the water, right?"

"Yes, it's possible. But both of those scenarios are unlikely."

"Why?" As soon as he asked the question, he wished he hadn't.

"Because accidental drownings usually involve witnesses," Dr. Collins said before he could withdraw the question.

"So, you're basing your expert medical opinion on the lack of witnesses?"

"No. My expert medical opinion is what is written in my report."

"That the cause of death is undetermined?"

"Yes."

"Let's talk about where the body was found. Are you familiar with the section of Moose Creek that runs through Middleton Falls?"

"Not particularly."

"What if I were to tell you it's swift water, with a series of ledges and boulders, and that the area is popular with whitewater kayakers. Would that make it more likely that the injuries to the body were postmortem?"

"No."

"Why is that?"

"Because except for the two head injuries that were noted, we found no other injuries to the body."

"But couldn't her clothing have protected her?"

"Only from minor impacts. If she had gone over some ledges, especially one as big as the falls, I would expect to see more damage to the body."

"Is there a scientific basis for that opinion?"

"Just my experience and training as a medical examiner and forensic investigator."

"Did you run any tests to determine whether Shannon had

been drinking prior to her death?"

"I ran tests, but I was unable to determine her blood alcohol concentration."

"Why?"

"The body had been in the water for too long."

"So it's possible that, when Shannon went into the water, her blood alcohol concentration was one hundred milligrams per deciliter or point one zero, isn't it?"

"Yes."

"And it's possible that her blood alcohol concentration was point two zero or even point three zero when she went into the water, true?"

"Yes."

"Isn't it true that a high blood alcohol concentration would make it more likely that Shannon's death was due to her own mishap?"

"In theory, but you have to look at all the circumstances."

Fred's redirect was brief. "Dr. Collins, based on the autopsy, is it possible that Shannon was assaulted, killed, and that her dead body was dumped in the river?"

"Yes."

"Is is also possible she was assaulted, knocked unconscious, and that her unconscious body was dumped in the river where she subsequently drowned?"

"Yes."

"Would either of those scenarios involve an accidental death?"

"No."

"And were there injuries to the body consistent with an assault?"

"Yes."

"Thank you, Dr. Collins. That's all I have."

When Dr. Collins left the stand, it was after eleven thirty. "I think we'll resume after lunch," the judge announced. "We'll reconvene at one o'clock and you can call your next witness then, Mr. Dutton."

"Actually, Your Honor, the prosecution rests."

"Well then, the jury is excused until one o'clock. I'll see the lawyers in my chambers."

Barry stood. "Excuse me, Your Honor. We'd rather wait until tomorrow to begin our case. Perhaps we could excuse the jury until tomorrow."

"Surely you have some witnesses you can put on today, Mr. Densmore?"

"I'd rather stick to our planned order, and our first witness is not due here until tomorrow morning."

The judge gave Barry a stern look. "Very well. Court is adjourned until tomorrow morning at nine o'clock. Gentlemen, my chambers."

In chambers, Barry made the expected motion for a judgment of acquittal. Judge Jenkins made the expected ruling and denied the motion. Barry reminded himself that the judge would have denied the motion even if he hadn't been pissed. And the upside was that he would have more time to prepare for the beginning of the defense case. Maybe he could even get a decent amount of sleep.

CHAPTER 58
Thursday, September 18, 2014

FRED SINCERELY hoped this would be the last day of the trial. He really was too old for this much stress. He should have turfed this case to one of his deputies.

For his first witness, Barry called Dr. Victor Lapitas who made his way to the witness stand and was sworn. Fred had been hearing about Dr. Lapitas for a few years. He knew that two of his deputies had cross-examined him in other cases and didn't like the man. Barry seemed inclined to use him in child abuse cases. Fred had deposed Dr. Lapitas by phone to save money. With only a brief report and a resume for reference, the deposition had been a waste of time. Fred was hoping there would be an obvious attack when it was time for cross-examination.

"Good afternoon, Doctor," Barry said. "Can you please describe your education for the jury?"

"Certainly. I received my Bachelor's degree in psychology from Dartmouth College and my Ph.D. in psychology from Princeton University."

Fred stood and the judge nodded in his direction. "Your Honor, I'm familiar with Dr. Lapitas. I'll stipulate to his qualifications."

Barry shook his head. "I'll be brief, Your Honor, but I'd like the jury to hear more about Dr. Lapitas' qualifications."

The judge nodded. "As long as you're brief."

"Dr. Lapitas, what did you do after you finished your training?"

"For twenty years I was a researcher and a professor of cognitive psychology at Rutgers University. For the past ten years, I have had a part-time clinical practice."

"For those of us who aren't scientists, what is cognitive psychology?"

"It's the scientific study of the mind and mental functioning."

"And what types of mental functioning does it refer to?"

"In general, cognitive psychologists are concerned with how we acquire, process, and store information."

"What was the focus of your research while at Rutgers?"

"Most of my research related to memory and the effects of stress on memory."

"Are you licensed as a clinical psychologist?"

"Yes. I am licensed to practice in New Jersey."

"Do you specialize in your clinical practice?"

"Most of my clients are people who suffer from post-traumatic stress."

"The defense now requests that Dr. Lapitas be qualified as an expert witness."

"The witness is qualified," the judge said.

"Dr. Lapitas, did you review any materials in connection with case?"

"I did."

"What did you review?"

"I reviewed recorded interviews of Greta Paraiso, Jenna Davidson, and Heather Turner."

"To be clear, which interviews were those?"

"There were at least two interviews of each witness. Officer Shores did the first interviews of Ms. Paraiso and Ms. Davidson by phone in December." Lapitas went on to describe the timing of the interviews before adding, "Both of Ms. Perkins' interviews were in person a few days apart."

"And what did you observe?"

"During the initial phone interviews, neither Ms. Paraiso nor Ms. Davidson described an assault. Subsequently, they did."

"Can you explain to the jury why this is relevant?"

"Oh, yes. It's actually fascinating. You see, contrary to popular belief, the human memory is not like computer memory. It's a very malleable thing."

"By malleable you mean?"

"Suggestible."

"You mean a person's memory can be changed?"

"It's been proven by several studies."

"Can you tell us about them?"

Lapitas grinned broadly and nodded. Fred thought he seemed too eager. "One of the first ones was in 1974. Researchers showed film clips of car accidents to test subjects. The subjects were later asked to estimate the speed of the vehicles. Subjects who were asked the speed when the cars *smashed* into each other gave higher estimates than those who were asked the speed when the cars *hit,* and both groups gave higher estimates than those asked about the speed when the cars *contacted* each other. The study raised the issue of question bias.

"It was followed by another study. This time one hundred fifty students watched a one-minute film that featured a car driving through the countryside followed by four seconds of a multiple-car traffic accident. Afterwards the students were questioned about the film. The independent variable was the type of question asked. Fifty of the students were asked 'how fast were the cars going when they *hit* each other?'. Another fifty were asked 'how fast were the cars going when they *smashed* each other?' The remaining fifty participants were not asked a question at all because they were the control group.

"One week later the students were brought back. Without seeing the film again they answered ten questions, one of which was a critical one randomly placed in the list: 'Did you see any broken glass? Yes or no?' There was no broken glass on the original film.

"The results are surprising. Overall, twenty-nine students or nineteen percent remembered the broken glass. Forty-seven percent of those asked the 'smashed' question as compared with approximately sixteen percent for the other groups."

"So what do these studies prove?"

"That the types of questions asked of a witness can affect how they remember an event to the point of witnesses remembering things that didn't happen, such as broken glass."

"Any other notable studies in this field?"

"There are many of them, but I'll only talk about a few more." Lapitas described in detail a study in which twenty-four people were told by a relative about several events relating to their childhood, including one that was fictitious. They were later asked to recall as much as possible. Twenty-five percent of the people remembered the false event, either partially or fully.

"So, what do these studies tell us?" Barry asked.

"That people's memories can be altered to include false events, and that they will remember those events with almost as much confidence and clarity as a true memory."

"So, in the study you just mentioned, twenty-five percent of the people remembered false events. Are the results on that consistent?"

"Actually, other studies have had higher numbers. Let me tell you about one more. A group of seventy-nine college students were told that they were participating in a study on reaction time during a computer typing exercise. They were told that under no circumstances should they touch the Escape key. In the middle of their tests the screen went blank. A highly distressed experimenter then accused the students of hitting the forbidden Escape key. At first, all the subjects denied touching the key, at which point the experimenter fiddled with the keyboard and announced that all the data had been lost and asked, 'Did you hit the Escape key?'

"Some of the subjects were also informed by a witness that they had done it; some were not. Overall, sixty-nine percent of the subjects confessed to having done something they did not do. Nearly all who believed there was a witness confessed."

"So what does the study tell us about memory?" Barry said.

"This study and others have shown us that social pressure and stress can decrease the reliability of someone's memory. Also, the belief that there is corroboration can affect the implanting of a false memory."

"So, can you apply what we learned from the studies to the case against Keenan Brody?"

"Of course. It's extremely telling that, in the first round of interviews, none of the witnesses described an assault on the night that Shannon disappeared. It would have been highly relevant, yet nobody reported it. Then, if you look at the transcripts of Officer Shores' interviews with the witnesses to the alleged assault, you can see that he planted the idea with his questions. In the second round of interviews, the students were again asked leading questions implying that there had been a physical altercation. In that round, two of the witnesses had vague recollections of Keenan grabbing Shannon. By the third interview, the witnesses were reporting more detail about the alleged assault than they had during either of the previous interviews."

"Okay, can you break this down for us, starting with the type of questions that would have planted the idea?"

"Yes. In the first round of phone interviews, Officer Shores asked questions like whether the witnesses had seen Shannon and Keenan fighting or arguing or if anything seemed wrong between them. Those questions would have planted the idea of a fight, even though nobody reported seeing one."

"Then what?"

"Then, in the second round, Officer Shores asked questions like, 'Did he get physical with her?' and 'Did you see them struggle?' At that point, the same witnesses who had not reported any sort of fight had vague recollections of an incident involving grabbing."

"But they testified in this courtroom that they remember an incident whereby Keenan grabbed Shannon hard enough to hurt her. How can you explain that?"

"After they reported their recollections of the grabbing incident, Officer Shores typed up statements for them to sign. He made the grabbing incident into a concrete event. The witnesses signed the statements, which would have further served to lock in their memories."

"But what about the detail they provided when they testified for the jury? Can you explain that?"

"Absolutely. After the witnesses reported their vague recollections, Officer Shores went back to them a third time. This time, he was looking for specific detail. He wanted to know if the grabbing incident was forceful enough to constitute an assault under the law. He again asked leading questions and again got more detailed statements."

"But there were multiple witnesses. Can more than one witness have had their memory altered to contain the same details?"

Lapitas nodded his head vigorously. "That's exactly what happens when witnesses talk to each other. Or when they read the same accounts, say, in media, such as Facebook. Their memories assimilate the details they learn from other sources."

"What about Heather Turner? She was only interviewed twice."

"It's harder to pinpoint where she got her misinformation. She may be highly suggestible. It could have also easily come from listening to other people talk about what they saw or reading Facebook speculation about Shannon's disappearance."

"Can you explain it more?"

"Yes. First of all, Shannon's disappearance would have been highly stressful for her friends, acquaintances, and even the student population in general. Shannon was missing, presumed dead. The police were interviewing people. Second, there was a lot of pressure on everyone to find out what happened to Shannon. As I said before, social pressure and stress have been shown to have an impact on memory formation."

"Are these true memories that form under these circumstances?"

"I don't doubt that the witnesses believe them, if that's what you mean. They weren't intentionally lying if they swore to the truth of them under oath."

"Thank you, doctor. That's all I have for now." Barry sat down.

Fred rose for cross-examination. He didn't have any great

ideas for debunking the science. He would have to try an attack on the man.

"You're a paid expert witness, correct?"

"Yes. I was retained by the defense."

"In fact, you have a business testifying as an expert witness, don't you?"

"I do. It's a part-time business that I do in conjunction with my part-time clinical work."

"How many hours per week do you devote to your clinical work?"

"Less than ten. About one day per week."

"And how many days do you devote to your expert witness business? Four?"

"It's usually less."

"So, when you testified earlier that you have a part-time clinical practice, you weren't telling us the whole truth, were you?"

Lapitas rocked side to side, sliding forward in his seat. "I wasn't trying to mislead anybody."

"Okay. In the interest of full disclosure, what percentage of your income do you derive from your business as an expert witness?"

"It's probably ninety percent."

"Because it's lucrative to be an expert witness, isn't it?"

"It can be."

"How much is the defense paying you for your testimony today?"

"Three hundred dollars per hour."

"And they also paid your travel expenses, correct?"

"Yes."

"So, what do you expect the total bill for your participation in this case to be all said and done?"

"About ten thousand dollars, maybe more."

"For about thirty hours of work?"

"It's likely more time than that. My billing rate is lower for review and preparation time."

"But, for that amount of money, you had better support the

defense theory, hadn't you?"

"I'm just here to educate the jury."

"Okay. Let's talk about that. How many times have you testified in the past ten years?"

"I don't know. More than a hundred."

"Have you ever been retained by the prosecution?"

"No, but I have been retained by plaintiffs in civil suits."

"But, most of your cases are criminal cases, aren't they?"

"That's true."

"And, again, you always testify for the defense?"

"Yes."

"Because they pay you to take their side, right?"

"No. Well, yes, but—"

"Thank you, doctor. That's all I have."

Barry rose for redirect.

"Dr. Lapitas, if you were asked by the prosecution to testify about memory in a criminal case, would you?"

"Yes, I would. I see my role as educating the court and the jury. Most of the research on memory runs counter to what people generally believe about how the human memory works. And our entire legal system was founded on the premise that the human memory is reliable. It's not."

"Why did you decide to become an expert witness?"

Fred knew Barry had recovered ground with his cross-examination. He wasn't going to let the defense win any more of it back. He stood. "Objection, beyond the scope of cross."

"Sustained," the judge said.

"Thank you, doctor," Barry said.

The court called a recess. Fred hoped the jurors had seen Lapitas for what he was—smoke and mirrors, a paid propagandist, nothing more.

CASSIE WAS glad for the opportunity to speak with Dr. Lapitas when he came into the conference room to introduce himself.

"Thank you for testifying," she said.

"I hope it was enough to help your son."

Keenan interrupted. "Doctor, why did you leave your job as a professor and become an expert witness?"

"Because I kept getting more and more requests from defense attorneys to testify. I realized that there was a need to educate the system. I couldn't maintain a full-time professorship and be gone all the time testifying, so I decided that it was time to turn the research over to the younger, more enthusiastic researchers. I feel good about what I do."

"Do you ever worry that you'll help get someone off who's actually guilty?" Keenan said.

"Never. It's ultimately up to the jury to decide whether there's enough evidence to convict. I only offer them a perspective on the eyewitness testimony. Besides, DNA has already proven that we've convicted far too many innocent people based on mistaken eyewitness testimony. I hate to think how many innocent people were probably executed. If one guilty person goes free here and there, it's still better than the alternative."

"Well, your testimony was an eye-opener for me," Cassie said. "I have to confess that when I first heard there were witnesses to an assault, I was upset with Keenan. I hoped it was a misunderstanding, that maybe he was unintentionally rough with Shannon. He kept denying that he ever laid a hand on her, and it would have been so out of character. I wanted to believe him, but it was hard. Now, I'm mad at myself for ever doubting him." She hoped Keenan would forgive her honesty.

"Most people don't realize that our justice system is outdated. It was created in a time when information spread more slowly. The internet and social media have taken over the way most people acquire information, so misinformation now spreads with lightning speed. We were convicting innocent people before Facebook and Twitter. Now, it's virtually impossible to tell what's true, that is, what people actually experienced, from what they believe they remember. Unless they're off the grid."

"It's like an invasive species," Cassie said. Dr. Lapitas looked puzzled, so she explained. "A single purple loosestrife seed can turn a marsh into a meadow of loosestrife. It spreads aggressively and chokes out competing plants. Before long the habitat changes and the wetland creatures migrate or die-off. What's left is a sea of purple flowers. It doesn't matter that it was once a marsh because it never will be again."

Lapitas' expression became a half-smile before he nodded. "I like that—misinformation invading the truth. All from a single seed." Lapitas wished them luck before he excused himself.

The break was only fifteen minutes, so they were soon back in their seats. Cassie felt the best she had felt since the trial had started. Dr Lapitas had been a great witness. She hoped the rest of the defense witnesses would have a cumulative effect and they would get to the end of the defense evidence feeling confident.

Next, Barry called Ken Brayton to the stand, and he was sworn.

"Good afternoon," Barry said. "Where are you from?"

"Chapel Hill, North Carolina."

"Where do you go to school?"

"Masterson College."

"What year are you in?"

"I'm a sophomore."

"Do you know Keenan Brody?"

"Only because of what I read in the papers and on the internet."

"So, you're not friends?"

"Nope."

"Ever even met him?"

"I don't think so."

"Did you know Shannon Dawson?"

"Yes, I did."

"How did you know her?"

"She sat with me and my girlfriend in cell biology freshman year. She was April's lab partner."

"Who is April?"

"Sorry. I'm nervous. April was my girlfriend last year."

"Where were you on the evening of Friday, December 20, 2013?"

"I went to a party on Maple Street."

"What was the party like?"

"It was a keg party."

"How many people were there?"

"It's hard to say. When I was there, there were at least sixty or seventy. But, people were coming and going all night."

"What time were you there?"

"I got there around ten o'clock and left around eleven o'clock."

"Did you see Shannon Dawson at that party?"

"I did."

"How did she appear?"

"She was drunk."

Fred jumped up. "Objection, Your Honor, there's no foundation."

"I'll lay a foundation," Barry responded.

"As long as you do, Mr. Densmore." The judge sounded impatient.

"What makes you say that?" Barry asked the witness.

"I know what drunk people look like. I've been around plenty of them. She was acting drunk. Loud, sloppy, having a good time."

"Did you talk to her?"

"Yeah. I remember she was ranting about how hard the cell biology final was. I remember because I was also worried about my grade, and I realized the next week that I was probably one of the last people to talk to her."

"Were you drinking that night?"

"No, sir. I don't drink."

"Do you ever drink?"

"I can't. I have diabetes. I was born with it. I've always had to be careful about what I eat and drink."

"On a scale of one to ten, where ten is unconscious, how

drunk was Shannon Dawson?"

"She was at least an eight."

"At approximately what time?"

"At around ten thirty."

"What about the rest of the party-goers?"

"Objection, calls for speculation. He's already said there were a lot of people there."

"Sustained."

"Did you notice who Shannon was with?"

"She was with a group of girls."

"Did you know any of them?"

"I recognized them, but I don't think I knew them."

"Can you describe how they were acting?"

"I think they were all drinking. As far as I know, I was the only one at the party who wasn't."

"Were they drunk?"

"I can't say for sure because I don't know how they were normally. But almost everyone there was celebrating the end of finals."

"Thank you. That's all I have."

The prosecutor rose. "Your Honor? Can I request a brief recess?"

"It's just about lunch time. Why don't you begin your cross-examination after lunch?"

"Thank you, Your Honor."

As soon as the jurors were out of the room, the prosecutor signaled to Officer Shores. Cassie and Greg came forward to meet Keenan.

"What was that about?" Keenan asked Barry.

"I think he wants dirt on Ken Brayton."

"Is he going to find any?"

"I don't know. I hope to hell not."

Everyone was quiet while Cassie passed out tuna salad sandwiches. She was trying to vary the lunch menu, like she did when they used to go camping as a family. But somehow it felt wrong to put effort into lunch when the occasions was so somber. Of course, people always put on big spreads for funerals too. Maybe that's what was wrong with this situation. It felt too much like a funeral lunch.

BARRY TOOK a bite of his tuna sandwich. He hadn't realized how hungry he was. As soon as everyone else was eating, he started his pitch. "I know we've been over this, but after the next witness, I think we should rest and give it to the jury. My gut says there's enough reasonable doubt there. We have a good shot at a not guilty verdict. I think it would be a mistake for Keenan to testify."

Keenan set down his sandwich. "But you told me right from the beginning that it would be my choice."

"It is, it has to be. But I have experience with this situation. We've given them enough that they have to be questioning the validity of the state's evidence."

"But they need to hear it from me that I didn't do it."

"I can talk about it during closing arguments. I can explain it."

"No. They'll always wonder if I had something to hide if I don't testify."

Barry looked pleadingly at Cassie and Greg. "Please. I know you're overwhelmed right now, but my gut says this is a mistake."

Keenan tossed the rest of his sandwich in the trash. "And my gut says they're going to convict me. I have to try to stop it."

Cassie buried her head against Greg's shoulder. Greg was staring at the wall. Barry looked at them, willing them to intervene. After a minute, he said, "Okay, but don't say I didn't warn you."

After lunch, Ken Brayton was reinstalled on the witness stand before the jury came back into the room.

Once the jury was seated, Fred approached Ken for cross-examination.

"You don't drink at all? Ever?"

"No, sir."

"But you went to a party where everyone was drinking?"

"Yes, sir."

"But you didn't need to drink because you were smoking marijuana, right?"

Ken looked uncomfortable. "I think I want to take the Fifth."

"Attorneys approach," the judge said. Barry and Fred went to the judge's bench and the white noise filled the courtroom. It was a brief conversation that went exactly as Barry expected it would. A minute later they were back at their respective tables.

"Mr. Brayton," the judge said, "the prosecutor has granted you immunity from prosecution. You are hereby compelled to answer."

Ken Brayton looked like he was going to vomit.

Dutton rose. "I'll repeat the question. Were you smoking marijuana at the party?"

"I was."

"How much marijuana did you smoke that night?"

"I'm not sure."

"Was it two joints or three joints? Or were you using a pipe?"

"We were passing around joints. I really can't say how much I smoked."

"Then it could have been a lot, right?"

"It wasn't that much."

"How often do you smoke marijuana?"

"Objection, relevance," Barry said.

"It's relevant to his memory," Fred said.

"I'll allow it," the judge said.

Fred resumed. "I repeat: how often do you smoke marijuana?"

"On weekends."

"Both days?"

"Sometimes."

"Are you familiar with the studies that show that long-term marijuana use can affect your memory?"

Barry stood. "Objection. He's not an expert medical witness."

"Sustained," the judge said.

"When you use marijuana, how do you feel?"

"Good. Relaxed."

"Isn't it true that, when you smoke marijuana, you get so relaxed that you lose touch with reality?"

"I don't know."

"And when you smoke marijuana, you don't pay as much attention to what's going on around you, do you?"

"I don't know, maybe."

"You know it's illegal to drive while you're under the influence of marijuana, don't you?"

"Yes."

"Because it impairs your ability to drive, right?"

"I guess."

"And you were definitely impaired when you were at that party, weren't you?"

"I don't think so."

Fred sat down and Barry immediately stood.

"What is your major at Masterson?"

"Neuroscience."

"What are your plans after graduation?"

"Objection. Relevance."

"I'm trying to rehabilitate the attack on the witness' memory."

"I'll allow it."

"What are your career goals?"

"I'm hoping to go to medical school."

"Are your grades good enough?"

"My GPA is three point nine."

"You ever experience any memory problems from your marijuana use?"

"No, sir."

"Do you have any doubts about your earlier testimony?"

"No, sir. Shannon was definitely drunk off her ass."

The look he gave the prosecutor as he exited the courtroom was definitely defiance. Barry hoped the jury didn't notice.

Barry called Greg Brody next. Fred objected, and there was a bench conference. While white noise filled the room, the attorneys argued.

"He can't testify," Fred said. "He's been sitting through the whole trial."

"He was on the witness list, and you didn't ask to have him sequestered," Barry said. "Besides, he's not going to testify about anything that's already been said."

"Then I object on the grounds of relevance."

"It's as relevant as Jack Dawson's testimony was."

The judge nodded. "He has a point. I'll allow the testimony. You can address any issues on cross, Mr. Dutton."

Barry beckoned Greg Brody forward and he was sworn.

"What is your relationship to the defendant?" Barry said.

"He's my son."

"Tell us about Keenan."

"He's our second child. He's always been a good kid. He loves to play hockey."

"About that—why hockey?"

"I think he got his love of the sport from me."

"You played?"

"Yes, I played for UVM. A long time ago."

"So, you don't find the game violent?"

"Checking may appear to be violent to the fans, but there are rules that make it safe for the participants." Greg turned to face the jury. "Keenan is not a violent person. He never has been. It's just not in his character."

"And what do you do now, Dr. Brody?"

"I'm a large animal veterinarian."

Barry produced a document from the counsel table. "I'm showing you Defense Exhibit E Can you tell the jury what that it?"

"It's a copy of our family cell phone bill from last December."

"Where did you get it?"

"I requested it from Sprint."

"What does it show?"

"It shows that Keenan made three calls to Shannon Dawson's cell phone on the morning of December twenty-first and then four more the next day."

"Thank you."

Fred rose, but did not leave the counsel table.

"Do you love your son, Dr. Brody?"

"I do."

"And you would do or say just about anything to keep him out of jail, wouldn't you?"

"I imagine so."

"I'm sure you would. That's all."

After Keenan's father had left the witness stand, Barry pushed the mute button on the microphone on the table and turned to Keenan.

"It's now or never. I still vote for never."

KEENAN MADE his way to the witness stand. He had no idea whether they would believe him, but he knew he had to testify. The problem was that, if he were them, he would probably convict him based on what he had heard during the trial.

Dr. Lapitas had been great, but there was just so much circumstantial evidence. He needed to explain as much of it as he could. They needed to hear from him that he didn't do this thing. They needed to hear from him that he had loved Shannon too much to ever hurt her. He hoped they would believe him.

He knew what he was supposed to do. Barry had reluctantly coached him. Very reluctantly. Which was part of why he was so nervous. He could feel everyone watching him, judging him. He had never felt so self-conscious in his life.

He raised his right hand and swore to tell the truth.

As rehearsed, Barry started with a few background questions, then got quickly to the meat of the testimony. They didn't want to keep him on the stand any longer than necessary.

"Tell us about Shannon Dawson," Barry said.

"She was beautiful and vibrant." Without meaning to, Keenan started to cry. "And I loved her."

"Tell us about the last night you saw Shannon."

"I spoke to her on the phone. She said she had something to tell me, but she needed to do it in person."

"Did you know what she needed to tell you?"

"I suspected she was planning to break up with me, but I wasn't sure. I mean, there's not a lot of things you have to tell someone in person."

"So, what did you do?"

"I decided to go to the party she was going to, see if I could run into her."

"Did you run into her?"

"Yes, sir."

"What did you observe?"

"She was drunk."

"How did you know she was drunk?"

"She was slurring her words, saying things that didn't make sense. I could smell the alcohol on her breath. I don't know, she was just acting drunk."

"What did you do after you saw Shannon?"

"I knew she had driven to the party because I had passed her car on the way in. I wanted to make sure she didn't drive home, so I asked for her keys."

"Did she give them to you?"

"Not at first. She got angry."

"What did you do?"

"I tried to calm her down."

"How?"

"I told her that I cared about her and I tried to hug her."

"Did it work?"

"It didn't exactly calm her down, but it convinced her to hand over the car keys."

"You said it didn't calm her down, what made you think that?"

"After she gave me the keys, she ran off."

"Did you follow her?"

"No, sir."

"What did you do?"

"I waited to see if she would come back."

"How long did you wait?"

"I don't know. It felt like a while, maybe fifteen minutes, but it could have been less."

"Did she come back?"

"If she did, I never saw her. In fact, I never saw her again after that."

"What did you do next?"

"I drove her car back to her dorm and walked home."

"Why did you do that?"

"I couldn't find Shannon's friends, so I was pretty sure they'd left. I knew she had a flight home the next day, and that there was something we needed to talk about. I figured it would make things easier if I drove her car back to the dorm for her. I was going to give her the keys when I saw her on Saturday."

"You said there was something you needed to talk about. When you saw Shannon, did she give you any idea what it was that she needed to tell you in person?"

"No, she never did."

"For the record, did you ever hit Shannon Dawson?"

"No."

"Did you ever grab her?"

"No, not other than the hugging, that is."

"Did you physically hurt her in any way?"

"No."

"Did you kill her?"

"No, I didn't."

"What did you do the next day?"

"I called her three times. I texted her twice. And I walked over to her dorm to return her keys. When I couldn't reach her, I put her keys in my desk and went home."

The prosecutor rose for cross-examination. Barry had warned Keenan that this was when things would get rough. Keenan took a deep breath and tried to look in the eye of the man whose only goal at the moment was to make him look guilty. Dutton's look reminded him of an alligator slinking through dark waters toward its prey—cold, calculating and focused. Supremely focused.

"You testified that Shannon told you she had something important to tell you, right?"

"Yes."

"Something that needed to be said in person, right?"

"Yes."

"So, you went looking for her, true?"

"Well, like I said, I went out hoping to run into her."

"You knew where she was going, right?"

"Yes."

"That's not really running into someone if you know where they're going and you go to the same place, is it?"

"That's how I thought of it."

"Or perhaps you're using that terminology because that's what you told Officer Shores the first time he questioned you, isn't it?"

"I don't recall."

"Isn't it true that the first time you spoke with Officer Shores, you told him you had run into Shannon on the night she disappeared?"

"I may have."

"I'm going to show you what's been marked as Exhibit 3. Please tell the jury what that is."

"It's a transcript of an interview."

"Whose interview?"

"My interview with Officer Shores."

"Why don't you read page three to yourself."

"Okay."

"Did you or did you not tell Officer Shores you 'ran into' Shannon Dawson the night she disappeared?"

"I did."

"And, it's different from what you told Evan Halliday, isn't it?"

"I'm not sure."

"You told Evan you went looking for Shannon that night, didn't you?"

"I might have."

"Let's see if we can't refresh your recollection again. Let me show you Exhibit 9. Can you please tell the jury what that is?"

"It's a transcript of my conversation with Evan Halliday."

"Please have a look at page 8 and then tell us what you told Evan Halliday about that night."

"I told him I went looking for Shannon."

"Okay. So, the first time you spoke to Officer Shores, you were downplaying your involvement, weren't you?"

"I don't know."

"Well, when he asked about your relationship with Shannon, isn't it true you denied she was your girlfriend?"

"Not really."

"Let me show you Exhibit 3 again. Isn't it true that your exact words to the officer were, 'She wasn't really my girlfriend?'"

"Yes."

"But she was your girlfriend, wasn't she?"

"I guess so."

"So you were lying to Officer Shores, weren't you?"

"I didn't mean to."

Dutton paused, leaving the words hanging. "Where did you go looking for Shannon on that Friday night?"

"To the party on Maple Street."

"Alone?"

"Yes."

"Because you weren't going to socialize, were you?"

"No, I was hoping to see Shannon."

"Because you were angry, weren't you?"

"I wasn't angry."

"Oh, right. You told Officer Shores you were ticked, but you were downplaying that too, weren't you?"

"No."

"Or maybe you weren't angry at first, but you were upset when you found out that Shannon had another boyfriend, right?"

"I didn't find out about Jake until weeks later. So, no, I wasn't upset."

"Okay, if you weren't upset, then why go looking for her?"

"I wanted to talk to her, find out what she had to say to me."

"But you knew it wasn't good news, didn't you?"

"I suspected. But I didn't know what it was."

"So, you were concerned enough that you went looking for her, but you weren't upset?"

"Yes."

"So, why not wait? You said you were planning to see her on Saturday before she left."

"I just wanted to know for sure what she had to tell me."

"So you decided to make her tell you, right?"

"No."

"You walked by yourself across campus to the party, right?"

"Yes."

"How long a walk was that?"

"About fifteen minutes."

"You spent that fifteen minutes getting angrier and angrier, didn't you?"

"No."

"Walking to Maple Street. That's a pretty memorable thing, isn't it?"

"I suppose."

"But when Officer Shores asked you where the party was less than a week later, you claimed that you didn't remember, didn't you?"

"Yes."

"That was one more lie you told to Officer Shores the first time he called you, wasn't it?"

"Yes."

Dutton paused for effect.

Keenan was kicking himself. He knew he should have told the officer the truth about the party the first time they spoke. But like everybody else, he didn't want to rat out the hosts. In retrospect, it was stupid. How was he supposed to know that less than a year later he would be sitting in this courtroom and what he thought was a random conversation would be evidence against him?

The prosecutor continued, getting closer for his attack.

"When Officer Shores searched your room, he found

Shannon's keys, right?"

"Yes."

"That might have been a good time to mention that you took the keys to keep her from driving if that had really been true, wouldn't it?"

"Yes, but . . ." Keenan brought his hands to his forehead, but brought them down suddenly when he realized it might make him look guilty.

"But, you didn't do that, did you?"

"No."

"Because you hadn't yet thought of that explanation, right?"

"No, it wasn't like that. You had to have been there."

Keenan remembered when Officer Shores had showed up at his room. When he recognized the officer waiting there, he had braced himself for bad news. But instead, the guy was in his face again, trying to make him look guilty for not letting him search Keenan's room. Keenan hadn't wanted to sign the consent form, but he was afraid if he didn't it would look like he had something to hide. He had forgotten completely about the keys. With the holidays and Shannon's disappearance, the keys had just been pushed from his mind.

Unfortunately, the prosecutor wasn't done with him.

"Isn't it true that the first time you told Officer Shores you were concerned about Shannon's ability to drive that night was on December thirtieth, ten days after her disappearance and the fourth time you spoke with the officer?"

"I think so."

Dutton nodded knowingly. "Okay. After you walked to Maple Street that night, you found Shannon, right?"

"Yes."

"And she told you about Jake, right?"

Barry stood. "Objection. Asked and answered."

Keenan answered anyway. "No, she did not tell me about Jake." His voice sounded shrill, angry, which was probably why his lawyer had not wanted him to answer. He needed to remember to keep his answers as short as possible.

"Sustained," the judge said, belatedly.

"You got upset, didn't you?"

"No."

"You yelled at her, didn't you?"

"No." Keenan tried to keep his voice even like Barry coached him, but it was getting harder and harder.

"You got physical with her, didn't you?"

"No."

"You grabbed her, didn't you?"

"I hugged her, that was all."

"And she ran off. Isn't that what you said?"

"She left quickly."

"She ran away from you, didn't she?"

"Maybe."

"Because she was scared of you, wasn't she?"

"Objection. Speculation."

"Sustained."

"And you followed her, didn't you?"

"No." Keenan shook his head.

"And you continued the fight, right?"

"No."

"And you hit her, didn't you?"

"No."

"Punched her on the left cheek, right?"

"No." Keenan was still shaking his head. He started crying.

"And she went down." Dutton paused. "And she hit her head, didn't she?"

"I don't know. I wasn't there."

"You knew you'd be in trouble for killing her, so you used her car to move her body, right?"

"No."

"You dumped her in the river, didn't you?"

"No."

"Then you drove her car back to campus, right?"

"I drove the car, but not the rest of it."

"That's right. You drove her car." The prosecutor started to sit. "One last question. What number is your hockey jersey?"

"Five," Keenan said. What difference did that make?

Dutton nodded and sat down.

Keenan looked pleadingly at Barry, whose face was grim as he stood for redirect.

"Why didn't you tell Officer Shores the whole story right up front?"

"I don't know. Even in the beginning, it felt like I was on the defensive. Then, when he came to my house on Christmas Eve, he actually accused me of doing something to Shannon. I couldn't even talk to him at that point."

"Why not?"

"It felt like he was accusing me of murder. Which it turns out he was."

"Why did you let Officer Shores search your dorm room?"

"I was trying to be cooperative."

"Were you concerned he would find Shannon's keys?"

"No, I really had forgotten about them."

"Why didn't you give the officer an explanation at that time?"

"He kept accusing me, twisting things. I didn't know what to do, but I didn't feel comfortable talking to him."

After Keenan had left the witness stand, Barry announced that the defense rested.

"Do you plan to present any rebuttal evidence, Mr. Dutton?"

"I do, Your Honor. And I need a few minutes to set up the AV equipment."

"Very well. We'll take a ten-minute break."

Barry and Keenan both used the bathroom before meeting back at the counsel table.

"I made it worse, didn't I?" Keenan said as they were washing their hands. He looked at Barry in the mirror.

"There's no way to know," Barry said without looking up. "What's done is done. Don't beat yourself up."

Keenan didn't believe him. "Who else is he going to use for a witness?"

"I don't know. I feel like I should, but I don't know what's coming."

CHAPTER 61
Thursday, September 18, 2014

FRED KNEW he was on shaky ground with his rebuttal, but he also knew that it would have a big impact if he got away with it. It had come to him while Greg Brody was testifying. He was surprised that Barry had made such a big mistake, a rookie mistake really, letting the dad talk about how nonviolent the son was. As testimony, it wasn't particularly believable, and it had opened the door for Fred's next move. He recalled Greta Paraiso.

"Ms. Paraiso, I'll remind you that you're still under oath," the judge said.

Greta bit her lip and nodded.

Fred began. "Ms. Paraiso, did you attend a Masterson College hockey game on November first of last year?"

"I did."

"What did you observe at that game?"

"I saw Keenan Brody get into a fight with a player from the other team."

"I'm showing you what is marked as State's Exhibit 10. What is this?"

"It's a video of part of that game."

"And have you watched that video?"

"Yes."

"And does it accurately portray what you observed?"

"Yes, it does."

"With the court's permission, I'd like to show the video to the jury."

Barry's voice boomed. "Objection, Your Honor."

The white noise came on and the judge beckoned the attorneys to the bench.

Barry was clearly pissed. "I have never seen this video. It was not included in any of the discovery I got. I want it excluded as a discovery violation."

"Is that true, Mr. Dutton?"

"Yes, Your Honor. But I only got the video in the last hour. I couldn't have turned it over because I didn't have it. I sent Officer Shores out during lunch to track it down after the defendant's father testified. I remembered Ms. Paraiso mentioned the incident in her deposition, so I brought her back. I had Officer Shores show her the video a few minutes ago."

"Mr. Densmore, did the witness mention the fight during her deposition?"

Barry shook his head slowly. "Possibly. I'd have to review the transcripts."

"Well then, I'm going to allow it. You knew about the fight even if you didn't have a copy of the video."

"But, Your Honor, it's more prejudicial than probative. There are multiple grounds for excluding the video. It's not even relevant. Hockey's a game, a sport. Not real life."

"You opened the door, Mr. Densmore. Let's watch the video."

Barry tried again, but despite trying the judge's patience, he couldn't keep the video out of evidence. He did, however, convince the judge to give a limiting instruction to the jury explaining that participants of contact sports consent to physical contact, so a fight on the ice wasn't necessarily an assault. For all the good it would do. The instruction would be buried in the post-trial boilerplate presented to the jury. Fred had to work very hard not to smile as he walked back to the counsel table and pressed the play button on the laptop.

The video was perfect. Dustin had gotten it from the archives at the college athletics office. Apparently, they kept videos of all the hockey games. It clearly showed Masterson

Number 5 in a brawl with Number 12 from the other team. The jury seemed enthralled by the graphic display.

It was three o'clock when the judge announced that the evidence was closed. He asked the jurors if anyone had a problem with staying late. When nobody objected, he said, "We'll take a fifteen-minute recess and return for closing arguments. I'd like the jury to begin their deliberations today."

BARRY WAS pissed. Mostly at himself. It was the obvious move. And he had missed it. How could he not have his head in the game when the stakes were so high? He used the fifteen minutes to splash some water on his face and go over his notes for the closing argument. It was more important than ever that the jury not see how frazzled he was. He wished he had longer to regroup.

Fred looked confident when he walked over to stand in front of the jury. Of course he did. He had ended the trial with an impressive and memorable display. Fuck!

Fred captivated the jury when he started talking. "Shannon Dawson was only eighteen years old when her life was ended. It was a life full of promise because, in her eighteen short years, Shannon had accomplished much. Here is a picture of Shannon in life." Fred clicked a remote and Shannon's prom picture appeared on the large screen. "She was an impressive figure skater, a brilliant student, a friend, a daughter. If her life had not been so tragically cut short, she likely would have become a doctor, like her father, and probably, some day, a mother herself. She would have given her parents even more reasons to be proud of their only child." Fred paused and looked toward Shannon's parents, who looked even more wilted than they had at the beginning of the trial. "But none of that is going to happen. None of Shannon's tremendous potential will ever be realized, because on December 20, 2013, her life came to an end in a few moments of uncontrollable rage."

"And here again is a picture of Shannon in death." Fred clicked the remote and the picture changed. "I apologize that it's disturbing."

"Shannon wasn't perfect. None of us are. Especially when we're only eighteen years of age and inexperienced in the ways of love. She made the mistake of falling in love with two young men at the same time. But that mistake should not have cost her her life.

"And yet it did. Because when the defendant found out he wasn't her only suitor, that he was not the only one she had been intimate with, he lost control.

"Ladies and gentlemen, the burden of proof is on the government in this case. As it should be. The judge will instruct you that all we had to do was present evidence of the defendant's guilt beyond a reasonable doubt. We have done that and more.

"You heard from three witnesses to the defendant's rage. Shannon's friends, Greta, Jenna, and Heather, described an angry defendant, grabbing and hitting, and Shannon fleeing. Were they reluctant witnesses, less than forthright with the police during their initial interviews? Probably. Does that mean that they inadvertently fabricated the testimony that helps establish the defendant's guilt? All three of them? It defies the odds. It's not reasonable to believe. Especially after watching the videotape of the defendant fighting with another hockey player. After you all saw the violence he's capable of.

"The defendant, on the other hand, his story has been inconsistent since the police first questioned him. Shannon wasn't his girlfriend . . . or she was. He ran into her . . . or he went looking for her. He forgot he had her keys . . . or he had them because he took them from her to keep her from driving. Which was it?

"And how did he know she was dead long before her body was found?" Fred paused here and took a sip of water. He was probably doing some mental organization, making sure he had hit all the highlights, but the act made him appear casual and highlighted his question at the same time. Well played, Barry thought.

"You also heard from the medical examiner. That evidence is clear. Shannon received two injuries to the head. The medical examiner has seen these types of injuries before. Lots of times. It's a common combination: a blow to the face delivered by a right-handed person, followed by a skull fracture when the person falls. These injuries are common in barroom brawls. And domestic violence cases. And you may have noticed from the hockey video that the defendant has a strong right hook.

"The evidence may be circumstantial, but it's overwhelming. The defendant was the last one to see Shannon Dawson alive. They had a fight in a public setting. She left. He followed her. Her keys were found in his dorm room. His fingerprints were found on the driver's side of her car. Her hair was found in the trunk. He lied to the police about his relationship with Shannon and about what happened that night. Innocent people have no reason to lie to the police.

"The defendant is a smart kid. He had to be to get into Masterson College. He had explanations for some of the evidence and his inconsistencies. But he also had the advantage of sitting in the courtroom, listening to the other witnesses. He had the opportunity to tailor his testimony to fit the evidence. It sounded rehearsed, desperate. Which, of course, he is. He's desperate to have a future, something that he denied Shannon of in a fit of jealous rage.

"Thank you."

This was it. Barry's last chance to turn this around. His last chance to talk to the jury before they decided Keenan's fate. He stood slowly and started talking as he made his way to the jury box.

"The prosecution has come up with a pretty compelling theory of how Shannon Dawson died. And based on the evidence you heard, it is one possible explanation. But there are others that would fit the exact same evidence.

"You heard evidence that Shannon Dawson was intoxicated on the night she disappeared and that she was an inexperienced drinker. You may also recall that the medical examiner was unable to determine her blood alcohol content.

"What if Shannon Dawson left the party by herself? Nobody actually saw her with my client after the party. What if they really did part ways at the house on Maple Street?

"If Shannon was heavily intoxicated, she could well have fallen into the cold water. All on her own. The medical examiner couldn't tell you for sure whether she drowned first or got the head injuries first. If she drowned first, then there is no way my client could have had anything to do with her death. That's a reasonable doubt.

"The medical examiner tried to argue against that doubt, but you may have noticed her argument was not logical. She believed that the death wasn't accidental because there were no witnesses. But what if the accidental death actually occurred because there were no witnesses? She couldn't tell you unequivocally whether the drowning or the head injury came first.

"It's just like the proverbial chicken or egg. We can't answer the chicken or egg question beyond a reasonable doubt. And you can't answer the head trauma or drowning question beyond a reasonable doubt. Circular logic notwithstanding, the manslaughter charge just wasn't proven by any standard, especially not beyond a reasonable doubt.

"The problem with the assault charge is similar. You heard from Dr. Lapitas how memories are formed. The human memory is incredibly unreliable. If you consider everything that Dr. Lapitas taught us about memory, you have to ask the question: Which came first? The suspect? Or the witnesses?

"In the first round of interviews, there was not a single witness who reported seeing my client assault Shannon Dawson. At that point, Shannon had been missing for several days. An assault just prior to her disappearance would have been highly relevant. But not a single one of the people interviewed mentioned it. The only one who used words like 'fight' or 'argument' was Officer Shores. And, as Dr. Lapitas explained, when Shores mentioned them, the ideas were planted. Those ideas spread. Through word of mouth. Through social media. And weeks later, when Officer Shores went back and interviewed the witnesses again, lo and behold, this time they remembered an altercation. And by asking leading questions, Officer Shores let the students know what an altercation might have looked like. Shores asked if Shannon was grabbed and hit. And a few students remembered that she was grabbed and hit. Most of them didn't because she wasn't. At a party full of people, only three people remember an incident resembling an assault.

"That's because, ladies and gentlemen, there was no assault. Just like there was no manslaughter. The witnesses now have memories of a fictitious assault because, like almost all human beings, their memories are imperfect. Dr. Lapitas described some interesting studies on human memory. Those studies prove that witnesses are frequently wrong. It doesn't make them liars. It just makes them human.

"And then there's the issue of motive. The prosecution paints a picture of Keenan as a jealous boyfriend. But there's one problem with the jealousy angle. He didn't know about Shannon and Jake. He told you he didn't know. And there's no direct evidence he did. Sure, there's evidence that Shannon was planning to tell Keenan. But there's also evidence that she didn't want to, that she'd been procrastinating, avoiding a confrontation. Without real proof of jealousy, there's no motive for anything. Not a homicide. Not even an assault.

"We may never know how this tragedy came about. And yet, the prosecutor has asked you to believe his version beyond a reasonable doubt. Because that's his burden: to prove what happened beyond a reasonable doubt. The prosecution did not meet its burden.

"There are too many unanswered questions. How come nobody saw Keenan and Shannon together after the party? Why weren't there more witnesses to the alleged assault? Why would Keenan go looking for Shannon the next day if he knew she was already dead? He sent her texts. He called her. He called her a lot during the first day she was missing. Because he didn't know she was missing. Because he didn't kill her. Just like he didn't assault her.

"He had no idea she was missing until Officer Shores told him on the phone. And, even then, he hoped there was an explanation. That Shannon was alive. But, when Officer Shores came to Keenan's home on Christmas Eve and told him that he, Keenan, was the last person to speak to Shannon, Keenan realized it was hopeless. It struck him. A girl like Shannon would not go days without using her phone. The phone that was always with her. The phone that she used constantly. If she wasn't using that phone, she was dead. And so, he stated the obvious. 'She's dead.' It wasn't an admission. It was merely stating the obvious. Officer Shores admitted he suspected the same thing himself.

"That's frequently the problem with police investigations. If the police have a suspect, it's not hard to make a case against that suspect. As Dr. Lapitas explained, all they have to do is ask the right questions, and they can create witnesses who remember events exactly the way the police want them remembered. It's not hard.

"It's actually quite easy to accuse innocent people of crimes. Fortunately, as jurors, you have the ability to prevent further injustice.

"What happened to Shannon Dawson, whatever that was, was a tragedy. But convicting Keenan Brody of a crime he did not commit would also be tragic. Unlike the police, you don't need to find someone to blame."

It was time to sit down, but Barry hesitated. He wanted to talk about the fight tape, but he couldn't think of a good way to do it. It was probably better to not bring any more attention to it. Was there anything he had forgotten to tell them? His mind was a blank. He looked at them all one more time before turning.

As soon as Barry sat down, Fred was up, clearly ready for his rebuttal.

"There aren't really any unanswered questions here. Just like there is no *reasonable* doubt. The medical examiner was clear. There may not be a medical test for drowning, but in her expert opinion, head trauma likely contributed to Shannon's death. And that trauma was consistent with a blow to the head, just like countless others she's seen." Fred gestured with his fist, a mock punch. "A blow to the cheek, followed by a fall and a hit to the back of the head. You've seen the defendant punch."

"There were no witnesses to Shannon's death because the defendant was smart. He was careful not to be seen. Just like he was smart by dumping Shannon in the river, knowing that the direct forensic evidence linking him to the homicide would be lost.

"Just like he was smart enough to try to cover his trail with text messages and phone calls. Those were smart moves that might have led the police investigation away from the defendant if the rest of the evidence didn't point in his direction.

"But we have three witnesses to the assault. Three witnesses who saw essentially the same thing. Their memories are slightly different. But that just proves they weren't coached.

"Sure, there were lots of people at the party. But they were there to celebrate the end of the semester. They weren't watching Keenan and Shannon argue. They weren't watching him grab her and hit her. They weren't watching him follow her away from the party. Fortunately, three people were paying attention. Three people saw the assault. They saw Keenan use enough force to hurt Shannon. They saw her leave. They saw him follow.

"The rest of the evidence may be circumstantial, but it is compelling. Fingerprints don't lie. And innocent people don't minimize their involvement to the police.

"Olivia and Jack Dawson won't get to spend any more Christmases with their only daughter." Fred looked at the Dawsons one last time. "But they will rest better after you bring her killer to justice.

"Thank you."

PART III
Judgment

CHAPTER 63
Thursday, September 18, 2014

OLIVIA STOOD in the gallery with her husband and watched the jury file out of the courtroom. The instructions to the jury had seemed tedious, too picayune. She hoped the jury wouldn't get so bogged down in technicalities that they lost sight of the big picture—that her daughter had been murdered.

After the judge had given them permission to sit, she reached over and put her hand on top of Jack's. He flinched, but she left her hand there anyway. She needed him right now, just like she had needed him during those early months after Shannon was murdered. He hadn't been there for her then. He was damn well going to be here for her now. The judge gave instructions to the attorneys and then everyone was told to stand again while the judge left. Jack pulled his hand out from under hers as he stood. The noise level in the courtroom started as a few lone voices, then became a din. Olivia watched as people trickled away. She wasn't sure what to do next, so she stood there feeling awkward.

"Is he going to get away with it?" Olivia turned toward Jack.

He just shook his head. After a minute, he said, "Whatever they do, it won't bring her back . . . I'm not sure it matters what they do."

"How can you say that? Don't you want justice for Shannon?"

Jack paused. "Of course," he said.

Olivia gritted her teeth. She was saved from responding by

Fred Dutton's approach. He showed them into a mini conference room near the courtroom.

"How are you both holding up?" Dutton asked.

"This was even harder than I expected it to be," Olivia said.

"I can only imagine," Dutton said.

"Seeing her . . . ," Olivia said. "Hearing them try to blame this on Shannon, having them make it sound like that boy is the victim here."

"It's what they do," Dutton said.

"They won't believe it, will they? The jury?" Olivia said.

"I hope not." The prosecutor shook his head. "I hope not."

"What happens now?" Jack said.

"We wait. It's four thirty now. Hopefully we'll get a verdict in a few hours. You don't have to stay here in the building. It could be a while, and I have your cell numbers. I'll call you as soon as I hear from the court."

Without discussing it, Olivia and Jack ended up in the bar of a grand old inn a block from the courthouse. It felt like alcohol was the only way to kill time and dull the pain of the past week. Jack raised an eyebrow when Olivia ordered a double martini, but he shrugged and said, "The same."

THE BRODY family crowded into a conference room. Cassie didn't blame everyone for wanting to hear what Barry had to say. They all needed a dose of his confidence.

"How long will they take?" Keenan said.

"There's a lot of evidence for them to weigh, and lots of messages to read. I think it'll be a while," Barry said.

"What happens if they convict me?" Keenan said.

"You'll almost certainly be taken into custody. If they convict you on the manslaughter charge, that is. If they convict on the assault only, it's hard to say whether the judge would make you await sentencing in jail. It would depend on his mood. Sentencing would be in a few weeks."

"So these may be my last hours of freedom. Hard to enjoy them, knowing they may be the last."

Barry just stood there.

This wasn't the assurance Cassie craved. She wanted to cry, but for Keenan's sake, she tried to think of something positive to say. "I feel like Mr. Densmore did a good job," she said. "Surely, they have to see how the whole thing was stacked."

Barry bowed his head. "It's hard to know how a jury perceives things. Let's just keep our fingers crossed. I'll call you as soon as I hear something. They'll keep this building open as long as the jury is deliberating, but my advice to you is to get out of here. Go somewhere else. Be with your family. I promise I'll call as soon as I hear anything at all."

DUSTIN AND the chief had come back to court to listen to the closing arguments. Dustin had flirted with an unattractive girl in the clerk's office and was promised a call when the court adjourned just before closings. The girl had delivered on her promise, and when the call came, the chief had insisted on going with him. They had sat on the same side as the Dawsons, but in the back row.

They were among the first to leave the courtroom.

"What do you think they'll do?" Dustin said in the cruiser on the way back to the barracks.

"I only saw part of your testimony and the closings. You probably have a better idea than I do."

"Fair enough. What did you think of the closings?"

"I think Fred's closing was stronger, but Barry scored some points."

"I'll be pissed if they acquit, won't you?"

"I'd be lying if I said I wouldn't be disappointed, but pissed? No."

"Why not? Nobody deserves to get away with murder."

"I agree, but do you feel like you did everything you could to make the case?"

"I suppose."

"Do you wish you had done anything differently?"

"Like what?"

"Well, do you feel like you did everything you could to find a witness to the killing?"

"I knocked on every door in the neighborhood. I ran down every lead. I don't know what else I could have done. I lived the investigation for months."

"Then you did your job. You can't create evidence that doesn't exist."

"Not according to that ex-professor, Lapitas. He tried to make it sound like I coerced the witnesses or something."

"Did you?"

"Of course not. Why would I try to frame some kid I don't know? That's bullshit."

"Maybe. But apparently judges and juries like him."

"That's just wrong. I'm beginning to think that the system is screwed up. It's supposed to be all about the truth, but it's not. It's about who has the better lawyer and who can hire the better expert witnesses. The O.J. Simpson murder trial proved it. Kill someone? No problem. Just hire the best that money can buy."

"I'm not ready to be that cynical."

"I wasn't. But Lapitas tried to make me into the bad guy. I'm no Mark Fuhrman. I'm one of the good guys."

"Don't take it personally."

"Easier said than done." Especially if Manny Rodriguez writes an article in the *Adams Gazette* that makes it sound like he tried to frame the Brody kid. That jury had better convict.

BARRY WENT back to his office. It was only a few blocks, but he had driven to the trial every day because of the heavy box filled with all the documents related to the case. He carried the box into his office and shoved it into the corner. He would need it for the appeal.

"You okay?" Marcy poked her head into his office. Barry sank into his chair.

"I don't know. This is probably the hardest part of the trial. The waiting."

"I have faith. You haven't lost one in quite a few years."

"Maybe I'm due."

Marcy sat down across from him. "I don't know that I've

ever seen you this worried."

"There's just so much at stake for this kid. I shouldn't have let the dad talk about his son's character. I should have explained to him why he couldn't do that. I paved the way for Fred to show this video of Keenan in a fight. It was a royal fuck-up on my part."

Marcy shrugged. "Everyone makes mistakes. It's probably not as bad as you think."

"And, I should have stopped the kid from testifying. If we had rested before he testified, I'd be feeling better about this."

"Did you try?"

"Of course." Barry steepled his hands and exhaled loudly. "I don't know. He had this driving need to testify. I advised him against it, but maybe I wasn't persuasive because I needed someone to blame if I lost."

"Is that what you really think?"

"I don't know. It's never productive to psychoanalyze yourself."

"So, stop."

"Okay. You want a scotch?" Barry got up and went his credenza. He held up two glasses.

"Don't you have to go back to court?"

"Maybe. Or maybe not until tomorrow. But, even if it's today, I won't have much to do. If he's guilty, I make a couple of standard motions, which the judge will inevitably deny. If he's not guilty, I congratulate him. The thinking part of this is over. The alcohol makes the waiting part easier. So, are you going to make me drink and wait alone?"

"Okay, I'll have one. But promise me you'll remember to eat tonight."

"Deal. Is there anything on this desk I absolutely need to deal with today?"

"Not in my judgment."

"It's probably better than mine."

They sat and sipped in silence.

"I believe him, you know," Barry said. "That he's innocent."

"I guessed that much. It's easier when they're guilty, isn't it?"

"It sure is."

FRED WALKED in the door of the State's Attorney's Office.

"You're back. How'd it go?" Carol said, looking away from her computer screen.

"You never know until it's over," Fred said.

Carol nodded. "What time did they start deliberating?"

"It was almost four thirty."

"Okay. I'll call it four thirty."

"It doesn't matter, you know."

"I know. It's just interesting to keep track. Based on my statistics, with a four-day trial, it should take at least three hours to convict. If it's less, it's probably an acquittal."

"I'm not sure I put much stock in your statistics."

"How dare you? My statistics are an office tradition, started by my predecessor's predecessor."

"Santa Claus is a tradition too. Doesn't make him real."

"Ah. But my statistics are just as reliable as Santa is."

Fred smiled. "I'll be in my office if the court calls."

Carol looked at her watch. "Okay. But I wouldn't expect a call before seven thirty."

Fred sat down and looked at the piles on his desk. There were phone messages from days ago. He had forgotten how much a trial can put you off your routine. He was trying to figure out whether it was worth it to try to dig out when Sanjiv, one of his three deputies, poked his head in the door. Fred filled him in on the trial and got updates on what he had missed over the past few days.

"Don't worry. We managed just fine without you."

"I wasn't worried. I know how to hire good people."

"Good luck with the verdict. I'm sure they'll convict." Sanjiv got up. Fred wished Sanjiv would stay and keep him company, but he couldn't ask. There was too much work to do to spend time sitting around, and the problem with being the boss is that people feel like they have to do what you ask them. Besides, Sanjiv probably wanted to get home to his kids.

Fred looked at his emails, deleting half of them, and prioritized the messages on his desk. Then, without even realizing what he was doing, he called Barry.

"Just want to make sure we're still friends," Fred said.

"I can forgive you if that's what you mean."

Fred laughed. "I thought we agreed years ago that work wasn't personal."

Barry sighed. "We did."

"Why does this case feel different?"

"I don't know. It's not fair to hold it against you, but I don't think what you did to this kid is fair."

"All I did was my job."

"I know you see it that way, just like the cops do."

"This isn't personal for any of us."

"Of course it is. You wouldn't be human if it was any other way."

"Maybe you're the one who's taking this too personally."

"You may be right. But I really do believe him."

"And I really don't."

"It seemed like you were willing to keep an open mind in the beginning."

"I always try to keep an open mind."

"So, what convinced you?"

Fred paused and pondered the question. He hadn't been convinced in the beginning. So, when did he change his mind? It might have been after he talked to the medical examiner. "I don't know," he said. "But I know I did the right thing. Can we agree that, whatever the verdict, we'll go back to weekly golf. At least until the snow flies."

"Of course. I just need a little time until this isn't so raw. Give me a few weeks."

"You're afraid you're going to lose, aren't you?" Fred said.

"I'm always afraid I'm going to lose. Aren't you?"

"I guess you're right. It's just been a while since I tried a case."

"See you back in court."

"Yup."

THERE WAS no verdict by six o'clock when the bailiff took dinner orders. The jurors enjoyed Subway sandwiches courtesy of the state. Finally, at nine o'clock, the judge let the jurors go home with the usual warning not to discuss the case with anyone or read anything about it. They were told to be back the next morning at 9:00 a.m. to resume deliberations. The lawyers and the defendant, still in their court attire, stood silently in attendance for the instructions. All the spectators from earlier were notably absent.

When Claire Hiller got home, her kids were in bed. Her husband was watching some stupid series on Netflix about a football team. He paused the program, holding the remote aloft as a way of communicating this should not be a long conversation. It was just as well, seeing as she wasn't supposed to discuss the case with anyone.

"Are you done with jury duty?" he said.

"No. I have to go back tomorrow. But I'm hoping it'll be the end."

"Okay, good. I ordered pizza tonight. You can make dinner tomorrow, right?"

"I should be able to." Claire nodded. She wished she could talk to someone outside the jury. It was hard not knowing what to do. It seemed like the jurors were split down the middle, but there was one juror, Tony Something, who was lobbying hard for a conviction. It just didn't feel right to Claire, but she was feeling the pressure to come to a decision. She could tell that all the jurors were feeling that same pressure. She had a feeling that, if the deliberations dragged on much longer, Tony would get even more persuasive and they would end up convicting. She certainly couldn't see herself as the lone holdout.

She wished she knew whether to believe that defense witness, Dr. What's-his-name. He seemed credible, but it could just be a load of hooey presented to the jury so that Keenan Brody could get away with killing his girlfriend. Just like Mr. Dutton had made it sound.

It would be wrong if she let him get away with murder.

CHAPTER 64
Friday, September 19, 2014

KEENAN LAY in bed and listened to Grandpa Armand snore. It was oddly comforting. He wouldn't have been able to sleep anyway. Grandma Helene was asleep on the bed next to his grandpa. She must be harder of hearing than she let on.

They both looked like they had aged a few years during the trial. His parents, too. At least his parents would probably still be around when he got out of jail. The odds were good his grandparents would both be gone.

Where would the jail be? Would it be close enough for his family to visit?

Would jail be as violent as they portrayed it on TV?

There was a feeling of urgency, so everyone was up and dressed early. Then, they sat in the motel rooms eating convenience store food and waiting for something to happen.

The hours ticked by one second at a time.

CHAPTER 65
Friday, September 19, 2014

W E HAVE a verdict," the clerk said when Barry answered his phone at 4:07 p.m. Barry immediately called Keenan's cell phone.

"You need to get to the courtroom as soon as possible."

"What do you think the verdict is?"

"I have no better idea than you do. But you need to hurry. The judge will consider it disrespectful if we make him wait."

When Keenan and his family walked into the courtroom ten minutes later, Barry was there waiting. Fred Dutton was in his place at the adjacent table. The Dawsons sat directly behind him. Most of the people who had been there for the trial had not waited around for the verdict. However, Manny Rodriguez from the *Adams Gazette* was in the gallery. He was talking to two other reporters who had either been waiting all day or had made nice with someone in the clerk's office.

Barry wished he could say something to reassure Keenan. But anything he said at that point would ring false, so he just put a hand on the kid's shoulder and nodded.

As soon as all the required people were present, the judge came onto the bench.

"Please remain standing for the jury," he said. He did not take a seat either.

THE JURORS were lined up on the other side of the door leading to the deliberation room. The remains of their lunch of pizza and salad were strewn around the room. It was clear nobody had wanted to disturb them by taking the time to clean up lunch.

A few people were chattering about work and kids and how much they had missed by spending most of the week at the courthouse. Most were too tired of the forced socializing. They stood quietly, just waiting to be allowed to go home. Claire Hiller was fighting to keep her composure. She wasn't sure whether she had done the right thing. She didn't know if she could live with herself. But the one thing she knew was that another day in the deliberation room would not have made the situation easier. That and she hoped she was never called for jury duty again. She had learned something about herself during the process—she didn't like having to judge other people. She had done it because it was her civic duty. Duty or not, once was enough.

The bailiff knocked on the door before he opened it. They all filed into the courtroom for the last time.

"Mr. Martin," the judge said, "I understand you have a verdict."

"We do."

"With regard to count one, voluntary manslaughter, how does the jury find?"

KEENAN HELD his breath. This was it, the moment that would determine the next fifteen years of his life. In reality, the rest of his life would probably be determined by the next few seconds. Would he get a college degree or a felony record? Would he eventually have a family of his own or live alone, labeled unworthy? His stomach cramped with dread.

CASSIE GRIPPED Greg's hand with both of hers and looked to the jurors for a sign. Many of them were looking down as if studying the carpet patterns. The rest were looking at the judge. Was it a bad sign that they were not looking at her son?

OLIVIA LEANED into Jack. Thankfully, he put his arm around her shoring her up. The enlarged photo of her daughter's face in death was etched into her memory. She hoped these next few moments would make it worth the nightmares she was sure to have as soon as she started sleeping again. *Make him pay. Please, make him pay.*

THE FOREMAN hesitated. "Not guilty," he said.

There was a collective gasp in the courtroom. While the judge took a few seconds to register the import of the words, the people in the gallery started to whisper and then talk. Cassie Brody sobbed loudly. Olivia Dawson shook her head angrily.

The judge gave them ten seconds before he banged the gavel firmly. "Order, please." He banged again. Three seconds later, the room had returned to silence, but the agitation of all the unexpressed emotions gave the air a humming feeling.

"With regard to count two, domestic assault, how does the jury find?"

This time there was no hesitation. "Not guilty," he said.

At the request of the prosecutor, the judge polled the jury.

EVERY TIME one of the jurors said "Not guilty," Keenan felt like a link was removed from an iron chain wrapped around his soul.

"Thank you for your service," the judge said. "We all appreciate the time and consideration you put into this case. All rise while the jury exits." The jury filed back to the deliberation room. As soon as they were gone, and everyone was again seated, the judge addressed Keenan.

"You are free to go, Mr. Brody. You may see the clerk of court about the return of your bail money. Good luck to you."

"All rise," the bailiff bellowed, and the judge left.

CHAPTER 66
Friday, September 19, 2014

T HAT'S IT?" Olivia Dawson said. That boy had murdered her daughter and gotten away with it? That couldn't be it.

"The jury didn't think he did it," Jack said.

"Of course he did it. How else could she have died?"

"Maybe someone else did it?"

"You don't believe that any more than I do."

"Or maybe . . ." The thought was left hanging as Fred Dutton approached.

"I'm sorry about that verdict. I tried to get you the result you deserved, but sometimes we just can't prove a case beyond a reasonable doubt."

"How could they have believed him? He murdered my daughter."

"I don't know. I've been doing this for many years, and I can't tell you what gets a jury to vote one way or the other."

"Is there anything else we can do? Are there other charges you can file?"

"I'm sorry. Now that he's been acquitted, double jeopardy keeps me from going after him again. You can consult a lawyer about a civil suit. The burden of proof is much lower, so you might have more success, but that's not my jurisdiction."

"We need to sue," Olivia said.

"Olivia," Jack said. "I think we should let it go."

"Our daughter is dead and you want to let it go?"

"I think Mr. Dutton gave it his best shot, but there's

obviously some question about whether that boy killed her. What if he didn't kill her? Suing him isn't going to bring her back. We have no good use for the money anyway."

"It's not about the money. It's about making him pay."

Jack glanced at Fred. "We can talk more about it later. Privately."

"Your husband is right. You don't need to make any decisions today. Except about what you're going to say to the press. You know they'll want a statement."

When Jack and Olivia walked out the front door of the courthouse, Barry Densmore, Keenan, and his family were already on the steps. A half dozen reporters were gathered, three with cameramen at their elbows.

"I will be speaking for Keenan and his family," Barry said. "Obviously, they are relieved that the jury believed in Keenan's innocence. It's a tragedy that Shannon Dawson is dead, but as Keenan has said all along, it is not a tragedy that had anything to do with him. Again, Keenan does not wish to make any statements at this time. Thank you."

"Did you get away with murder, Keenan?" a reporter shouted.

"You can tell us, you know. They can't try you again," another said.

"For the last time. I did not kill Shannon," Keenan said before his parents closed ranks and pulled him away from the reporters. The reporters quickly turned their attention to the Dawsons, who were standing side by side at the top of the steps.

"How do you feel about the verdict, Mr. and Mrs. Dawson?"

"It's a travesty," said Olivia.

"Are you upset with the jury, Mr. Dawson?"

"I'm sure they did what they thought was right."

"Are you saying that Brody might be innocent?"

"Only that boy knows whether he killed my daughter," Jack said. "The rest of us can only look at the evidence. I don't necessarily agree with what the jury did, but I don't blame them for it."

"Are you saying you thought it was a weak case?"

Olivia stepped in front of her husband. "I have no doubt that boy killed my daughter and I know that he will rot in hell for it eventually. In the meantime, I hope he thinks of her and feels guilty every day for the rest of his miserable life. He may have fooled the jury, but he didn't fool me, and he can't fool God."

"Will you be filing a civil suit?"

Jack grabbed Olivia and pulled her away. "We have no more comments at this time," he said.

As soon as they were away from the reporters, Olivia hissed, "Why did you say those things? That boy doesn't deserve anything resembling vindication. There's a big difference between not guilty and innocent."

"It's time to let this go."

"Let it go? Our daughter is dead. We'll never have grandchildren now. Are you serious? Let it go?"

"Look, I understand why you're angry. A guilty verdict would have meant closure. Now we'll never know for sure what happened to Shannon that night. I don't like that any more than you do. But we have a choice. We can let it define the rest of our lives or we can move on."

Olivia shook her head, her expression like vinegar on her tongue. "I don't understand you."

"I know. I'm not sure you understand anyone. Maybe that's part of your anger. You realized during this trial that you didn't even understand your own daughter."

Olivia started to cry.

Jack shrunk. "I'm sorry. I shouldn't have said that. You were a good mother to Shannon."

"No, I wasn't. If I were, she wouldn't have crossed the country to go to college, and she'd be alive right now."

"Don't do this to yourself. Shannon loved you. She was just at the age when kids assert their independence. It's part of becoming an adult."

"She never made it."

"I know. And it's not fair. But ultimately it may not be anyone's fault."

"I'll never forgive him."

"Nobody's asking you to. For now. But eventually, you may have to for your own sake. Come on. Let's go back to the hotel and see about getting a flight back to California. You'll probably feel better when you get home."

"I want to sue him."

"I know. But I'm not going to let you."

FRED WASN'T sure where he had gone wrong. He always told his young deputies that you learn more from your losses than your wins, and he'd always believed it. That meant that there was a lesson for him somewhere in the rubble. He wondered if his mistake went all the way back to jury draw. Maybe there had been a rogue juror on the panel. He probably should have kicked that guy Anthony Brennan.

Manny Rodriguez was sitting in Fred's visitor chair, a notepad in his hand. "Keenan Brody was acquitted of all charges. Do you have any comments for the people of Adams County?"

Fred nodded. "I believe in our system of justice. We have stringent standards for convicting people of crimes because it's better to let guilty people go than to convict the innocent."

"Are you saying that you think Keenan Brody got away with a crime?"

"Only he knows the answer to that. And I don't need to know to do my job. My job is to present the evidence to the jury and let them decide. I don't feel bad about the way it turned out because I know I did my job."

"Anything else?"

"Yes. I am honored that the people of this county have entrusted me with the job of protecting them, and I will continue to do that job as long as they see fit."

CLAIRE HILLER watched her son Brian slap-shooting tennis balls at a net in the driveway. He was a pretty good hockey player, not the best on his team and probably not in the same league that Keenan Brody had been at that age. Brian didn't have a future in hockey, but she hoped and expected he would go to college and get a good job. He would have a future. And now, thanks to her, Keenan Brody would as well. She hoped he deserved the second chance, but that really didn't matter. They hadn't proved he was guilty beyond a reasonable doubt. Or maybe they had. She only knew that what she had learned on the internet had scared her too much to allow her to convict him.

That night in the middle of deliberations, while her husband watched TV, Claire Hiller had done something that she felt sure the judge would not have wanted her to do. She had googled "eyewitnesses and memory." She kept telling herself that it wasn't technically a violation of the judge's instructions. He had told them not to look up anything to do with the case. She hadn't googled Keenan Brody. She'd just done a little research of her own.

She had learned that the studies that Dr. Lapitas had described were the tip of the iceberg. She read about all the people who were convicted on the basis of eyewitness identification and later exonerated by DNA evidence. The problem with the case against Keenan was that there was no DNA evidence to exonerate him or prove his guilt unequivocally. If they convicted him, he would spend the rest of his youth in jail. She just couldn't do that to him. Not based on the evidence that had been presented in court.

Claire had hoped the other jurors would get to the same place on their own, but the next morning when they voted, it seemed they were going the other direction. What had been a vote of six to six the night before became a vote of seven to five in favor of conviction. By that point, they were all on a first-name basis. People just wanted to be done and Tony was pretty persuasive. She held her tongue until after lunch when the vote was eight to four in favor of conviction.

Then, she had done something she didn't know she was capable of doing. She started standing up for Keenan.

"I know you all want to get out of here, but there's something fishy about the way the police handled the investigation," Claire said.

"I thought Officer Shores seemed honest," Kathy said.

"I'm not questioning his integrity," Claire said. "But I think there's something to this memory stuff. I think that eyewitnesses alone are just not reliable enough."

"I believed them," Tony said. He reminded Claire of a football player in her high school class who had always seemed like a bully.

"That's exactly what the doctor guy said." Claire sat up straighter. "That they would be believable because they believed it themselves, but that doesn't mean it happened."

"Sounds like a load of crap." Tony crossed his arms. "They're not going to make up witnessing an assault. My cousin got date raped. Nobody believed her, and the guy got away with it."

"I'm sorry about your cousin," Claire said. "But this is different. You have to wonder why the witnesses didn't report the assault when she was first missing." Claire said.

"They forgot," Tony said.

"Really? What if they didn't remember because it wasn't planted in their memories yet? Just like the doctor said."

"You believed him?"

"I do. I'm not going to convict this kid."

"You didn't seem so firm about this yesterday," Tony said.

"I thought a lot about it last night."

"But what about that video?" Craig said. "You saw him beat up that guy on the ice."

"That's just part of hockey. It happens all the time," Claire said.

"If it was part of the game, he wouldn't have gotten a penalty," Craig said.

"There's a big difference between taking a swing at a guy wearing a face mask and helmet and taking a swing at your girlfriend," Claire said.

Everyone had looked at her blankly, seemingly not sure what to make of the hockey mom. Ironically, she had never thought of herself that way. The mothers of her son's teammates had sometimes seemed too loud and aggressive, taking the game too seriously. Too mother-bear-on-steroids. Well, if that's what it took to get people to do the right thing, she would have to dig deep and find her own inner bear-on-steroids.

Slowly, the jurors started to swing her way. She kept at them until it was nine to three in favor of acquittal. Tony clearly didn't like the idea of a not guilty verdict. "We can always tell them we couldn't come to a decision," he said.

"The judge said we need to agree," Claire said. "I think a hung jury is a last resort."

"I had a friend who had jury duty and they couldn't agree," Kathy said. "The judge made them keep trying for three days. I'm pretty sure that if we don't agree, they have to do the whole trial over again."

"I'm not going to convict," Claire said. "If we have to stay in this room for two more days, so be it."

Tony gave it another try. "I think Keenan Brody is a liar. And a murderer. The prosecutor showed us how many times he lied or misled the cops during the investigation. If he had nothing to hide, why'd he lie?"

Claire knew the answer. "He's just a kid. A scared kid.

Imagine it was your kid. Does everyone agree that the strongest evidence in the manslaughter charge is the assault?"

There were quite a few nods.

Claire had an idea. "I think we've been going about this wrong. We keep voting on the manslaughter charge because it's at the top of the page and that's the order they gave it to us. Let's focus on the assault for a while."

Tony was shaking his head.

"How many of you think Shannon told Keenan about Jake?" Claire said.

Ten jurors raised their hands.

"Based on what?"

"The assault," Craig said.

"That's just it. Like Mr. Densmore said, it's all circular. Did anyone find anything in the texts they gave us proving that she actually told him?" Claire said.

"I read all the documents pretty thoroughly and no." Kim said.

"Does anyone think they proved that he knew beyond a reasonable doubt?" Claire said.

There was a lot of head shaking. "No," Craig said.

"Okay, if we start with the proposition that he didn't know, there's no motive. All the witnesses were partying. Isn't it possible that the argument over the keys got misremembered as an assault?" The response was mostly tired shrugs. "Let's vote on just the assault. I don't think they proved it beyond a reasonable doubt."

Tony collected and tallied the folded papers. "Eleven to one," he said. "Look, it's clear you all want to acquit on the assault. Unlike some people, I'm not willing to be the lone holdout."

"Does anyone think that if he didn't assault her, he might have still killed her?" Claire said.

"There's the keys, the hair in the trunk," Tony said.

"But no blood," Craig said. "She had a cut on her face that might've left blood. And the hair could have been there for years."

"He might have used something to keep the blood from getting in the trunk," Tony said.

"And then kept the keys?" Kathy said. "If he was that careful, he would have gotten rid of the keys and wiped down the car." Claire was glad that the others were making the arguments. She had been uncomfortable doing so much talking.

"You know, I think that's what's been bothering me," Craig said. "Everybody watches *CSI* so we all know that if you want to get away with a crime, you have to be careful about trace evidence. The kid did nothing. If he was going to go to the trouble of getting rid of the body, he would have done more to hide it. It's almost like there's too much evidence."

Tony had made a few more arguments for convicting before throwing up his hands. "You all want to acquit. Let's just do it and get out of here."

BARRY WAS relieved more than anything. He knew it had been a close call. In some ways, he was surprised by the verdict. He had definitely been off his game.

The trial had taken so much out of him. Maybe it was time to retire. Who was he kidding? He couldn't afford to retire for a few years yet. Besides, he already had another client that might be innocent. Maybe he should hire an associate, train him or her for a few years and then think about passing the baton. That could work.

Barry was on his way to Brattleboro. He didn't know whether his son would see him or not, but he had to try.

He waited half an hour in the visiting room before Sam appeared.

"The trial must be over," Sam said.

"We won," Barry said, nodding.

"I didn't ask."

Barry shrugged and decided to wait him out. It didn't take long.

"You always win, don't you? It must be so hard for you, having a son that's a loser."

"You're not a loser. You have a disease. It's not your fault you're bipolar."

"You had me committed."

"No, you did that to yourself. By refusing your meds."

"You sure made it easy for them. You didn't even come."

"I was in the middle of trial. Someone's life was in my hands."

"Your clients always come first, don't they? What about my life? Do you have any idea what's been going on in my life?"

"Was this some sort of test? Because if it was, I clearly failed."

"I don't know. Maybe."

"I'm sorry I let you down. I hated doing it. But if I had to do it all over again, I would do it the same way. It's my job."

"I know, Dad. It's always your job."

Sam got up and walked out.

KEENAN HAD gone home with his family after the trial. He could have gone to the dorm and gotten settled in for classes. He was already two weeks behind, but he needed time to regroup, sleep in his familiar bed, be surrounded by people who didn't doubt him. The morning after the verdict, he went for a walk with his mother.

"I can't believe it's finally over," Cassie said.

"I'm not sure it is. I'm sure there are still a lot of people at Masterson who think I killed her. Several of them think they saw me assault her. I may still have to face the judicial board. It's so screwed up."

"You don't have to go back to Masterson, you know. You can always take a semester off and transfer somewhere else. You could stay home and go to Lyndon State."

"I thought of that. But you didn't raise a quitter, Mom."

"Under the circumstances, I, for one, would not consider you a quitter."

"I want to play hockey this year. If I transfer now, I'll have to sit out a year and my skills will get rusty. That's if I can even find another school with a hockey program as good as Masterson."

"I can't believe what you went through."

"Sometimes I can't either. And then I remember that Shannon is dead, and it all gets real again."

"I wonder what really happened to her."

"Me, too. I guess we'll never know."

"I feel bad for her parents."

"They really hate me."

"It's understandable. Like Barry said, they need to blame someone."

"I know. It's just hard to be the blamee." They stood and watched as the dogs took off across the field chasing a scent. "I've decided to change my major."

"Really? To what?"

"Psychology."

"Dr. Lapitas made an impression on you."

"I want to be a researcher. I want to help other people accused of things they didn't do."

"So, why not be a lawyer?"

"There are plenty of lawyers. But according to Barry, there are only a handful of psychologists willing to testify for defendants about problems with memory and eyewitnesses. Besides, I still don't understand how this could have happened to me. I need to know more. I need to try to fix the system."

"I thought you were thinking about being a writer."

"I do like to write, and I already have a lot of credits toward a literature degree. Maybe I'll take a double major."

"Sounds ambitious. I'm proud of you Keenan."

"Thanks, Mom. Especially for being there through all of this."

"I would have been there even if you had been convicted. Every visiting day."

"What a scary thought. How close I came to losing everything."

"Keenan?"

"Yeah?"

"I would have been there even if you were guilty."

Keenan looked at his mother and wondered if she still had her doubts.

CHAPTER 68
Wednesday, October 1, 2014

OLIVIA STOOD in the doorway of Shannon's bedroom. She had snooped in the room so many times those first few months when Shannon had gone off to college. She had thumbed through Shannon's high school yearbook, reading the notes from Shannon's friends, relishing the photos of her beautiful, smiling daughter at school events, among friends. She had pawed through Shannon's box of keepsakes, wondering about the significance of movie ticket stubs and other seemingly useless trinkets. She had cherished the skating medals and certificates as if she had earned them herself. Which she had, in a manner of speaking.

She knew her previous snooping had been a technical violation of Shannon's privacy, but she had justified it to fill her own emptiness, loneliness. Oddly, now that there was no moral reason to stay out of Shannon's room, and her emptiness was a yawning cavern, it felt wrong to go in.

All last summer, when Olivia had been home awaiting the trial, she had kept the door closed and tried not to think about what was behind it. In fact, she'd kept a lot of metaphorical doors closed during that time of limbo—friends, clubs, even her regular yoga class. She just couldn't pretend to be a normal human being when she didn't feel like one. She wasn't sure why she decided to open the bedroom door today or whether she would actually go in.

Jack came and stood beside her in the doorway. "We should donate Shannon's clothes to Goodwill. Or something."

"You're in an awfully big hurry to write off your daughter. But you wrote her off months ago, didn't you?"

"How can you say that?"

"You weren't there! I spent months trying to get justice for Shannon. And you weren't even there."

"It wouldn't have made a difference to her if I had been there. She was already dead."

"You didn't know that."

"Yes, I did. And so did you."

Olivia fought the sob, but it escaped. "You know, I might have been able to forgive him if he'd just admitted what he did. He probably didn't mean to kill her. I know that. But if he'd just told someone, we wouldn't have spent all those months wondering what happened to her. Hoping." Olivia looked down at the floor. She was surprised when she felt Jack's arms around her.

"Why are you so sure he killed her?"

Olivia pushed Jack away and clenched her fists. "Didn't you listen to the evidence? She broke his heart. And he's a violent, angry young man. Of course he killed her."

"What if you're wrong?" He was using his reasonable clinical tone. She hated when he used that tone on her.

"What if I'm right, and he does it again?"

"What if you're wrong, and he went through hell?"

"How dare you!" She felt the drop of spit as it left her mouth and saw Jack flinch as it hit his cheek.

Slowly, Jack wiped his cheek with the back of his hand. "He was found 'not guilty.' You can't change that. Nothing is going to change that. You need to focus on what you can change. And stop blaming me for being realistic. Would you be happier if I had stayed in Vermont and given up my practice? Would you be happier if we'd defaulted on the mortgage and lost our house? Would more loss have canceled out the loss of Shannon? Or just made it worse?" Jack turned and walked away.

Olivia wondered if he could be less supportive. No wonder so many couples divorced after losing a child.

CHAPTER 69
Saturday, October 11, 2014

KEENAN WOKE up in his dorm bed tangled in his sheets. In his nightmare, Shannon had been floating down the river, her eyes open underwater, her blond hair spread across her face. He ran along the shore trying to reach her, but he kept slipping on the ice. Shannon got farther and farther away.

He looked around his single room. It was smaller than the double he'd had to himself last semester, but it was enough.

It came to him that it was the first day of ice at the rink. Normally, this day gave him a boost of energy, but today he wasn't even sure he wanted to go. So much of hockey was the camaraderie. But even since his acquittal, it felt as if his teammates were going out of their way to avoid him. Just like everybody else.

The college judicial board had briefly resumed their witch hunt the week after the trial. Barry had given them transcripts of Dr. Lapitas' testimony and delivered a persuasive speech, reminding them repeatedly that Keenan had been acquitted. They ultimately decided it was outside their jurisdiction to consider the matter.

Not quite as good as another not guilty finding, but it meant that his financial aid and place on the hockey team were intact. He was determined to take advantage of those opportunities, even if it meant feeling like a pariah. Besides, he had so much work to do with the extra courses he was taking to add the psychology major. He didn't have time to socialize even if he'd wanted to, although he found time to have lunch with Aarav a few times a week.

His parents had let him take the old Subaru back to school. He'd used it to go home every weekend since the trial. That was probably why he wasn't welcoming the beginning of hockey season. It would be harder to go home. It would be longer between his times of feeling normal. In fact, the next time he would be home would be Thanksgiving.

He remembered saying good-bye to Shannon a year before as she left to go to New York City with Amy. How would things be different if she had come home with him instead? If she hadn't slept with Jake, would they have stayed happy together? Would she have run away from him the night she disappeared? He knew it was useless, but he couldn't help but think about all the things that could have been different that might have kept her alive.

And he missed her. Despite all the pain she'd caused him, he missed her.

FRED HOISTED his golf bag onto his shoulder and waited for Barry so they could walk to the eighth hole together. Fred was glad his friend had finally agreed to play.

"I can't even beat you at golf these days," he said, shaking his head.

"You're just having a bad day. It happens to the best of us."

"You mean bad year."

"If you're talking about the Brody case, the facts weren't on your side. You can only work with the facts you have."

"No, you can only work with the facts that are admissible. He did it, you know."

"I really don't think so."

The two men walked in silence for a few minutes.

"How's Sam?" Fred said.

"He's still at home. I think if he had another place to go, he'd leave. It gives me a little more time to get him to forgive me."

"I GOT the final bill from Barry today," Greg said. He and Cassie were eating dinner alone. Their two younger daughters were at hockey practice.

"I'm not sure I want to think about money right now," Cassie said.

"We can talk about it later."

"The problem isn't going away anytime soon. How bad is it?"

"I guess it's a matter of perspective. We still have our son."

"And I'm grateful," she said and truly meant it. In fact, whatever the bill was, she would have gladly paid even more. "Just say it."

"Barry used up the last retainer and we owe another fourteen thousand dollars."

Cassie exhaled. "Have you figured out how much this whole thing cost us?"

"We gave Barry three retainers. I think they were ten thousand, forty thousand and eighty thousand. So, a hundred and forty-four thousand dollars. Plus the ten grand for Dr. Lapitas."

"How are we going to pay that back? Kaitlyn starts college next year."

"We could sell some of this land."

"But it was a wedding present from my dad. It's been in my family for generations. He'd kill me."

"He's the one who suggested it. Bert Charbonneau needs another hayfield. One of the ones he's been leasing is getting converted to a strip mall. We could sell him twenty acres and get enough to pay off most of the second mortgage we took out."

"I can't sell the pond. You know how much the kids love to skate there."

"I know, but they're not going to be around for much longer."

"I want them to be able to come home to it. Why don't you see if Bert wants to lease our land as long as we can still use the pond?"

"That might be enough to cover the interest, but it won't pay off that loan."

"I could get a job."

"You have a job."

"Another job, on the side."

"What would you do?"

"I don't know. The bakery had a sign. I could work there part time and still spend the afternoons tending my plants and sending out shipments."

"Doc Beaulieu is planning to retire," Greg said. "I'll see if I can take over some of his clients."

"You already work so hard."

"I can work harder for a while."

"And you can stop waiving so many of your bills."

"You're an amazing woman, Cassie Brody. No wonder Keenan seems so resilient."

"It must be our French Canadian stock."

Greg laughed. "You don't think it comes from my Irish ancestors' hardiness?"

"Surviving a few famines and plagues is nothing compared to what Keenan went through," Cassie said. "Seriously, he's hurting. He just does a good job hiding it."

"I know. We're all hurting and we're all trying to hide it."

"When I think about what he went through, how he must have felt, I want to scream. It was bad enough watching it."

"Have you talked to him more about getting some counseling?"

"I've tried, but I don't want to push him."

"Hopefully, he'll ask for help when he's ready," Greg said. Cassie nodded, but didn't mention that she already had a list of therapists who specialized in PTSD.

ARE YOU safe?" Olivia said to the woman sobbing on the other end of the line. It was the first question she was supposed to ask anyone who called the domestic violence hotline.

"I think so. I mean, he left."

"What if he comes back?"

"I don't know."

"Is there some place you can go to be safe tonight?"

"Not really. Besides, the kids are already in bed."

Olivia's heart ached. So many of the women who called the hotline had children in the house. She wanted to scream at them, tell them to get their heads out of their asses and get their kids to safety, but she had learned to hold her tongue. She had spent two full weekends attending the domestic violence training offered by the local women's shelter before she started volunteering at the hotline. The training stressed that the victims of domestic violence were in the best position to decide what was their safest course of action. When, if ever, it was safe to leave.

"Okay. Why don't you tell me what happened to make you so upset?"

Olivia listened carefully to the woman's story before explaining some options. She wanted to encourage her to go to the police and file charges against her abusive boyfriend, but the program guidelines on that were clear. Filing charges was frequently not the best choice. The system usually did little more than slap perpetrators on the wrist, and angry boyfriends were known to retaliate. Olivia knew that the system needed reform, and she was determined to get involved.

A month ago, Olivia had made a large donation to the local women's shelter in Shannon's name. It felt like the right thing to do, and she was proud of the choice. It was also a compromise she had made with Jack. She agreed not to sue Keenan Brody, and Jack agreed to let her donate the money they would have spent on Shannon's education to causes of her choice in Shannon's name. The shelter donation had been the first. And she hoped to use the money strategically to improve the response to domestic violence in her county. But first, she needed to learn more about domestic violence. She began volunteering at the shelter one night a week, and when there was a vacancy, she had been offered a spot on the board of directors. It might not be much, but it felt like she was at least doing something.

And it was probably saving her marriage. It was too soon to tell.

Olivia rarely spent time with her friends anymore. She could no longer relate to them. Besides, she was making new friends among the women who volunteered their time at the shelter. Her new friends were so passionate about helping others that they ignited a spark that had been smoldering in her soul during the many months she spent in Vermont trying to get justice for Shannon.

Her new passion would never take the place of her lost daughter, but it gave her a reason to get out of bed in the morning. And maybe someday she would save someone else's daughter.

JACK HUNG UP the phone. Olivia had just called to say she would be staying late at the shelter again. A woman had come in with kids in tow, and Olivia wanted to help get them settled for the night.

He hadn't seen Olivia so determined to do something since she had tried to get pregnant with Shannon. Olivia had wanted to be a mother so much. For two years she took her temperature, kept charts, and unromantically told him when it was time to have sex. Eventually Clomiphene had worked for them. But only once.

Olivia had been a good mother to Shannon. Despite her tendency to smother. Another child probably would have helped with that. Or a job to challenge her. It was probably partly his fault for encouraging her to quit her job when Shannon was born. By the time Shannon went off to kindergarten, he was making a good living and there was no reason for Olivia to go back to work.

Both having money and being a stay-at-home mother had changed her, made her world smaller.

It was good to see Olivia committed to something other than Shannon. It reminded him of the Olivia he had fallen in love with more than two decades ago. That young Olivia had been passionate and outspoken, a frequent writer of letters to the editor. They had met when she was handing out campaign fliers for a local senator who favored stricter drunk driving laws. Jack had pretended to be a fellow supporter and offered to help her. She never knew that he'd never heard of the candidate before.

Or maybe she did. He chuckled.

CHAPTER 71
Wednesday, December 3, 2014

DUSTIN LOCKED Nate in his crate after his morning walk. He'd had the puppy for a month. Nate looked like a cross between a Golden Retriever and a Boxer. Sergeant Patterson had found him in the dumpster behind the police station. A shivering, whimpering ball of matted fur. What kind of person does that to a helpless creature? At least he'd been left in a place where someone might find him. The person must have had a glimmer of conscience.

The kids loved the puppy. Joanne was not a dog person, so they'd never had one. Whenever they came into the apartment, they went straight for Nate. They took turns having him sleep on their beds at night.

The puppy had given him an excuse to put off buying furniture. Everyone knows that puppies chew. Even still, the place looked better than it used to. He'd bought three giant beanbag chairs to go in front of the TV and some posters for the walls. He'd also bought bed frames for the kids' mattresses. His own mattress was still on the floor, but he didn't care. The divorce was final, so he had nobody to impress.

The divorce trial had been the worst experience of Dustin's life. He had felt like he was on trial, defending his choices, his lifestyle. He wasn't a criminal for Christ's sake. He was a cop. A good one, even. But Joanne had made it look like he was an irresponsible parent just because he worked a lot of hours, fed the kids popcorn for dinner sometimes, and had no furniture.

The icing on the cake had been when Joanne had testified

that Sienna had told her that Dustin was looking at pictures of naked women in front of their daughter.

At first Dustin had been stunned. Then, he realized she was talking about the autopsy photos that Sienna had seen by mistake. During a break, he explained it to his lawyer. Bob Kessler didn't have a reputation for being in Barry Densmore's league, but he seemed to be on Dustin's side.

"Shit, Dustin," Bob said. "I don't know which is worse. You getting caught looking at girlie mags or letting your kid see autopsy photos."

"It was a mistake. I thought she was asleep."

"Honestly, I think we should let it go. The judge will assume it was girlie mags. He probably looks at those himself."

"But, I think we should tell the truth."

"And, you'll play right into Joanne's argument that you work too much and pay too little attention to your kids."

"But—"

"We're not going to lie. We're just not going to correct a misperception."

"What's the difference?" Dustin had said.

Bob had shaken his head. "This is a court of law, not a court of truth."

THE CHIEF looked up when Dustin knocked on his open door. "Got a sec?" Dustin said.

The chief was catching up on his mail, so he was glad for the excuse to talk to Dustin. He gestured toward a chair. "What's on your mind?"

"I have a few weeks of unused vacation time and comp time. I'd like to take a big block of it this coming summer."

"How much are we talking?"

"Four weeks. It's how long I have the kids."

"You know they have summer programs for kids, right?"

"I want to do something special with them. Go somewhere. I know it leaves the department short. That's why I'm asking in advance."

"What are you planning?"

"A camping trip. Out west. I'm thinking Yellowstone, Grand Canyon, maybe Mount Rushmore."

"Sounds ambitious."

"It is. That's why I need the extra time."

The chief nodded. "Are you still upset about the Brody verdict?"

"It's wrong that he got away with it, but I can't let it define my life. Just like I can't let this job define my family. That's why I need to make the most of the time I have with my kids."

"If I don't give you the time off, are you going to quit?"

"Probably not."

"Okay, then I'll make it work." It would be a stretch, but he knew the past six months had been especially rough on Dustin. Divorce always sucked. And devoting your life to an investigation and watching the defendant walk, well, it was demoralizing. "Just promise me you won't quit. I don't have anybody else that can fill your shoes." In fact, the chief had been thinking that Dustin would make a good sergeant.

"It's a deal."

"Hey, Dustin?"

"Yeah?"

"What are you going to do with the dog while you're traveling?"

"Take him, of course."

The chief smiled. "I was going to offer to watch him for you."

"Thanks, but, not a chance. He's part of the family."

BARRY HAD made a chicken stir-fry for dinner. He wasn't much of a cook, but stir-fry was one of his three "specialties" and Sam had promised to be home for dinner.

He was setting the table when Sam walked in. Barry instantly smelled the alcohol on Sam's breath. In frustration, Barry thrust the silverware onto the table. It clattered and skidded in different directions. An errant fork landed on the floor.

"Why are you so set on self-destruction?"

"It's just the way I am. Haven't you heard? I'm bipolar."

"Stop making excuses. There are plenty of bipolar people who lead normal lives."

"That's what I'm trying to do. Lead a normal life. Have a beer like a normal person."

"That's not what I meant, and you know it. Why don't you get your act together and finish college?"

Sam raised his chin and glared, but the defiance didn't ring true. In fact, the look reminded Barry of Sam's difficult early teen years so much that Barry realized Sam might be as confounded by his mental health disorder as he had been by teenage hormones. Barry forced himself to soften his demeanor before he picked up the fork from the floor and tossed it into the sink. "I know I let you down back in September, but we can't turn back the clock. I'm here now and I'm trying, so talk to me. Tell me what's going on."

"You don't want to know."

"I asked because I do."

"You won't want to hear it."

"I promise I won't judge. Try me."

"Okay. You asked for it." Sam paced. Barry waited him out.

"I know something about that girl. The one they found in the river."

"Shannon Dawson?"

"Yeah."

Barry blinked rapidly as the import registered. "Do you know how she ended up in the river?"

"Not exactly, but I was there."

"Wait a minute . . . wait a minute . . . you were *where*?"

"Down at the river. The night she drowned."

"How do you know she drowned?"

"I heard her."

"And you didn't help her?"

"What happened to not judging?"

"I'm sorry. Just—please tell me what you know."

"I was down at the river with Kurt and Joey. Near the walking bridge upstream from the falls."

"What were you doing there?"

"Drinking and smoking pot."

Barry could see Sam searching his face for a reaction, so he willed himself not to react. "What did you see?"

"It's more what I heard. Or thought I heard. I thought I heard a splash, and then someone calling for help."

Barry pondered the implication. Shannon was alive when she hit the water. And she went into the water above the falls. She was conscious before she either drowned or was killed going over the waterfall. That meant she wasn't killed or knocked out and dumped in the river like the prosecution claimed during the trial. It meant that Keenan Brody was almost certainly innocent. Not that Barry had had many doubts by the end of the trial.

"Did you check it out?"

"Not really. It was dark. It looked like there might be someone in the river, but the current was moving fast, and I couldn't be sure."

"And you didn't do anything?"

"What was I supposed to do? Jump in the river? It was December, for Christ's sake."

"You could have investigated. Called the police. Something. Anything!"

"There you go, judging again."

"Okay. Let me ask it this way—why didn't you do anything?"

"We were stoned, Dad. It didn't seem like it was our problem. Kurt and Joey were so messed up, they probably don't remember it. Besides, if I'd called the police, they just would have arrested us for possession of marijuana. You told me after the last time that you wouldn't be able get me out of trouble again. In case you've forgotten."

"But you might have been able to save her!"

"You think I don't know that now. You think I didn't realize it a long time ago when they found her body. That maybe I'm more guilty than that guy you represented."

"It's not a crime to not save someone. But it's wrong, very wrong."

"You really can't stop with the judgments, can you?"

"Do you really hate me that much? So much that you'd let an innocent man go to jail. You realize your testimony would have helped prove he didn't do it."

"You got him off."

"And what if I hadn't? Would you have come forward?"

"Maybe. Probably. I'm telling you now, aren't I?"

"Why are you telling me now?"

"I don't know. Maybe because you finally asked."

"I always ask how you're doing."

"But you don't mean it. I've been living with you for two years. You're almost never here."

"I thought you wanted me to leave you alone."

Sam shrugged. "Are you going to tell anyone?"

"About your sin of omission?"

"Yeah."

Would it be an ethical violation to keep the secret? Technically not. But morally? It wouldn't be Barry's first venture into the gray zone. And if he could go there for his clients, he ought to be able to go there for his own son. "No, it's too late to do Shannon or Keenan any good. And it would do a lot of harm to you, to our family, if this got out."

"So, it's all about you again."

"No, Sam, it's all about you. You're going to have to live with what you did, or rather didn't do. And self-destruction is not the answer."

"You have no idea how hard it's been. Sometimes I just want to be someone else."

"You're right. I don't know what you've been dealing with. But I've been doing defense work long enough to know drugs and alcohol don't solve problems, they create them."

"You sound like the counselors at Brattleboro Retreat."

"I probably do." Barry was tempted to give a long lecture, a rant really, but he knew he would only feel better temporarily, and it would definitely discourage Sam from talking to him more. He looked in Sam's eyes and this time saw the guilt and worry he frequently saw in the eyes of defendants after they confessed their crimes and begged for his help. Sam had been carrying a heavy burden. "You hungry?" he said.

"I can always eat," Sam said and started putting the silverware in its proper place.

Things between them were nowhere near resolved, but it was a start. And no matter how tempting, he would have to keep Sam's secret. Because if it got out, another downward spiral was almost certain.

Keenan Brody and his family deserved to know the truth. Shannon's parents had deserved to know the truth a long time ago. Even Fred would probably feel better if he knew the truth. But none of them would ever know.

Was he committing his own sin of omission? Maybe, but he was also being a father.

"If it helps," Barry said, "we've all done things we're not proud of."

"Thanks," Sam said and sat down. "And, by the way, I don't hate you."

CHAPTER 72
Friday, September 23, 2016

KEENAN WIPED the sweat from his brow with the edge of his T-shirt before he unlocked the door to his studio apartment. His regular evening run had left his gray shirt a few shades darker. Compared to Vermont, it was warm in Irvine, California, even though the sun had set an hour ago. Not that he was complaining. The change of climate somehow seemed appropriate, to go along with all the other changes he had made starting last month.

He had finished his degree at Masterson College by sheer force of will and a love of hockey, but hadn't bothered to attend his college graduation. Graduation was a necessity, not a cause for celebration. Besides, he'd only had one true friend to celebrate with. And, by that point, he had already been accepted into the highly competitive psychology Ph.D. program at UC Irvine. The Statement of Purpose essay he had written for his application to the program had included an intimate account of his trial and a heartfelt plea to be allowed to explore human memory formation.

He opened some windows and stood before his fan while he guzzled a bottle of Gatorade. His apartment would probably be cooler if he dared leave the windows open when he was out, but he wasn't yet comfortable in his new urban environment. He showered before organizing his lecture notes from the day. He almost couldn't believe that he had attended a lecture by the legendary Elizabeth Loftus. Her research on memory had been groundbreaking.

The heat in the apartment and the throb of his fan conspired to make it difficult to do any more reading, so he gave up and got ready for bed. It was definitely easier to read in the air-conditioned library.

After he clicked off his bedside light, he thought of Shannon, as he always did, before falling asleep. Recently, he also wondered how her mother would feel about him being only a county away.

Shannon struggled against her wet clothing, trying to keep her head above the water that marched onward and boiled, sweeping her downstream. The falls rumbled.
She was swimming now, fighting the water with all her strength. The falls thundered.
"Keenan!" she cried, as she went over the edge.

Keenan awoke with a start. He knew now that Shannon had drowned by accident, not because she was depressed, or suicidal, as he had often guiltily imagined. He knew now that she had called to him, and that meant that she had loved him and trusted him up to her last breath.

A feeling of calm came over him. Acceptance. That's what it was. He had studied the stages of grief in his early psychology classes. It could be nothing other than acceptance.

As he went through his morning routine, he continued to feel different, lighter.

"Thanks, Shannon," he said aloud as he picked up his backpack. Today, he would see if Marnie wanted to have coffee with him after class. She was cute, with adorable dimples, and a bouncy walk. It was time. And, he was pretty sure she'd say yes.

AUTHOR'S NOTE

When I set out to write this novel, I wanted to show how a person whose only mistake was to cooperate with the police could be made to look guilty of a most serious crime. At first, I was focused on police investigation techniques and how a suspicion based solely on statistical likelihood and/or a stereotype can become leading questions designed to explore that suspicion can become the memory of the witnesses questioned.

But as the story developed, I realized that, in our current culture, the police are not the only ones at fault for the spread of misinformation. They may be the ones to plant the seed, but social media is a place for opinions and speculation as much as fact. And once an idea becomes widespread, it becomes its own truth.

Thus, in my mind, the title of this novel refers both to the inadvertent spread of misinformation by investigating officers and also the intentional spread of misinformation by our gossip-loving culture enamored of social media. With its lightning speed, social media has done much to increase awareness of police misconduct and civil rights violations, but it's wise to remember that it's a double-edged sword.

My good friend the fictional Dr. Lapitas again makes an appearance in this novel. As always, his expert testimony is based on actual studies by researchers in the field of cognitive psychology and memory proving the unreliability of human memory and the ease with which false memories can be planted. And yet, most jurors in criminal cases will make their decisions without any inkling of this research.

I also note that the premise of this story is based on the case of Nicholas Garza, who disappeared from the campus of Middlebury College during his freshman year in 2008. His body was found several months later below the falls on Otter Creek in downtown Middlebury. In that case, the body was pristine and there were witnesses who acknowledged that they had seen him drinking large quantities in the hours before his disappearance. Thus, the official conclusion was accidental drowning based on intoxication, despite inconclusive toxicology test results. It occurred to me that, if Nick had been a female with a stereotypical boyfriend and the body had been damaged before becoming wedged, the results of the investigation may have been different. Regardless, what happened to Nick was a tragedy, and his death should provide an impetus for change in the culture of drinking secrecy that has done nothing to encourage responsible alcohol consumption on college campuses.

ACKNOWLEDGMENTS

I again find myself indebted to friends who helped to refine this story by reading drafts and sharing their considerable experience and expertise. Amy Rast and Antonia Losano have my eternal gratitude for editing help. Thanks also to Tom Yurista, Sarah Kearns, Barbara Kolysko, Betsy Cartland, Sarah Star, Kathy Hall, and Naomi Smith.

Special thanks to my editor, Barbara Bamberger Scott, who gave the story a better ending.

CPSIA information can be obtained
at www.ICGtesting.com
Printed in the USA
LVOW12s1632190417
531396LV00004B/684/P